STONE COLD DEAD

ALSO BY JAMES W. ZISKIN

Styx & Stone

No Stone Unturned

STONE COLD DEAD

An Ellie Stone Mystery

JAMES W. ZISKIN

SEVENTH STREET BOOKS®
AN IMPRINT OF PROMETHEUS BOOKS
59 JOHN GLENN DRIVE • AMHERST, NY 14228
www.seventhstreetbooks.com

Published 2015 by Seventh Street Books®, an imprint of Prometheus Books

Stone Cold Dead. Copyright © 2015 by James W. Ziskin. All rights reserved. No part of this publication may be reproduced, stored in a retrieval system, or transmitted in any form or by any means, digital, electronic, mechanical, photocopying, recording, or otherwise, or conveyed via the Internet or a website without prior written permission of the publisher, except in the case of brief quotations embodied in critical articles and reviews.

This is a work of fiction. Characters, organizations, products, locales, and events portrayed in this novel either are products of the author's imagination or are used fictitiously.

Cover image © Can Stock Photo Inc./gsagi
Cover design by Jacqueline Nasso Cooke

Inquiries should be addressed to
Seventh Street Books
59 John Glenn Drive
Amherst, New York 14228
VOICE: 716–691–0133
FAX: 716–691–0137
WWW.SEVENTHSTREET BOOKS.COM

19 18 17 16 15   5 4 3 2 1

Library of Congress Cataloging-in-Publication Data

Ziskin, James W., 1960-
   Stone cold dead : an Ellie Stone mystery / James W. Ziskin.
      pages ; cm
   ISBN 978-1-63388-048-1 (softcover) — ISBN 978-1-63388-049-8 (ebook)
   1. Women journalists—Fiction. 2. Missing children—Investigation—Fiction.
3. Nineteen sixties—Fiction. I. Title.

PS3626.I83S76 2015
813'.6—dc23

2014047612

Printed in the United States of America

To Mom, who I wish were here to read this,
and to Dad, who—I'm happy to say—is.

CHAPTER ONE

SATURDAY, DECEMBER 31, 1960

The room was hot to begin with. It was a huffing, pipe-knocking, radiator heat. The kind that desiccates the air and smells like blistering iron and rust. That I was wrestling with a strapping young man on the sofa didn't help matters, serving only to fog up the nearby window. I wouldn't have opened it, even if I'd had a free hand; it was freezing cold outside.

Mrs. Giannetti downstairs was sure to hear. Such a light sleeper. Judgmental landladies always are. She'd be thumping a broomstick on her ceiling at any minute, or worse, banging on my door for the chance to look me in the eye.

"Is everything all right, dear?" she'd ask, affecting genuine concern, all the while bobbing and weaving like Jake LaMotta to see past me into the apartment.

"Yes, Mrs. Giannetti," I would pant. "Just beating a rug."

"At two in the morning? Well . . . Happy New Year."

Yes, it was New Year's Eve, and I was ringing it in drunk, my skirt hiked halfway up my thigh, my blouse tousled, with said strapping young man pressing his lips to mine. Seaman Apprentice Eddie Robeleski was home from the navy for the holidays. I had met him earlier in the evening at a party thrown by Phyllis Cicero, one of the girls from the steno pool at the paper. Eddie and I had chatted, flirted, and enjoyed a snootful together. Then, as midnight struck, he planted a sloppy kiss on my mouth and suggested we ditch the party. What he lacked in technique, he made up for in enthusiasm. Fooling nobody, we sneaked out to my car, which barely started in the cold, and I fishtailed my way through the snowy streets as Eddie blew in my ear and endeavored to separate me from my brassiere.

When it comes to eligible bachelors in New Holland, a single girl feels as if she's arrived an hour late for a bargain basement sale, and all that's left to pick through are the plus sizes and factory seconds. To wit, middle-aged, never-been-married carpet weavers slash bowling heroes; embittered, ready-to-retire thirty-year-old math teachers; local farm boys with their flattops, sunburned arms, and coarse hands; and divorced philanderers, after the one thing the female of the species possesses that they do not. It's enough to make a girl despair. Or at least concede. So when a handsome sailor appears at a New Year's Eve party, you don't quibble that he's only twenty-one years old (three years younger than I.) And Eddie certainly was handsome. Tall and well built, with toned biceps and a broad chest. Sure, he was quiet, but not socially backward. He had a sweet smile, good teeth, and his zeal boded well for a winning finale to the evening's program. Plus he'd already finished one tour of duty in the navy—had crossed the equator twice and managed to escape without a tattoo—so he was a man of the world by New Holland standards. The fact that he was shipping out in two days was a bonus; he wouldn't be around long enough to become cloying.

I shook Mrs. Giannetti out of my mind and—anchors aweigh—abandoned myself to the sailor. I wrapped my arms around his neck and drew him to me. But just then, there really was a pounding at the door.

We froze. Entangled in each other's limbs on the sofa, we wheezed quietly so as not to be heard, and we listened. My heart was thumping in my chest, and Eddie's arms—sturdy though they were—wobbled slightly in consequence of his exertions as he held himself aloft over me.

The radiator hissed in the dark, and the knocking at the door resumed.

"Who's that at this hour?" whispered Eddie.

"The landlady," I said, disengaging myself from our enterprise and wriggling out from under him.

"Don't answer it," he said, but I knew better. Mrs. Giannetti would use her own key if I didn't open up, no matter the hour or the likelihood of an embarrassing discovery.

I tucked in my blouse, straightened my skirt, and tried to smooth my unruly curls. I glanced in the mirror at my flush complexion. My red face and the smell of alcohol were a dead giveaway of what was going on. I told Eddie to wait in the bedroom.

But as things turned out, it wasn't Mrs. Giannetti at the top of the stairs after all, but a strange woman in a clear plastic rain hat and a dark coat. In the dim light of the landing, I could smell the wet wool of her overcoat, the vague odor of time and wear. Her eyes were pink, like a white rabbit's, as if she had a cold, hadn't slept, or had been crying. Maybe all three. She looked to be somewhere in her late thirties, a little worse for wear—what my friend Fadge so delicately describes as "ridden hard and put away wet." But in her severe face, you could almost discern the shade of a once-fresh beauty whose light had faded with the passing years. Life had been hard on her, that much was clear.

"I think you have the wrong place," I said, holding the door fast between us. "There's no party here."

She sniffled, staring at me. "I'm not looking for a party," she said, her upstate twang an ideal candidate for a phonological study. "I'm here because you didn't answer my calls."

"I beg your pardon."

"I left messages for you down to the paper, but you didn't call me back. My name's Irene Metzger."

I blinked at her. "Sorry. Doesn't ring a bell. Are you sure it's me you're looking for?"

"You're Eleonora Stone, that girl reporter from the *Republic*, aren't you?" I nodded. "I called you about my daughter." She paused and drew a short breath. "Darleen Hicks."

Now *that* name I knew. Darleen Hicks was a ninth grader from the wrong side of the tracks. She'd disappeared nearly two weeks earlier, shortly before Christmas, having missed her bus home from school. No one knew anything more.

The investigation never really got off the ground, and the hunt cooled off quickly with the Christmas holidays. Both New Holland chief of police, Patrick Finn, and Frank Olney, sheriff of Montgomery County, liked their investigations short and sweet, and a down-and-out fifteen-year-old girl from the farming hills beyond the South Side didn't merit much of their attention. They probably figured she'd run off with some hood who'd have her pregnant within a week.

"Please," I said, hoping Eddie Robeleski had the good sense to stay out of sight, and I opened the door. "Won't you come in?"

I invited her to sit at my kitchen table and offered her a cup of coffee.

"I'd rather something stronger," she said.

I fetched some Scotch from the cabinet in the parlor and pushed a tumbler across the table. I offered ice but she said she'd manage as is. Suited me fine; I wouldn't have to risk freezing my hand to the metal lever prying the ice out of the tray.

"Sorry to barge in on you like this, Miss Stone," she began once she'd taken a good swig of whiskey and lit an Old Gold. She paused to pick a bit of tobacco from the end of her tongue. "But the cops won't do a thing to help me find my Darleen."

"What can I do?" I asked.

"I seen your articles in the paper about that Shaw girl. Jordan Shaw. So I figured you could do the same for Darleen. Investigate and write stories to help find her." She hesitated a moment, brushing the tablecloth absently with her right hand. "I can't pay you."

I was flattered but still no more confident that I could do anything to help her. Who knew if there was anything to be done anyway? My guest waited for me to say something.

"You don't have to pay me," I said, embarrassed for her. "Could it be she went somewhere with someone?" I asked, trying to steer her away from talk of money.

"Don't tell me she's run off. I've had a bellyful of cops saying she's run off with some older fellow and that she'll come home when she's good and ready."

"But can you be sure? I mean, maybe . . ."

"Impossible," she interrupted. "Darleen would never do that. She had no reason to go. A mother knows." Her expression was assured, her tone commanding, brooking no dissent.

For all I knew, Darleen Hicks had skipped town with some older guy. It wouldn't have been the first time a foolish young girl had done so. And I didn't know Irene Metzger from Adam. How could I be sure she knew better than experienced cops like Frank Olney and Patrick Finn?

"Okay," I said, throwing a glance over my shoulder. No Eddie. "Let's start at the beginning. When did Darleen disappear?"

"Wednesday, ten days ago," she said swallowing a mouthful of smoke. "December twenty-first. She left for school like always, took her lunch pail, and caught the bus at the end of our road about six fifteen. Her class was going on a field trip to the Beech-Nut factory up to Canajoharie that day. I had to sign a permission slip."

"Was she excited about the trip?" I asked.

"Would you be?" Her voice, pickled and scabrous, rasped like tires over loose gravel.

Probably not.

"Of course, she does like chewing gum," she granted. "Especially that Black Jack gum. She's always chewing that disgusting stuff." She took a drink as if to wash down the taste of the foul chewing gum then drew another deep drag on her cigarette. "But Beech-Nut don't make that brand."

"When did you realize Darleen had gone missing?"

"About five thirty that evening. She doesn't always catch her bus, but she always manages to make it home for supper. We eat at five."

"You live out in the Town of Florida, don't you?" I asked, vaguely recalling a story I'd read in the paper. "That's pretty far from the junior high school. How does Darleen get home when she misses the bus?"

"Well, I don't like it at all, but sometimes she takes rides from strangers."

My eyes popped open.

"Or taxis," she continued. "At least part way, if she's got some pocket money, which ain't often. She's a clever girl, though. Always finds a way to get by, even without money."

"That sounds dangerous," I said, wondering how Darleen hadn't disappeared earlier.

"You think I don't know that?" she asked. "I tell her the same thing all the time, but she's stubborn. And her stepfather said he'd beat her silly if she missed the bus again. But girls are girls."

(Stepfather. . . . And a beater besides.)

"Do you have any other children?" I asked, making a mental bookmark to return to the stepfather.

She shook her head.

(Black Jack gum. I was sure I'd heard that recently. It was itching my brain, but not germane to the matter at hand. I pushed it to one side.)

"What about neighbors? Any men living in the area?"

"Why, sure, there are men around. It's farm country."

"Any of them close by?"

"Walt Rasmussen owns the next farm over. He's a giant. Must be six foot nine or ten. And as unpleasant as he is tall. He's about sixty-five. Then there's Mr. Karl and his wife on the other side. They have a son, too. Bob Jr. About twenty-five years old."

"Nice enough people?"

She shrugged. "Suppose they are. Walt Rasmussen had a disagreement with Dick over the property line a few years ago. He said our fence was a couple of feet on his side, but Dick don't make mistakes like that. He's careful that way. We're not friendly with him, but I don't know that he's ever talked to Darleen."

"Anyone else in the area?"

"There's Pauline Blaine and her two boys who live not too far. She's a widow."

"How old are the boys?" I asked.

"Small. Maybe the older one's ten."

"Is Dick your husband?" I asked, shifting gears, and she nodded. "Tell me about him."

"Dick? What do you want to know about him for?"

"I want to know about everyone Darleen knows, starting at home."

Irene Metzger didn't much like it, but she explained that Dick Metzger was her second husband. She'd lost her first, Gene Hicks—Darleen's father—in the closing days of the war in the Pacific. Dick was forty-five, a simple, dirt-under-his-nails, hard-working Joe, struggling to make something of his small dairy farm. He had borrowed money from every bank in town, each to pay the last, enough to hold off foreclosure at least until spring. He had a plan to buy some good cows from a neighbor, and things would turn around soon. I didn't see it.

"How long have you been married?"

"Fourteen and a half years," she said. "Dick and Gene were childhood friends. When Gene was killed in action, Darleen wasn't even born yet." She paused then explained that Darleen was born December 9, 1945, the consequence of her husband's last furlough in February of that year. Irene Metzger wanted to be sure I understood the timeline. "Gene was home in February, you see. Nine months earlier," she said, punctuating the math with a sharp tap of her finger on the table. "Anyways, when Gene was killed, I was six months along. A war widow, living on aid. Then Dick come back from overseas and stopped by to see me. He helped me out, and we got married a year later."

"How is he with your daughter?"

"He's a good father to her," she began then suddenly caught on. She frowned at me. "I don't know what you're driving at, but you got the wrong idea about Dick. He loves Darleen like she was his own. Always treated her like his own daughter. He's sick about this thing. Drove me over here at one in the morning and is waiting downstairs in the truck. That's how much he cares."

"He didn't adopt her?"

"Of course he did," she said.

"But she didn't take his name?"

"I wanted her to, but Dick thought it wouldn't be right for Gene's memory. Like I said, they were fast friends, and Dick wanted Darleen to keep her father's name."

"Why don't you invite him up?" I asked, wanting to have a talk with him. "He must be freezing."

"No, he don't want to come up," she said, draining her glass and stubbing out her cigarette. She'd smoked the whole thing right down to her brittle, yellowed fingertips, wasting none of it. "He wouldn't be any help in this; he don't know about girls."

I regarded her with suspicion, and she picked up on it right away.

"Look," she said, "Dick is a good husband and father. Why do you have to go suspecting him?"

"I don't suspect him," I lied. Of course I suspected him. He might well be Father of the Year, but other stepfathers before him had put a bull's-eye on his back in cases like this. "I'd still like to talk to him. He might know something."

"Don't waste your time," she said simply.

I sighed, poured a short drink for each of us, and asked if Darleen had a boyfriend.

"She took up with a boy last spring. Joey Figlio." She pronounced it FIG-lee-oh. "He's in Darleen's class, I think. Lives near the hospital on the West End. I had to stop her from seeing him last month because things were getting too serious all of a sudden."

"And you don't think Darleen might have bucked and taken off for a while with him?"

"Nope," she said, lighting another cigarette and sucking half of it down in one gasp. "I told you, she didn't run away."

I must have appeared skeptical, because she offered more without my asking: "She couldn't have run off with him because he's up to Fulton over in Johnstown. Locked up in reform school since the beginning of

December. He snuck out, though, and Dick found him hiding in our barn the night Darleen disappeared. You see, he was waiting for her to come home, too."

"Okay, so she didn't run away with her boyfriend," I said. "Does she have any friends?"

"There's a couple of girls she rides the bus with. Susan Dobbs, Carol Liswenski, and Linda Attanasio. And there's Edward, a boy who's had a crush on her since the seventh grade."

I stood and fetched my grocery pad and pencil from the counter near the icebox. I wrote down the names. I also noted the neighbors, Rasmussen and Karl. Under normal conditions, my memory is as faithful as a dog and as trustworthy as the mighty Jeep, but this night, I feared the whiskey might prevail and blur everything in the morning.

"Now, about your husband," I said. "I really would like to talk to him. Since he's just downstairs . . ."

She seemed to ignore me.

"If you want my help, you'll have to let me do things my way," I said. "You can say what you want, but I need to believe what you tell me. And the only way I can do that is to satisfy my doubts."

Irene Metzger sat quietly, slouched a bit to one side, fixing me with her stare. I couldn't tell if she was riled or just considering my words. Finally she spoke.

"I'm sorry if you don't like what I'm telling you, but I know my daughter. And my husband."

I shook my head; I had drunk enough whiskey for two New Year's Eves, there was an eager young man waiting in the next room, and this lady wasn't cooperating. She wouldn't allow that her daughter might have run off or—if she hadn't—that her husband might have a darker side than she could ever imagine.

"Okay," I said, shrugging my shoulders. "I'll think about it."

"Think about what?" she asked, alarmed.

"Whether I can help you or not."

A grimace, bitter and disappointed, curled slowly across her upper lip and flared her right nostril. She tried to hide it.

"You mean you *won't* help me," she said.

I said nothing, just stared at her.

"I'll talk to him," she said, almost in a whisper. "Can't promise anything."

"And I'll make some inquiries," I said. "Then I'll be in touch. Give me a few days."

"I brought this," she said, producing an envelope. "It's Darleen's school picture. In case you can use it."

"Thanks," I said, pushing it to one side on the table.

I accompanied her down the stairs in my stocking feet. Shivering on the porch, I watched her climb into an old, faded-green Ford pickup at the curb. Judging by the looks of it, the truck must have been the first one to roll off the assembly line after the war. Or maybe it had been through the war. For a couple of seconds, while a dim glow shone from the dome light, I could see the man at the wheel inside. He looked hard, like sunburn, chewing tobacco, and a three-day beard. My stare met his pale eyes for a short moment, and I froze. He aimed a piercing look at me, expressionless, almost dead like a lizard's. The dome light went off as Irene Metzger yanked the door closed with an icy, metallic bang. Then Dick Metzger pushed the starter, shifted into gear, and eased away from the curb.

I stood there in the cold for another minute, watching the red taillights recede down Lincoln Avenue. My encounter with Irene Metzger had unsettled me. Convinced her daughter had not run off, she must have feared the worst. She must have been sure Darleen had met a terrible end. What other explanation could there have been? I remembered some of the chances I had taken as a teenager. I had been lucky in my games of Russian roulette, while Darleen Hicks, it seemed, had spun the cylinder and come up with a bullet in the chamber. Irene Metzger's pain must have been cruel, incorporating both grief and uncertainty. A heavy sadness welled up in my chest as I thought of my own parents, both gone, and the wayward girl I had been. The wayward girl I still was.

Damn! Eddie Robeleski. He was still upstairs. When I returned to the warmth of my apartment, I found him standing there, lipstick smeared over his face, his shirttail hanging out.

"Come on over here," he said with a big grin, and he reached out both arms for me.

"Oh, God," I said, rubbing my temples. "I'm sorry, Eddie, but you have to go now."

CHAPTER TWO

SUNDAY, JANUARY 1, 1961

I don't normally suffer from hangovers. That's the blessing, or perhaps the curse, of holding one's drink. But this day I woke up slowly, my mouth a little dry, one nostril hermetically sealed, and my eyes crusted shut by the sandman. The new year had dawned, and I had slept through the morning.

A confirmed heathen, I usually spend my Sunday mornings lingering over coffee, a hard roll and butter, and the newspapers at Fiorello's across the street. Fadge, the proprietor and my dearest friend in the world, was sure to be there on New Year's Day, albeit late. Not because it was New Year's Day, of course, but because it was morning, and he always ran late. He usually rolled up to the curb in his '57 Nash Ambassador at eight thirty. Unshaven and (sometimes) unwashed, he would trundle across the seat to the passenger's side like a walrus undulating across an ice floe, the car rocking on its struts beneath him. The driver's door was dented shut, so he always dismounted from the right-hand side. Barely four years old, the car was a disgrace. From the day he'd driven it off Bob Frank's Hudson-Nash lot on Division Street, Fadge had abused it through neglect of maintenance, willful flaunting of the laws of physics, and a demolition-derby style of driving. Vinnie Donati, a local mechanic, once begged Fadge to tell him what he had against the car.

But this frigid New Year's Day, I was curled up on the sofa under an afghan watching George Blanda lead the Houston Oilers over the Los Angeles Chargers in the inaugural AFL Championship Game. There were no college bowl games due to New Year's falling on a Sunday, and the NFL had finished up the week before, so I settled for the new league's championship. Just one of the boys when it came to sports.

By six I still hadn't dressed and didn't see the use of changing from my

17

flannel pajama bottoms and terrycloth robe; I'd be ready for bed before too long.

I heated up a forty-nine-cent Salisbury steak frozen dinner. Having withered in the heat of the oven and long since given up the ghost, the steak sat mired in an epoxy of reduced gravy, like a mastodon trapped in the La Brea Tar Pits. The mashed potatoes had stiffened to a grayish plaster, and the peas and carrots had somehow come out sodden toward the edge of the tray and dried out in the middle. I lost my enthusiasm for the meal and left it to clot before me on the coffee table.

I rose to change the channel, and the television threw a fit. Jack Benny warped and skipped rhythmically from the bottom of the screen to the top, and neither the vertical-hold knob nor the rabbit ears remedied the situation, despite my repeated fiddling. I switched off the set and plopped back down on the sofa, wrapped the afghan around my shoulders, and gazed up at the painted tin ceiling and alabaster light fixture above me. In moments like this, I especially appreciated these unexpected touches in such a simple duplex.

I tried to will time to pass. It was too early for bed and too late to make anything of the day. I turned my head, and my eyes fell on the unopened letter on the end table beside the sofa. Not ready to deal with that.

Across the room to my right, a pair of mahogany pillars framed a wide passageway between the kitchen and the parlor. Two waist-high hutches with glass windows and shallow drawers anchored the columns. I assumed the cabinets had been designed to display books or curios. Picture Hummel figurine knockoffs or pressed-glass swans trying to pass as crystal. But the hutches were, nevertheless, well built and tasteful. I kept my liquor in the one on the right.

The cabinet beckoned me, as surely as if it had crooked a finger. It wasn't yet seven, but I'd waited long enough. Answering the siren's song, I poured myself a thimbleful of Scotch, then, after a moment to consider properly the miserly amount, I topped it off with another two fingers and some ice. The first sting of whiskey, the sip you take before the ice has had a chance to melt and dilute the kick, that's the one that reminds you it's alcohol, reminds you why you drink. With each passing glassful, you think less and less that it's booze. It dissolves into a simple beverage, transforms as if by alchemy into a social lubricant, something to hold in your hand and raise to your lips every so often. It loosens the binds of your corset, and makes you smarter and more attractive. You sparkle with charm. Personality in a bottle. At least for me. But once the burn of that first undiluted swallow has faded in your mouth, your guard drops, you drain the bottle, and end up snoring on the sofa hours later, fully clothed, with the Indian-head test signal glowing blue from the television set across the room. That's still better than waking up with a stranger in your bed. Or you in his.

Two whiskies later, the letter was still there on the table.

I pulled a record at random from the bookshelf and placed it on the hi-fi: Brahms's "Academic Festival Overture," the one that ends with an old German university drinking song: "*Gaudeamus Igitur.*" I raised my empty glass in a toast to nothing. Then I refilled it. I must have been really smart and beautiful by nine o'clock, when I popped the spring cap off a new fifth of White Label and poured myself another drink. Then Fadge showed up with a pizza and a couple of quarts of Schaefer beer.

"About time you showed up," I said, giving him a New Year's peck on the cheek and grabbing the pizza. "I was about to drown."

He pulled off his coat as I dug into the pizza.

"What's that?" he asked, nodding at the envelope on my kitchen table. It was the one Irene Metzger had left me.

"Nothing," I said, picking it up and tossing it to the counter next to the toaster.

"How come you didn't come by the store today?" asked Fadge a while later, once we'd settled in on the sofa with our drinks.

"I was busy," I said. "New story I'm working on."

He eyed the empty bottle in the wastebasket. The recently opened one stood without shame in plain sight on the table before us.

"Tough, working on a Sunday," he said. "And a holiday to boot."

I shrugged. "Yeah, well, you know how it is. You worked today, too."

"Sure, but I didn't get as much done as you did."

We stared at each other. Fadge was no saint and wasn't judgmental either. I couldn't believe he would begrudge me a lazy Sunday of overindulgence.

"How was that party you went to last night?" he asked after a suitable moment of discomfort had passed.

"It was all right," I said. "What did you end up doing?"

"Worked till about eleven thirty, then closed up and went over to Timmy Gallo's."

"Sounds like fun. Did you ring in the New Year there?"

"I wouldn't exactly say we *rang* it in. I drank beer with Timmy's father-in-law, Lou, and we watched Guy Lombardo."

"No girls?" I asked, mugging a pout.

"Timmy's wife changed their one-year-old daughter's diaper on the coffee table in front of the TV. Does that count?"

I shook my head.

"I was so hard up, I drove back here around one thirty to peep through your windows, but someone took away the ladder."

"And after I'd left the curtains open for you . . ."

"Your light was on anyway, so I figured you were busy."

I had to tread carefully now. Joking was fine as long as I didn't cross certain lines. Fadge was sweet on me—I knew that much—and I didn't want to parade my indiscretions in front of him.

"I had an unexpected, late-night visitor. A lady named Irene Metzger."

Fadge took a gulp from the quart of beer and waited, watching me, his eyes bulging from an overactive thyroid. I sensed he didn't believe me. A doubt crawled into my mind: What if Eddie Robeleski had stopped by the store and bragged of his conquest? Why wouldn't he want to blacken my name? I had left him high and dry, after all. Or what if Fadge really did have a ladder?

Okay, that was paranoia. Fadge was a true pal. Even if we did crack off-color jokes about sex, he'd never so much as made a pass at me, and he'd never inquired about my attachments. Still, a girl likes to give the impression of propriety, even if she's only kidding herself. So what if Irene Metzger showed up later than I'd said? Would Fadge rather hear that I'd been breaking commandments with a twenty-one-year-old sailor on shore leave? What kind of floozy do I take me for?

"Who's Irene Metzger?" he asked.

"Have you heard about that junior-high-school girl who disappeared ten days ago? Darleen Hicks."

"Sure," he said. "I read the papers. What's she got to do with it?"

"This Irene Metzger is her mother."

"So what did she want with you at one thirty in the morning? And on New Year's Eve."

"She wants me to help find her daughter. She says the police don't care, and she read all my articles on the Jordan Shaw murder."

"How proud you must be," he smirked.

"Jealous. Anyhow, she thinks I can help find out what happened to Darleen."

"So what does she think happened?"

"The only thing Irene Metzger's sure about is that her daughter didn't run off. And that her husband, the girl's stepfather, couldn't possibly be a suspect."

"Isn't it always the stepfather?" asked Fadge. "I read *Lolita*."

"You read *Lolita* because you heard it was all about sex."

"True," he granted. "A little disappointing in that regard."

"Serves you right."

"So you've talked to him?" asked Fadge.

I took a sip of my drink. "Not yet. Irene Metzger wouldn't hear of it. She insisted he knows nothing about Darleen's disappearance."

"What else did she tell you?"

"Not much," I shrugged. "Boyfriend's up at Fulton. Couldn't have had anything to do with this, according to her. There are a couple of men who live nearby. Nothing to point to them yet, though."

Fadge rose to get the second quart of beer from the icebox. He asked if I wanted another drink, but I'd had enough. When he returned, he sat down beside me on the sofa, placing his beer on the end table.

"Can I use this as a coaster?" he asked, showing me the unopened letter.

"No, I need that," I said, reaching for the envelope.

He drew it back and squinted at the postmark. "This was mailed a month ago. You haven't even opened it." Then he read the return address: "'Berg and Raphael Statuary.'"

I snatched it away and tucked it into the pocket of my robe. "There's a coaster right in front of you."

"Take it easy," he said. "I didn't mean any harm."

Fadge sipped his beer pensively. A long silence settled over us. I was thinking about Darleen Hicks. I don't know what was on Fadge's mind.

"Her mother said she sometimes took taxis home when she missed the bus," I offered finally. "And sometimes she took rides from strangers."

"There's your ending," said Fadge. "Probably jumped into the wrong car. Wouldn't be the first time."

"Yeah, I thought of that, too. But her mother says she's smart and resourceful. Never got into trouble before."

"She tell you anything else?"

I thought some more. "Just that Darleen chews Black Jack gum. Yuck. And I know I've heard that recently, but I can't remember where."

"You're kidding, right?"

I looked up at him, waiting for an explanation.

"You really don't remember?" he asked. "A couple of weeks ago at the high-school basketball game. You were drunk and got sick in the girls' room. You told me a girl chewing Black Jack gum held your hair while you puked into the garbage can."

What a humiliating reminder. Though it stung, Fadge was right. Partly right.

"I wasn't drunk," I corrected. "And it was the toilet, not the garbage can. I had the flu."

"And a pint of whiskey in your purse," he said. "You told me so yourself."

I waved him off. "The bottle was unopened. Intended for later. It was the flu."

The memory returned instantly. I had drawn photo duty for the Friday-evening basketball game. Our sports-page photographer, Gabe Morrissey, was in Herkimer, covering local kegler Casimir Nowicki in a regional bowling tournament. Better him than me. My editor, Charlie Reese, assigned me to the basketball game over George Walsh, who'd just emerged from football season and was convinced that a basketball field goal counted for three points.

The New Holland Bucks, in the midst of their most promising season in a decade, were squaring off against the Gloversville Red Dragons in a Friday-evening tilt. Charlie wanted some action shots of Teddy Jurczyk— Teddy J., the straight-A freshman sensation who had turned around the Bucks' season after a dismal start, leading them to seven straight wins.

Teddy had been marooned at the far end of the bench, collecting splinters, while the coach's son, Dickie Mahoney, started at guard. Then Dickie came down with tonsillitis. A tall, wiry kid with a crew cut, pale-white skin, and an Adam's apple that called to mind Ichabod Crane, Teddy Jurczyk looked more like the scarecrow man in a Charles Atlas ad than a basketball star. But he was a natural: one of those players who made opportunities for himself and his teammates; handled the ball like a wizard; and led the team in scoring, assists, and steals. While almost all the other players launched workmanlike, two-handed set shots, Teddy soared high and let fly grand, arcing jump shots. Deceptively fast, he glided over the polished hardwood in his tight satin shorts, dishing out assists and sinking baskets by the dozens.

Charlie had instructed me to come back with some good action photos and a pithy, post-game comment from the kid, who—I was sure—would be tongue-tied talking to a girl reporter.

At halftime, the score was tied at thirty-two. Teddy J. was leading the way with fourteen points and five assists. I had been running a temperature since morning, but the nausea was new. I had felt like hell all through the first half, but the real trouble began just as the referee tossed the ball skyward for the second-half tipoff. A crawling, cold sweat on my neck, general discomfort of my insides, and a swallowed gag convinced me that the evening was not going to end well. I had the good sense to spring from my seat in the second row, climb over my fellow spectators, and dash for the exit before it was too late. I bounded up the stairs to the corridor ringing the gymnasium above and shouldered my way through the door of the girls' bathroom. There were three or four girls primping in the mirror, but I hardly took notice. I made a beeline for the first stall. My nausea was cresting, and there was no time to lose. The first stall was locked. I lurched toward the second, covering my mouth and squinting through watering eyes. It was free, but filthy. Summoning God knows what determination (and intestinal fortitude), I managed to dive into the third stall before the floodgates released their plenty. After three or four healthy heaves, I became aware of two firm hands holding my long curly hair clear of the rush of vomit. Or nearly, as I discovered a few minutes later.

Once the convulsions had subsided, and I had wiped my mouth and nose with a wad of tissue, I collapsed against the wall of the toilet and closed my eyes. A gentle hand stroked my head, and I heard a soft voice comforting me. I opened my eyes and turned to see my savior: a pretty girl with green eyes and dark hair, pulled back on both sides by tortoise-shell barrettes, leaving long bangs hanging down to her eyebrows in front. She was about fourteen or fifteen, with red lips and a pink nose from the cold weather. She smiled at me, and that's when I saw the silver braces on her teeth and the black chewing gum sticking fast to them like a thick tar.

"Are you okay now?" she asked. I nodded. "I sent my friends to get the nurse. Can you stand up?"

"Just help me to the sink," I said. "I want to splash some cold water on my face."

The young girl lifted me off the floor and guided me to the bank of washbasins where she released me and let me fly solo. Grasping the porcelain sink with both hands to steady myself, I examined my reflection in the mirror. I looked away; didn't want to throw up again. I dug into my purse, looking for a comb, and removed the pint of Dewar's and placed it on the edge of the sink. Then I pulled out a lipstick, a package of gum (Doublemint), and my Leica, before I finally located the comb at the bottom.

"I have to go now," said the girl. "The nurse will be here soon."

I washed my face and slipped a stick of gum into my mouth. A few minutes later, I had combed my unruly hair and painted my lips. I was presentable, if somewhat green. Repacking my purse, I realized the bottle of whiskey had vanished.

The kindly nurse, Mrs. Golnik, and the faculty chaperone, Miss Barnett (one of the girls' gym teachers), escorted me to the infirmary. Mrs. Golnik clopped down the corridor in her sturdy heels, supporting my left elbow, while Miss Barnett squeaked along in sneakers and a Jack LaLanne jumpsuit, holding my right. To complete my embarrassment, the assistant principal, Mr. Brossard, arrived to investigate the incident. I assured them I was fine to see myself home, but they insisted I call someone to pick me up. Since it was Friday, I knew Fadge would be up to his fat elbows in the usual ice cream, hot fudge, and egg creams, so he was out of the running. I dreaded calling Charlie Reese. His wife, Edith, always sounded put out when I phoned, and, all things being equal, I preferred to keep my boss in the dark about my more spectacular bouts of public disgrace.

"I'm fine now, really," I said, giving it one last try. "I can drive myself home."

Miss Barnett volunteered to accompany me, but she was a bit too keen and transparent in her motivation. Mrs. Golnik stood before me, flashed a light into my eyes, then grasped my jaw firmly in her right hand and cocked my head upward to examine my pallor. She flattened the back of her fingers against my forehead to gauge my temperature, then frowned, gave a curt shake of her head, and said no. Mr. Brossard, a stocky man in his mid-thirties, considered the options from a few feet away. He stood there squarely in a plain brown suit and wingtip shoes, arms crossed over his ribs, legs splayed just beyond their normal stance, like a football coach watching his charges practice.

"You don't look well, miss," he said finally. "We can't let you leave by yourself."

"Ellie?" a voice called from the doorway. "I thought I saw you. What are you doing here?"

Stan Pulaski: deputy sheriff, ardent admirer, and my hero. Thank God. Stan would drive me home and probably pay me a few compliments on the way, too. "Gee, Ellie, your hair looks nice with sick in it."

Mrs. Golnik and Mr. Brossard were satisfied with my escort and gave me their blessing to go. Miss Barnett sighed as I took my leave.

Stan drove me home in his cruiser and helped me up the stairs. My landlady, Mrs. Giannetti, witnessed the whole thing, and I heard all about it the next day.

"What were the charges, dear? Well, at least you were completely dressed."

I wanted to invite Stan in for a coffee, but I felt like vomiting again, and he was on duty besides. He left me at my kitchen door, bowing and replacing the cap on his head.

Fadge nudged me from my thoughts. "Anyone home?"

"Sorry," I said, putting the memory aside. "Do you suppose that girl was actually Darleen Hicks?"

"Kind of a long shot, isn't it?"

"Maybe. But she was chewing that awful gum. About the right age . . ."

"Wasn't that after she disappeared?" asked Fadge.

I shook my head. "No, the basketball game was the sixteenth, a Friday. Darleen Hicks disappeared on Wednesday the twenty-first."

"Could have been, then," shrugged Fadge.

"Wait a minute. Her mother left me a photograph."

I jumped from the sofa and scooted to the kitchen, where I grabbed the envelope and pulled out the picture. A teenage girl, smiling, with hair falling off her shoulder. There was something impish in her eyes. Just a bit naughty perhaps. Her lips were open just so, and you could detect the braces underneath. She was pretty. And she was the girl who'd held my hair and stolen my whiskey.

MONDAY, JANUARY 2, 1961

My New Year's lethargy flowed into the next day. I was still on the sofa, still wrapped in my robe, watching the Rose Bowl and working my way to the bottom of a bowl of Chex Mix. Okay, to be honest, it was just some stale Wheat Chex cereal from the box. No nuts, no pretzels, just cereal. I love football, but even I realized that any self-respecting fan should have already showered, breakfasted, and dressed for the game. Down from the highs of my New Year's revelry with Eddie Robeleski, and sullenly aware of the letter I was avoiding, I felt deflated and withered, filled with self-reproach for wasting another day doing nothing. And still I had no spark to drag myself to the bath. Then something strange happened.

Washington was leading Minnesota 17–0 at the half. I watched with eyes half shut as the Huskies' cheerleaders began to lead a typical flip-card routine with their fans on the Washington side. Black-and-white squares spelling out inanities for the edification of the opposite side of the stadium and the national TV audience. I was about to take a snooze when I noticed the Washington student section was holding up some kind of funny-looking, bucktoothed creature. Looked like a beaver. Then, on command, they flipped their cards and spelled out "SEIKSUH," Huskies spelled backwards. (I'm quick with anagrams and word puzzles.) The roaring crowd seemed to lose some of its volume, no doubt thrown off stride by the funny beaver and the backward spelling. But the next stunt silenced everyone inside the Rose Bowl, including the television announcers, Mel Allen and Chick Hearn. For some obscure reason, the Washington fans were showing their school pride by spelling out "CALTECH" for all the world to see.

I sat up, confused at first, leaned closer to the set to see better, then burst out laughing. Caltech didn't even have a football team, but they had just won the Rose Bowl. The prank lifted the fog I'd been under since I'd sent Eddie Robeleski packing New Year's Eve. Skipping the second half (Washington won 17–7), I showered and dressed in a hurry. It was a Monday, after all, even if it was a holiday. If a gang of Caltech eggheads could infiltrate the Rose Bowl and steal the halftime show on national television, I could get off my duff and start asking some questions.

CHAPTER THREE

My company car, a 1955 red-and-black Dodge Royal Lancer, sat cockeyed in the street in front of my apartment, its right front tire mashed against the curb, where it had skidded to a stop New Year's Eve. Not my best parking effort. A glaze of frost, spotted like lichen on a rock, dappled the black hood, windshield, and roof. It was cold. A sunny, biting cold that sears your nostrils with every breath. Your mouth moves like a ventriloquist's, as if you've been punched in the lip and shot full of Novocain. I jumped inside the car, praying it would start, and turned the key. Not always first at the post, the engine roared to life this day, eight cylinders thrumming under the hood as I pumped the gas pedal for encouragement. It took a full five minutes before the heat finally made some headway with the frost on the windshield. The wipers swept a half-thawed patch of glass clear so I could see. I shifted into gear and pulled away from the curb, heading down Lincoln toward Market Street, where I turned south. At the bottom of the hill, past DeGroff's TV and Radio Repair, the New Holland Hotel, and the Masonic Hall, the Mill Street Bridge spanned the Mohawk, connecting New Holland proper with its South Side. A steel truss affair, the gray bridge arched like a behemoth's spine above the icy river fifty feet below. Like New Holland itself, the Mill Street Bridge was grim and industrial, form and function as one, with little thought for trimmings or frills.

On the opposite end of the bridge, the Coezzens Broom Factory anchored the west side of Mill Street, and the Mueller Linseed Oil Company held down the east. I drove up the hill, past the armory and the home of a fellow with whom I'd had a brief, ill-fated fling two years earlier. His mother didn't appreciate the finer points of my "Jewiness," to use her word, and my forward behavior eventually proved too much for his conservative sensibilities. He broke it off via telegram. Funny how guilty he felt after the sin, not while we were breaking the commandments (number seven, in particular). It was just as well; as sinners go, he was fairly passive. A girl doesn't want to do all the heavy lifting herself.

At the top of the hill, I turned west on Route 5S, heading toward the open farmland of the Town of Florida. My first stop was a gray clapboard house, set back about a hundred yards from the road on a solitary stretch of County Highway 58. A fine powder of dry snow had blown into the road, stretching its long fingers to reach the other side. You could see the wind at play in the drifts, sculpting and brushing its handiwork in the bitter cold. The gentle hills, lit by a low winter's sun, spread out for miles to the west, buried in white from the recent snowfalls. A dented tin mailbox on the side of the road read "W. Rasmussen." Beside that stood a *Republic* newspaper box, leaning to the side about thirty degrees short of perpendicular.

I turned into the narrow drive, tires crunching over packed snow and gravel, and approached the gray house. A giant man in coveralls, work boots, and a red-checked hunting jacket emerged from the adjacent barn before I'd even reached the house, as if he'd been standing sentry, waiting to ward off trespassers. Fresh from some heavy exertion in the barn, the big man glared at me as I climbed out of the car. Steam rose from his ruddy head, shorn close to the skin like a spring sheep. He looked to be in his sixties or seventies. He was at least six feet eight and burly, easily three hundred pounds: the biggest man I'd ever seen. A small, bloody ax dangled from his right hand. I nearly lost my nerve, but I'd come this far.

"Well?" he said, as I pulled my wool overcoat tight about my neck. The late-afternoon sun was blazing behind him, and I squinted through the glare to see him.

"Mr. Rasmussen?" I asked, eyes fixed on the ax. No response. Just a frozen, iron face staring back at me. "My name is Ellie Stone. I'm a reporter with the *Republic*."

Still no reaction.

"I see you're a subscriber," I continued, referring to the newspaper box I'd seen at the head of the drive.

"I don't much like the idea of girl reporters," he said. "What do you want?"

"Sorry," I said. "I hope you won't cancel the paper over it."

"What do you want?" he repeated.

"I came to ask you about Darleen Hicks."

"Who?"

"Darleen Hicks," I repeated. "Dick Metzger's daughter."

Rasmussen sauntered over to the porch where he stood before a frozen tree stump. He flipped the ax into the air like a juggler, catching it again by the handle once it had completed a single rotation. If he wanted to intimidate me, he'd succeeded.

"Why ask me?"

"She disappeared two weeks ago. Do you know anything about her?"

"Nothing," he said, weighing the ax in his hand.

"Never met her?" I asked, trembling as much from the cold as from fear. My God, I wanted to run. "Never laid eyes on her?"

"Sure, I seen her a couple of times," he said. "Couldn't describe her, though."

"Have you seen her recently? Maybe with someone else? A boy? A man?"

He shook his head.

"Do you have any family here, Mr. Rasmussen?"

"My wife died eight years ago."

"You don't have any children?"

He shook his head once, then took a step toward me. His huge, windburned face twisted quizzically. "Are you that girl reporter who wrote about Judge Shaw's daughter?"

"Yes."

He considered my answer for a moment then repeated that he didn't like the idea of girl reporters.

I didn't know exactly how to respond to that, so I asked him about his dispute with Dick Metzger. Rasmussen cocked his head to one side.

"So I'm supposed to have killed his daughter 'cause he put a fence a couple of feet on my property?"

"Who said she was dead?"

Rasmussen clapped the ax into the frozen stump with a sharp chop. He glared at me, eyes smoldering. Clearly he was not used to girls talking to him this way.

"I mean, why do you think she's dead?"

"She's been missing without a word for two weeks," he said. "She's dead, and you know it, too. You're barking up the wrong tree if you think I had something to do with it."

"What's in the barn?" I asked, marveling at my audacity. This guy had a bloody ax, for God's sake.

"What's that?" he asked, easily as surprised as I by my effrontery.

"You came out of the barn with a bloody ax in your hand. I was wondering what you were doing in there."

"You come snooping around on my property uninvited, accusing me of killing a little girl . . ." He shook his head woefully. "Why don't you go home and bake some cupcakes?"

"Thank you for your time, Mr. Rasmussen," I said, my breath freezing in the sunny air.

"You'll leave my property now."

In the rearview mirror, I could see the giant man watching me from the porch until I'd turned back onto 58 and lost sight of him.

A half mile farther down the road, I rolled to a stop at a rusting mailbox. The name "Metzger" was stenciled on the side in rough block letters. I sat inside the car staring up the long, unpaved drive. The house was not visible from the road, hidden by a small hill and tall trees. The sun was still hovering over the horizon to the west, but I was parked in near darkness. I could feel the outside temperature dropping along with the waning daylight. The exhaust from my Royal Lancer billowed white in the air, rode forward on the wind, passing over the entire car, and scattered somewhere beyond the nose of the long black hood.

This was where Darleen Hicks had waited for the school bus, where she had climbed aboard for the last time on December 21. I made a mental note to find the driver and interview him about that day. Why had Darleen missed the bus that afternoon? Maybe he would know something.

For now, though, I wanted to meet the other neighbors: the Karls. Their house was another three-quarters of a mile past Dick and Irene Metzger's farm. It was dark when I turned down the road that led to their place. Another weathered, blistered clapboard farmhouse, this one a pale blue color. Languishing half buried in the snow, the carcasses of three fossilized vehicles—a long-dead tractor and two old pickups—welcomed visitors. No Negro lawn jockeys here. The leaning porch was stacked on one side with fragments of old, busted furniture—wooden chairs, a dilapidated table, a disemboweled sofa, and a couple of galvanized steel tubs, dented and filled with rags—and at least two cords of firewood, neatly stacked, on the other. A *Town & Country* cover photo.

I pulled the handbrake and switched off the engine. A biting wind whipped over the landscape, carrying waves of fine, fallen snow to new destinations. I popped open the door and felt the cold rush under my overcoat. Climbing out of the car, I pulled my coat tight and hurried toward the porch. I slipped and skinned my knee.

"Are you lost?" a voice called through the raw wind. I looked up from my bleeding knee to see a man standing in the warmly lit doorway of the house, between the woodpile and the broken furniture. Dressed in a red waffle-knit thermal undershirt and overalls, bib and brace unhitched and hanging from his waist, he studied me deliberately. He looked to be about sixty.

I shook my head, pushed up off the ground, and brushed my knee clean. The stocking was ripped clear through.

"Sorry for the intrusion," I said. "I wanted to ask you some questions about Darleen Hicks."

The man frowned, rubbed his stubbled chin, then waved me toward him. "Come on in," he said, "before you catch your death. We'll clean up that knee, too."

The house was warm, almost steaming. A potbellied stove blazed in the sitting room, and the oven was belching heat in the kitchen where he led me. There, a thick, gray-haired woman of about fifty or fifty-five was stirring some meat stew and boiled potatoes on the stove. She looked surprised to see me. A man in his mid-twenties gazed up at me from the table. His greasy hair, cut down almost to the scalp on the sides of his head, had been chopped coarsely, as if by hedge sheers on the top. He smiled a crooked-toothed grin at me but didn't get off his duff to say hello.

"Sorry, I didn't get your name," said my host.

"Ellie Stone," I answered. "I'm from the paper."

"The paper? What happened to Lenny?" he asked.

"Who?"

"The paperboy," he said.

"Oh, no. I'm not the papergirl. I'm a reporter for the paper, looking into Darleen Hicks's disappearance."

"A girl reporter?" he laughed. "No kidding?"

I blushed and nodded.

"I heard of her," said the young man at the table. "She wrote all those stories about Judge Shaw's daughter just a couple of weeks ago."

The father, a stocky man with thick, yellowing-gray hair slicked back on his head, cackled to himself.

"Well I'll be a monkey's uncle," he said, marveling at the wonders of the modern world. "A girl reporter . . . What's next? A colored mayor?"

"Please have a seat, miss," said the lady. "I'll make you a plate."

The father scrambled to pull out a chair for me, and I sat down.

"She skinned her knee falling on the ice," he said to his wife. "Get her a bandage, Doris."

The son leapt from his chair and circled around in front of me, gaping at my legs, which I clenched together to protect my modesty. He was as eager as a bird dog and not shy about showing his enthusiasm.

"I'm Bob Karl," said the old man, as his wife dabbed my knee with some Mercurochrome. "That's my son, Bob Junior, and my wife, Doris."

The son and heir continued to drool over my legs, but his mother was blocking his line of sight. Once she'd patched my knee, I tucked my legs out of view under the table. The show over, Junior returned to his seat.

"That's right, Bobby," said Doris. "You sit next to our guest. You two youngsters will have plenty to talk about, I'm sure."

I didn't share my hostess's confidence.

While the mother had been tending to me, a small calico cat had wandered into the kitchen and jumped onto the counter. She was interested in the stew, but it was too hot. Doris Karl shooed the cat away, but she didn't seem too bothered by the prospect of sharing her supper with Puss.

"You ought to throw that cat out of here," said Mr. Karl, dipping his head to see over the lenses of his reading glasses. "We got company, after all."

"Let her be," said his wife. "Edna caught a mouse this afternoon, right behind the breadbox. Didn't you, Edna? Good girl," and she gave the cat a pat on the head.

"She *is* a good mouser," granted Mr. Karl. "Now how about some supper? Miss Stone, please join us."

"I'm sorry," I said, thinking of the mouse behind the breadbox and Edna, the cat who'd killed it. "I've got a dinner date this evening." A complete lie. They offered me milk instead.

"I don't understand how people can eat so late," said Mr. Karl. "Girl reporters and supper at seven o'clock . . . I'm in bed reading the Good Book by that hour."

Mrs. Karl ladled out steaming portions of mouse stew into three yellow bowls. She smoothed her apron, sat down, and reached out both hands, one to her husband and one to her son. Before I knew what was happening, Junior and his father had each grabbed one of my hands. I nearly gasped.

"Lord Jesus," intoned Karl *père*, eyes clenched shut, "be our guest, and let thy gifts to us be blessed. Amen."

The other Karls echoed the amen then looked at me.

"Amen," I offered.

Mr. Karl smiled, tied his napkin around his neck, and dug in. After about two minutes of spoons clicking and lips slurping, he took a breath and regarded me queerly.

"Didn't you say you come to ask about Darleen Hicks?"

"That's right," I said, grateful for the opening. "As you must know, she disappeared from school two weeks ago. I was hoping you could tell me something about her."

"What for?" asked the father.

"Well, so I can help find her."

He took another mouthful of stew and chewed, looking off into space. His wife frowned.

"But you're just a girl," she said.

"I'm a reporter for the paper," I reminded her. "And Irene Metzger asked for my help."

"I seen her articles in the paper," repeated Junior. "She wrote all about Jordan Shaw's murder."

The mother shook her head and returned to her stew. "I don't like talk of killing, especially at suppertime. Girls shouldn't get caught up in things like that."

"Have you ever seen Darleen with any men or boys?" I asked the group, braving Mrs. Karl's disapproval. "Do you know anything about her that might help me locate her?"

Mr. Karl said he'd seen her from time to time on the road and doing chores. And she'd delivered a pie to him in September, compliments of her mother.

"Real nice of Mrs. Metzger to think of us," he said, eyes beaming. "She's a fine-looking woman, too."

Mrs. Karl bristled in silence.

"What about Darleen?" I asked. "Did any of you see her leave home the morning she disappeared?"

"Not me," said the father. "But, Bobby, didn't you say you seen her getting on the bus that day?"

Bobby had his chin in his bowl, spooning the last of the stew into his mouth. He looked up, startled.

"I was spreading some hay for the horse over by the fence," he said. "She was walking to the bus stop on Fifty-Eight. The girl, not the horse."

"You can see her property from here?" I asked.

"Not from here," said the father. "But the horse pen is over that way. Still kind of far, though. How'd you see her from there?"

Bobby wiped his mouth with his napkin and said the horse had wandered over to the boundary. "Likes to scratch himself against the fence. I went after him and seen the girl walking down her drive."

"Did you speak to her?" I asked. He shook his head. "Isn't it dark at that hour? How could you have seen her?"

"Maybe I just heard her. She walked down the drive like always and got on the bus five minutes later."

"Like always? Are you always up and chasing horses at that hour?"

"Well, yeah," he said, stumped by my question. "We rise early around here."

"So you did or didn't speak to her?" I asked.

He looked at his mother then his father. They offered no advice.

"I didn't talk to her, no. I never spoke to her much. She was just a kid, you know."

The Karls finished their supper quietly after that, topped it off with coffee and some Minute Tapioca pudding. (The empty box was standing on the counter, between the stove and the mouse's breadbox.) I sat there fidgeting, waiting for an opportunity to bolt out the door. When they finally pushed back from the table, patted their stomachs, and began picking their teeth, I seized my chance.

"Well, thank you for your time and hospitality," I said, rising from my chair. "And the milk."

The mother and father glared at me as if I'd drunk from the finger bowl. Mr. Karl and Junior reached out their hands and took mine before I could make good my escape. All three shut their eyes again and squeezed hands. I was yanked back into my seat.

"Give thanks to the Lord," wailed Mr. Karl, "for he is good. His mercy endures forever. Amen."

"Amen!" That was me. "Well, I'll just go now. Don't get up. I know the way out."

They did get up—all three of them—and waved goodbye from the porch as I climbed into my car. They stood there watching as I turned the key, pumped the gas, and turned the key again.

"Please, start!" I begged. I tried again. "Start, you no-good . . ."

I pumped and turned three more times, until the engine groaned like a dying swan and fell silent. She was dead. I banged my head on the steering wheel. Exhausted though the battery may have been, it had the strength to bleat one last whimpering cry from the horn. That summoned Mr. Karl to the car. I cranked down the window, and the frigid air rushed in.

"Sounds like a dead battery," he said. "Come back inside, and Doris will get you something to eat. You're going to miss your dinner date."

Like fun I was.

"Can't you give me a jump?" I asked.

"Sorry. Lost my truck three months ago to the bank. I got a tractor in the barn, but the fan belt's busted. Battery's dead besides. Just like yours." He smiled.

I remembered something about a horse but thought better of it.

"Do you have a phone, Mr. Karl?"

"That we got," he said and stood aside for me to open the car door. "Of course it's a party line, and Mrs. Norquist usually does her telephoning after supper. We can visit while we wait for her to finish."

Back inside, I declined all offers of nourishment, planting myself next to the plain, black phone, which sat atop a lace doily on an end table. Mrs. Norquist was indeed monopolizing the line. I checked in from time to time, lifting the receiver hoping for an operator, but getting an earful about Mrs. Norquist's late husband instead. Finally, when my hosts left the room, I grabbed the phone and interrupted the call.

"I beg your pardon," she said. "Who's that?"

"It's CONELRAD, ma'am. We've issued a warning. Please go to your bomb shelter or root cellar. Whatever you've got."

"I thought CONELRAD was a radio warning," she said.

The old bird was sharper than I had expected.

"We've recently added telephone warnings as a new service in the event of nuclear Armageddon."

"Oh, my!" she gasped. "Lillian, this could be it," she said to the woman on the other end of the line. "If this is it, Godspeed. If not, I'll see you at bingo on Thursday."

I tapped furiously on the cradle until the operator came on. I gave her Fadge's number and waited for him to pick up. It was a Monday evening in January, not his high season. When he answered, I told him I needed a ride, no excuses.

"I'm working," he said in his defense. "Can't you call a cab?"

"I'm stuck out here with Ma and Pa Kettle and their halfwit son," I whispered frantically. "Get your fat ass out here and rescue me now!"

"How can I resist such a polite request? Where is this place?"

I gave him the directions, and he said he thought he could find it.

"But you're going to be beholden to me," he said. "And I'm not talking a peck on the cheek, either."

"Let's see how fast you get out here, then we'll negotiate the payback."

My hosts reentered the room just as I hung up. Mrs. Karl was carrying a plate of powdered-sugar cookies and a steaming pot of tea. Mr. Karl was beaming at me. Junior was nowhere to be seen.

"Thank you so much for letting me use your phone and wait in the warmth," I said.

"Our pleasure, miss," said Mrs. Karl.

"Parcheesi?" asked the father.

"Oh, my! Parcheesi!" I smiled. "May I use the powder room?"

"We don't have fancy facilities," Mrs. Karl explained as she led me back behind the kitchen. "There's just the one john," she said. "It's back here behind Bobby's bedroom."

We passed through the kitchen, past Edna, who, tail twitching, looked ready to pounce on something in the corner. Mrs. Karl showed me into a cold, dark bedroom.

"Just through there, dear," she said, switching on the light and pointing to a crooked door.

She left me alone. The small room, colder than the rest of the house, was fitted with a single bed, heaped with heavy blankets, rumpled and poorly made; a dim lamp on a small wooden table; an old braided rug, whose dark colors were difficult to identify in the low light; and an eerie collage, which hung on the wall behind the bed. The upper right-hand side of the three-by-four-foot work of art was decorated with 4-H clovers in felt, construction paper, and metal buttons. Intermingled with these, three pairs of shoelaces dangled from thumbtacks. I couldn't fathom a guess. Below the laces, there was a yellowed school certificate of some kind and several black-and-white snapshots of a forsaken farm, most likely the Karl Ranch, though the photos were so dark and small it would be nearly impossible to tell. Locks of brown hair—God knows whose—were held together with a faded ribbon and taped to the collage. And there was a filthy, crumpled neckerchief, knotted and stapled to the background. A Zorro mask, a red paper poppy flower, and a tin sheriff's badge. Several varicolored, shiny stars dotted the canvas here and there, self-awarded praise by the artist, perhaps, or a constellation as dim and odd as its maker. But the dominant feature of the collection was a hundred or so pictures of ladies in girdles, brassieres, and underwear, cut lovingly from the pages of the Sears catalog. Wrinkled from the globs of paste used to hold them captive forever, the models were arranged at different angles, with great care taken to mix sizes and shapes, presumably to lend artistic panache to the creepiness.

A shiver ran up my spine, and I was pretty sure it was the collage not the temperature of the room. I crept to the bathroom, peered inside, and thought better of it. I was going to have to wait until I reached home. But that didn't mean I wouldn't milk my time away from the Karls for all it was worth. I stalled, staring at myself in the mottled mirror, examining my manicure, and touching up my lipstick.

When I finally opened the bathroom door, Junior was standing there, not two feet away. I quite nearly fainted. Only the certainty that he would perform unspeakable, hill-folk perversions on my person if I were to black out kept me conscious.

"Excuse me, miss," he said, grinning as he pushed past me. "Nature calls."

It was seven fifteen, and I was furious and frightened at the same time. I really wanted a drink, and not a glass of milk. That fat rat Fadge hadn't shown up yet, and it seemed Mr. Karl had ideas of fixing me up with his 4-H, Zorro pervert of a son. It had reached the point where the old man wouldn't take no for an answer. He wanted me to come for supper the next evening (afternoon, really) and then attend some kind of backwoods dance with Junior at the Town of Florida volunteer firehouse Saturday night. Finally, I took the path of least resistance and told him that, being Jewish, I wasn't allowed to drive or dance on Saturday, our Sabbath. He blanched, his wife choked, but Junior smiled his cretin's grin. Either he didn't understand or didn't care. Or maybe he'd heard Jewish girls were easy.

"But supper tomorrow sounds swell!" I said brightly, unable to resist. "I'll bring the Mogen David wine. What time shall I come?"

"Actually, miss," said Mr. Karl with a rueful shake of his head, "we don't partake."

We sat in awkward silence for ten minutes more until the lights of a car flashed through the parlor window and across the wall behind me. I jumped up off the sofa as if it were electrified and thanked my hosts once again.

"I'll send a wrecker tomorrow for my car," I said to the stunned couple. I wriggled into my coat. "Shalom!" The door closed behind me.

"Where the hell have you been?" I asked, once I'd slid into Fadge's Nash.

But it wasn't Fadge at the wheel. It was his crony and old school chum, Tony Natale. Tony lived two doors down from me on Lincoln Avenue, and I often saw him at Fiorello's. Once he'd asked me out, but I turned him down. I just couldn't have accepted; it would have killed Fadge.

"What are you doing here, Tony? Where's Fadge?"

"He couldn't leave the store. Just be glad I wasn't busy."

"Right. What do you have to do? Address the UN?"

"You wanna walk home, Ellie?"

"Drive, Tony."

CHAPTER FOUR

TUESDAY, JANUARY 3, 1961

I got an early start the next morning, phoned Dom Ornuti's Garage to have my car towed in from the Karl farm, then met Fadge for coffee across the street. He was in a foul mood due to the persistent cold and slow business.

"I forgot to thank you for sending Mr. Charm to pick me up last night," I said, sipping my coffee at the counter.

"That's right," he said. "You owe me, remember?"

"I took care of your pal Tony," I said. "Get your payment from him."

Fadge sulked. He was sitting a few stools away, flipping through some bills. He grunted then impaled the lot on a spindle in front of him.

"All paid?" I asked, trying to engage him.

He snorted with derision. "Yeah, they'll get paid when I rob a bank."

"Are things that bad?"

He shrugged. "I'll be all right once spring comes. And besides, they know they can't cut me off or they'll never get their dough."

"Speaking of owing," I said, feeling guilty, "I think my tab for last week is a dollar eighty-seven."

I placed a single on the counter, counted out some change, and slid it over to him. He didn't bother to check it. Just stuffed it into his pocket. No wonder he had trouble making ends meet; I'd seen him use the cash register as his personal wallet. Whenever he needed money for pizza or beer or records, there was a drawerful of cash waiting for him.

"If nobody buys ice cream in the winter," I said, "why don't you just close the store and drive to Florida for a couple of months?"

"I can't go south for the winter because I don't want my regulars taking their business to Mack's Confectionery while I'm gone."

"But you told me yourself that these cheapskates only buy the newspaper and the occasional quart of milk. What do you make on a news-paper? A penny?"

"Some of them buy a cup of coffee, too," he said, casting a sideways glance my way.

"Okay, I'll take a dollar's worth of penny candy, a pack of cigarettes, some gum, and two of your dirtiest magazines."

"How sweet of you to finally buy one. But I don't need your charity."

To prove I was serious, I swiveled off my stool and examined the chewing-gum display opposite the counter: Wrigley's Spearmint, Doublemint, and Juicy Fruit; Beech-Nut Peppermint and Pepsin; Life Savers of all colors and combinations; Adams Chiclets and, of course, Black Jack gum. I picked up a package of Black Jack and turned it over in my hand, examining the black-and-blue label, thinking of Darleen Hicks.

Fadge noticed and asked how my investigation was going.

"Nothing much so far," I said. "She's got some pretty weird neighbors, though. Last night I met the folks who live on either side of her farm out in the Town of Florida. Say, why do they call it Florida anyway?"

"I forget why. We studied about it in the seventh grade. Has some-thing to do with Ponce de Leon, but I don't remember."

"Anyway, the one neighbor was almost seven feet tall," I said. "The others were that strange Karl family. I suppose I could picture the son as a homicidal psychopath. And the giant was juggling a bloody ax for my entertainment. He's a scary one."

"That must be Walt Rasmussen," said Fadge. "He comes in here a couple of times a year. In the summer, of course. He always gets a double banana split in a booth as far back as he can."

"Let's not aggrandize, Fadge. You've only got four booths."

"He likes the last booth if he can get it, El, okay?" he sneered. My heart jumped; my brother used to call me El. "You can sit at the counter with the pimple-faced boys from now on."

"You'll always make room for me," I said, pushing Elijah's memory to one side. "You'd kick six double sundaes out of a booth for me, wouldn't you, Ron? Even if I just wanted a glass of ice water."

"Sure," he smiled. "Next time, you'll have your ice water in that little room in the back. You know, the one with the porcelain chair."

We had a good chuckle over that one. Fadge's sense of humor hadn't progressed beyond the bedroom and the bathroom, but I didn't mind. He was my favorite guy in the world.

"So what were you saying about Walt Rasmussen?"

"Nothing. Just that when he comes in, he orders a banana split and likes the back booth. Then when he leaves, he gets a quart of hand-packed ice cream to go. Butter pecan if we have it. Otherwise, coffee."

"Friend of yours?"

"No. That man is friendless in the world. But he won't let anyone else wait on him but me. Once, Tommy Quint asked him what he'd have, and Walt almost made him cry. Poor Tom. For some reason Walt puts up with me waiting on him. Maybe because I own the place, and someone has to take his order. He's a funny one. Parks that pickup truck of his at the curb, climbs down, and lumbers in here in his muddy boots. And he always shows up late at night, around eleven or eleven thirty. Just before closing."

"Why's that?" I asked. "A vampire?"

Fadge shook his head and seemed to be thinking hard about his answer. "The kids stare at him, you know? They can be so mean, the little bastards. They stare at him like he's some kind of freak because he's so huge. They peep around corners, laugh with each other, point at him. And Walt just sits there in the booth, as big as Goliath, looking straight ahead and ignoring them. But you can tell it's burning him up. Like maybe he'd like to squash those kids like bugs and be rid of them."

"Or maybe wring their necks and chop up the bodies in the barn?" I said.

Fadge shrugged. "Imagine what it must be like to go through life having people point at you like you're a sideshow attraction."

I'd met the guy. I wasn't feeling too much sympathy for the man who'd waved an ax in my face.

A horn sounded outside. It was Vinnie Donati from Ornuti's Garage at the wheel of my Royal Lancer, which he'd just towed back from the Karl farm. I abandoned Fadge and ran out to meet Vinnie as if he were a beau picking me up for a date.

"All set, Ellie," he smiled, as I climbed into the passenger seat. "Drop me back at the garage, and she's all yours."

"Thanks, Vinnie," I said, flashing my best smile at him. "What was the problem this time?"

He slipped away from the curb and took a left at the corner of Lincoln and Glenwood. "Dead battery," he said. "And some wiring went bad. Same old thing. This was a good car until it was totaled."

"What do you mean, *totaled*? I asked Charlie Reese about accidents, and he swore there was only minor body work done on this car."

"I'll let you in on a little secret if you swear you won't tell," said Vinnie, giggling like an idiot. "This car was pulled out of Winandauga Lake last summer."

"What?"

"You know Fred Blaylock?" he asked.

"I should. He's the associate publisher at the paper."

"Well, he had dinner and some drinks one night last August at Maraschino's in Mayfield after the races in Saratoga. I heard he lost a hundred and sixty-two bucks. Anyways, to drown his sorrows, he had a few too many Old Fashioneds with his steak dinner and mistook the boat launch for Route Twenty-Nine on his way home. Drove right into the lake." He laughed and slapped the steering wheel. "Poor car ain't been right since."

I glared at him. "Not funny, Vinnie!"

He swallowed his grin, knitted his brow, and cleared his throat. "Electrical problems," he pronounced soberly.

"And that must be where the mildew smell comes from."

"Most likely," said Vinnie. "Consider yourself lucky, though. We had the car in the shop for at least a month after Fred Blaylock drove it into the lake, trying to make it right again. When we dried her out, the horn used to blow when you made a left turn. People on the street would look. Every time I took her for a test drive, I waved and smiled back at them so I wouldn't look like an idiot."

I noticed Mrs. Pindaro shuffling along on the icy sidewalk with her pug, Leon, on a leash doing his business, and I reached past Vinnie and blasted the horn. The dog yelped and leapt into a snow bank.

"What'd you do that for, Ellie?" he asked as if I'd doused him with cold water.

"Wave, Vinnie," I said sullenly, crossing my arms and turning away. "You look like an idiot."

I fumed, thinking of my boss, Charlie Reese. He'd assured me the car was all right when he'd given it to me a month earlier. (Someone had cut the brakes of my Belvedere, resulting in a crash that could have killed me.)

"Gee, Ellie, I'm sorry," said Vinnie finally.

"Why didn't you tell me this a month ago?" I asked. "This car's been nothing but trouble."

He patted my shoulder and told me not to be upset. "Come on. You didn't really think they'd give such a nice car to a girl, did you?"

∂☉

Theodore Roosevelt Junior High School squatted stubbornly on the corner of Division and Wall Street, flanked by the Lutheran church to the east and Porter's Funeral Home to the west. Located at the bottom of Wall Street's steep hill, a few blocks from the river and the Mill Street Bridge, the junior high was a hulking, five-story mass of grayish bricks, long since discolored by grime and soot. It was joined at the hip to a second, newer building that easily surpassed its companion in both size and homeliness. Large rectangular banks of steel windows were tilted open, venting excess radiator heat into the frigid winter air. The school had a drab, industrial look, like a carpet mill or a prison. A small annex filled half of the empty lot adjacent to the communicating buildings. The remaining blacktop, scarred with faded parking stripes, was fenced in with two rusty, netless basketball hoops on either end.

It was just after eight a.m. Two school buses were idling along the curb of Division Street on the north side of the school, their tailpipes chugging exhaust into the cold air. I parked on the flats of Wall Street on the west side of the prison yard, just opposite the cigar store, and made a dash for the school and the warmth inside.

The corridors were deserted, as classes had begun a few minutes before. I made my way down the dull terrazzo floor, looking for someone to direct me to the principal's office. A janitor told me I was on the right path.

"Good morning," I said to the tall, middle-aged lady in a poodle cut with short bangs. Quite fashionable if your name was Mamie Eisenhower. Hers wasn't. The Bakelite nameplate on her desk read "Mrs. Worth, Secretary."

"I'd like to speak to a student," I said.

"Is that so?" she asked, subjecting me to close scrutiny. "What about?"

"It's a personal matter," I answered.

"And who are you, if I may ask?"

"Of course," I chirped. "My name is Ellie Stone. I represent the *New Holland Republic.*"

She rose and walked over to a desk to engage another middle-aged lady in a powwow. The second woman looked over her horn-rimmed glasses at me from a distance, shrugged, and said something to Mrs. Worth, who moved on to a frosted glass door marked "Ass't. Principal" in black lettering. She knocked and, following a muffled grunt from the other side, let herself in. A few moments later, she reappeared and asked me again who I was and what I wanted.

"My editor wants me to do a feature on Teddy Jurczyk, the basketball star."

The woman eyed me guardedly. "And who are you again?"

"My name is Ellie Stone. I'm a reporter for the *Republic.*"

She made her way back to the office with the frosted door and, after a minute, she returned and invited me to follow her. "Mr. Brossard will see you now," she said.

I remembered that name immediately from the basketball game at the high school. He seemed like a decent enough man. I only hoped he hadn't formed a bad opinion of me, based on the vomit in my hair.

"*You're* Miss Stone?" he asked. "Do you remember me?"

"Of course," I said, surely blushing. "What are you doing here at the junior high? Aren't you the high-school assistant principal?"

"Oh, no. That's Mr. Brooks. He was ill that night and asked me to fill in for him," he explained. "All the administrators are required to chaperone basketball games from time to time."

"Your lucky night," I said. "You got the sick girl. Sorry about that."

He smiled and waved it away, held a chair for me, then took his own seat behind his desk. I smoothed my skirt over my knees, wet my lips, and waited for an opening.

"So you're here to do a story on our Teddy J.?" he asked, rocking in his chair. "He's quite a phenomenon, isn't he? And only a freshman."

"I'll say. It's not often a freshman makes the varsity squad. And he's the best player on the team."

"Best player in the county," he corrected.

"By the way, I've been wondering why the freshman class is part of the junior high and not the high school. That's unusual, isn't it?"

"Simple explanation," he said. "The high school's too small to house four classes, so the freshmen are here."

"I see. So tell me more about Teddy."

"Well, did you know he's an honors student at the top of his class? Best scores in the school on the Iowa Tests. We think he's going to be a writer someday. Brilliant in English."

I smiled back at him for a moment, then I gave up on the charade.

"Yeah … Mr. Brossard, I'm not really here to talk about Teddy Jurczyk," I said.

Brossard was confused. "Sorry?"

"I'm investigating the disappearance of a student of yours: Darleen Hicks. I believe she's a ninth grader here."

The change of gears had thrown him. He gaped at me, cocked and shook his head as if to clear out the cobwebs.

"I'm making general inquiries into her disappearance. Her mother is convinced she didn't run off, as the sheriff believes."

Now he was peeved. Brossard leaned forward in his chair and stared me down, as he might do to a truant student.

"What game is this, Miss Stone? Why the pretense of talking about Teddy Jurczyk?"

"I apologize. I don't know why I said that." Truth be told, the disorienting effect had been my intention. It's an old Indian trick I use often when interviewing. He settled back in his chair, watching me, drawing out the silence to intimidate me. I really don't mind silence; it gives me time to collect my thoughts.

"Yes, Darleen Hicks is a student here," he said finally. "What is it you want exactly?"

"I'd like to speak to some of her friends and others who might know her. Her teachers, for instance."

Brossard pursed his lips and tented his fingers as he thought it over. Then he shook his head.

"I don't like the idea," he said. "It would be very disruptive."

"For the girls or the teachers?"

"Both. Did the paper send you here?"

"Actually, it was Mrs. Metzger, Darleen's mother, who asked me to help find her."

Brossard was softening now that the shock of my bait-and-switch was wearing off.

"I remember the day it happened," he said. "It was a Wednesday, and her class went to Canajoharie to the Beech-Nut factory. I remember because it was also the day of the superintendent's Christmas banquet. The entire administrative staff was invited to Isobel's. I had ziti and meatballs."

"That's nice," I said, wondering what that had to do with the price of tea in China. "About Darleen Hicks . . ."

"It is a perplexing case," he said.

I crossed my legs and leaned forward. "In what way?"

"People don't simply disappear. She either had a plan to run away or someone made plans for her."

"Foul play?" I asked.

"What else?"

"You don't think she ran off?"

"That's the most likely possibility, but she would have needed help."

"Money . . ." I offered.

He nodded. "And transportation."

I mulled over his assessment for a minute then asked him again about Darleen's friends. He frowned as he considered it.

"I still don't like the idea of you talking to the girls. They're young and impressionable."

"You're probably right," I said, thinking I could easily visit Darleen's friends on my own away from school. "What if we compromise? May I speak to a couple of her teachers?"

∂⊙

Brossard arranged for me to meet Darleen's algebra teacher, Mr. Vernon, during his free period at ten a.m. Mrs. Worth escorted me to the newer building, passing through a communicating hallway on the second floor, and we climbed the stairs to the teachers' lounge on the third.

"That's him over there," she said, pointing to a tall, balding man in a dark-blue suit, serving himself some coffee from the stainless-steel perco-lator. He was bent over about twenty degrees, searching for the cleanest sugar cube in the bowl to drop into his cup. Once he'd made his selec-tion, he stood up straight and twirled a spoon through his coffee. Then he turned and spotted us in the doorway. He must have been warned of my visit, because he scowled. In fact, he produced the physical equivalent of a groan, making me feel as welcome as a sneeze. He trudged over to a worn armchair and placed his coffee down on a heavy wooden side table. Then he drew a handkerchief from his vest pocket and proceeded to dash it against the chair's seat several times. At least that's what I assumed he was doing. From my vantage point at the door, his large bottom blocked my view and any chance for a true eyewitness account.

"I'm afraid you'll find he's a pill," Mrs. Worth whispered in my ear.

Her confidence surprised me, and I must have looked puzzled. Then she gave me a gentle nudge. "Go get him," she said. "Girl reporter." And she winked. No smile. Just a wink.

I still looked confused.

"Jordan Shaw was in my Girl Scouts troop," she said. Then she turned and left.

I cracked a small grin back at her, though she didn't see it. Then I made my way over to the seated Mr. Vernon. I stretched out a hand and introduced myself. Vernon neither accepted my hand, nor invited me to have a seat in the chair on the other side of the wooden table. I took it anyway.

"Thank you for agreeing to talk with me," I said once I was seated, knees tucked safely together. He wasn't looking.

"I didn't exactly have a choice, did I?" he grumbled, lighting a cigarette.

I had no coffee, so I lit a cigarette as well, and we settled in for our chat.

"I'm investigating the disappearance of Darleen Hicks," I began. "I understand she's a student of yours."

"Great work so far," he said, looking away from me.

"Can you tell me anything about her?" I asked, ignoring his crack.

"What's to tell? She was a rotten student with a miserable attitude. There are dozens like her here, all headed for jail or the welfare line."

I studied him as he sipped his coffee. He hunched his shoulders and blinked his eyes rapidly as he raised the cup to his lips. I noticed the sprinkling of dandruff on the shoulders and lapels of his jacket, as well as some flakes trapped in the slicked-down hair of his head.

"What are you looking at?" he asked, and I shook the distraction from my head.

"Tell me about Darleen in particular," I said. I had learned not to let the subject dictate the direction of the interview.

"I didn't like her, if that's what you mean. She was a silly girl who didn't pay attention in class. She chewed gum incessantly. Used to stick it under her desk. Disgusting habit."

"I see. Anything else you remember about her?"

"She failed fractions."

"Why do you refer to her in the past tense?" I asked.

Vernon had tired of me. He sneered, picked himself up, and trod off out of the lounge. I was writing some notes in my pad, about to leave, when another teacher, a woman, approached me.

"Excuse me," she said. "Are you inquiring into Darleen Hicks's disappearance?"

Her voice was a crackling falsetto, her dress a baggy flower print. She was about sixty and smelled of rose water.

"My name is Adelaide Nolan," she said, taking Vernon's vacated chair. "Darleen was in my English class last year."

"What can you tell me about her?" I asked, stubbing out my cigarette.

"Well, she's a spirited girl, but she has a good heart. I remember that she felt sorry for Oedipus."

"How's that?"

"She felt sorry when Oedipus poked his own eyes out. We were reading Sophocles, and Darleen thought that Oedipus was a little too hard on himself. After all, he didn't *know* Laius was his father and Jocasta was his mother."

"Still," I said, "one can understand his horror at the discovery . . ."

"Of course," she said, taking a sip from her tea. "But Darleen didn't quite grasp the concept of Greek tragedy."

"Excuse me, Mrs. Nolan, but why are you telling me this?"

"Because of Joey Figlio."

I remembered that Irene Metzger had told me about him. He was Darleen's boyfriend.

"Joey Figlio was in the same class," she continued. "A bad egg, that boy."

She sipped some more tea, and I waited for the punch line. After thirty seconds had ticked by, I cleared my throat.

"Oh, sorry," she said after my prompting. "A smart aleck. I gave him detention once."

"What for?"

"It was for Oedipus again. He made a tasteless joke in class when

Darleen Hicks said she felt sorry for Oedipus. As I told you a moment ago, Darleen asked me why poor Oedipus should blind himself. And I said how would you feel if you killed your father and married your mother?"

"And then?"

She pinched her nose and sniffed. "From the back of the room, Joey Figlio started singing '*I want a girl just like the girl that married dear old Dad.*'"

I couldn't quite suppress the laugh that snorted through my nose. Adelaide Nolan stared daggers at me and pursed her lips in disapproval. I apologized, but continued to struggle to stifle a smile. Joey Figlio had unsuspected wit. Mrs. Nolan quickly changed her opinion of me.

"I'm sorry," I choked. "Please continue."

She shrugged her shoulders. "That's it. That's the story."

"Excuse me, but why did you tell me about Joey Figlio, then?"

"Because you should be questioning him, not her teachers," she said. "He's no good, that one. Do you know that he writes obscene poetry? Disgraceful. Poems about Darleen. Go talk to him, and you'll find out what happened to that poor girl."

CHAPTER FIVE

I stopped by the paper to give Charlie Reese an earful about the Royal Lancer. I had always thought it was too nice a car for me, and now I had the proof. Millicent Riley, the publisher's secretary, said Charlie was in a meeting with Mr. Short. That was my signal to scram. Artie Short hated me, and I was happy to return the sentiment.

"Not so fast, Miss Stone," Millicent called after me. "Mr. Short said he wanted to see you when you came in."

I froze. What did he want with me? I'd been keeping my nose clean for weeks, if you didn't count getting sick at the high-school basketball game.

"Can't you tell him you haven't seen me?" I asked.

She shook her head. "Why would I do such a thing?"

"I don't know, to be nice just once?"

She buzzed her boss inside the office. "Miss Stone to see you, Mr. Short." Then she glanced at me and said, "You may go in now."

"Look what the cat dragged in," mumbled Short as I entered. "I didn't know Miss Stone still worked here. Haven't seen her in weeks."

"Now, Artie, she's been a good girl," said Charlie. "She's been covering the basketball games and the City Council meetings for me. Doing a darn good job, too."

Artie waved a hand at Charlie. "Our Miss Stone knows we're old friends," he said with a scowl, pointing at a chair for my comfort. "Isn't that right, Miss Stone?"

"Like Martin and Lewis," I said.

"I called you in here to discuss this missing-girl case," he said, ignoring me. "What's her name, Charlie?"

"Darleen Hicks."

"Yes, Darleen Hicks. She's a ninth grader who disappeared a couple of weeks ago. Charlie wants you to look into this. I'm not convinced, of course. Seems like a lot of nothing."

"By the way, what were you working on this morning?" asked Charlie. "I'll reassign it."

"Actually, I was working on the Darleen Hicks story."

The two men exchanged glances. Charlie shrugged.

"Don't you know what your staff is doing?" Short frowned, taking a seat at his desk.

Charlie threw me a withering look.

"Darleen's mother came to meet me and told me the whole story. She asked me to help her."

"What have you got so far?" asked Short as he shuffled through some papers.

"I've interviewed the mother, the neighbors, and two of her teachers."

"What's next?" he said, not even looking at me.

"Her friends," I said. "A couple of girls and her boyfriend." I paused. "Then there's her stepfather. And of course the sheriff."

Short rose from his desk and began digging through a filing cabinet against the wall. "I still don't think there's much of a story here," he said, his back to me. "If I did, I'd put George on it, you can be sure of that. He wrote the first couple of stories on this when it happened. He says it's a dead end. And I don't like the idea of wasting manpower." He turned halfway around to look at me. "Or should I say *girl* power in this case?"

"There could be something to this disappearance," said Charlie. "Let's give her a week to dig around."

Artie Short yanked some papers from the filing cabinet and returned to his desk. He wrinkled his nose, as if something in the room smelled bad, and cocked his head.

"I don't like it," he said, shaking the papers in my general direction. "But if she doesn't neglect the basketball and other assignments . . ."

That was our cue to leave. Charlie and I stood and made for the door. Short called after him, "I'm expecting her to deliver on this. I don't like wild-goose chases."

Charlie and I filed out of Short's office and headed toward the newsroom. We didn't speak as we went, but we both knew a debriefing was in the offing. I followed him into his office and leaned against the bookcase.

"Well, that wasn't so hard," he said. "Now you'd better get something on this story, or Artie will kill it."

"And if I do find something, he'll hand the story back to George Walsh," I said.

Charlie had no answer for that. Instead he asked me what I had learned so far. I filled him in, saying I wasn't even sure if she'd been the victim of foul play or if she'd simply run off.

"Is there any legwork I can do for you? Anyone giving you trouble? Or maybe there's someone you can't reach?"

I shook my head. "I can manage. But speaking of your help, I know the car you got for me was pulled out of the lake last August. Thanks a lot."

He stared dumbly at me for several seconds. Then he got that trapped-animal look in his eyes.

"Sorry about that, Ellie," he said finally. "I just couldn't swing another. As it is, after you drove the first car into the tree, Artie wanted to take it out of your salary."

"You make it sound as if I hit the tree because I was primping in the rearview mirror. Someone cut my brakes, Charlie. They were trying to kill me. Not like Fred 'One for the Road' Blaylock. What's he driving these days, by the way? Something shiny and brand new, I'll bet."

"I told Artie it wasn't your fault, but he's old-fashioned. Doesn't like the idea of women in the workforce, let alone behind the wheel. That's why you've got to lie low and keep up with your other assignments."

I pouted, dissatisfied with the car discussion. "Why can't Georgie Porgie take some of what I'm doing? Local theater, for example. The Mohawk Valley Players are doing *South Pacific* this year. Give that to George. But don't tell him how the war ends; you'll spoil it for him."

Charlie said nothing. He often indulged me, especially where George Walsh was concerned. George was Artie Short's son-in-law and strutted around the newsroom like the cock of the walk. George's antagonism toward me was well known to all at the paper. He routinely tried to insult me by talking down to me in meetings and asking me "to be a good girl" and fetch him some coffee. He stopped doing that once he noticed the coffee I'd given him had an odd taste.

But when it came to getting the better of George, it was mostly George who did the heavy lifting anyway. His miscues were legend at the paper, like the time in June of 1959 when his headline proclaimed, "Ingmar Bergman Knocks Out Floyd Patterson in the Fourth Round." (He even got the round wrong.) Twice he referred to Pat Summerall as the placekicker for the *San Francisco* Giants, who don't play football. And in general, his sports stories rang false; his shallow knowledge of the games and awkward grasp of their lexicon always bled through the ink. He wrote strange headlines like "Speed-Ball Ace Timmy Vardon Twirls Two-Hit Gem in New Holland Tilt." Georgie's articles had the mawkish, homespun feel of a *Boys' Life* story from 1925.

Walsh and his father-in-law hated me, never more so than during the Jordan Shaw investigation just a month earlier when George tried to muscle in on my story. In the end, despite his aversion to me, Artie Short had to hold his nose and go with the girl reporter over his own son-in-law.

"I'll try to get you another car," said Charlie.

"Forget it. I love that car now, mildew and all. It's mine."

"There must be some help you could use. I can put Norma Geary at your disposal."

"Norma? From the steno pool?"

"She's smart, Ellie. And eager. She can make calls, run errands, get you coffee. Give her a chance."

"But isn't she a little old?"

Charlie frowned. "She's younger than I am."

"That's not saying much. You're Methuselah's older, uglier brother, Pops." I could get away with that remark because Charlie was the handsomest, most dignified gent in the city. Tall and trim in his broad-lapelled pinstripes, he looked like "Dad" in a pipe-cleaner ad, and he was proud of his full head of silver hair.

"I'm fifty-six," he announced proudly. "And you'll get here one day, so watch what you say. Poor Norma lost her husband last year and had to find a job. She's got a retarded son to care for."

He looked pathetic.

"Okay, spare me the waterworks. I'll take her."

Norma Geary was seated at a desk near the back of the steno pool, head cocked to the right, reading from a sheet of handwritten paper clipped to a stand. She tapped furiously on an old black Smith-Corona with green keys, while all around her, younger women were clicking along on much newer machines. There were even a couple of stylish electric IBMs for the fastest girls. But Norma didn't seem to mind. In fact, I fancied I could see a small grin on her lips as she typed.

"Are you Norma Geary?" I asked.

She continued typing without looking up at me. "Yes, and you're Miss Stone."

How could she read, type, and speak at the same time? And to top it all off, she was chewing gum.

I told her Charlie Reese had said she might be interested in helping me on the Darleen Hicks story. She stopped typing mid-word and beamed at me.

"Yes, Miss Stone," she said. "I'd like that very much."

I had an hour and a half to kill before the junior high let out. Not enough time to drive to the reform school and back, so I thought of my old friend, Sheriff Frank Olney. I wanted to talk to him about Darleen Hicks, but there was more to do still.

"Norma, would you be able to look up a couple of things for me?" I asked, once she'd set up her desk in the City Assignments area where I sat. "I need copies of the *Republic* from December twenty-first, twenty-second, and twenty-third."

She scribbled the dates silently in shorthand on a pad. Then she looked up at me over her round glasses, which were tethered to her neck by a long, golden chain.

"Yes, miss," she said. "What else?"

"And the Canajoharie paper, too. Same dates. You'll probably have to drive out there. I can get you a voucher for gasoline."

"Yes, miss," she said again, making a note. "The *Courier Standard*."

"Then I need the addresses and phone numbers of these girls." I handed her the list of Darleen's friends. "And finally, can you call the Fulton Reform School and make an appointment for me for tomorrow morning? I'd like to talk to a student named Joseph Figlio."

"That's a rough place," said Norma, finishing her notes with a flourish that broke her pencil nib. "I'll take care of it."

"So that's it," I said. "It's not too much?"

"Not at all," said Norma.

The Montgomery County Administration Building was a few miles north of New Holland. I swung onto Route 22 and sped toward the Town of

Poole. No problems from the Royal Lancer now. I patted the dashboard and encouraged her. Then I switched on the radio and heard the last strains of Johnny Burnette singing "You're Sixteen." "Western Movies" came on next, and I'd had enough. I twisted the knob to off and enjoyed the frozen landscape in silence. Why did I even bother with the radio? I was becoming as particular as my father when it came to music. Another thought to push to one side.

"Eleonora!" boomed Frank Olney when I entered the warm office building. He knew I hated that name. He was standing over Deputy Pat Halvey, reviewing some papers. "What are you doing here?"

"I just wanted to see my favorite cops," I said.

"Like fun you did. Let's see, what cases have we had recently that might interest a clever reporter like you?" he asked, scratching his bald head. "It wouldn't be that teenage girl who ran off, would it?" He squinted an accusatory eye at me.

"You see right through me, Frank," I smiled.

"Yeah, well, you're pretty transparent that way, aren't you? I'll bet you think she didn't run off at all. You think there was foul play."

"I don't know what I think yet. But I'm here to cover the bases."

Frank hunched over and started to pour himself a mug of coffee from the percolator when he realized the machine was empty.

"Damn it, Halvey," he roared at the deputy. "I told you to make sure there was always coffee. Now what can I offer Ellie?"

"There's a doughnut," said Pat. "And we can make some tea."

"Tea? What is this? A garden party? Make some damn coffee!" Then he motioned for me to follow him inside to his office.

"Sorry, Ellie, the coffee will take a while," he said, lowering himself into his swivel chair. "Now what can I do for you?"

"Irene Metzger came to see me New Year's Eve," I began. Frank groaned. "She asked me to look into her daughter's disappearance."

"That woman is a nuisance," said the sheriff. "She's been pestering me for more than two weeks. Called me at home on Christmas."

"Have a heart, Frank. She's worried sick. Lost her only child."

The sheriff waved a bearish hand at me. "Run off is more like it."

"Can you give me a little background on the case? Who did you talk to?"

"Just about everyone, I suppose. Her friends, family, teachers. I really did look into this, Ellie. No one knows a thing. The girl just disappeared."

"What about her boyfriend?" I asked.

"Yeah, I talked to that little JD. If anything bad happened to her, he'd be my prime suspect. But like I said, she's just run off somewhere."

"But he's got an alibi, doesn't he? He's been locked up at Fulton for a couple of weeks."

Frank smirked. "I guess you didn't know he slipped out the night before Darleen Hicks went missing. They caught him two days later and took him back to Fulton," said Frank.

"What about the bus driver?" I asked, changing gears. "Did you talk to him?"

"Just to ask if he'd seen her that afternoon. He insisted she got on the bus. Remembers seeing her climb on before he drove off. But no one else said she was on the bus. Later on, he changed his mind and said he's not sure if she ever boarded the bus at all."

"That's puzzling."

Frank shook his head. "He's an old drunk. Obviously can't remember straight. In fact, when I questioned him, he said he parked the bus just behind the snow hills near the Metzger farm to take a half-hour nap after finishing his route. That's baloney, of course. He was drinking is more likely."

"Snow hills?" I asked. "What's that?"

"The county plows the snow, collects it if it doesn't melt, and dumps it in a clearing at the end of that road. That's where the bus driver says he took his nap."

Frank gave me the driver's name and address: Gus Arnold, sixty-one, a former city sanitation worker. He lived by himself in a trailer next to Drusek's Scrapyard, northeast of town off Route 29.

"You can find him at the school district depot around five," said Frank. "That's off Grove Street on Polack Hill. Try to catch him before five fifteen, or he'll be halfway to the bottom of a fifth of rye."

I told Frank of my plans to pay a visit to Fulton to speak to Joey Figlio.

"The hell you will!" he said. "Damn it, Ellie, you can't go up there alone. It's not safe for a young lady. I'll send Stan or Halvey with you."

"I can take care of myself," I said, feeling touched and annoyed at the same time. "They have guards at Fulton, don't they?"

"It's too late to go over there today anyway," grumbled Frank. "They'll be locking down those animals in an hour or so."

Polack Hill, so delicately named for the Polish folk who lived in the
humble duplexes around Upper Church Street, dominated the city's
East End from above. On the corner of Church and Tyler, St. Stanislaus
Church stood white and tall, bounded by the Polish-American Veterans
Club on one side and the Lithuanian Club on the other. Nearby, Jepsen's
Lumber spread out over four entire city blocks, its tall green fence
surrounding the yard like a palisade. You could hear the shrill buzz of the
saws and the banging of hammers inside; smell and taste the smolder of
fresh pine passing under the spinning teeth of the blade; and—if there
was no rain—you could see the fine sawdust hanging in the air and feel
it settle on your hair.

I drove two blocks past Jepsen's to the intersection of Tyler and Grove,
where a chain-link fence, crowned by a tangle of rusting barbed wire,
stretched around a large gravel parking lot. An orange-and-black metal
sign read "New Holland School District Vehicle Depot." Inside, dozens of
yellow school buses, spattered with the frozen brown-and-gray residue of
slush and salt, huddled on the uneven ground in the bitter cold.

I parked at the curb and waited in the warm car, working up the
courage to open the door to the cold. Just to mock me, the radio played
"Theme from a Summer Place." I smoked a cigarette and waited. It was just
five, already dark, when an empty bus rumbled up to the gate, negotiated
the bumpy bit of cracked sidewalk between the street and the parking lot,
then juddered its way toward the other buses. A stocky man, dressed in a
red-checked hunter's cap (flaps down), blue dungarees, and a dark-green
field jacket, emerged from the bus. Lugging his gray lunch pail in his meaty
hands, he trod off to the dispatcher's cabin next to the garage. I switched
off the radio and climbed out into the cold.

"I'm looking for Gus Arnold," I announced to the two men inside.
One was a slight man, about thirty, with slicked-down wavy hair and a
thin, tired mustache. He was seated at a heavy wooden desk with a nameplate that identified him as "S. Pietrewski, Dispatcher." The other man was
the bus driver I'd just seen pull into the parking lot. Both stared at me. I
could see their frozen breath in the cold room.

"Gus Arnold?" I repeated.

"That's me," said the driver. His broad face was red from the cold, and his bulbous, pocked nose betrayed a fondness for drink.

"My name is Eleonora Stone. I'm a reporter for the *Republic*."

"What do you want with me?"

"I'm investigating the disappearance of Darleen Hicks. I believe she rode your bus."

"Yeah," he said hesitantly. "I already talked to Sheriff Olney about that. He said she ran off."

"Would you mind answering a few questions for me?"

He looked at the dispatcher, who didn't seem to like the idea of one of his drivers mixed up in a story like this. He squinted at me through the low light.

"Do you remember seeing Darleen that day?" I asked, ignoring the dispatcher's scrutiny.

"Yeah, I seen her get on the bus in the morning like usual."

"What about that evening? The sheriff said you remembered seeing her on the bus."

Gus Arnold twitched, wiped his nose with his hand, then shook his head. "I must have remembered wrong. She didn't get on the bus that afternoon."

"Are you sure?" I asked.

He frowned and whined at me that there were a lot of kids, wearing heavy coats and winter hats. He couldn't be expected to remember every one of them every day.

"But the sheriff said you were certain Darleen was aboard the bus that afternoon. Then you changed your mind. What would make you doubt your memory now?"

"I seen her in the morning, but not in the afternoon," he repeated.

"Did she have friends on the bus?" I asked, moving on. "Who did she sit with?"

"There was a couple of girls, I guess. They got off at the same stop. The one before the Metzger farm. There's the Dobbs girl and the Liswenski girl. I don't know their first names."

"And you dropped those girls off that day?" He nodded. "What time was that?"

"Same as always," he fidgeted. "I finish my run around four twenty or so."

"I can show you the log from that day if you don't believe him," volunteered the dispatcher. "Right here," and he flipped back several pages in his ledger to the date in question.

I ran my finger down the column, searching for G. Arnold. It was there. Route number 17, bus 63, South Side and the Town of Florida.

"It says here you returned the bus to the depot at six eighteen p.m.," I said, and Gus Arnold blanched.

"Let me see that," said the dispatcher, rising from his seat. He scanned the ledger then looked to Gus for clarification. "That's right, you got back late that day. Where were you?"

Gus Arnold looked terrified, his eyes open wide, revealing a network of bloodshot capillaries in the whites.

"The streets were icy," he said.

"But you were more than an hour late," I said.

"And I had a flat."

"That's true," said the dispatcher. "There was a big puncture in the tire."

I knew that was a lie. Frank Olney had said that the bus driver had taken a nap near the snow hills beyond Darleen Hicks's house. Maybe he was lying to the dispatcher to save his job. Or maybe he had other reasons to lie. I kept quiet; I would confront him about his story at a more appropriate time.

The dispatcher eased himself back into his seat and fixed his glare on the driver. He said nothing, but I could tell he was thinking hard on something.

"You changed the tire yourself?" I asked after a long, awkward silence.

Gus Arnold nodded but wouldn't look at me. I glanced at the dispatcher, who was still staring at Gus, a troubled look of doubt on his face, as if he was wondering how well he knew this man.

CHAPTER SIX

It was after eight, and I was already slouched on the sofa, working on my second drink of the evening. *Laramie* was playing on the television. No volume, and I wasn't paying attention. I didn't like westerns, especially on TV. Between sips of whiskey, I nibbled on some slimy canned asparagus spears and a cold slice of ham. Dinner. The phone rang. I didn't recognize the voice at first. It was Norma Geary.

"Sorry to interrupt your evening," she said.

"Where are you?" I asked.

"At work. I just wanted to give you your schedule for tomorrow."

"Schedule?"

"You've got a nine a.m. appointment with Joey Figlio at the Fulton Reform School for Boys," she began. "Maybe you should write this down."

I rummaged through my purse for a pencil and paper, wondering who was working for whom. "Ready," I said, and Norma gave me the agenda:

9:00 a.m.: Joey Figlio at Fulton Reform School
11:00 a.m.: City Desk meeting in Charlie Reese's office
12:00 p.m.: Lunch with Norma Geary at Wolfson's to review requested editions of the *New Holland Republic* and *Canajoharie Courier Standard*
1:00–3:00 p.m.: Work on Hicks story for Thursday's edition
3:30 p.m.: Meet Darleen Hicks's friends at junior high school

"Good job, Norma," I said, quite impressed. "But what are you doing at work? What about your son?"

"I'm leaving now. Toby will be waiting for me at home. He likes to watch *Dobie Gillis* on Tuesdays."

I said goodnight, feeling wretched for being two drinks into my evening ritual while Norma was still at work and her son, Toby, sat waiting with Dobie Gillis and Maynard G. Krebs for company.

WEDNESDAY, JANUARY 4, 1961

About eight miles west of New Holland, a cluster of single-story buildings huddled behind a high fence at the bottom of a hill: Fulton Reform School for Boys. Probably lush green in summer, the place was now barren, desolate, and white. A line of naked elms, their brittle, gray branches spreading like fans against the sky, fronted the school's metal fence like pickets. The school looked like a lonely outpost in hostile territory.

The guard let me through the gate and instructed me to check in with the officer on duty, who was expecting me inside the main building. He searched my purse for contraband, confiscated my nail file, and asked if I really wanted to take a camera in there.

"More than likely you'll get it stolen," said the skinny young man in a green uniform and cap.

I left my precious Leica and billfold with the guard, who stashed them in a box below his desk. He smiled and waved me past, then pointed me in the direction of the visitors' room.

Fulton wasn't really a prison, so guests and inmates mingled in many of the public areas. A dark, heavyset man, smelling of stale perspiration, showed me to a large, cold room outfitted with long wooden tables and benches. The high, steel windows looked like the ones I'd seen at the junior high school, only these had a sturdy metal grating between them and the inmates below.

"Wait here," said my escort, and he disappeared through the swinging doors.

I sat down at one of the long tables. Ten minutes later, the doors swung open again, and some students started drifting in. A rough-looking bunch, they sauntered over to different tables and slouched into their seats, eyeing me the whole time. After a few minutes of quiet study, three got up and began circling me like buzzards. The boldest of the three sized me up and took the seat opposite. I tried to avoid his stare, but he twisted and contorted himself like a bird doing a mating dance until he'd attracted my eye. He was small and wiry, with dark, curly hair and a football mustache above his lip: eleven hairs on each side. He had the hardened look of a wretch. Young, but let's face it, already lost.

"Hey, you, pretty chick," he said. "Hey!"

I ignored him. He reached across the table and flicked my nose. I recoiled then froze in place. His buddies closed in. The oldest of them was all of sixteen, but I was scared.

"What's your name, baby?" asked one of the boys behind me. I didn't look to see which one.

"Scram, Dooley," said the boy across from me. "I was here first."

Where was that smelly guard who'd shown me in? Another boy touched my hair from behind me. I jumped.

"Screw you, Frankie," said the voice at my back. "Maybe you saw her first, but I'm here now, so shove off," and he gave my hair a quick twirl with his hand.

Yet another boy sat down next to me and grinned. His incisors were gray with decay where they touched his canines. His breath smelled, too. With no help in sight, and seriously fearing the worst, I took a gamble.

"Okay, who wants to be first?" I blurted out. The boys all gave a start. "You, Breath of Death?" I said to the one next to me. "Have you ever even kissed a girl before? And Frankie here doesn't count." Their jaws dropped, and the other boys roared with laughter. "You think this is funny?" I said, turning to face the boy who'd twirled my hair from behind. "Hairy palms, gaunt, sallow expression . . . You'd better cool it with the self-abuse, or it will fall off."

Howling laughter from across the room, and red faces all around me. Breath of Death and Hairy Palms crumbled instantly under the weight of derision from their mates and lost their swagger. Still the boldest of the bunch, Frankie didn't budge. He just smirked at me.

"I'm not going anywhere," he said, fixing me with his eyes.

I leaned forward and placed my elbows on the table before me, returning his stare. I tried to reflect his animus back at him and force him to blink. But that wasn't working. Then I laughed, I don't know why. It was one of those nervous, uncontrollable explosions that snorted through my nose. That made things worse. The laughter turned into a fit. My eyes watered, I pointed at Frankie in derision, and slapped the table. I must have looked crazy, and everyone in the room was watching.

"Cut it out!" said Frankie, but I laughed harder and louder. "I said shut up!"

I'd unnerved him. He broke off his glare and glanced around to gauge the reactions around him. He sneered some more, yelled at me again to can it, but I was beyond reason now. Then he swore and called me an unflattering name. He pushed away from the table and screamed, "Weirdo!" as he threw his hands in the air.

He began to walk away, and his fellow reprobates directed a chorus of jeers at him. But he had one last salvo to fire as my laughter finally subsided.

"I'll come looking for you when I get out of here," he snarled. "And you'll get yours."

Frankie exited stage right, and the assembled quieted down. I had won the round, but beneath my self-satisfied smile, I was trembling. My God, why had I taunted him so? A rush of panic overcame me, and I had to drop a pencil underneath the table so I could bend over and hide the tears I could not control. I wiped my face as I pretended to reach for my pencil. Then I righted myself and stared down at my notebook, praying no one had noticed. Slowly, I caught my breath and willed myself to calm down, if only in the interest of self-preservation. I really needed to control my more daring impulses.

Just then the smelly guard returned with a boy in tow.

"Where have you been?" I asked. "I was nearly manhandled by these delinquents."

He shrugged his indifference. "Cry me a river, sister. Here's the kid you wanted to see," and he ambled off somewhere, surely to scratch himself against a tree.

The kid standing before me was short with longish, unkempt hair. His eyes were big pools of brown, desperate and angry. He had full, red lips, chapped and raw from the dry cold.

"Are you Joey Figlio?" I asked.

"Yeah. Who wants to know?" he said, taking the seat opposite me at the table.

"My name's Ellie Stone. I work for the paper. Darleen's mother asked me to help find her."

"They told me a reporter was here to see me. I wasn't expecting a Girl Scout." And he chuckled.

"That's funny," I said, playing along. "You can have a good laugh over that one when I drive home, and you're still stuck in here."

That wiped the smirk off his face. He fidgeted in his seat, scowling for a moment, then asked me what I wanted.

"I'm trying to find out what happened to Darleen. I assume you'd like to help me."

"I know what happened to her," he mumbled. "The only way you can help is to get me out of here so I can get the guy that did this to her."

"Did what exactly?" I asked.

He gazed at me with those big brown eyes. I couldn't tell if he was seething mad or about to cry.

"You know as well as me that she's gone," he said softly.

I had to admit that a happy conclusion was growing more unlikely by the hour. Darleen had been missing for two weeks in the middle of a frigid cold spell. Chances that she was alive were slim, unless she'd actually run off with an unknown man, as the sheriff maintained. Like Darleen's mother, Joey seemed to have accepted the worst as well. Irene Metzger just wanted to know what had happened to Darleen and to close the book on her poor daughter's life. Joey Figlio wanted something more.

"You said you wanted to get the guy who did this," I prompted. "You said it as if you knew who he was."

Joey stared deep into my eyes, unblinking, and said he did.

"Mr. Russell, the music teacher," he said quietly. "I'm going to get out of this crazy place, with its crazy food and music, and I'm going to kill him."

"This place is crazy?" I asked.

"They make us eat funny food and listen to stupid music," he said as if no further explanation was required.

Joey Figlio warmed to me after that, as if confiding his murderous intentions had made us confederates. His JD, wise-guy veneer melted away, replaced by a sort of inflamed ardor, a sensitive yet volatile passion for everything he cared about, most of all Darleen. Like a fervid partisan or an artist who knows nothing of compromise or half measures, Joey Figlio screamed earnest zeal. But at the same time, you knew he was deeply disturbed. He leaned back in his chair and rocked slowly, staring at the floor as he chewed on the rough edge of a fingernail.

"You drive?" he asked.

"Yes. Why?"

"Not all girls know how to drive."

"Maybe not, but I do."

"Have you ever piloted a plane?"

"No, and I've never captained a ship either. Can we change the subject? I'm here to ask you about Darleen."

He shrugged, as if resigned to being told what to do by everyone. "Okay," he said. "Shoot."

"How long have you known her?" I asked.

"About two years. Since seventh grade. We were in different schools before then."

"Where did you meet?"

"I met her my first day of seventh grade and fell in love with her."

"Isn't that rather young?" I asked, thinking how sweet it was.

Joey didn't answer. He just stared off into space, inscrutable, lost in some tender memory of his beloved or vengeful fantasy of murdering her killer. It could have been either one with this boy. Barely an adolescent, he was contending with painful adult emotions that he was ill-equipped to handle.

"But she wasn't your steady back then, was she?"

He shook his head, perhaps ruing the lost months and the love they might have shared over a social studies or arithmetic book.

"Just since last May," he said softly. "We flunked English together."

"Mrs. Nolan's class?" He seemed surprised that I knew. "Sophocles can be tough."

He chuckled. "I wrote 'Eddie Puss' on my test, and Adelaide failed me. Old hag."

"Poor woman," I scolded, thinking he would have surely failed anyway. "She liked Darleen, though."

Joey shrugged then demanded a cigarette. I asked if the students were allowed to smoke, and he nodded.

"At least until one of the guards catches us. They steal them and smoke them themselves."

"Tell me about Darleen," I said, offering my cigarette case; he grabbed several, stuffed all but one into his breast pocket, and slipped that one between his lips. I held out my lighter, hoping he'd give it back when he was done. He lit his cigarette, turned the lighter over in hand, examining it distractedly, then pushed it gently across the table to me.

"What was she like?" I asked, opting for the past tense.

"She was the coolest girl. We were going to run away together, take off for Florida. I was going to find a job, and we were going to get married."

"How old are you, Joey?" I asked.

"Fifteen. Sixteen in May. I got held back in the third grade. How old are you, Ellie?"

Joey Figlio had no concept of propriety. He lacked discretion and placed no limitations on his speech. He would boldly ask you uncomfortable questions or bare his soul without invitation, no matter how personal or unwanted the information was. He was a naïf, a child—and perhaps a slow-witted one—fiercely proud of his high passions and unafraid to cut off his nose to spite his face, as my mother used to say. I couldn't decide if he was retarded or wildly intelligent, but he had a flair for theatrics.

"I understand you write poetry," I said. "Would you show me your poems about Darleen?"

"I asked you how old you are," he repeated.

"Twenty-four," I answered tentatively. "Now about your poetry. Would you show it to me?"

"No," he said. "That's private between me and Darleen."

"I won't tell anyone, promise. I love poetry. Maybe I could give you a critique."

He just stared at me, his eyes almost dead, emotionless. He was truly odd.

"When did you last see Darleen?" I asked, changing gears.

"That's two questions in a row," he said.

"You can ask me one next. When did you last see Darleen?"

"The last time was about a month ago. They sent me up here on December fifth."

I tried to look him in the eye, but he was focused on something else again.

"I heard you broke out of here the day before she disappeared. Did you see her then?"

"My turn. What kind of car do you drive?" he asked.

Okay, I knew the drill now.

"A Dodge Royal Lancer. Red and black," I said. "Did you see Darleen during the two days you were on the lam?"

"Yeah, I saw her. I was lying to you. I hitchhiked to New Holland then took a bus over to the South Side and walked five miles to Darleen's place. Hid out in her stepfather's barn for two nights before that old crank caught me. But Darleen brought me some beef and macaroni before that. It sure was good, but not enough. They don't give us beef here. How did you manage to get such a nice car? Is your dad rich or something?"

That took me by surprise. Just the mention of my father could still knock the wind out of me. I tried to bury it. "Company car," I croaked. "Did you see her the day she disappeared?"

"Where do you live?"

"I'm not telling you that. You seem to be quite good at slipping your jailers here, and I don't have any beef and macaroni to offer you. Besides, it's my turn to ask the question. Did you see her the day she disappeared?"

He thought a moment, then nodded. "Yeah, I saw her. She came to the barn and gave me some bread and butter and milk, then she said she had to go. She said she'd bring me some gum or something from Canajoharie. Of course, she never came back. Then her father caught me about eight o'clock that night and called the cops. They brought me back here. You got a boyfriend or are you married?"

"Neither. Did you notice anything out of the ordinary that day? Was Darleen upset about anything?"

"She was okay, in a good mood. Nothing strange, except that weird neighbor of hers."

"Bobby Karl?"

"Yeah, that's him."

"What about him?" I asked, realizing I'd just managed two questions in row.

"He was watching her from the fence when she went to catch her bus. I don't think Darleen knew he was there, but I saw him. His shadow anyways."

Then he asked me why I didn't have a boyfriend.

"You're pretty," he said. "Are you some kind of prude or something?"

"I have dates, but no one steady," I answered. Prude, indeed. "Did Darleen ever mention this Bobby Karl to you?"

"Lots of times. She said he stared at her a lot from across the fence. One time, when her ma gave her a haircut, Darleen said he stole some of her hair before she could sweep it up. She saw him through the screen door as he was taking it."

I remembered the lock of hair tied up with yellow ribbon that I'd seen on Bobby Karl's queer collage and wondered if it might have been Darleen's.

Before leaving, I had a word with the principal, Dr. Arnold Dienst, about Joey Figlio. Dienst was a tall man of about fifty, with an equine face and large, probing eyes, homely but kind. Dienst told me Joey was an unusual boy, even for Fulton.

"He's a loner. Hasn't bonded with any of the boys here at the school. And he won't take any tests, so we don't know anything about his intelligence, though I suspect he's an imbecile, perhaps even an idiot."

"I heard he writes poetry," I said. "Do you know if he keeps it here?"

"That's news to me," said Dienst. "I'm not sure he knows which side of a pencil to write with, but I suppose it's possible."

"Can you search his belongings for it?"

"That's rather irregular, Miss Stone. What do you hope to find anyway?"

I said I didn't know. "He won't tell me much. I was thinking maybe his poetry might be more illuminating."

Dienst scribbled something into a pad on his desk, squinting sideways to focus better as he wrote. His eyeglasses must have been for distance, not reading.

"I can't search his things without good cause. But if anything were to come to light, I would reconsider the question," he said.

"What did he do to land up here anyway?" I asked.

"The first time he stole a car," said the principal, whose nameplate identified him as a PhD. He struck me as a caring, intelligent man. How had he ended up in this forsaken backwater? "Then he started a fire somewhere or other. Thankfully, no one was hurt. I'd like to bring him out of his shell, but he's resisting me. Some specialists have recommended electric shock therapy, but I am not a believer in such barbaric methods. I prefer a more humanistic approach. That's where I disagree strongly with the board here. They're either for corporal punishment or psychotherapy. The causes of juvenile delinquency and its treatment are both poorly understood, even in the institutions and research centers across the country. It's not a facile matter of beating discipline and good behavior into a child. Nor should we be tempted to spare the rod in the name of progress. Some juvenile delinquents are born, but I suspect many more are made. And I believe the child can ultimately decide for himself what behavior is most advantageous to him, provided we give him that opportunity. What's sure, at any rate, is that a child gone wrong is never a lost cause. That's why we encourage arts and crafts, music, and education here at Fulton."

"That's progressive," I said. "Have you observed positive results in your students? Is it working?"

Dienst smiled and shook his head. "It's not so simple. We have thieves, arsonists, forgers, what have you. Even sexual deviants. That's a problem exacerbated by grouping teenage boys together with no outlet for their sexual urges. Sex is, after all, a normal human function. But we must guard against perversion and unhealthy behaviors."

Why was he telling me this? All I'd asked was if it was working.

"Each case is different, you see," he continued. "So to formulate conclusions and categorize them so broadly and vaguely as success or failure is a sophistic exercise."

I took that as a no.

"Do you know anything about what Joey Figlio did when he escaped?" I asked, deciding not to share my other thoughts.

Dr. Dienst harrumphed. "Which time?"

I retrieved my camera and billfold from the guard, then braced myself at the door, pulled my collar tight, and made a dash for my car. The cold hit me like a slap, stinging my eyes and blistering my lips. I heard the guard laughing at me as I hurried through the snow, but at least I didn't slip. The car door handle crackled stiffly from the frost but opened after two sharp yanks, and I ducked inside. The Dodge groaned to life, and I rubbed my gloved hands together for warmth before gunning the engine and driving off. I wanted to shake the dust of the Fulton Reform School from my heels as soon as possible. Depressing hole. Plus, the faster you drive, the sooner the heat kicks in.

I swung onto Kendall Road and headed toward Route 5, about six miles ahead. My City Desk meeting was at 11:00, and my watch showed 10:40. No problem, I thought. Plenty of time. And I had a good trick ready for Georgie Porgie, too: a clever scheme involving George's new Pontiac and three boxes of wet cotton balls. He'd be driving around in a white cloud until the spring thaw. I had a good chuckle just thinking about it. Then I felt something cold on the right side of my neck. And it was sharp.

"Just keep driving," said the voice behind me.

CHAPTER SEVEN

I gasped and nearly drove off the road, but a hand slipped around my clavicle and held me steady. Once I'd come down from the ceiling, I began panting furiously, my mind careering in search of an out. The pressure on my throat caused me to gag, and my passenger ordered me to stay calm. Why hadn't I locked my doors? Better still, why had I taunted a pack of poorly supervised juvenile delinquents? I pictured myself plunging over the shoulder of the road in a spectacular, fiery, cartwheel of doom, coming to a tortuous, painful end: me slumped over the steering wheel, my jugular sliced clear through, as the car eventually scraped slowly to a halt against a snow bank beside the road. I knew without looking that it was that mutant, Frankie Football Mustache, holding the blade to my throat.

Imagine my relief when I glanced in the rearview mirror and discovered that my stowaway was actually Joey Figlio and not Frankie or one of his inbred chums.

Employing an abundance of caution and attention to his feelings, and staring straight down the icy road as I drew deep, calming breaths, I asked Joey to take the shank away from my neck.

He eased the pressure slightly and informed me that it was a knife, not a shank.

"Where would I get a shank?" he asked. "I took a knife from the cafeteria."

"Take it off my neck, Joey!"

He complied but then told me to pull over up ahead.

"Pull over? What for?"

"Sorry, but I'm going to have to steal your car."

I told him I had no intention of pulling over, and he stuck the knife against my neck again, this time a little harder. I sensed it was only a butter knife, but he could still cut my throat with it.

"Pull over now," he said and he meant it.

I rolled to a stop and yanked the parking brake.

"Now get out," said Joey.

I reeled around to look at him, sure that he was joking. But he looked annoyed.

"Come on, hurry up," he said, shooing me with his free hand. "I got to get out of here."

The heater had just started working its magic, so I wasn't keen on leaving the warmth of the car.

"It's ten degrees outside," I said, but he wasn't moved.

He climbed over the seat from the back and landed next to me with a heavy bounce. Before I could react, he'd reached past me and pushed open the door, inviting a blast of arctic air inside. Then, the rotten little thug shoved me out onto the ground. The very cold, hard ground. I rolled a few feet into the road, righted myself, and scrambled back to the car on my knees. I reached out for the door handle, intent on fighting for my warm car, and managed to grab hold of it just as Joey pulled the door shut. The engine roared, louder than I would have imagined possible, and the tires spun on the frozen shoulder, firing gravel and ice like buckshot behind them. The wheels soon found their traction, though, and the car shot forward, taking me with it.

God knows what I was thinking, but I held fast to the door for about twenty yards, skidding along through the frozen slurry of snow, salt, and dirt covering the road, tearing my stockings and skinning my knees as I went. I'd seen plenty of local kids skitching in the frozen streets. After a cold snowfall, they'd lie in wait along the side of the street until a slow-moving car rounded the corner. Then they'd dart into the road, grab the rear bumper, and crouch down low, knees bent, boots skating over the snowy surface. It looked like fun. Too bad I was wearing heels, one of which had fallen off when Joey hit the gas.

Once I'd accepted the bitter fact that Joey had no intention of redressing his ungentlemanly conduct and inviting me back inside, I let go of the door handle and tumbled several rotations before rolling to a stop in the middle of the road. I'd nearly been run over by my own car and had a tire track on the tail of my overcoat and a black scuff on my forearm to prove it. Now, lying on the frozen pavement with only one shoe, torn stockings, and scraped knees, I watched the taillights recede into the white distance, a blowing mist of snow swirling behind my warm car as it disappeared. I dusted myself off and, sitting on my frozen rear end, cursed the little JD who had quizzed me about my driving, asked me the make and model of my car, then stolen it out from under me as if performing a table-cloth trick.

It was bitter cold. I hadn't seen so much as a barn since driving away from the reform school, let alone a house or a filling station. And the school was at least three miles back. I struggled to my feet and examined the sorry state of my person: bloodied knees soaking through sagging, torn stockings; white gloves tattered and soiled with slush, about a shovelful of which had been forced down my collar as the car dragged me and was now melting down my back; and one broken shoe in the middle of the road some sixty feet behind me. I limped and hopped back down the road to retrieve the shoe, soaking my foot in the process. Then I started to worry about frostbite. I rubbed my right foot furiously, but the sopping stocking meant my efforts were futile. Now my gloves were wet, and my fingers stung from the cold. I sat down beside the road and cursed Joey Figlio.

I huddled in my overcoat for warmth, pulling my head and feet inside, as I debated whether to wait where I sat or hobble three miles ahead to Route 5 and potential salvation. Either way, it was even money that I would die where I sat or somewhere further on up the road. For, make no mistake, if the cavalry didn't arrive soon, I would freeze to death with one shoe on and one shoe off. My greatest regret was that I wouldn't be able to drag Joey Figlio to hell with me. I tucked my chin into my chest and shivered, my rear end already turning numb. And then I heard the crunch of rubber tires on frozen snow and the crackle of a two-way radio.

I poked my head out of my coat to see the headlights of a sheriff's cruiser staring dumbly at me from fifteen feet away. The door popped open, and Stan Pulaski stepped out looking like Randolph Scott climbing off his horse.

"Ellie!" he called once he'd recognized me. "What happened to you?"

I struggled to my feet and limped toward him. He made a move to receive me in his arms, but I tacked to the left and the passenger-side door of his cruiser instead. In a trice, I was inside the humming car, propping my right foot against the heat vent on the floor for warmth.

"What the heck happened?" asked Stan once he'd joined me inside the car.

"God . . . damn . . . Joey . . . Figlio . . . stole . . . my . . . car," I chattered. "He's got a ten-minute head start. Go!"

Stan threw the car into gear and swerved into the road, gaining speed as he floored it.

"Sheriff Olney was right to have me follow you," said Stan, eyes fixed on the straight, white road. "He told you to stay away from Fulton."

"Never mind that," I said. "Get on the radio and tell Frank to meet us at the junior high school."

Stan threw a quick look at me before shifting his attention back to the slippery road. "The junior high? What for?"

"Joey Figlio's going to kill a music teacher named Mr. Russell if Frank doesn't get there first."

Stan plucked the mic from its perch and radioed headquarters. Pat Halvey answered, chewing on something, and Stan started to explain in cop-talk that a perp was heading south on Kendall Road in a stolen vehicle. I'd heard enough and snatched the mic from his hand.

"Pat, this is Ellie Stone. Put Frank on the horn now!" I said.

After a few moments, the sheriff's booming voice came over the radio.

"What the hell's going on, Ellie?"

I didn't have time to explain about my car. I told him to get down to the junior high school before a fifteen-year-old juvenile delinquent killed a music teacher with a butter knife. Frank tried to ask for clarification, but I assured him a man would be dead within twenty minutes if he didn't move fast.

I replaced the mic in its cradle just as Stan veered onto Route 5 and hit the gas. My right foot was still freezing, despite the heater's best efforts. Stan's eyes were still fixed on the road, so I shimmied down in the seat, raised my skirt to mid-thigh, and rolled the right stocking down and off my leg. Then I removed the left one and tossed them both to the floor. Sure enough, Stan stole a glimpse and nearly drove off the road.

"I need a favor from you," I said to Stan as I examined the scrapes on my knees. Not too bad. They looked worse than they were.

"Anything for you, Ellie," he said, glancing again at my bare legs.

"When we get to the junior high, give me your gun. I'm going to shoot Joey Figlio between the eyes."

∂◯

We skidded to a stop in front of the junior high school fifteen minutes later. Three county cruisers and four city black-and-whites surrounded the building's exits. My red-and-black Dodge was sitting innocently next to the main entrance on Division Street, the driver's side door opened wide with four cops milling about, doing little more than freezing in the cold.

"I see you've found my car," I said to be friendly. They just stared at me quizzically. "The kid stole my car," I explained. "This is it. I'd like to take it when I've finished here."

"You'll have to talk to the chief, Miss Stone," said one of the men in blue. I'd seen him a few times before. Tall and nice looking. I've got a thing for cops.

"You know my name?" I asked.

He smiled. "Your press card is in the glove box."

Inside the school, I found Frank Olney and Patrick Finn, New Holland police chief, holed up with the ancient principal, Clarence Endicott, Louis Brossard, and a fifth man I didn't know. Frank acknowledged me from across the room with a short nod then turned his attention back to the conference. I was waiting quietly near the door for the huddle to break, when the secretary, Mrs. Worth, motioned for me to join her at her desk.

"Who's the man with the mussed hair in the houndstooth jacket?" I asked.

"That's Mr. Russell," she said. "Ted Russell, the music teacher Joey Figlio attacked."

"Where's Joey now?" I asked, wanting to chain him to my car's bumper and drag him through the ice and snow back to the Fulton Reform School for Boys.

"Got away. But not before he tackled Mr. Russell in the hallway and tried to slit his throat. He would have, too. Mr. Brossard arrived just in time."

"Oh, my, that's what I feared he'd do. Was Mr. Russell injured?"

"No," she said, dismissing my concern with a wave of her hand. "Mr. Brossard pulled Joey off before he could do any real harm. Managed to slice Mr. Russell's tie in half, though."

"I thought he looked a little too casual for a teacher. Any idea why Joey wanted to kill him?" I asked, wondering if others shared Joey's suspicions about him.

She almost said something then held back. I smiled to encourage her, but she wouldn't say.

"I know about Mr. Russell and Darleen," I whispered.

Mrs. Worth adjusted her glasses as she pretended to read a sheet of paper she'd just taken from the Ditto machine. The smell of volatile solvent gave me an almost Proustian nostalgia for my school days. I inhaled deeply and was transported back to a sixth-grade social-studies test and Mrs. Jelkin's permanent wave and black, laced Oxfords.

"Miss Stone," whispered Mrs. Worth, interrupting my memory. "Everyone has heard that rumor."

Suddenly Chief Finn, red face, white hair, and bushy eyebrows, noticed me and tried to shoo me away, insisting I had no business there. Frank informed him in his world-weary way that I was there to see him.

"What do you want with her?" asked Finn, a barrel-chested Irishman in a tight, blue pinstriped suit.

"She's the one who called us," said Frank. "If she hadn't, you'd have a homicide on your hands, Finn. I phoned the school as soon as I heard, and the assistant principal saved Russell's life. So you can thank me and her for doing your job for you."

"Is she the gal from the newspaper? Artie Short told me about her," said Finn, glaring in my direction. Then to me: "Hey, sweetie, next time try keeping track of your car, will you? Look at the trouble you caused us."

"Come on over here, Ellie," said Frank. "Let's hear what happened."

Finn looked me up and down, grinning like a bully. Frank opened the principal's door and escorted me in. When the police chief tried to follow, Frank blocked him with a bearish arm.

"Get lost, Finn. And learn some manners when you're talking to a lady."

"So Joey made good his escape?" I asked.

"Yeah, he was gone before we got here," Frank drawled. "He must have been driving like a bat out of hell. We showed up here about twelve minutes after your call. Finn took an age to get here."

"It's a pretty good car," I said, "if you don't mind that Fred Blaylock drove it into the lake last summer. Still smells of wet sometimes."

"Forget about that. We've got to find that kid before he hurts someone. You talked to him for a while. Where do you think he'll go?"

"He won't go home," I said. "The last time he broke out, he stayed in Darleen Hicks's barn."

"You think he'll go there?" asked Frank.

I shook my head. "No. No Darleen. I'm sure he'll be skulking around Ted Russell's house tonight. If I were you, I'd set a trap for him there."

Frank thought on it, and I could tell he liked the idea. And I had a feeling he might want to have the press along to document his triumph.

On my way out of the office, I met Assistant Principal Brossard, who was giving Ted Russell some kind of talking to, but I couldn't tell if the intensity of his words was due to anger or concern for his well-being.

"Good afternoon, Miss Stone," he said, wiping his brow with a handkerchief. "I understand it's been an interesting morning for all."

"Mine had its excitement," I said. "Though no more than Mr. Russell's."

Ted Russell was a handsome man. Just under six feet tall, with an athletic build and wavy brown hair, he had a soft, angular quality. His eyes were a prepossessing blue—cerulean blue—and they squinted just so when he smiled, which he was doing to great effect at that very moment. He had a large, red scratch on his neck. If I found him attractive, I wondered if an impressionable, young girl like Darleen Hicks might have done the same.

"Do you two know each other?" asked Brossard.

"I haven't had the pleasure," said Russell, extending his right hand to me. He stared deep into my eyes with the practiced tenacity of a seducer. I knew that look well. "You have me at a disadvantage, miss."

"Eleonora Stone," I said. "Ellie Stone."

"I've heard that name somewhere," he said, holding my hand, it seemed, until he remembered.

"Miss Stone is a reporter for the *Republic*," volunteered Brossard, who was the forgotten man in our conversation.

"That's it," said Russell, and he released me gently, managing to graze his fingers over my palm as he did. "You're that girl who wrote all those articles about the Shaw murder case, aren't you?"

I blushed.

"May we help you, Miss Stone?" asked Brossard, interrupting the lingering gaze between Mr. Russell and me.

"As a matter of fact, I wanted to get a statement from Mr. Russell for the paper. For the article I'm writing."

Brossard seemed fine with the idea, but Russell demurred politely, saying he'd rather not make a big deal about Joey Figlio.

"But I wasn't going to ask you about the attack," I said. "At least not exactly."

"Then what do you want to ask me?"

"I'd like to know about your relationship with Darleen Hicks."

Russell choked. Louis Brossard stood by as I stared at Russell, waiting for some kind of coherent answer. Finally he managed a smile and a dismissive wave of the hand.

"I'm afraid you're mistaken, Miss Stone," he said. "I had no relationship with Miss Hicks beyond that of a teacher. Joey Figlio had the crazy idea that there was something untoward going on, but it wasn't true."

I asked Brossard if the school's administration had known anything about Joey's accusations before today.

"It's true that we were aware of the rumor," said Brossard. "Principal Endicott asked me to investigate the matter last fall. I spoke to the girl, several of her classmates, Mr. Figlio, and, of course, Mr. Russell."

"And what did you conclude?" I asked.

"Both Darleen Hicks and Mr. Russell denied that anything of the kind had ever happened."

"I would never do that with a student, Miss Stone," said Russell with an apologetic smile. "Really, I'm not that kind of man."

∂⃝

Outside the school, I found Chief Finn leaning against my car, smoking the stub of a foul-smelling cheroot, giving some instructions to his men. My handsome cop was listening intently to his boss, but not so much that he didn't cast a glance my way.

"Am I keeping you from something, Palumbo?" Finn asked with all the feigned sweetness he could muster. My handsome cop flushed red and cleared his throat.

"No, Chief."

Then Finn pushed off my fender and reeled around to find the source of Palumbo's distraction. His eyes came to rest on me.

"You?" he asked. "What do you want?"

I pointed timidly to the car and mumbled that it was mine.

"Sorry, what'd you say? I didn't hear you."

"I said that's my car," I repeated, a touch more forcefully.

"Sorry, miss," he smiled, cigar squashed between his lips. "Evidence. You can't have it till I'm done with it."

He turned back to his men, a couple of whom laughed, while others looked away. Officer Palumbo stiffened, his broad chest growing before my eyes, as he frowned at his chief. Finn took notice and strutted over to the handsome cop.

"You got something to say, Palumbo?" he asked.

Palumbo looked past him and said no. Finn stepped back, regarded him up and down, then sneered.

"Who do you think you are? Vic Mature?"

The same couple of cops laughed, no doubt to curry favor, and Finn smiled at them, relishing his power.

"You and your guinea good looks," sneered Finn, turning back to Palumbo. "You think that girl over there is gonna swoon over you 'cause you look like some wop actor?" He laughed then looked at me. "Wait till you're off duty to chase after Jew girls."

That was unexpected. I gasped, and the cold air bit my lungs. Finn looked to his men as if expecting applause, then I felt a soft touch on my shoulder. I jerked my head to see who was there. It was Frank Olney, his smoldering eyes fixed on Finn.

Frank stepped around me, boots crunching on the frozen slush, and approached the chief, who was still admiring his own wit and basking in the approbation of his sycophants. Then Finn turned back toward me, no doubt to fire off another enlightened bit of bigotry, and saw Frank approaching. His smile vanished from his chapped lips, and his red face froze.

"Key," said Frank, holding out his hand.

Finn took a half step back. I wasn't sure whose jurisdiction we were in, but Frank was claiming it.

"I'm not asking again," said the sheriff, his meaty paw still waiting for the key.

The policemen behind Finn fidgeted, except for my handsome cop, Palumbo, who stood like an obelisk, gazing straight ahead. Finn frowned, huffing hot breath into the frigid air. His lip curled a touch as he squinted at the big man before him. Finally, he smiled and shook his head.

"If you want to take over this investigation, you're welcome to it," he said, trying to save face. "I sure as hell don't want it."

He slapped the key into Frank's hand, thinking he'd scored a point or two, or at least escaped with his pride. But the sheriff caught his hand as he tried to withdraw it and held it fast when the chief tried to pull it away. He squeezed it for about ten seconds, refusing to let go, and Finn resigned himself to captivity.

"Thanks," said Frank finally. "I'll be happy to bail you out on this one if it's more than you can handle," and he flung the pink hand away as if it were mucus stuck to his fingers.

Frank Olney may have seemed like just another big fat guy. But, like those huge professional wrestlers, he was a tough fat guy: a brute who could twist your arm off and beat you over the head with it. And in spite of our rocky start on the Shaw murder case, he'd become *my* tough fat guy.

The police chief waved goodbye over his shoulder and sauntered over to his car as if nothing had happened. Just as if he hadn't been schooled by Big Frank Olney.

"Here's your key," said the sheriff once the city cops had decamped. "You'll want to move your car before Finn gives you a ticket."

"Thanks, Frank," I said, beholden, trying to catch his eye to express my gratitude. I was making him uncomfortable in the process.

"Go on," he said, patting me on the shoulder to be rid of me, and trudged off to his cruiser.

I climbed into my frigid car, slipped the key into the ignition, and pulled the door closed. There was a thud, and the door banged open again. I yanked it a second time with the same result. Several attempts later, I bowed my head, drew a sigh, and cursed Joey Figlio and Fred Blaylock. My car door would not close properly, thanks to Joey for leaving it open and to Fred for driving it down the boat launch into the lake.

I moved the Dodge into an empty space next to the school buses in the parking lot. I managed to secure the door by holding it shut and locking it. The latch still didn't hold, but at least the door wouldn't wave in the wind.

My whole day had been turned on its ear. I'd missed my City Desk meeting and lunch with Norma at Wolfson's, and I was bruised like an old peach kicked down a hill. But I was in the perfect spot to meet Darleen's friends. I located bus number 63 idling a few feet away from my car. Some students had already boarded the bus to escape the cold, but most were milling about, stealing a few more minutes with their friends on the blacktop before heading home for the day.

Gus Arnold was reading the newspaper in the driver's seat, his big right boot crossed over his left knee, exposing half a meaty calf beneath his green work pants. He didn't notice me when I climbed aboard, but once I'd said hello, he did a double take and nearly fell out of his seat.

"What do you want?" he asked.

"I'd like to take a ride, if I may."

He didn't like the idea, but I told him I only wanted to see the route and talk to Darleen's friends. He probably figured he'd rather have me on his good side than not, and he reluctantly agreed.

"Can you drop me here on the way back to the depot?" I asked.

He grunted assent then excused himself to smoke a cigarette outside, anywhere but with me.

Teenage girls are an intimidating lot. There's no social group more confident in its own superiority with less reason to justify it. They hold dominion over their peers, parents, and innocent adult passersby—men and women alike—bullying and disarming all with sniggering ridicule. A well-placed sigh, histrionic yawn, or a roll of the eyes can inflict more damage, knock the wind out of one's sails, better than any punch in the stomach. A group of adolescent girls rules without pity or challenge until a teenage boy appears. Kryptonite. The bravado melts into simpering and subservience. I knew this for sure about teenage girls, because I had been one not too long before. And they didn't scare me.

I asked a couple of girls where I could find Susan Dobbs. They pointed to the back of the bus and a pink-faced girl in a faded red coat and green-and-yellow rubber hunting boots—the kind that lace up to midcalf. The look was provincial, even for New Holland, but it was bitter cold outside. Still, I wouldn't have been caught dead dressed like that, especially in front of boys.

"Are you Susan Dobbs?" I asked. She looked up at me, mouth agape, sniffled, and said yes. "Mind if I talk to you about Darleen Hicks while we ride?"

Susan looked to her friends for guidance, but they just chewed their gum and shrugged.

"You're that lady who threw up at the basketball game," she said finally, smirking as she did.

"That's right," I said, smiling back. "And you're the girls who stole my bottle of whiskey, aren't you?"

Susan's smirk disappeared.

"And you two?" I asked the other girls. "Which one of you is Carol Liswenski, and which one is Linda Attanasio?"

They didn't like that I knew their names and that they had stolen my liquor. They identified themselves reluctantly.

"Darleen's the one who took your bottle, honest," said Linda Attanasio. "We told her not to."

"I don't care about the whiskey, girls. I want to talk to you about Darleen. My name's Ellie. I work for the paper."

"Are you a secretary or something?" asked Susan.

"I'm a reporter, working on a story about Darleen's disappearance. I'm trying to find out what happened to her."

The girls exchanged glances, mugged surprise, and probably didn't believe me. Then the bus door closed, and the tired engine groaned to life. The bus lurched forward.

"What do you want to know?" asked Susan.

"First, there's some confusion over whether Darleen was on the bus the day she disappeared. Did she ride the bus with you that day?"

All three girls insisted that Darleen was not on the bus when it left the school, despite what Gus the driver had initially told the police. There was an awkward silence.

"What aren't you telling me?" I asked. They remained silent. "Okay, you've said very carefully that Darleen was not on the bus when it left the school. Was she on the bus before it left?"

Carol blurted out yes. "She was on the bus with us, waiting for the driver to get in, but she saw someone outside she wanted to talk to."

"And she got off the bus," said Susan.

"Who was it she wanted to talk to?" I asked, and the three girls shrugged. "You didn't see? She didn't say?"

"She always had an eye on someone," said Susan.

"Or someone had an eye on her," added Linda.

"What about Joey Figlio? I thought he was her steady."

Again the shrugs.

"Were they going steady or not?" I repeated.

Carol volunteered that they had been going out, but Darleen seemed to have grown tired of him.

"Why was that? I asked. I weighed my words carefully for the next question. "Did Darleen have any older boyfriends?"

The three girls exchanged looks yet again, tacitly searching for consensus on their answer. Susan finally spoke.

"Sure, there were older fellows who were interested, but Darleen wasn't tired of Joey for that. He was just a weirdo."

"These older fellows," I began. "Any names you might know?"

"We wouldn't want to get into trouble for saying," said Susan.

"Wow, sounds like it's someone important. Like the mayor."

They laughed.

"No, nothing like that."

"You can tell me, you know. I don't reveal my sources. Besides, I can't print someone's name without corroboration." They looked confused. "I won't tell anyone that you told me."

"Well, there was someone who kept calling her," said Susan. "He used to call her up and pester her. Ask her to meet him."

"Do you know who that was?"

She shook her head. I tried to get them to say Mr. Russell's name, but they wouldn't rise to the bait. I hinted and led them by the nose, but his name just wouldn't fall. Finally I asked outright if they'd heard rumors about him and Darleen.

"There was some talk about three months ago," said Susan. "But Darleen said that was all guff. Of course, we didn't exactly believe her."

"Yeah, we all thought she was lying to cover up," added Linda. "I always thought she was sweet on Mr. Russell. And he seemed sweet on her, too. Always calling on her in class. Always kind of looking her way. But Darleen said no."

The bus rumbled over the Mill Street Bridge and began to climb the big hill, fan belt squealing and exhaust belching as it went. Once we'd reached the top, Gus Arnold pointed us west on Route 5S, into the gray gloaming of the late afternoon. I watched the white landscape drift by for a couple of minutes.

"What do you think happened to Darleen?" I asked the girls finally, as we eased to a stop on the side of the road to disgorge a smallish kid in a red-checked hunter's cap. He slipped on the ice as the bus pulled away, and the kids roared with laughter. The poor boy's lunch box opened and spilled his thermos into the highway. I watched him scramble to retrieve it as a big Chrysler bore down on him. The kids on the bus groaned in disappointment as the boy dashed to the safety of the shoulder, only to slip and fall again just as the Chrysler blew past him, leaving a cloud of snow in its wake.

"That was rather mean," I said to the girls, referring to the laughter.

They shrugged. "Yeah, but it was hilarious. You have to admit."

I thought about it. Had I grown too old to laugh at a harmless pratfall? The kid had looked pretty funny, twice landing on the seat of his snow pants. And he seemed unhurt, at least physically. Still, poor kid.

"Now, about Darleen," I said. "Do you girls live near her place?"

"I get off two stops before Darleen," said Susan. "About three miles away from her house. Linda and Carol get off at the stop before Darleen's."

"It's about a mile from my house," said Linda.

"Have you ever met her neighbor Bobby Karl?"

"That creep next door?" asked Susan. "Such a weirdo."

"How so?"

"We had a sleepover about two months ago, the four of us. Darleen's stepdad was building a bonfire for Halloween. Darleen said he did it every year, and it was fun. A big hay bonfire. But Darleen said he did it to burn all the garbage he was saving up all year."

"And you saw Bobby Karl that night?"

"He was hanging around, gawking at us. Well, Darleen, mostly. And talking nonsense about calving and tractors. Who cares?"

"Was he weird in any other ways besides talking about livestock and farming machinery?"

"Not really."

"Did he speak to Darleen that night?"

"No he just was hanging around, scratching his scabby arms."

"And what about the other neighbor? Mr. Rasmussen? Did you ever see him at Darleen's?"

"The giant?" asked Susan.

Carol laughed. "No, we decided to call him Gargantua, remember?"

"Oh, yeah, that's right," said Susan. "Darleen came up with that one."

"Never mind that it's not nice to call people names, did you ever see him while you were visiting Darleen?"

"Darleen said you could see him from space," said Susan, and the other two girls giggled.

"Were you in space, or did you see him at Darleen's?" I asked, a little less nicely the third time.

"We saw him maybe once or twice when he was plowing his field," said Linda. "He never spoke to us, except once to say stay off his land."

"Were you on his land?"

"No."

"Okay, anything else you can tell me about your visits to Darleen's place? Did she get along with her stepfather, Mr. Metzger?"

Susan shrugged and said they got along okay. "He was pretty strict with her, though."

"How about you, Carol?" I asked. "What did you think of Mr. Metzger?"

"He was kind of scary," she said, wincing and showing her braces.

Susan glared at her.

"What?" asked Carol. "He *was* scary, wasn't he? I mean, I couldn't even sleep after that."

"Why don't you shut it, Carol?" said Susan.

Once Gus Arnold had dropped Linda and Carol at their stop at the mouth of County Highway 58, he threw the bus into reverse and began to back out onto Route 5S.

"Wait a minute," I called from the back. "Aren't you going to drive your full route?"

I'd been timing the drive and didn't want to guess at the total if he skipped Darleen's stop.

"But there's no more kids to drop," he said, looking at me through a mirror above him. "I'm taking you back to the school to get your car."

"No, I'd like to run the full route, please. It will only take a few minutes more."

Gus Arnold scowled, I imagined, though all I could see were his eyes in the mirror. He made a big show of throwing the bus into first gear and wrestling the steering wheel back into place. We rolled through a large pothole, nearly knocking me out of my seat, then proceeded peaceably over a pack of mostly white snow toward Darleen Hicks's house.

Five minutes later, the bus slowed to a stop in front of the rusting mailbox labeled "Metzger." It looked frozen shut, the red flag bent down permanently or at least until spring and warmer temperatures would free it from the frost's grip.

Gus Arnold slouched against the steering wheel, disinclined to face me as he awaited instructions. I joined him at the front of the bus and asked him how long he usually paused at Darleen's house.

"What?"

"Do you wait here or do you drive away once she's off the bus?"

"I drive away, what do you think?"

"Then let's move."

Gus Arnold shook his head in disgust. I don't know what hold I had over him, but he was doing as I asked. He released the clutch, and we jerked into motion.

"You go straight from here?" I asked, leaning on the back of his seat as I looked out the windshield.

"No room to turn around here," he said. "Metzger's road is too narrow."

"I saw a no-outlet sign back there. How do you get out of here?"

"There's an opening about a mile ahead. It's big enough to turn the bus around."

We drove for about three minutes over the bumpy road, through an ever-narrowing alley of thick pines, until we reached a cul-de-sac. The trees had been cleared and the ground leveled about a hundred yards deep into the woods. But there was barely thirty yards available for the bus to turn around due to the mountains of snow dumped into the dead end by county plows. Like ridges of a true mountain chain in miniature, some of the snow banks rose as high as fifteen feet, their peaks rugged, speckled with dirt, salt, and gravel. The snow hills stretched nearly eighty yards deep and forty yards across. They looked like a paradise for little children to play in, ripe for adventure and filled with fantasy.

"Are these snow hills here every year?" I asked to make conversation.

Gus grunted as he twisted the big steering wheel around to complete his one-eighty. "County's been dumping snow here for years," he said, and the bus rumbled back onto 58.

"The sheriff says you took a nap here after finishing your route the day Darleen Hicks disappeared. Is that true?"

He seemed unnerved. "Well, not exactly here," he said. "On the other side of the hills. That way," and he pointed past the snow toward the woods beyond.

"How do you get to the other side? There's no road."

"You got to drive back to the highway and turn west. There's a turnoff about a quarter mile past here."

"Do you take naps there often?" I asked.

He drove on, shoulders hunched as he leaned over the steering wheel. "I like the quiet. No one there to bother me."

We passed Darleen's house again, and I watched it melt into the dark behind us. I turned forward to take in the view through the windshield, looking past the driver. Ahead, on the side of the road, a giant figure stooped to grab the post from his mailbox. We rolled past him just as he righted himself. Walt Rasmussen glared through the bus's windows; he was almost tall enough to look me in the eye and give me a fright. It was as if he'd recognized me in the dark.

I sat quietly for the ride back into town. The giant had spooked me. Gus Arnold dropped me off at the junior high school at 4:47. The bus depot was perhaps ten minutes farther. That made for about thirty-five minutes from the end of his route back to the depot. I knew he hadn't changed a flat tire that day. And if he'd finished his route at four twenty, then snoozed for thirty minutes, he should have been back at the depot by five thirty. That left nearly an hour of his time unaccounted for.

CHAPTER EIGHT

I put my feet up on the ottoman and hoisted a stack of newspapers onto my lap: the ones that Norma had collected for me. My feet were stinging from the exposure to the cold that morning. I wriggled my toes, trying to urge some warm blood into my feet. I squirmed in my seat, searching for a comfortable position for my sore bottom. It felt as if I'd been kicked by a mule. I cursed Joey Figlio again then reached for my drink on the end table.

The television was humming quietly; the second act of *Hong Kong* was just beginning after a commercial. I didn't know much about the show, but I kind of had a thing for Rod Taylor, and I liked the exotic setting. Better than *Wagon Train*, which aired opposite it. From the top of the pile of papers on my lap, I unfolded the *Canajoharie Courier Standard* from Wednesday, December 21. The front page proclaimed, "First Day of Winter" and "Christmas Decorations Pageant Lights up City." There was a dark photo of Main Street with garlands and festooned streetlights. And there was a second photo accompanying the "First Day of Winter" story: a view of the Mohawk River, completely frozen over, from Lock 12 in Tribes Hill.

I picked up the December 22, edition of the *Republic* and scanned the local news. Nothing noteworthy had happened in the city the day before, if you didn't count the mayor's toy drive for the poor. But then I noticed a group photo of the school superintendent's annual Christmas banquet at Isobel's Restaurant on Division Street. The administrative staff of the entire district was assembled, from grammar-school, junior-high, and high-school principals and assistants to secretarial staff. I recognized Principals Keith from the high school and Endicott from the junior high. At a table near the middle of the room, I could make out Mrs. Worth, the secretary from the junior high, sitting with Louis Brossard.

"A Merry Christmas to All" read the caption. "Superintendent Mitchell Plays St. Nick." The article said the dinner had broken up at ten p.m.

Then the phone rang. It was the sheriff.

"We just got a tip someone saw a kid prowling around near Ted Russell's place," he said. "I'm heading there now. You want to come along?"

"Do I?" I said, sitting up and dumping the papers on the floor.

"You can't ride with me. I've got to run up to Fonda afterwards, so you'll have to follow in your own car. Two minutes, Ellie. Be ready. I won't wait."

Two minutes was plenty of time to grab my camera and four rolls of film, and wrap myself in my overcoat. Then I downed my drink in one go: antifreeze for the cold evening ahead.

Once in the car, I rubbed my cold gloves together, started the engine, and cranked up the heat. The driver's side door was still frozen and wouldn't close properly, but the lock held it in place. Mrs. Giannetti emerged from her door in an overcoat and boots, yoo-hooing to me as I waited in the car for Frank Olney.

She inched across the icy porch and down the steps, steadying herself on the rail, then scurried up to my car and tapped on the window. "Going out, dear?" she called through the glass.

"Yes, Mrs. Giannetti," I said, leaning across the seat to roll down the passenger window.

"A date? On a night like this?" Her breath froze as it left her mouth.

I looked at her pointedly. "A date?"

She shrugged. "I just thought that since you have so many dates . . ."

She stood there for a few moments before she spoke again, and I let her, wondering how long she could brave the cold. Finally, realizing I wasn't cooperating, she shivered and caved in.

"You're always running off somewhere and staying out late."

"I spend most evenings at home watching the television," I corrected her.

"And enjoying a nice drink of something," she added. "That's fine, of course. I'm all for it, but the delivery boy from Corky's has a loose tongue. He tattles to Mrs. DiCaprio about my one little bottle of crème de menthe. I sometimes like a cordial after supper. Just a sip," she said, indicating a small measure with two fingers of her gloved hand. "If he gossips about me, I can't imagine what he must say about you."

My ears were burning in the cold. I craned my neck to see down the street, wondering how Frank's two minutes had stretched to four.

"Has the delivery boy said anything to you, Mrs. Giannetti?" I asked.

"Oh, no, nothing. It's just that, well . . . A girl wants to be careful with her reputation, dear."

"I've heard that."

Finally, the sheriff's county car rounded the corner onto Lincoln and accelerated toward my salvation. When he pulled to a stop at the curb next to me, I cranked down the driver's side window.

"Follow me, Ellie," he said.

"Are you in trouble, dear?" called Mrs. Giannetti as Frank gunned the engine. I rolled up the windows and shifted into gear to follow him. The air was bitter cold as we cruised along Route 5 at sixty-five miles an hour. Blasts of dry, needle-sharp snow streaked past the windshield, and the defroster struggled to keep the glass clear. The frozen rubber of the wipers rattled back and forth, skittering over the ice, occasionally dislodging a small chunk and sending it hurtling over the roof into the frozen darkness behind me.

Route 5 runs east to west along the north side of the Mohawk, from Albany past Buffalo to the Pennsylvania state line. We were heading east toward Schenectady, but we weren't going that far.

About four miles past the city limits, an old inn sat on a hill just above the highway. Recently restored by an ambitious transplant from Florida, the Kasbah was a fanciful interpretation of a North African souk, complete with turrets with onion-shaped domes, like an old Russian church. Somehow, somewhere along the way, the new owner had decided that Russian was exotic enough to pass for North African, and the Kasbah was born. I'd had drinks there twice with a handsome engineer from General Electric.

Just below the Kasbah, perpendicular to Route 5, the tiny village of Cranesville climbed Cranes Hollow Road into the hills above the Mohawk. Consisting of perhaps two dozen homes, Cranesville was a sleepy hamlet where nothing ever happened. Until now.

Sheriff Frank Olney pulled off to the side of Cranes Hollow Road, turned right, and crawled up a narrow lane that snaked through the trees above Eva's Kill, a trickle of a stream that ran down from the hills into the river. Three of his men were already there, sitting quietly in the warmth of their darkened cruisers. When Frank arrived, they popped their doors and climbed out. I saw Vinnie Brunello, Stan Pulaski, and Pat Halvey.

I left my car twenty yards farther down the hill, as the width of the road prevented me from finding a spot closer to the sheriff's. Narrow enough in summer, now the little road barely allowed one car to pass in either direction due to the mounds of snow and ice encroaching onto the pavement.

I grabbed my camera from the backseat, slung it over my shoulder, and climbed out of the car. Having forgotten about the frozen door, I slammed it shut only to see it bounce back open with a metallic thunk. I sighed, thinking some wicked thoughts for Charlie Reese, and pushed the door gently closed. It held.

Frank was dispensing instructions to his deputies when I arrived, ordering them to fan out around the house at the end of the lane. He wanted them to beat the bushes and locate Joey Figlio.

"Ellie and I are going to talk to Ted Russell," he said. "You boys come find me there once you've finished."

The modest clapboard house was a one-story dwelling, painted red, with a plume of smoke rising from its single chimney pipe. Frank knocked at the door. A hand pulled back the shirred curtain in the sidelight, and I could see Ted Russell's eyes peering out. He opened the door and invited us in.

"Thank you for coming, Sheriff," he said, taking our coats. "And what a nice surprise to see you again, Miss Stone."

"So, a neighbor said she saw someone prowling around outside," said Frank once we were seated in the parlor around the Franklin stove, opposite an upright piano draped with multicolored Christmas lights. "What about you? You see anything?"

Ted Russell glanced my way, blushed a bit, then cleared his throat and nodded. "I was having my supper and heard something out by the garage. I looked out the kitchen window and saw someone dart into the woods. I can't be sure, but I think it was Joey Figlio."

"When was this?" asked Frank.

"About an hour ago. A little past seven."

Frank looked at his wristwatch. "Do you always eat so late?"

I had to smile to myself. Coming from New York City, I was not accustomed to the early dinnertimes in New Holland. Seven was indeed a late supper for these parts, where most folks ate around five or five thirty.

Frank questioned Ted Russell for thirty minutes more, leaning back in the chair he'd been offered, lazy and patient, but calculated. Without his host's noticing, he brought the subject around to Darleen.

"Funny, though, that Joey Figlio would think you were interested in Darleen Hicks," he said from his seat.

Ted Russell cleared his throat again and dismissed the idea. "Just idle gossip, Sheriff," he said. "A single teacher is vulnerable to such accusations. Kids say terrible things about teachers."

"So no fire with all that smoke?" asked Frank, then he glared at Russell a good while, making him squirm in his chair.

"What do you think, Ellie?" Frank asked me. "Were there stories like this when you were in school? Or is Mr. Russell here a particularly attractive target."

Ted Russell looked at me, probably wondering what I was doing there, and if that was good or bad for him.

"My teachers were mostly old maids," I said with a smile.

"But she was a student of yours, along with this Joey Figlio, wasn't she?" asked Frank, turning back to our host. "Did you notice anything about their relationship? Were they going steady?"

"I suppose they might have been," said Russell. "I don't normally pay attention to ninth graders' love lives."

"Not normally," mocked Frank.

"No, sir."

"When did you last see Darleen Hicks?" I asked.

"I'm not sure," said Russell. "It must have been the week she disappeared."

"Wasn't she in your music class?"

"Yes."

"Then surely you saw her the day before she disappeared: Tuesday. Unless you saw her the next day."

He shook his head adamantly. "There was the field trip on that Wednesday, wasn't there? I couldn't have seen her Wednesday because she wasn't at school."

"You seem to be up to date on her whereabouts," added Frank.

"I read about it in the papers," said Russell.

"You might have seen her in the parking lot Wednesday," I offered, catching him off guard. "Darleen returned to the school to catch the bus home after the field trip."

Ted Russell looked uncomfortable, but why not? He was being grilled by the sheriff and the press at the same time without his lawyer present. He managed an apologetic grin and repeated that he hadn't seen Darleen at all on that Wednesday.

"Where were you that afternoon?" asked Frank. "What time did you leave school and where did you go?"

Russell tried to recall but could not produce a convincing alibi. He said he'd left school at his normal time. Probably about three forty-five or four. He said he'd returned home but doubted anyone saw him or could corroborate his statement.

The sheriff's men arrived at the door, having scoured the area, which they pronounced clear of Figlios. Frank asked Ted Russell if he felt confident of his safety. Russell shrugged and said he supposed so.

"I'll leave a man here for the night," said Frank, pulling his coat on. "I hope you appreciate it, 'cause it's cold out there. Tomorrow you'll be on your own if this kid doesn't show."

Ted Russell nodded his head, helped me into my coat, and saw us to the door.

"I appreciate your help, Sheriff," he said then caught my hand. I looked up at him startled, and he smiled. "Come back later," he whispered so Frank wouldn't hear. "Good night, Sheriff. And thanks again."

Outside, I asked Frank if he'd thought about searching Darleen's locker.

"Sure. I'll look into it," he said, climbing into his car. I doubted he thought it was worthwhile.

I backed down the hill, knocking down a couple of trash cans as I went. No harm done, and it was too cold to stop to right them again. I turned west onto Route 5 and accelerated, intending to pour myself into a warm glass of Scotch as soon as I got home. The car responded, but there was a voice behind me.

"Stop the car now." Joey Figlio.

Twice in one day! I felt ice-cold metal against my neck and took my foot off the gas.

"You're not going to take my car again," I warned as I continued down the middle of the road.

"Pull over," he said. "We're not going through this again, are we?"

"Come on, Joey, be reasonable," I pleaded. "You can't leave me out here. I'll freeze."

Then he nicked my neck with his blade, and I screamed.

"Pull over or we both die in the wreck," he said. "Darleen's gone. I don't have much to live for except to avenge her."

I pulled to the shoulder, wishing I had Stan Pulaski's gun. I'd never fired one before, but I was sure I could put a bullet between Joey's eyes at close range. I'm not normally a violent person, but for the first time in my life, I felt I could kill a man.

The car came to a rolling stop, crunching heavily over the snowpack. I sat at the wheel, seething, holding my gloved hand to my bleeding neck. It was just a scratch, really. The night was absolutely still, frozen, and deserted on Route 5. No cars coming or going. We were four miles from New Holland, and I was not keen on walking them. The wipers continued to rattle back and forth over the ice, and I waited.

"Move it," he said, shoving me to the passenger side, as he climbed over the seat.

I slid over, hoping for some kind of opening to take the knife out of his hands, but in reality I doubted I could overcome him anyway.

"Now get out and start walking," he said.

"Joey, I'm not getting out of this car," I said. "Not again. It's five degrees out there."

He shoved me again with his right hand, which was clutching the knife. I flailed, slapped at his arm, and tried to hide my face. Then I remembered the door. The door that wouldn't close. I leaned back and, risking knife wounds to my ankles, kicked him as hard as I could with both feet. I pushed and kicked and thrust, knowing that everything depended on it. He yelled in protest, recoiled, moved back against the driver's door, which opened obediently, and Joey Figlio suddenly found himself on the frozen pavement. There was no time to lose. I scooted across the seat, threw the car into drive, and gunned the engine before I'd even squared myself behind the wheel. The tires spun, and the car jumped forward. Joey was on his feet again, but I was already out of reach. Soon I was roaring down the highway, driver's door flapping open and shut in the icy wind, as I watched Joey Figlio recede into the black night of the rearview mirror. I hooted and hollered in victory. I'm not proud of it but, if I'm honest, I have to confess that I actually wished him frostbite and worse for the trouble he'd caused me that day.

About a half mile down the road, I slowed and pulled over at a lonely phone booth. I jumped out and quickly dialed the sheriff's office to inform them of Joey's reappearance and whereabouts. Deputy Wycek patched me through to Frank over the radio.

"Joey Figlio tried to steal my car again," I panted into the receiver once I had the sheriff on the line. "He's about a quarter of a mile behind me on Route Five, heading toward the city."

"Got it, Ellie. Sending Stan right now," said Frank. "Get in your car and get out of there."

I hung up and climbed back into my warm Dodge. Shifting into drive again, I threw a glance in the rearview mirror, and what did I see but Joey Figlio jogging out of the darkness into view. He was yelling for me to wait. With sadistic relish, I released the brake and pulled away from the shoulder. Driving no faster than ten miles an hour, I maintained a safe distance from my pursuer, who never got any closer than ten yards or so. I accelerated when needed, braked when I felt a carrot was in order, then gunned the engine again to leave him in my cold dust. I marveled at his persistence. I reveled in it. He just wouldn't give up. He ran desperately, lunging to reach the car, but falling short each time as I teased him with a well-timed acceleration. Pulling him along like a yo-yo, I continued this strategy for about ten minutes, laughing at his stamina and stupidity, until I saw the cherry top appear on the horizon behind us. In two minutes, Deputy Stan Pulaski had corralled a frozen and exhausted Joey Figlio. I threw the car into reverse and backed up fifty yards to enjoy my victory.

"Add attempted murder to the charges," I told Stan. "That little JD tried to cut my throat."

Joey Figlio stared vacantly at me from the fender of Stan's cruiser, huffing in the frozen air. His eyes told me nothing.

By the time I'd made a statement at the sheriff's office, it was nearly eleven. Joey Figlio would spend a night in the county jail before a morning appearance with the family-court judge. Joey was, of course, a minor. I was scheduled to attend to give testimony against the rotten little thug.

I turned south out of the County Administrative Building's lot and pointed my Lancer down Route 22, confident there was no juvenile delinquent waiting in the backseat. I intended to have that Scotch, and perhaps two more, and curl up on the sofa with the newspapers Norma Geary had collected for me. The Wilkens Corners Liquor Store appeared on the horizon to my right, a diffused white glow in the frigid night. I pulled into the gravel lot and climbed out. The door was still frozen open, but I wasn't worried about Joey Figlio anymore.

A fifth of Scotch safely tucked into my overcoat's hip pocket, I climbed back into my car and reversed onto Route 40. Change of plans. Instead of heading south, I turned across Wilkens Corner Road, then down Upper Church Street to the East End, where I picked up Route 5. Ten minutes later, I was knocking on Ted Russell's door.

CHAPTER NINE

Ted Russell was hardly the answer to my prayers, but I wasn't asking for much. I just wanted to see where the evening could go with a handsome man and plenty of booze. There was always the chance it could lead to something unexpected or provide a temporary elixir for the tedium of the bitter-cold winter.

My host was happy to see me, if eyes lighting up like the flash of an H-bomb meant what it used to. He took my coat, poured me a drink, and shoved a log into the Franklin stove in the parlor. He put some Nat King Cole on the hi-fi: "Pretend." Before the second track came on, his arms were around me, and moments later my drink was orphaned on the side table, surely leaving a ring as the ice melted and the glass sweated. Ten minutes after that on the rough rug, I lifted myself onto my elbows, pushed my hair out of my face, and reached for my clothing. Ted huffed and puffed, red-faced, and covered himself with the afghan from the sofa.

"Wow," he said, wiping his brow. "That was . . . wonderful. Was it good for you, too?"

I smiled and patted him on the shoulder.

"Let me get you a fresh drink," he said, jumping to his feet, but I stopped him.

"I've got an early start tomorrow," I said. "I should be going."

THURSDAY, JANUARY 5, 1961

By the time I'd parked my Lancer on County Highway 58, the heater was cooking with gas, but the car hadn't quite reached toasty. It was still dark, the air frigid, but I had a hot cup of coffee inside me. No breakfast. The mailbox had no name on it, but I knew it was Carol Liswenski's house.

I'd watched her climb down from the bus the day before. Now, with an arctic breeze blowing across the road, I saw her emerge from the long drive leading to her house. She was wrapped in snow pants, rubber boots, and a blue coat with a gray faux-fur collar. She clutched a plaid lunch pail in one hand and three or four books strapped together in the other. I switched on my headlamps, startling her, and I inched the car closer.

"Don't be frightened, Carol," I said through the window. "It's me, Ellie Stone from the newspaper."

She shivered in the cold, squinting into the glare of my headlamps, and waited for me to say something.

"Climb in until the bus gets here," I said. "It's warm. Come on."

Carol didn't hesitate. She jumped in and soaked up the heat with relish.

"What are you doing here at this hour?" she asked.

"I couldn't sleep," I said.

"So you're waiting outside my house for me?"

"I have to see Mrs. Metzger later. I'm a little early."

She shrugged and switched on the radio. She seemed happy with Anita Bryant singing "My Little Corner of the World." I wasn't.

"Since I have you here, I wanted to ask you something," I said. "You told me that Darleen got off the bus in the parking lot at the junior high the day she disappeared."

"Yeah, that's right. What about it?"

"You also said she got off the bus to talk to somebody. Can you tell me who that was?"

Carol ran her tongue over her braces as she thought it over. Then she shook her head and said she didn't see who Darleen had spoken to. I still felt she was hiding something and asked her again.

"Was it a student? One of Darleen's boyfriends? A teacher, perhaps?"

Carol almost said something, but just then the headlights of the school bus appeared over the crest of the hill in the distance. It was about a half mile away, and I knew I had only a few moments left to question her.

"What about Darleen's father, Mr. Metzger?" I asked. "You said he was scary. What did you mean by that?"

"Nothing," she said. "Here comes the bus. I should go now."

"You've still got a minute," I said. "No sense waiting in the cold. What happened at the sleepover?"

She thought about it for several seconds then said she'd promised not to tell.

"Susan doesn't want you to tell, is that it?"

Carol nodded. My face remained calm even as my insides roiled. How could I get her to talk before the bus arrived?

"I think Mr. Metzger is kind of scary, too," I said. "He stared at me with those eyes. I didn't like it one bit."

"He came into our room," said Carol suddenly. "We were talking and giggling when we were supposed to be sleeping, and Mr. Metzger came into the room without knocking."

"And? What happened?"

"He told us to quiet down and go to sleep."

"What's wrong with that?" I asked.

"Then he came over to the big bed where we were and kissed Darleen good night."

I turned up my nose at the thought of that man kissing his stepdaughter good night, but I still didn't see how that qualified as scary.

"On the lips," added Carol.

Worse. I know some people kiss their children on the lips—midwesterners, I'd heard—and there's nothing untoward about it. But I could never understand it. My parents had been free enough with good-night kisses, but they always planted them on my cheek or forehead.

The bus was just a hundred yards away when Carol turned to me, almost in desperation, and made me swear not to breathe a word to anyone.

"I promise," I said. She hadn't really told me anything I would want or need to share. "I won't tell about the good-night kiss."

But I soon found out that her plea for my silence wasn't for what she'd already told me, but for what she was about to say.

"Darleen always has a bath before bed. She said her father insisted on it. So after Mr. Metzger kissed her, he kind of sniffed her head a bit, and told her to go have her bath. She didn't want to, since us girls were all there, but he made her go. When I went to find Darleen twenty minutes later, Mr. Metzger was standing outside the bathroom, looking through the crack in the door at Darleen. He caught me and stared at me, real mean-like. I was so scared. I ran back to bed."

The bus arrived at the mouth of her drive, and Carol opened the passenger door. The dome light came on and she glanced at me in terror for one brief moment. Her cheeks were red, and her eyes were wet.

"Please don't tell anyone I told," she said and jumped from the car to run for the bus.

"Miss Stone," said Irene Metzger, clutching her sweater to her throat as she stood in the doorway. "I wasn't expecting you. Please come in."

The Metzger house was a drab collection of worn-out furniture, faded wallpaper, dim lights, and stale odors of fabric and farmers. It was chilly inside; the fireplace yawned empty and cold in the center of the sitting room, and the potbellied stove in the corner sat in disuse, as if forgotten or broken.

"Let's go to the kitchen," said Irene Metzger. "It's the warmest room in the house."

She offered me a cup of coffee from a chipped enamel-coated pot on the counter next to the giant utility sink, used for laundry and dishwashing. We sat at the wooden table, and Irene Metzger lit a cigarette.

"Have you come with news about Darleen?" she asked.

"Actually, I wanted to ask more than tell," I said.

She looked disappointed.

"Well, I've spoken to the sheriff, the assistant principal, the bus driver, Joey Figlio, your neighbors, and Darleen's friends."

"And?"

"So far, not much to go on. No one will admit to having seen her after three o'clock that Wednesday."

"What about that teacher of hers? The music teacher who was so sweet on her?"

"Mr. Russell?" I asked, and she nodded, taking a deep drag on her cigarette.

"He claims there was nothing improper about his relationship with Darleen. The assistant principal backs him up on that."

"Then why did he telephone her at night?"

"Ted Russell phoned Darleen?" I choked. "Are you sure of that?"

Irene Metzger tapped her ash into a tin tray before her. "I don't know.

That's who I suspected it was. He called lots of times, or someone did. Used to call her in the evenings. It drove Mrs. Norquist to distraction."

"Just to be clear," I began, "you can't say for certain that Ted Russell telephoned Darleen, but you suspect it. Why?"

"Well, her friend told me."

"Which friend was that? Carol Liswenski?"

Irene nodded. "I could always count on Carol to tell me the truth when Darleen was unwilling. Carol told me about the rumors going around school about him and Darleen. When I asked Darleen, she denied it."

"But you believed Carol, not Darleen?"

"Well, yeah," she said, a tad defensive. "You know how it is with girls. They lie when it suits them."

I thought about Carol and her reluctance to talk. Sure, I'd managed to get her to tell me about Mr. Metzger, but I sensed she was holding back on what happened in the parking lot the day Darleen disappeared. If she'd opened up to Darleen's mother, why not to me? I resolved to corner her again and get an answer out of her.

"Is your husband at home?" I asked.

"No, he's out in the fields. He's an early riser."

"Will he be back soon?"

"I'm afraid not," she said. "Why do you insist on talking to him?"

"Can I find him outside somewhere?" I asked, ignoring her.

"He's building a new shed for the horses and cows. Out by Rasmussen's property line. He said he was pouring cement today."

"In this cold? Isn't that . . . The temperature . . . Sorry, but isn't this the wrong time of year to be pouring cement?"

Irene Metzger shrugged. "Dick knows what he's doing. I never question him on men's work."

"I was wondering if I could have a look at Darleen's room. Would you mind?"

She pushed the butt of her cigarette into the astray and said sure. "I don't know what you think you'll find, but be my guest."

She led me out of the kitchen, down a narrow hallway, to a set of stairs behind the kitchen.

"This way," she said.

The steps groaned with each footfall, and I imagined flakes of dust, dried paint, and varnish falling like snow into the cellar beneath the staircase. I held the railing tightly as we climbed for fear that the whole thing might collapse under our weight.

At the landing above, a larger hallway opened up, and I could see four doorways, two on each side.

"That's Darleen's room," said Irene Metzger, motioning to the first door on my right. "Dick—my husband—and I use that room there," she said, indicating the door opposite and farther down the hallway. "That's the bathroom over there," she said, pointing to the door next to Darleen's.

If Carol Liswenski was to be believed, that was where Darleen took her nightly baths under the watchful eye of her scary stepfather.

"What's that room there?" I asked, motioning to the fourth door, the one directly opposite Darleen's.

"We don't use that room," said Irene Metzger. "There's nothing in there. We used to store Dick's mother's things in there, but we gave it all away to his elderly aunt a few years ago."

"May I have a look?"

"See for yourself," she said, opening the door to reveal an empty room. "Told you there was nothing there."

We moved on to Darleen's room. The small wooden doorknob, probably once a beauty, had been painted over white so many times that it now looked lopsided and large. Irene Metzger reached out and turned it briskly, pushed open the door, and we entered the bright room. The curtainless windows faced south, and lots of light was pouring in, even if the sun was weak. Above the flaking wainscoting, the walls were papered with a cream-and-gold-colored pattern of stripes and fleurs-de-lis. The floor was bare slats, the finish long since worn away, leaving a dull, soft surface. An old dresser stood between the two windows, and there was a writing desk, blistered and warped, with papers and books on top. Darleen's narrow bed anchored the opposite wall, a threadbare, white matelassé cover stretched over the mattress, while a line of four naked Kewpie dolls sat listing in different directions on the single pillow.

I gazed out a window across the barren landscape. A virtual whiteout, the view was interrupted only by a dark line of fencing, a dilapidated barn, and a small, dark blot about a hundred yards from the house behind a copse of bare trees. A solitary figure moved stiffly around the dark spot, performing tasks that I could not identify from such a distance.

"May I look at Darleen's things?" I asked, still staring out the window.

"I'll leave you to it, if you don't mind," she said. "I've got work to do. I'll be in the kitchen if you need me."

I waited for her footsteps to recede down the stairs before beginning my search. I started with Darleen's chest of drawers, pawing through her clothes: underwear and dresses, shoes and blouses. If she'd run away, she left with little to wear. I lifted the radiator cover near the window, but only found a radiator underneath. On the shelf over the desk, there were perhaps twenty books. I turned them over and fanned the pages, hoping something besides a bookmark would fall out. There was nothing. I stopped to look out the window at the frozen, tar-gray shingles of the porch roof. The window provided an ideal escape route for a rebellious teenage girl, I figured, but there was nowhere to hide anything out there.

Darleen's desk presented a jumble of odds and ends. Marbled composition books, loose sheets of homework, schoolbooks, a pack of letters, jacks, and Black Jack gum wrappers woven into long chains. Putting those to one side for the time being, I ducked my head below the desk and examined the underside, looking for hidden notes or mementoes. Aside from several globs of hardened, black chewing gum, still no luck.

I picked up the packet of letters from the desk, untied the ribbon binding them together, and shuffled through them. Some were insipid notes from her friends, Susan, Carol, and Linda, chronicling their daily activities, crushes, gossip, and homework assignments. Other letters had been written by someone named Edward, short, but spelled correctly with proper punctuation and unexpected vocabulary.

"I saw you and Linda walking to social studies after study hall," read one from two years earlier. "How was Mr. Bellows today? He looks like an endomorphic walrus with those whiskers, don't you think? See you."

There were two unsigned letters that seemed out of place. Written by an adult hand, they, too, were short, but lacked Edward's attention to the inessential.

"Meet me tomorrow in the usual place after the drama club meeting before you catch your bus. Make it look accidental."

The other one said simply, "Saturday at the agreed place and time." Neither was dated.

Inside one of the small desktop drawers was another pack of letters. Scrawled by a juvenile hand and seemingly spelled by a caveman, these were written by Joey Figlio. The ardor surprised me, though I might have expected it after my conversations with him the day before. As I read the raw missives, I reminded myself that fifteen-year-olds could be just as passionate, if not more so, than adults. Their emotions rage without the perspective and rationale that come with experience. That doesn't make them any less potent. Joey's love wheeled and careered out of control, spinning like a palsied top, erratically, without boundaries or proportion. He was pure id, like a cat, and with the claws. His professions of love exploded off the page, without shame or self-consciousness. Despite the bad spelling and lack of any sense of irony, Joey Figlio emerged a hot-blooded lover. I found it cute and dangerous at the same time.

I will lick the sweat off your skin and you will lick mine until we are united as one in spirit and sole. Two hearts beeting together as none have ever beet before. Yours and mine in sickniss and hell. I will hang myself for you, Darleen, even if you betray me and stole my rope. You are mine and be long to me.

And there were poems—truly bad ones—but not obscene as Mrs. Nolan had described them. And Joey had plans for the future. In September, he wrote of dropping out of school to get a job as soon as he was sixteen in May of 1961. Then he and Darleen could get married and move into an apartment in Jacksonville, Florida, with three older guys Joey knew. Wow, I thought. Every day a honeymoon.

In October, after Darleen joined the drama club, Joey was talking about running off with her to California. He had an uncle who worked as a custodian in Bakersfield and, Joey was sure, Darleen could be a famous movie star. To him, Bakersfield and Hollywood seemed interchangeable. In November, he was begging her to run off anywhere: Florida, California, Nevada. I had nothing in Darleen's hand to indicate her state of mind vis-à-vis Joey Figlio. If she'd written any responses to his love letters, they would have been with him. But I did uncover a locked diary that looked to be a couple of years old. Irene Metzger was downstairs, so I forced the lock. The leather strap gave way without too much trouble, and I opened the diary to read. But there was nothing to see. Darleen had made the last entry three years earlier: musings on things like the Girl Scouts and what she wanted for Christmas and her birthday. Nothing about boys or running away. I spent a stray moment wondering why she had stopped maintaining a diary, but figured she'd lost interest and moved on to other things.

In the center drawer I found some travel brochures for California and Nevada. The Hoover Dam and Hollywood studio tours. Darleen had circled Paramount Studios and Disneyland on the cartoonish map. On the Nevada brochure, she'd marked the Sands, Tropicana, and Frontier casinos in Las Vegas. I wasn't sure how a fifteen-year-old Darleen thought she could gain entrance to a casino, but clearly her tastes ran in that direction. I shrugged, admitting to myself that I, too, would have wanted to see the same places at her age.

I came across three worn folded-paper fortune-teller games, the kind young girls make with their friends to amuse themselves. Under the flaps were such oracles as, "You will kiss a boy" and "You will break his heart." There was also, "You will lose your socks in gym class." These fortune tellers, probably two or three years old, provided no clues to Darleen's recent state of mind.

Then I found a brown envelope with a paper inside. I retrieved it and unfolded it, not knowing what to expect. It was a receipt for $43.20. A Trailways bus receipt for a ticket, one way to Tucson, Arizona. Ten more minutes of searching the room produced no bus ticket. I plopped down on Darleen's bed and held the receipt before my eyes. I stared long and hard at the paper, running through all the scenarios its presence suggested. In reality there was only one. With no accompanying ticket, what else could I deduce but that Darleen had used it? What further proof did I need? She'd run off, just as the sheriff had said, just as I had suspected. But as sometimes happens when the truth presents itself, we can't quite believe it. Still, I smiled, uneasily, knowing that this pointed to the best possible ending under the circumstances. Despite Irene Metzger's assurances to the contrary, it appeared her daughter had skipped town, most probably with an older boy.

I made my way down the narrow stairs and rejoined Irene Metzger in the kitchen.

"Find what you were looking for?" she asked, glancing up from her mending.

"Maybe," I said, taking a seat across the kitchen table from her. "Does Darleen know anyone in Arizona?"

Irene Metzger's eyes narrowed and she glowered at me. "You're back on the idea that she's run off, aren't you? I already told you there's no way she did that."

I produced the bus receipt and laid it gently on the table between us. She eyed it for a long moment, before glancing up at me. I could read the turmoil in her eyes. Was this good news? Or false hope? She was probably asking herself how well she knew her own daughter.

She took the slip of paper and pored over it, her eyes ranging back and forth over the print, twitching as she examined both sides. "Where did she get that kind of money?" she mumbled finally.

"Did she have an allowance?" I asked. "A part-time job of some kind?"

Irene Metzger shook her head in a daze. "We gave her forty cents a week for her chores. And even that was difficult. These are tough times on the farm."

"That's not a small amount," I said. "Especially if times are hard."

"That's her doting father. He's hard, but with a soft spot for his little girl. He insisted on raising her allowance from twenty to forty cents a week about three months ago."

A regular Daddy Warbucks, I thought. Forty cents a week seemed extravagant for a farmer on the wrong side of luck. But even at that rate, it would have taken Darleen about two years to save up forty-three dollars. I, too, wondered how she had managed to accumulate such a sum.

Irene Metzger sat immobile, receipt in hand, staring dumbly across the room, struggling to make sense of it.

"Mrs. Metzger?" I asked.

She shook back to life, her face white, and fumbled for a cigarette from the crumpled package on the table. It was empty.

"Damn it," she whispered.

I produced one from my purse. Not her brand, but she wasn't about to beg off.

"So," I asked as she inhaled deeply. "Does Darleen know anyone in Arizona? Perhaps someone with forty-three dollars?"

I could see that she was rattled.

"What is it?" I asked.

"It was last spring," she began carefully. "Before Darleen took up with that Joey Figlio."

She looked straight ahead, fixing her gaze somewhere between her nose and the stove against the wall. "There was this boy," she continued.

"Wilbur Burch. His family has a farm in Fort Hunter, back in the woods near the old Erie Canal lock. He was older than Darleen." She paused to draw on her cigarette, still looking at nothing in particular.

"How much older?" I prompted.

She shrugged. "Eighteen or nineteen."

"You didn't mind that Darleen was seeing a grown man?"

"Of course I did," she said. "And Dick went through the roof when he heard and put an end to it right away. He said Wilbur wasn't good enough for Darleen and threatened to kill him if he didn't stay away from her."

"So he's in Arizona now?" I asked.

"He's stationed there at some big army base. There was a notice in the paper about four months ago."

The family court was located in the County Administration Building, just one floor above the sheriff's office. Judge Anthony Albertone, a portly man of about forty with slick, black hair and a Thomas Dewey mustache, entered the room at precisely 10:00 a.m., climbed the two steps up to the bench, and motioned absently for the assembled to take their seats. He retrieved some papers from a leather case, unfolded his half-moon spectacles, and began to read. Then he cleared his throat. He said nothing for the next few minutes, absorbed as he was with his reading, but he had cleared the airways just in case the urge moved him. At length, he whispered something to the bailiff, who nodded and stepped over to the door to the left of the judge. He disappeared inside, only to emerge a few seconds later pushing Joey Figlio before him.

Joey wasn't shackled—as I had hoped and expected—and looked like a kid heading to school. He shuffled over to the large table in front of the bench wearing a wrinkled blue-and-white panel shirt, buttoned up to the collar, sleeves not quite reaching his bony wrists; brown slacks; and a pair of old, black leather shoes. He looked ahead, seemingly without seeing, with the same witless void in his eyes and anesthetized expression on his face. If he saw me, he didn't show it.

I'd covered family court for the paper many times in the previous three years. In my experience, New Holland courts worked pragmatically and often quickly, especially in juvenile cases. It wasn't unusual for the arraignment and fact-finding hearing to take place one after the other without adjournment. That's why I was present, in case I had to give evidence against my aggressor, that dirty little JD, Joey Figlio.

Stan Pulaski was seated a row behind me. All business, he nodded at me without smiling. He was also in attendance in the event he'd be called to testify about the arrest. Behind Stan, a couple of tired-looking old men and three ladies wrapped in heavy winter coats appeared to be ready for a warm snooze out of the cold. The salacious details of the case might prove to be an entertaining bonus. From a seat near the door, a severe man in his late forties, looking somehow startled and angry at the same time, stared at me as if to trying to see through me. His hair was cropped close to his head, but still stuck up in thorny defiance, and I was sure his pillow played a greater role in his grooming than did his comb. I leaned back and asked Stan Pulaski who the gruff-looking man was, and he told me that it was Joey's father, Orlando Figlio. As Judge Albertone tapped his gavel to call the court to order, Dr. Arnold Dienst, principal of Fulton Reform School, slipped through the door and took a seat next to Joey's father. The two exchanged a silent look. They might have been through this before.

The court clerk asked all to sit, and that's when I noticed Joey's lawyer. Oh, God. It was Steve Herbert, a man I'd been seeing casually until I decided I'd rather pluck my fingernails out one by one than spend another night in his arms. Wasn't this some kind of conflict of interest? Shouldn't he recuse himself? He threw me the slightest hint of a smile and blinked slowly in a way to suggest everything would be all right. I can't say for certain, but I must have blushed crimson.

The judge announced that this was an arraignment of Joseph Figlio, a minor, accused of multiple probation violations, grand theft automobile (two counts), and assault with a deadly weapon (the butter knife, two counts). The judge cleared his throat once more and asked Joey if he understood the charges lodged against him. Joey shrugged.

"Is that a yes or a no, young man?" asked Albertone.

Steve Herbert whispered in Joey's ear, and the boy told the judge, "Sure, I guess so."

"You guess so?" asked Albertone. "Some of these charges are felonies. These are very serious offenses, young man."

"Yeah, but I'm a minor," said Joey, much to the consternation of his counsel. "I can't get into too much trouble on account of I'm not an adult."

The judge was taken aback but didn't have an answer for him. At length, he asked the defendant for his plea.

"Innocent," said Joey, without consulting his lawyer.

"Very well," said the judge. "In that case, I will remand the boy without bail to the county jail until the fact-finding hearing can take place."

"Your Honor," piped up my pal Steve Herbert. "We ask that the defendant be remanded to the Fulton reformatory instead. Dr. Arnold Dienst, principal of that facility, is present in the courtroom today and will assume responsibility for the boy."

Damn Steve Herbert! Whose side was he on anyway?

"That's correct, Your Honor," piped up Dienst from the back of the room. "I will guarantee the boy's detention until the fact-finding hearing."

"Wait a minute," I said, jumping from my seat. "If the floor is open to all, I've got a few things I'd like to add to the record."

"Sit down, miss!" ordered the judge. "I'll have order in this courtroom. Now, who are you, exactly?"

"Eleonora Stone, Your Honor. I'm the person whose car that little delinquent stole," I said. "Twice."

"Allegedly, Your Honor," interjected good old Steve.

"All right," said Albertone. "Procedure will be followed in my court. Now, I see no reason to set bail, as the defendant was already under an order of detention at Fulton at the time of these offenses. Do you have anything to add, Mr. Herbert?"

Joey Figlio tapped Steve Herbert on the shoulder and leaned in to whisper something in his ear. Steve stood and addressed the judge.

"My client would like to ask the court a question," he said.

Judge Albertone frowned, but allowed it. Joey stood and dug his right hand into his trouser pocket to retrieve a wadded-up piece of paper.

"I want to show you that that lady, Ellie Stone, can't charge me with nothing," he said. "She wrote me love letters and asked me to take her car."

"What?" That was me, on my feet again. "Your Honor!"

"It's all right here, sir," said Joey, taking a few steps forward and holding out the sheet of paper. The court clerk took it from him and handed it to the judge.

I looked to Steve Herbert for some assistance, but he was watching Judge Albertone, who was reading the paper Joey had produced.

"'Dear Joey,'" read the judge. "'Please come to my car and I will help you escape from Fulton. You can take my car and drive it to wherever you want.'"

At this point, I decided to sit down and keep my mouth shut. Joey's letter was speaking eloquently enough for me.

"'Also, thank you for the knife for my kitchen,'" continued the judge. "'It's a nice present 'cause I said I wanted one for spreading butter on my toast.'"

Judge Albertone peered over his reading glasses at Joey, who looked as inscrutable as ever. "Young man, are you telling me that that young lady over there—Miss Stone, is it?—wrote this letter to you?"

"Yeah," said Joey. "She digs me."

"Miss?" the judge asked, looking to me. "Please spell your full name."

I stood and complied.

"Thank you," he said then turned back to Joey. "The handwriting on this letter is an abominable scrawl, written in pencil, with many misspellings of simple words. Furthermore, if I am to believe you, Miss Stone has misspelled her own name." He paused to let his words register. "What do you have to say about that?"

Joey sat silent for a moment, then opined that I was probably too emotional and girlish to get the spelling right.

"Her own name?" asked the judge, incredulous.

Joey shrugged. "Sure. Look at her. She came here today to beg my forgiveness for getting me pinched by the cops."

Judge Albertone sighed and put down the paper. He shook his head in woe and pursed his lips.

"The defendant will be remanded to the Fulton Reform School for Boys until the date of the fact-finding hearing, which I will schedule for next week. I request that counsel make a recommendation so we can avoid an actual hearing. As for you, Mr. Figlio," he said, staring down my nemesis, "you will not leave the school grounds, and you will keep your distance from Miss Stone. And, for God's sake, stop stealing automobiles."

"Yes, sir," said Joey. "But please tell her to stop bothering me. My heart belongs to another."

The judge cracked a smile and shook his head. "Miss Stone, the court hereby instructs you that Mr. Figlio's heart belongs to another. Try to cope with it." He pounded his gavel and declared the hearing adjourned.

Joey was escorted from the room, and Dr. Dienst followed him out.

Orlando Figlio stayed put in his seat, still watching me in startled anger. Steve Herbert sidled up to me.

"I'll bet you weren't expecting to see me," he said, smiling broadly, flashing his perfect white teeth.

"I certainly wasn't expecting you to double-cross me," I said. "That kid should be locked up in the county jail until they can ship him off to Attica."

"Come on, Ellie," he said, waving a hand at me. "You're overreacting, don't you think? And I was doing my job. The kid deserves a proper defense, doesn't he?"

"He didn't throw you out of your car onto the frozen road."

"He's not a bad kid, Ellie. Come on, let's go somewhere quiet for a couple of hours. I don't have any appointments until after lunch."

"Start holding your breath, Steve," I said.

"Don't you mean, 'Don't hold your breath'?"

"No, Steve. I was suggesting you asphyxiate yourself," I said and turned on my heel.

As I approached the door, Orlando Figlio stood and blocked my exit. I took a step back and scanned the room for the bailiff. He'd already decamped. Why had I been so rude to Steve Herbert?

"Is there a problem, sir?" came a voice behind me. Stan Pulaski. "Is he bothering you, Ellie?"

"No problem, Officer," said the man. Then to me, "I don't mean no harm, miss. I'm that no-good boy's father, and I just want to apologize for the trouble he's given you."

"It's all right, Stan," I said, dismissing my champion, who seemed unsure about leaving me. He stepped away but watched intently as Joey's father and I sat down on the bench to talk.

"He's just no good," said Mr. Figlio, shaking his head. "I've tried to reason with him, tried beating some good behavior into him, but nothing works. He's just a stubborn little so and so."

"Can you tell me about his girlfriend?" I asked. "Darleen Hicks."

"He never brought her around much. Once or twice. She was quiet. Didn't say much at all to my wife and me. I thought she was a little slow, if you know what I mean."

"Did they seem happy together?" I asked, wondering how Darleen could seem slow when standing next to Joey Figlio. "Your son says they were in love."

Orlando Figlio scratched his head, his scruffy eyebrows arching and eyes yawning wide open as if pulled up by strings. "What do kids know about love? Besides, Joey wouldn't have told me nothing anyway. We don't talk much."

"What about his mother? Did Joey confide in her?"

He shrugged. "Sure, I suppose he did. Mother's a boy's best friend, after all."

"Do you suppose I could speak to your wife about Joey?" I asked.

He eyed me with suspicion. "What do you want to know about Joey for anyway?"

"I'm not in love with your son, if that's what you're thinking," I said. "I'm investigating Darleen Hicks's disappearance, and Joey told me they were planning to get married and run away together. Maybe he said something to your wife."

Orlando Figlio thought about it then said he didn't like the idea. "What do you mean, 'investigating'? What's a girl like you got to investigate? I just wanted to apologize to you for what my boy did. I didn't think you'd want to start playing policeman."

"I'm a reporter for the paper, Mr. Figlio, not a cop," I said, reaching out and touching his arm. "Trust me. I'm looking for Darleen. I don't want to investigate Joey."

He smiled at me and blushed. His teeth were long and gray, but his crazy eyes sparkled, the result of my hand on his arm, surely. There was something about the soft touch of a girl's hand that he liked. He said he would ask his wife.

"But she's in Cobleskill visiting her aunt. That's why she ain't here. She'll be home Sunday."

"Fine," I said. "I'll be in touch."

FRIDAY, JANUARY 6, 1961

The next afternoon, I was at my desk, rolling another sheet of paper into the Underwood. Norma Geary was leaning over my shoulder, waiting for the final version of my story to spirit away to Composition.

"It's not going to get written any faster with you hovering over me," I said as I began to type.

"Harry's waiting," she said, referring to our typesetter. "If you want this in tomorrow's edition, it's got to go now. The entire paper is put to bed except your story and the basketball-game story, which, by the way, is also yours."

"Jeepers, I must be good," I said. "How much do they pay me?"

Norma feigned a smile. "They've left space for your basketball story. Harry said he'll fit it in tomorrow morning before going to print. Now, about your Darleen Hicks story . . ."

There wasn't much left for me to write about except the Trailways receipt and everything its very existence suggested. Once finished, my article would all but close the disappearance of the ninth grader.

George Walsh entered the newsroom and waddled over to his desk a short distance away. He threw a sour look my way then inspected the nibs of several pencils before finally selecting one.

"What are you doing here, Stone?" he asked as he scribbled something on a sheet of paper before him. "I thought Charlie sent you out on basketball duty." He chuckled. "Better you than me."

"Funny. That's what Charlie said, too," I answered, and George's smirk vanished. Norma snorted back a laugh.

"Are you lost, Mrs. Geary?" he asked. "Mighty far from the steno pool, aren't we?"

"Mr. Reese assigned me to Miss Stone," she said. "I'm her assistant."

George's eyes nearly popped out of their sockets, and he could muster no speech. After huffing and puffing himself breathless, he grabbed a sheet of carbon and rolled it backwards into his electric typewriter—no accompanying paper—and began banging away.

"You're going to be late for the basketball," Norma said.

"Leaving now," I mumbled. "This one's not ready yet. Just notes, mostly. Take this one instead," I said, shoving a two-page report on the city council's last meeting at her.

Georgie Porgie noticed his blunder with the carbon paper and tore it from the machine. He glanced at me to see if I was watching and, like a snoozing cat that's fallen off the sofa, pretended nothing had happened.

"All right, then," said Norma. "You'll have to finish the Hicks story tomorrow." George Walsh's ears pricked up. "It can wait one more day."

I slipped what I had of Darleen's story into the drawer of my desk, grabbed my coat and purse, and hurried out the door, trying to remember if I had enough Scotch at home for after the game. I turned to wish Norma good night, and noticed George Walsh glaring at me. I was sure he'd be complaining to Artie Short about my assistant as soon as I'd gone.

The New Holland Bucks and the Mont Pleasant Red Raiders of Schenectady took to the court at seven. A full house cheered them on as the boys ran through their pregame layup and passing drills. I was courtside, loading film in my camera and scouting the opponents as they warmed up, placing names to the skinny frames for my recap later on. Minutes before the tip-off, Coach Mahoney gathered his charges around the bench to review the game plan. Once he'd finished and the boys had broken their huddle, I corralled Teddy Jurczyk on the bench as he tightened his shoelaces. I introduced myself and asked if I could speak to him after the game for the newspaper. He looked a little frightened, but then smiled shyly and said sure. Just then, Ted Russell, of all people, tapped me on the shoulder.

"I've tried to phone you, Ellie, but you're never home."

Teddy Jurczyk blushed, and I cursed my bad luck for running into the music teacher.

"Yes, I'm on duty, Mr. Russell," I said, now blushing myself and surely fooling no one.

"Working on the Darleen Hicks story?" he asked. "At the basketball game? Don't tell me you're interviewing suspects here," and he chuckled. Teddy gave a visible start. "Anyway, how about we catch a bite to eat somewhere after the game?"

I really wanted to cast my eyes downward and beg off demurely or somehow discourage his advances. But I didn't. I didn't even answer him. I was too busy studying the horrified look on Teddy Jurczyk's face. The color had drained from his red cheeks, his mouth hung ajar, and his troubled eyes betrayed a roiling agitation within.

"Ellie? Uh, Miss Stone?" said Ted, perhaps realizing for the first time that I didn't want to broadcast our acquaintance publicly, at least not in front of a subject I had to interview later on.

"Ted, I'm sorry but I'm covering the basketball game here," I said a little too sharply. "Please."

He looked wounded, but got the hint. He apologized for the interruption and wished Teddy good luck for the game.

Teddy picked up a towel and wiped his brow, still not quite in control of his emotions.

"Teddy," I said to him. He looked at me. This kid needed a pat on the back. "Teddy, you can do it," I said. "Go out there and win this game for us."

"I hate that name," he said, almost in a whisper, then turned and dragged himself out to center court.

CHAPTER TEN

I watched the carnage from my seat behind the New Holland bench. Teddy Jurczyk put on the worst performance of his brief career. Two points, one of nine shots made, two double dribbles, a walk, and all three free throws missed. The visitors took full advantage of Teddy's troubles and raced to a 34–16 halftime lead. The hometown crowd went from boisterous anticipation of a victory at tip-off—a win would lift the Bucks into a tie with Albany for first place in the Class A league—to dismal and surly silence by halftime. And some of the discontent was directed at me.

"That girl was talking to Teddy just before the game," said a man a couple of rows behind me. "She said something to upset him. Probably from Schenectady."

"Why doesn't she sit on their side?" asked a woman near him.

I tried to shrink into my seat, but the people near me inched away. I made a big show of standing and reloading my camera, displaying my press badge prominently, and yelling encouragement for the home team when the players appeared on the court for the second half. Teddy didn't fare much better after the intermission, though, finishing with just seven points in a crushing defeat, 59–37. Though it was my assignment, I had little interest in torturing the poor kid by rehashing his dreadful performance with an interview about basketball. But judging by his reaction to Ted Russell's comment, I wondered how well he might know Darleen Hicks. Even if I thought the case was settled, I like my stories to be complete, and I felt the need to have one more answer from Teddy Jurczyk.

Teddy evaded me temporarily when the final whistle blew, disappearing into the locker room before I could grab him, but I'm not so easily discouraged. I parked myself outside the locker room, endured the snide remarks of a couple of high-school boys, who joked about me waiting for my boyfriend to finish showering. They laughed, thinking they were clever, congratulating each other for their wit.

"Yes, I'm waiting for my boyfriend," I said. "Where are your dates?"

Their mirth soured, and they slunk away.

Just then the locker room door swung open and Coach Mahoney stepped out. He walked right past me without noticing my presence. It was too much to expect that he might recognize me as the reporter who'd interviewed him four times in recent weeks about the team's progress. I was just a skirt in the corridor. Then Teddy emerged, shuffling, eyes cast down to the floor, a small canvas gym bag in his hand. He didn't see me until I called to him. He stopped, looked back at me, and nearly ran. But what was he running from?

"May I speak to you, Teddy?" I asked. "Nothing about the game. We all have off nights."

He didn't know what to say. He was just a fifteen-year-old boy, after all. Little artifice, no sophistication, and a reluctance to talk to strange girls.

"I don't know what happened to Darleen," he volunteered.

"Tell me about her," I said.

"What's to tell?" he asked, setting his gym bag on the floor. "She's a swell girl. In my homeroom since seventh grade."

"Did you see her the day she disappeared? Maybe in the parking lot near the buses?"

He shook his head. "No, she was on a field trip that day."

"She came back to the school to catch her bus," I corrected. "And if you and Darleen were in the same homeroom, you must have gone to Canajoharie, too."

He stood silent. His crew cut, still wet from his shower, glistened in the fluorescent light of the corridor. He wanted to go, run, put as much distance between him and me as possible. But he was too polite for that.

"Did you go to the Beech-Nut factory that day?" I asked.

Teddy didn't answer right away. He just stared at me, chewing his lower lip. Finally, he nodded.

"Yes, I went to Canajoharie that day," he said softly. "But I didn't even talk to Darleen on the bus or at the factory. And I didn't see her after that, either."

I must have looked skeptical, because he repeated his story. Then he said he had to go.

"I can't talk here. Some of the fellows are still in the locker room. They'll be out any minute."

"Can you meet me at Fiorello's later tonight?" I asked. "Around eleven. We can talk privately there."

Teddy didn't like the idea, but he nodded okay.

〰

I walked briskly toward my car, parked on the southeast side of the lot outside the high school. The weather report called for warming temperatures the next day, an end to the brutal cold spell we'd been under the past three weeks. But that was small consolation this night; it was freezing. I saw groups of kids huddling in the dark, smoking, joking, waiting. One girl caught my eye. Susan Dobbs was holding court with Linda Attanasio and four other girls. She was in charge, that much was clear, as the girls focused their attentions on her.

I thought about stopping to ask a question, but then remembered the bus receipt and told myself it was too cold to tie up loose ends. Then a dark station wagon rolled up to the group, blasted the horn, and Susan waved goodbye to her friends. I could see the man at the wheel, surely her father. About forty, with a hunter's cap on his head and several days' stubble on his chin, he lit a cigarette as Susan and Linda climbed in. Never even looked at them. And Susan didn't look at him. He just threw the car into gear and drove off. Susan waved out the window to her friends as they went.

I slipped into my car and emitted a long shiver that rose from deep inside of me. Then I loosed a scream and lunged for the door. There was someone else in the car.

"It's okay, Miss Stone," came a girl's voice from beside me in the darkness of the passenger seat. "It's me, Carol Liswenski."

"Oh, my God," I panted. "You gave me such a fright! I thought you were someone else. What are you doing in my car?"

"Sorry," she said with a sheepish smile. "It was just so cold waiting for you, I thought I'd wait in here. Your car door is broken, by the way. Did you know that?"

"Yes, I was aware of that," I said, my breathing slowly returning to normal. I wasn't sure my heart would ever recover. The specter of Joey Figlio, juvenile-delinquent car thief, lying in wait for me in my car, ready to take me on another joyride, terrified me more than I would have expected. He was just a kid, after all. Yet he had happily left me to freeze to death on the side of the road, then tried to do it again, all in one day. I thought with dread of the lax security at Fulton Reform School, the ease with which Joey routinely slipped his bonds. When would he come for me again? What was stopping him?

"Are you all right, Miss Stone?" asked Carol. "I didn't mean to frighten you. It's just that I lost my ride. Could you drive me home?"

"What happened to your ride?"

"Susan Dobbs and I came to the game with her boyfriend, Pete Keppler. He's sixteen and has a car." She said it to impress me. Didn't work. "Then they had a fight, and she left with Rick Stafford."

"And Rick didn't give you a ride home?" I asked, certain that the man driving Susan away was not her new boyfriend. "She ditched you?"

Carol shrugged. "Yeah, well, she was sorry about it, but you know how it is."

No, I didn't know how it was. I had forgone a few trysts with some dreamy boys in my younger days to look after a friend: Janey Silverman on one of our boozy nights cruising lounges on Manhattan's Upper East Side. Janey didn't hold her liquor as well as I did, and there were plenty of men all too eager to take full advantage of an underage girl. We were scarcely older than Carol Liswenski and Susan Dobbs, yet I never abandoned my friend for a guy. And to top it all off, I had to figure out why Carol was lying to me about Susan.

"Fine, I'll take you home," I said, starting the car. "But you're going to have to help me out with something."

"I will if I can," she said. "Mind if we listen to the radio?"

By the time we'd reached the Mill Street Bridge, I'd suffered through Dion and the Belmonts, the Hollywood Argyles, and Andy Williams. Carol loved them all. Then, when Brook Benton and Dinah Washington came on, finally giving me something I could enjoy, she turned her nose up at "A Rockin' Good Way" and changed the station. I switched off the radio.

"You said you would help me," I said. "I need you to tell me who Darleen spoke to when she got off the bus the day she disappeared."

Carol was having none of it. "I already told you I didn't see who it was."

We'd reached the top of Mill Street, and I turned west on Route 5S. I sensed something fishy about the entire conversation, but this was no time to stop. I wanted to see how much more information—truth or lies—I could get from her.

"Do you know Wilbur Burch?" I asked as we gathered speed along the highway.

Carol jerked her head to look at me. "Why do you ask about Wilbur?"

"Just something I heard about him and Darleen. Weren't they getting serious about five months ago? Before he shipped out for the army?"

"I don't know anything about that," she said, turning away to the window.

"They didn't stay in contact after he left? By mail, perhaps?"

Carol scoffed then said Darleen didn't read or write letters. "She didn't bother with that kind of thing."

The paper was quiet at ten, except for Composition and Bobby Thompson in the photo lab. As the *Republic* was an evening paper, the presses in the basement wouldn't be active until the following morning. I handed a roll of film from the game to Bobby to develop. Nothing too exciting— we weren't the Schenectady paper after all—and I left a note for Ralphie Fisher, sports editor, to choose any two shots he liked. I sat at my desk and rapped out my story in record time. Try as I might, there wasn't much I could embellish about the home team's performance. The Red Raiders had dominated from the opening tip-off to the final whistle. Gerald Washington, Mont Pleasant's six-foot-four-inch center, scored nineteen points and pulled down seventeen rebounds. He also blocked seven shots, including one of Teddy Jurczyk's. I didn't mention that in my article.

I pulled the last page of my piece from the typewriter at a quarter to eleven, retrieved a folder from my desk drawer, and slipped the story inside. I filed the carbon copy for my records and stood to leave. I had an appointment with Teddy Jurczyk in fifteen minutes. But then I stopped. One of those queer sensations that something was off beam seized me just as I was buttoning my coat. Turning to look over my shoulder, I fixed my gaze on the desk drawer. I slid it open and checked the contents. Everything seemed normal. Even my story on Darleen's bus receipt was there. But it was face down in the drawer, not the way I'd left it, I was sure. I was being paranoid. The cleaning lady, Luba, must have straightened things out. I grabbed my purse and camera and headed for Composition on my way out.

Fiorello's was slowing down when I arrived a few minutes after eleven. Only a few straggling teenagers in the booths. In summer you could find some older patrons at this hour, stopping in for a late-night sundae or banana split. But in the dead of a January cold spell, no one was buying ice cream.

I took a seat at the counter and asked Fadge if anyone had been looking for me.

"Aren't these boys a little young for you?"

"I'm serious," I said as he placed a mug of vanilla ice cream and hot fudge in front of me. "And I didn't order this."

"That means the calories don't count."

"Is that your strategy for dieting?" I asked.

He called me an unflattering name then asked who was looking for me anyway. I leaned across the counter to whisper the name discreetly.

"Poor kid," he said. "Had a bad night from what I hear."

I nodded. "He looked spooked out on the court. But I don't want to talk to him about basketball. I have a sneaking suspicion he knew Darleen Hicks pretty well."

"Well, he hasn't been in," said Fadge, noticing a kid near the cigarette case opposite the candy display. "Hey, Zeke! Get away from those cigarettes. If I catch you stealing, you're banned for life."

"I wasn't going to steal anything," said the kid. Fadge knew most of the kids by name. "Honest, Fadge. I was just waiting for Joe. He's in the bathroom."

Fadge turned back to me. "Damn Joe Biggins. I didn't see him buy anything, and now he's using the bathroom."

"Your office," I said, just as the front door opened, and Pat Mahoney, the basketball coach, strolled in. He made a beeline for me.

"Hello, Miss Stone," he said. "Can we talk for a minute?"

I exchanged a glance with Fadge, who motioned to the last booth in the back, near the pay phone. It was the only clean table. The other booths had just cleared out a minute before, and the place was empty except for Coach Mahoney, Zeke, Joe, Fadge, and me. Oh, and Bill, the retarded dishwasher. "Retarded" is perhaps not the right term, since Bill was probably closer to an idiot savant. He was busy smoking a stogie over the soapy sink in the back room. His lips were moving in some kind of private conversation with himself. Bill was sweet, but he'd pinch your behind if you weren't careful. I always made it a point to face front when he was in the room.

"You're probably wondering why I'm here," said Mahoney once we'd slipped into the booth. He was about forty, a little pudgy around the waist, with a receding hairline. He had nice eyes.

"Actually, I was expecting Teddy Jurczyk," I said. "Do you know if he's coming?"

Mahoney made a face, as if I was putting him out. "Look, miss," he began, "I know you got a job to do, and I want to be polite and respectful. But can I ask you to please leave Teddy out of it?"

"I beg your pardon," I said.

"You really upset him tonight," said the coach.

"Is this about the basketball game?" I asked, incredulous. "You're asking me to leave him alone because I put him off his game? Are you aware a fifteen-year-old girl is missing?"

Mahoney held up his hands to stop me. "Whoa, there," he said, his face flush. He was trying to control himself. "I wasn't talking about the game. I was talking about what happened *after* the game. You ambushed him outside the locker room. The kid came to me crying."

"Oh," I said, feeling like a cad. "Sorry about what I said, Coach."

"Look," he said with a little smile, "I like to win like any other coach. Heck, I start Teddy over my own son because I know he gives us a better chance to win. I guess that's kind of obvious. But I care about these kids, you know. Win or lose. And this investigation has upset him."

"But I haven't asked him anything yet," I said in my defense. "Just if he knew Darleen."

Mahoney looked deep into my eyes. "It's a school of nine hundred students total. Everyone knows everyone else. And they're in the same homeroom, so, yeah, he knows her. Can't you leave it at that? He hasn't done anything wrong."

I considered his argument, all the while trying to figure out how I would get the information I needed. Coach Mahoney seemed like a decent man, and I didn't want to lie to him. But I wanted to talk to Teddy about more than his silky jump shot.

"Will you do me this favor, miss?" asked Mahoney, his eyes saying please.

I reconsidered. In light of the bus-ticket receipt, did I really need to dig any further? I was convinced, after all, that Darleen had run off to Arizona to shack up with some buck private. Why not let it go?

"Okay, Coach," I said. "I'll leave him alone."

Mahoney was relieved and gave me a broad smile. He patted my hand and thanked me. "Now you'll have more time to write your bake-sale and garden-party stories," he said, piercing my heart.

I know he meant well, but I nearly slapped him.

"Coach," I said finally, "sometimes it's better just to say thank you and nothing else."

Once Mahoney had driven off, Fadge joined me in the back booth. "What did he want?" he asked, slipping into the seat opposite me. To tell the truth, he didn't so much slip as stuff.

"Oh, nothing," I said. "He asked me to stop scaring his star player."

"Teddy Jurczyk? What did you do to him?"

I waved off the question. "It doesn't matter anyway," I said. "The story's over. It looks like Darleen ran off after all. I found a bus receipt in her room. One-way ticket to Tucson."

Fadge pondered it a while, then suggested we go get a pizza at Tedesco's.

"It's only eleven thirty," I said. "You're going to close up early? What if you get a rush on penny candy?"

"Very funny," he said. "Just for that, you can pick up the bill to cheer me up."

He squeezed out of the booth and shuffled toward the front just as the door opened. I slid off the bench and looked to see who was delaying my midnight pizza. There, filling up the doorframe from floor to ceiling, stood Walt Rasmussen, looking like the Colossus, Helios, straddling the harbor of Rhodes. Okay, I'm embellishing, but he was huge.

"Hey, Walt," said Fadge. "What'll you have? A little cold for your usual, isn't it?"

He shook his head and squinted in my direction. "Nothing for me tonight, Ron," he mumbled. "I come to talk to that girl."

My knees threatened to collapse beneath me. This was the man who'd shown off his ax-juggling skills for my benefit. I had no idea what he wanted with me, and I didn't care to find out.

Fadge turned to look at me, mugged bewilderment, then told Rasmussen he could use the back booth. I wished he'd asked me first.

I was trembling as I retook my seat. If Fadge had trouble fitting into the booth, Walt Rasmussen almost ripped the table off the wall squeezing inside. His mammoth belly stretched the limits of the undershirt he wore under his open, checked flannel, fighting the edge of the linoleum table for dominion over the space. The wooden bench seat groaned under his weight, creaking in protest as he settled into a comfortable position. Folding his rough, red hands on the table between us, he towered over me, glaring in silence at me as he breathed through his nostrils like a horse. Unconsciously, I shrank deeper into my seat, and he appeared even larger.

"You wanted to speak to me, Mr. Rasmussen?" I asked once the silence had become too much to bear.

He grunted something deep and gruff that I took for a yes. Then he unfolded his hands and placed them flat on the tabletop.

"I saw that girl that day," he announced. "Dick Metzger's daughter." His voice was rich and gravelly, and his small eyes peered out from his great ruddy cheeks at me, unsettling me at such close proximity. But I was determined not to blink or look away.

"Where did you see her?" I asked.

"It was along the highway. Route Five-S. She was getting out of a taxicab."

"What time was that?"

"It was about four. I was in my truck, driving back from the feed store, when I saw her."

"Did you notice anything else? Anyone else in the vicinity?"

He shook his head. "She got out, and the taxicab drove away. She looked put out. Annoyed. The road was empty at that hour, and it was already almost dark."

"Did you stop to see what was wrong?" I asked.

"Why would I do that? It's none of my business what her problems are. I just saw her on the side of the road, and I thought I should tell you about it."

I couldn't figure why he felt that way, but at least he was being friendly. For him.

"How far was she from home?" I asked. "Close enough to walk?"

"Only about two and a half, three miles," he said.

"Three miles?" I gasped. "And you didn't offer her a ride?"

"Like I said, it's none of my business what her problems are. She looked healthy enough to me. It's not like she was bearing burdens. She had no books. Just her lunch pail."

I had to remind myself that Darleen was in sunny Arizona. None of this mattered. Or did it? I kept thinking back to the receipt. Still, I had a couple of more questions for him.

"What can you tell me about Bobby Karl?" I asked.

Rasmussen just stared at me. He didn't move except to breathe through his nose. Then he said he didn't know the first thing about Bobby Karl.

"His father's farm's on the other side of Dick Metzger's. That's all I can tell you."

"You never saw him with Darleen Hicks?"

"Nope."

"One last thing," I said. "Why are you telling me this? I thought you didn't like the idea of girl reporters."

"I still don't like the idea. It ain't natural. But I thought I should tell you what I knew anyway. I felt bad about keeping it to myself when you come out to see me. So now I've cleared my conscience. Maybe you can print your story and help find out what happened to her."

"I already know what happened to her," I said. If he was surprised, it didn't show on his face. "I think she ran off."

SATURDAY, JANUARY 7, 1961

With the morning came the break in the weather we'd all been waiting for. After three long weeks of bone-chilling cold, the temperatures rose into the fifties by afternoon. These January thaws were common in these parts people told me as if perhaps I'd arrived on the banks of the Mohawk from some far-off, tropical land. New York City was, after all, just two hundred miles south of New Holland. We sometimes got the breezes from the north. The warmth was a welcome respite from the snow and ice of December.

I drew duty covering the executive-board meeting of the local council of the Boy Scouts of America in Canajoharie. Not much less interesting than a City Council meeting, and it was short and easy to write for Monday's edition. I scribbled the details in my pad and figured Norma could simply type it up without changes. I enjoyed the drive back to New Holland along the river, smiling to myself as I passed the turnoff for the Fulton Reform School for Boys. It warmed my heart to think of Joey Figlio locked up inside those walls. And if he were to escape and steal my car, I would never freeze to death on a glorious, sunny winter's day like this one.

When I arrived back at the paper, the City Room was empty, except for George Walsh, who was typing away furiously at his desk. He saw me enter, sneered my way, then returned to his task. I left my story from the Boy Scouts' meeting for Norma on her desk. That's when I noticed a folder of her notes on the Darleen Hicks piece left open next to her typewriter. I picked up the first sheet of paper and read.

"Monday: Call CO at Fort Huachuca re. Wilbur Burch and Darleen Hicks. Confirm her arrival. Check bus schedule. E. S. to Arizona?"

There were phone numbers and names of army personnel, secretaries, and addresses. I hadn't asked her to do any of these things, but my Norma was a self-starter, it seemed. I also had no intention of going to Arizona, even if Artie Short had been willing to pay my fare. For me the story was over. But I thought the answers might be of interest to Irene Metzger. She might want to contact her wayward daughter. I closed the folder and replaced it in Norma's filing cabinet behind her desk.

"Why don't you take a picture? It lasts longer," I said to Georgie Porgie who, I noticed, was watching me.

I spent Saturday afternoon doing laundry and watching the NFL consolation game, the marvelously alliterative Bert Bell Benefit Bowl. A bit anticlimactic, but not a bad game. The Lions beat the Browns 17–16. After some ironing and some housework, I worked my way through a couple of crosswords I'd been neglecting. It felt good to be free of Darleen Hicks's sad story, even if I had wasted a few days on it. I relaxed in front of the television, watching the news then *Perry Mason*. I kind of had a thing for Paul Drake. Something about his checked sport coats and white hair. After the wild courtroom confession at the end of the last act, I got up to pour myself a drink, happy to spend a quiet Saturday evening alone. But the cupboard was bare. Well, not exactly bare, but there wasn't enough whiskey to see me through the night and Sunday, too. The prospect of a dry Sunday made me shudder. Damn blue laws.

Remembering Mrs. Giannetti's admonition about the delivery boy's gossip, I pulled on my coat and grabbed my purse. Clark's Wine and Liquors on Brookside wasn't the cheapest, but it was the closest to my apartment. Clark Robinson, a colored man with one arm, was the proprietor. He didn't ask questions or make small talk. He just stuffed your bottles into a bag and took your money. Two fifths of Dewar's would see me easily through the weekend, unless I had company.

I drove home and parked opposite Fiorello's as usual. The place was hopping, with teenagers spilling out onto the sidewalk, enjoying the warm weather after so much cold. I thought I'd stop in to see Fadge at the end of the evening, but for now I had an appointment with a tumbler and some ice.

I climbed the stairs and paused at my kitchen door, fumbling with the keys, squeezing my parcel to my side so as not to drop it. It wasn't until I'd unlocked the door and pushed my way inside that I noticed—too late— that I was not alone. From the dark of the vestibule, a thin figure slipped inside behind me. I shrieked, but he shushed me. I switched on the light, ready to bash that damn Joey Figlio on the head with one of my bottles. But it wasn't Joey at all.

"Frankie!" I cried. The little JD who'd threatened my life at the reform school. "Stay away from me!"

"It's okay," he said, holding out his hands to indicate his good intentions. He looked small, scared, and hungry. "I'm not going to hurt you."

We stood there frozen for nearly a minute, each terrified of the other. His chest rose and fell as he huffed for air, as if he'd just run a four-minute mile. I held my breath waiting for some kind of explanation of why he was gasping in my kitchen.

"Can I have something to eat?" he asked finally. "I haven't eaten since yesterday."

"What are you doing here?" I demanded.

"Please, just give me a cracker or something. Then I'll tell you."

In the freezer, I found some Swedish meatballs I'd frozen in October after a truncated dinner date with a handsome young pediatrician who'd recently moved to town. After a few drinks, he made the mistake of sharing his politics with me. Not only did he not end up in my bed, I threw him out without his supper.

Frankie stuffed some potato chips into his mouth and washed them down with a beer as the meatballs warmed on the stove. I gave him some bread and butter to accompany the meatballs, wondering if he was going to kill me once his strength had been restored. I watched from a distance as he ate. The angry young man I'd met at the reform school looked more like a frightened boy in my kitchen. His greasy hair, wet with sweat, clung to his head making him look even smaller. His football mustache was gone, and his checked shirt was wrinkled and perspired. Funny how checks on this kid didn't do it for me the way they did on Paul Drake.

Finally he finished, wiped his hand across his mouth, and said thank you.

"What are you doing here?" I demanded again.

"Don't be sore, Ellie," he said. "I mean, Miss Stone. Like I said, I won't hurt you."

What game was this, I wondered. I moved a step closer to the table, and Frankie stiffened in his seat. I was beginning to think I had nothing to fear from this kid.

"Okay, Frankie, let's get some things straight. At Fulton, you told me you'd come looking for me when you got out. And you said I'd get mine. Now you tell me I've got nothing to worry about. What gives?"

"I was just saying that up at Fulton," he said, averting his eyes from my stare. I waited for more. "I had to say that, don't you see?"

"No, I don't. Why?"

"I've got a reputation to protect inside," he said. "You made me look like a fool. If I'd have let you get away with it, my life would be ruined. I got to be the toughest kid there, or I'll wind up the sissy to some guy with ideas that he wants a girlfriend."

I didn't know what to say.

"So you see I had to act tough with you." He paused, looked down into his lap, then continued. "Honest, I'd never hurt you, Ellie, 'cause I'm in love with you."

"What?"

"It's true. Ever since that day, I can't stop thinking of you. You're so pretty and smart and you got real guts. I just had to bust out of there to see you, if only for a few minutes."

The last thing I needed or wanted was a sixteen-year-old boyfriend. And a juvenile delinquent to boot. And yet I couldn't help feeling a little flattered.

"But I taunted you," I said. "I called you names and mocked you."

"That's okay," he smiled, beaming at me now. "I kind of asked for it. I was pretty rude to you. But I didn't mean it, Ellie. Not a word. At least not at the end."

"Look, Frankie, I don't know what to say. Or what to do with you. You can't stay here, and you can't . . ." I searched for the right words. "You know we can't . . . You know that, don't you?"

He cast his eyes down again. I felt I'd torn his heart out.

"I know that," he said softly. "At least for now."

"Oh, Frankie," I said. "No. Not now, not later."

"Is it because I'm too young?"

I chewed on that one for a moment. The age difference would never change. Maybe I should go with that. But it was actually so many other things. For one, I barely knew him. For another, what I knew of him did not help his cause.

"Yes," I said finally, patting him on the shoulder. "We're just too far apart in age."

Frankie seemed to be weighing my words then shook his head. "No, you'll change your mind someday, I hope. I can wait for you. It's not like I'm meeting any girls up at Fulton."

"You know I'm Jewish, don't you?" I asked, playing my trump card. It didn't work quite as well as it had with the Karls, but it derailed his love song for a bit.

"Really?" he said, his face twisted like a screw. "You don't look Jewish. My old man said all Jews had hook noses and fat lips."

"Well, there's another reason we can't be together, Frankie. Think of your father. He'd never accept me."

"He's dead."

"Frankie, what am I going to do with you?" I asked again, changing the subject. "You've got to get out of here."

"I know," he said. "But will you do me a favor?" Oh, God, I thought. What was he going to ask? "Would you call the cops on me? That way when they take me back, the guys will believe I went through with my threats. I'll still be top dog."

"Okay," I said. "I suppose I could do that for you."

"And you'll tell the cops I tried to, you know, do stuff to you?"

"I won't say that."

He frowned. "Okay, well, would you mind if I yell and swear at you when they take me away? Don't be shocked, but I'm planning to say some real bad things. But that doesn't mean I don't love you."

I smiled gently and said, "Sure, Frankie. You can swear and scream at me when they come to take you away."

Frankie was pleased. "Oh, I almost forgot," he said. "Joey Figlio asked me to give you something."

Frankie fished a crumpled piece of paper from his pocket and pressed it into my hand. I asked him what it was as I flattened it on my kitchen table.

"He said it was something to help your investigation. He said if he couldn't kill that teacher, he wanted you to make sure he pays for his crime. Sounded pretty weird to me, but he's a strange kid, that Joey."

"You're telling me," I mumbled.

"What's it say, anyway?" he asked.

"It's a love letter to Darleen Hicks," I said, dazed by what I'd just read. "The girl who disappeared three weeks ago."

"A love letter from Joey?"

"No," I said, feeling the skin crawl on my neck. "It's from Ted Russell."

CHAPTER ELEVEN

I had to submit to the drama Frankie wanted to play, accompanying him down the stairs, where we waited a few minutes for the law to show up. We didn't say anything; Frankie just stared at me with a goofy expression on his face. Then the sheriff pulled up at the curb, and we knew it was time to go. Frankie smiled sweetly at me, told me he loved me, then stepped outside and loosed a bloody scream. Frothing at the mouth, spitting like an alley cat, he yowled in protest and flailed his arms as two deputies corralled him. Bellowing my name at the top of his voice, right there on Lincoln Avenue, he threatened to come back and slit my throat, before performing unspeakable acts on my dead person with all his appendages, his mouth, and a stick. An impressive display of profanity, perversion, and vitriol from such a young thug. What a performance! I didn't mind too much going along with his scheme, except that he was doing it in front of a crowd of at least sixty teenagers loitering outside Fiorello's. My good name and respectability echoed off every house in the general vicinity. The violence and volume of his tantrum shocked me for real, even though he'd warned me, which only made the hysteria more believable for the bystanders. So many witnesses to my embarrassment, including Fadge and his crony, Tony Natale.

As Frank Olney prepared to slap a pair of handcuffs on the kid, Frankie flashed me a quick high sign and an impish smile. Once he'd cuffed him, the sheriff shoved Frankie into the backseat of his cruiser, deliberately bouncing his head off the doorframe as he did. Now it was Frank Olney's turn to give me a smile.

The crowd dispersed slowly once the sheriff had driven off with Frankie. Mrs. Giannetti sidled up to me on the porch. She'd seen everything, but could manage no speech. Not one snide remark. Finally, after a few moments of awkward silence had passed, she reluctantly forfeited her chance to shame me and slipped back inside her door. Fadge approached to see if I was all right.

"What the hell happened?" he asked, joining me on the porch.

"Don't worry about it," I said, shaking, and not from the cool air. "It was all an act."

He stared at me for a long moment, trying to gauge the level of my upset. "You want me to close up and stick around for a while?"

I scoffed with a forced smile. "Don't be silly. I'm fine. I just want to go to bed."

He looked uncertain, but finally wished me good night and crossed the street to the store. I trudged up the stairs, damning myself for what I'd done with Ted Russell, author of love notes to fifteen-year-old girls. I wanted to be alone.

SUNDAY, JANUARY 8, 1961

I awoke Sunday to find one of the new fifths of whiskey I'd bought half empty. If that wasn't enough, the original bottle—the one I'd been sure wouldn't last the weekend—was dead in the trash can. Whiskey doesn't give me headaches, but I still felt fuzzy-headed. And ashamed. Not so much for the liquor I'd consumed, but for the reason I'd drunk it. How could I have done such a thing? How had Ted Russell managed to fool me?

I spent hours in bed, the pillow over my eyes, sleeping off my regret. Slumber provided a temporary tonic for my self-reproach. As long as I was unconscious, I could dream of other things. I lowered the shades and closed the drapes, shrouding the bedroom in total darkness. I felt anonymous and invisible to the world outside, and I liked it. I imagined myself in a strange city, holed up for days in a nondescript hotel, selected so randomly no one would ever be able to find me. With doors bolted and curtains drawn, no one could possibly know where I was, what I was doing, or what I'd done, and that comforted me. I would still have to face myself and the truth once I finally got out of bed, but for now, I wallowed in the indulgence of escape and solitude.

The phone rang a few times throughout the afternoon, but I didn't answer. It may have been Charlie Reese or Sheriff Olney, but it was probably Fadge, wanting to know if I was okay. I told myself I'd drop in at the store in the evening then rolled over and fell back asleep.

Around ten p.m., I showered and dressed in a black skirt and cotton blouse. I didn't bother with lipstick, figuring I didn't need to impress Fadge. The store was empty when I walked in a half hour later. Fadge was putting off the end-of-day sweep of the floor and was holding down a stool with his rear end and the edge of the counter with his fat elbow. We chatted for a few minutes about the sudden warm weather, then he asked about the previous night's scene with Frankie. I really didn't want to talk about it, but I had no excuse not to. At least until Frank Olney strolled into the store.

"Just the girl I wanted to see," he said, taking the seat next to me at the counter. He nodded to Fadge, "Hi, Ron. How's business?"

"I've got two customers, Sheriff, and neither one of them has ordered anything."

"Do you want us to order something?" I asked. "That would mean you'd have to get up and do some work."

He considered it a moment then waved us off. Frank jerked his head toward a booth, silently inviting me to join him for a private powwow. We settled into my usual booth at the back of the store.

"You okay?" he asked.

"I'm fine," I said. "So what's up? You didn't come here to buy me an ice-cream soda."

"Tomorrow morning at nine, I'm going to the junior high to search Darleen Hicks's locker. How'd you like to come along? It was your idea, after all."

I sighed. "I'm not sure, Frank. It seems a waste of time," I said, steeling myself to break the news that I'd been holding out on him. "I should tell you that I visited Irene Metzger and found some new information. Darleen had a bus ticket to Arizona. You were right all along. She just ran off to meet a fellow."

Frank stared at me for a long time, breathing a little heavier with each moment that passed. At length, he fidgeted then began with great care: "I wish you'd told me sooner. But that doesn't mean your story is finished. You've got a girl that's run off."

"Sure," I said. "But this story is a dead end, Frank. I just want to forget it."

"Something else is bothering you. I think it's those Fulton boys. First Joey Figlio, now Frankie Ralston. I tell you, we can keep them away from you, Ellie."

Joey. Damn. Wallowing in my self-reproach, I'd completely forgotten to contact Orlando Figlio. What did it matter, anyhow? Darleen was gone. No need now to pay social visits on the Figlios.

"I'm not worried about Frankie Ralston," I said. "He's harmless."

"Well, Joey Figlio's locked up tight at Fulton. No need to worry about him either."

"That school couldn't hold him if he had a handle. Arnold Dienst told me he's escaped on several occasions already. Fulton is no Alcatraz."

"I'll ask the city police to watch your place. You'll be fine."

"You're going to ask Chief Finn to look out for me?" I said.

"Okay, if it'll make you feel better, I'll check in with Fulton to make sure your boy's still there."

Frank pushed his way out of the booth, forcing a squeal from the table, then sauntered over to the phone booth and stuffed himself inside. He didn't close the folding door. Probably had forgotten his shoehorn and figured it was too much trouble without it. I heard the jingle of change slipping down the slot then the whir of the dial as he wrenched it around and around. He asked in his deep voice to speak to a night guard. A few moments later, he squeezed back into the booth opposite me and smiled.

"Everything's fine. Said there hasn't been one escape today. So stop worrying about Joey Figlio and Frankie Ralston."

I picked at my fingernails and probably chewed my lip. He was far off the mark; I was thinking of Ted Russell and just wanted to slither away.

"Ellie, my dad taught me to finish what I started. No matter what. He said he didn't mind if I didn't do anything at all. But if I started it, I had to finish."

"Cool your jets, Frank," I said finally, thinking it was preferable to waste an hour pawing through a junior-high-school girl's locker than to explain the true reason behind my gloom. "I'll go with you tomorrow."

"Don't take it so hard. There'll be other stories. Better ones. I shouldn't say this, but you're good at this newspaper stuff. You run circles around George Walsh."

I grunted a thank-you.

"Eight forty-five okay? I'll pick you up," he said, sliding out of the booth like the Queen Mary down the launch.

MONDAY, JANUARY 9, 1961

I rose early the next morning and packed a bag of clothes: a couple of skirts, blouses, shoes, toiletries, and underthings. After some toast and coffee, I emptied the perishables from my icebox into the trash, then I settled down on the sofa and picked up the letter Fadge had wanted to use as a coaster. It had been sitting there unopened for nearly a month. I had been either too busy or too stubborn to open it. I knew what was inside, of course, but some things are just hard to look at.

December 1, 1960

Dear Miss Stone,

As discussed in our first meeting in February of this year, a proper burial is an essential tradition in the completion of a life. The ritual honors the departed in a holy ceremony and provides a measure of solace and peace for the loved ones left behind. We encourage mourners to show respect for the departed by fasting, sitting shivah, and donating to the needy or religious organizations of their choosing.

We also implore you not to neglect an important part of this ritual: the selection and placement of the headstone. You will recall that we showed you a wide variety of options in February, and you expressed interest in a simple granite marker. I'm writing now to remind and beseech you to consider finalizing the arrangements at your earliest convenience. The yahrzeit is fast approaching, and you should not fail to mark this solemn occasion.

Please telephone or wire us with any queries you may have in this time of somber reflection and remembrance. We, at Berg and Raphael Statuary, are at your service, should you require assistance.

Sincerely,
Moises Rafael

I folded the letter back into its envelope and tucked it into my purse.

I waited on the porch, soaking in the warmth of the day. It wasn't exactly swimsuit weather, but the forecast called for temperatures touching sixty by early afternoon. The sheriff arrived as promised at a quarter to nine. I climbed into the car and smiled good morning. Frank switched on the radio: instrumental rubbish not rising to the level of swing or jazz. It sounded old and dusty. The kind of stuff you'd hear in a men's barbershop. He maintained silence for the ten-minute drive to the school.

We met Assistant Principal Brossard in his office a little after nine. He offered us coffee, but I wanted to get the search of the locker over with. I had places to go. Still, I wanted to have a word with him privately about Ted Russell. If I was bothered about my own indiscretion with the handsome teacher, I was outraged that he may have had his way with a fifteen-year-old girl. But I had to speak to him alone, away from the sheriff.

Brossard led Frank and me to a bank of gray lockers in the first-floor corridor. There we met a Negro janitor, who was carrying a long metal bolt cutter. Brossard consulted a slip of paper in his hand for the number of Darleen's locker. A moment later, standing before number 432, Brossard nodded to the janitor, who made short work of the padlock, clamping the jaws of the bolt cutter around the shackle and biting it off with a smart click.

"Thanks," said the sheriff, pushing past the assistant principal, "I'll take it from here."

"Are you sure you don't need some help?" he asked.

"I can manage," said Frank, without even looking back over his shoulder as he yanked the locker door open.

Reluctantly, Brossard shoved off, taking the janitor with him, and left us alone in the corridor. Frank stood there a moment staring at the contents, blocking my view. Then he snatched a composition book from the shelf inside and flipped through it.

"You want to have a look?" he mumbled as he read.

"Not really," I said. "I mean, what's there to see? Just the messy left-overs of a girl who ran away."

"That might sound good in your story. The human angle, you know."

I stepped up to the locker and peered inside. There were school books, a pencil box, and a sweater dangling from a hook. A small vanity mirror hung on the inside of the door, alongside black-and-white pictures of Ricky Nelson, Bobby Rydell, and Fabian, clipped from teen magazines and pasted to the metal. Darleen had scrawled love notes to each of them.

"Ricky, my darling! Marry me!"

"Fabian, I'm yours forever!"

"Bobby, take me away!"

Lots of exclamation points.

Sticking out from behind Fabian was a small black-and-white snapshot. I plucked it from its perch and examined it. It was a blurred photograph of Joey Figlio standing next to an old car. I didn't believe he had any connection to the car; it was just there. Joey looked witless and unimportant, common and unremarkable, even more so when compared to the practiced poses of the heartthrobs with whom he shared Darleen's wall of fame. Scrawled across the back of the photo in a rough hand, Joey had written, "You're mine forever. If I can't have you, no one else will."

I showed it to Frank, who gave me a knowing look.

"If I wasn't sure she'd run off to Arizona," he said, stuffing the photograph into the breast pocket of his shirt, "I'd arrest that kid on suspicion of murder."

I turned back to my search. At the bottom of the locker, a pair of white sneakers and a crumpled, sweaty gym suit lay in a tangle on the floor. Black Jack gum wrappers, folded into long chains, hung from the shelf, stretching three-quarters of the way down to the floor of the locker. On the underside of the shelf, Darleen had left gobs of black gum stuck to the metal. Disgusting.

At the back of the locker, a light-weather jacket sagged from a hook. Going through the motions, I frisked it. There was something weighing down the right-side pocket. I reach inside and pulled out a pint bottle. It was Dewar's White Label, not quite empty, and I was sure it was the one stolen from my purse the night of the basketball game. Darleen and her friends hadn't yet acquired a taste for the stuff, it seemed, judging by the amount left in the bottle after three and a half weeks. But then I remembered that Darleen had disappeared on the twenty-first, just five days after the game. It looked as though she'd been sneaking slugs of whiskey between classes. I had done the same at Riverdale Country School. Janey Silverman was in the habit of pocketing the odd bottle of booze from her uncle's shop on Fifteenth Street and Fifth Avenue, Paramount Liquors. Whatever was closest to the door, she told me years later. I had assumed she was taking it from her father. The selection was a bit of a grab bag; never the same liquor twice. But Janey didn't particularly like drinking and hardly ever touched the stuff. She ended up giving it to me, and I put it away, one sip at a time between classes, just as Darleen Hicks had done.

"What's that you got there?" asked Frank. I pushed aside the memory.

"Whiskey," I said, handing him the bottle.

Frank harrumphed. "Wonder where she got that."

"How should I know?" I said a mite too insistently.

I stood on my toes and reached deep inside the locker to retrieve a small cosmetics bag from the back of the shelf. Lipsticks, eyelashes, pimple cream, Midol, and blush. There was some talcum powder and a hairbrush as well. I dived in again, this time fishing out a canvas pouch, the kind banks and businesses used to carry money. I opened it up and dug inside. The first thing I found was a well-worn envelope with unused hall passes, unpunched lunch tickets, and excuse slips for a variety of absences, from influenza to menstrual cramps, all with Irene Metzger's name and signature at the bottom. But there wasn't a date on any of them. Darleen Hicks was a fair hand at forgery.

I found some simple jewelry: earrings, a couple of friendship rings, a pendant, and a charm bracelet. Then I pulled a large coin purse from the bottom of the pouch. It was heavy in my hand.

"Find anything?" asked Frank.

I uttered a short gasp.

"What is it?" he said, joining me to see.

I opened the purse for him to see. "It's money, Frank. A lot of money."

He glowered at the wad of bills in the purse; he knew as well as I what it meant.

"There's no way a girl would run away and leave all this money behind, is there?" I asked, dreading the conclusion that was dawning on me.

"I don't think so," said Frank. "I'd better count it; this has to be official now."

He pulled the wad of bills from the purse with his meaty fingers, clamped the money under his arm, and retrieved one last item from inside the bank pouch: a stamped envelope from Fort Huachuca, Arizona. It was addressed to Darleen Hicks, general delivery, New Holland, NY. Inside there was a short letter, a small blue square of paper, and a third sheet of thin paper.

"This is a New York State driver's license," said Frank, giving it close scrutiny. "Forged. Says she's seventeen years old." He handed the license and the purse back to me to hold while he dug into the wad of cash.

"These things look pretty easy to fake," I said, referring to the driver's license. "All you need is an eraser and a black pen." I slipped it back into the envelope and pulled out the thin piece of paper instead.

Frank grunted agreement as he counted the money. "There's ninety-seven dollars here," he said once he'd thumbed through the bills twice. "Where does a fifteen-year-old girl get that kind of money?"

"Probably the same place she got this," I said, handing him the paper from the pouch.

"What's that?" he asked.

I sighed. "It's Darleen's bus ticket."

Besides the unused bus ticket, there was a short letter in the envelope, written in a clumsy chicken scratch, dated November 20, 1960.

Dear Darleen,

I saved up enough to buy the ticket. With the hundred dollars I wired you and this ticket, there's no reason we can't be together and get married right away. A hundred dollars! If you got the fake driver's license like you said, we're set now, baby girl. I'll meet you in Tucson in four weeks. Don't miss that bus!

Yours always,
Wilbur

Frank procured a new padlock from the janitor and slapped it on Darleen's locker to secure its contents. Then he hustled me down to the principal's office along with the new evidence. This was my chance to have a word with Brossard about Ted Russell. I got lucky; Frank needed to make a phone call to the jail to bark some orders at Pat Halvey. The sheriff plunked himself down at Mrs. Worth's desk, and I slipped behind him and knocked on Brossard's door.

"Come in," he called from inside. He looked up at me quizzically when I entered. "Miss Stone. What is it?"

"I need to speak to you about Mr. Russell," I said, taking the seat before him. Brossard waited. My face felt flush. "I have reason to believe he was behaving badly with Darleen Hicks. Perhaps other students as well."

Brossard let loose a short laugh. He stared at me, brandishing a half-cracked smile for several beats. Finally he asked me what reason I had to believe such a thing.

"I've come into possession of a note. A handwritten note from Ted Russell to Darleen Hicks. A love note."

Brossard's smile fell, and he leaned forward in his seat. "Now that's a very serious accusation, Miss Stone. I've already told you that I investigated the allegations and found them to be false. Both Mr. Russell and the girl insisted there was nothing."

"I've got the note."

"Did you find it in her locker just now? May I see it?" he asked.

I shook my head. "I don't have it with me."

"And you're certain it was written by Ted Russell?"

"Yes," I said. "It was signed by him."

Brossard looked troubled. He eased back into his seat and frowned at something out the window. "What did the note say?" he asked, his voice slow and gruff. Suddenly, he sounded as if he had smoker's cough.

"It said, 'Darleen. Each time I see your bright face, my heart leaps.' And it went on for a bit after that."

Brossard banged the table with his hand and shot out of his chair. He paced back and forth at the window for about thirty seconds before drawing a restorative breath and turning to me.

"I just can't believe it," he said, dismissing my evidence. It had sure looked as though he believed it a moment before. "It's not possible," he continued. "I've known Ted—Mr. Russell—for two years. We socialize. We've bowled together. He took me under his wing and showed me around town when I arrived here from Hudson. I interviewed Ted and the girl, and I tell you I'm sure there was nothing between them. There must be some mistake."

"Hudson?" I asked, veering off course. "Are you from Hudson?"

"No," he said. "I'm from Yonkers originally, but I was deputy headmaster at a small denominational boarding school in Hudson. St. Winifred's."

"Why did you leave? I'm always interested to know how people end up here in New Holland."

He shrugged. "It was a good opportunity. I would like to be a principal or superintendent one day. St. Winifred's was a bit of a dead end."

"Do you have a sample of Mr. Russell's handwriting?" I asked, returning to the subject at hand.

"I think this has gone far enough. I'm not going to give any handwriting samples. Not Mr. Russell's and not mine."

"I didn't ask for yours."

He stared at me. His nose twitched just ever so, then Frank Olney walked in.

"I meant I would no sooner give my handwriting sample than I would Mr. Russell's," he said.

"There you are, Ellie," said Frank. "What's all this about handwriting samples?"

"Miss Stone is under the mistaken impression that Mr. Russell misbehaved with Darleen Hicks," said Brossard.

"Her and me both," said the sheriff deadpan. "It does look suspicious."

"Nevertheless, it's false," insisted Brossard. "You must be mistaken, Miss Stone. That love note is surely from someone else."

"What love note?" asked Frank.

"Frankie Ralston gave it to me," I said through my teeth. "I forgot to mention it to you."

"All right," said the sheriff, lips pursed, exhaling through his nose. He wasn't happy to learn about the note this way. "Let's go, Ellie."

"What about Darleen Hicks's locker?" asked Brossard. "Did you find anything new?"

Frank stared at him long and hard. "Nothing at all. Just girl stuff."

Frank zoomed up Market Hill, heading for Route 40 and the jail. "Ellie, I've got to ask you nicely not to mention anything about this money and bus ticket for now," he said. "Nothing in the paper, please. Sometimes we have to withhold information from the public so as not to tip off the bad guys. This proof satisfies me that Darleen Hicks did not run off to Arizona, or anywhere else for that matter. And I don't want anyone who might have been involved with her disappearance to know that we know that. I'm happy to share information with you when I can, and you can print it when it's time. But for now, I'm asking you to play ball. Is that clear?"

I wasn't sure what to say. The sheriff had been cooperative with me—a true gem—ever since the Jordan Shaw murder investigation got under way, but my job was to bring in the story. Should I—could I—put my responsibility aside and do the right thing? It was the right thing, after all. If a few days of silence from my side could help nab a kidnapper or a murderer, then it was my duty as a citizen to go along with the law. Why, then, did I feel that I was betraying my profession? Torpedoing my own career? I wanted to break this story.

"Ellie?" he asked, rousing me from my thoughts.

"Of course, Frank," I said. "I'll keep this quiet for now."

He nodded in satisfaction. "I need you to give a statement on the bus receipt you found at the Metzger place. And I'm going to need that love note."

∂◯

Twenty minutes later, I was sitting across from Deputy Pat Halvey, dictating my account of how I'd found the receipt in Darleen Hicks's room. After a couple of minutes of watching Pat hunt and peck at the keys, I elbowed him to one side and assumed control of the typewriter, completing my own statement while Pat fetched me a cup of tea. Once I'd finished, the sheriff packed me off with Stan Pulaski, who had orders to retrieve the receipt from Darleen's room at the Metzger farm, as well as the love note from my place on Lincoln Avenue. Stan waited in my kitchen, hat in hand, as I made several photographs of the crumpled note in the other room. I watched Stan drive off, thinking about the packed bag I'd left upstairs. The trip I had planned would have to wait for now.

It was after eleven by the time I walked into the City Room. Norma Geary looked distraught, her face ashen as she caught my eye. Then Charlie Reese strode in.

"Where have you been, Ellie?" he demanded, his voice tight and impatient. "I called you five times yesterday, and now you show up three hours late for work, and on a Monday morning. You know how Artie Short feels about tardiness after the weekend.

It was true. The publisher had met a statistician from the university in Albany who espoused a theory that employees ditched work, pretending to be sick, on Mondays and Fridays, thereby extending their weekends and defrauding their employers. That set Artie Short on a crusade to prove we were all slackers. He collected his evidence over the next six months then called a general meeting with the staff to present his findings.

"People," he began, frowning, clutching a few sheets of paper in his right hand. "I stand before you today to report that I have been concerned about absenteeism in this place for quite some time. So concerned, in fact, that I have compiled data from the past several months." He held the papers up for all to see, crushing them in his tight, sweaty grip. Then he cleared his throat, adjusted his glasses, and continued. "You will be interested to know that the staff of this publication seems to think it normal to take things easy, play hooky, and shirk its working responsibilities, on Mondays and Fridays in particular." The crowd of employees glanced about at each other in confusion. This was news to me as well; my attendance had been nearly perfect for two and a half years. "The statistics do not lie," he continued. "Eighteen percent of all absences occur on Mondays," he announced, reading from the wad of paper in his hand. "Eighteen percent!" he said, shaking the document at us. "And fully sixteen percent of absences are recorded on Fridays." He paused to glare at his audience.

I raised my hand. Artie Short took notice and gave a start. He actually looked stunned that anyone, let alone I, would interrupt him in the middle of an all-hands chewing-out. His mouth hung open, and his eyes betrayed both anger and surprise. He stared at me for a long moment, saying nothing. Bobby Thompson, standing at my side, inched away from me.

"What is it?" hissed Short at length.

"Excuse me, sir. You said that sixteen percent of absences occur on Friday?" I asked. The publisher gaped at me but said nothing. "And eighteen percent on Monday?"

"That's what I just said, yes. What is your point, Miss Stone?"

"Just that Friday and Monday account for forty percent of the workweek, yet only thirty-four percent of the absences. It seems to me that Tuesday through Thursday are the real problem."

Artie Short recoiled, twitched, then huffed, looked around, searching perhaps for someone to contradict my math. When no one volunteered, he throttled the papers one last time, shaking them at the employees.

"Precisely my point, Miss Stone," he said with an unconvincing nod. "The shirking is a problem all week long. Correct it immediately, people. I will be monitoring your absences."

"I was home," I said, returning to Charlie Reese's question. "I wasn't feeling well."

He gave me a knowing look, but didn't dare suggest I had been drinking.

"What's the big crisis anyway?" I asked.

"George Walsh has been nosing around your story," said Charlie. "He's got a big scoop, and Artie Short has pulled you off, in part because we couldn't locate you yesterday for your input on what George found."

"Off the story? He can't do that."

"He already has," said Charlie, waving a hand at me in frustration and turning to face the window.

"What does George have that I don't?"

"Read it and weep," said Charlie, tossing some pages onto my desk. "This will be in this afternoon's edition."

I snatched the story off the table and read. It only took seconds to realize what kind of scoop George had landed. Mine. His article told the tale of Darleen Hicks's bus ticket. "Missing Girl a Runaway" he led. A receipt for a one-way fare to Tucson, Arizona, had been found in her bedroom. She was thought to be in the company of an enlisted man at the nearby Fort Huachuca army base, and the *Republic* was spearheading the effort to locate the wayward girl there and bring her home "to the bosom of her modest, salt-of-the-earth, loving mama and papa."

"Charlie, this is my story," I said, punch drunk. "I mean, I didn't write this schlock, of course; it's classic George Walsh, with the melodrama and the references to 'this newspaper' and 'your humble correspondent.' But this is my research."

"Can you prove that?"

"He must have gone through my notes. I saw him skulking around here the other day. I'd almost finished the story, and I'd left it and my notes in my desk."

I yanked open the drawer and rifled through its contents, but my story and notes were nowhere to be found. Georgie Porgie must have removed them in anticipation of my reaction.

"My notes are gone," I said. "But Norma knows. She can tell you I wrote it all down."

"That's true, Mr. Reese. Miss Stone showed me her notes, and we discussed the entire story on Friday."

"If that's so, why didn't you finish it? Or tell me?" asked Charlie.

I didn't have an answer for that. There was the basketball game Friday, but that didn't explain Saturday or Sunday. I should have written the article then, but I was glad I hadn't. The truth of the matter was that Darleen Hicks had never boarded any Trailways bus for Arizona. The actual ticket was safe with the sheriff, locked away in his safe, along with ninety-seven dollars in cash. I couldn't say any of this to Charlie, or even to Norma. For the time being, I had to bide my time and take my lumps as they came.

As things turned out, I didn't have to wait very long.

Artie Short entered the City Room with George Walsh following behind. The publisher strode up to me and smirked right in my face.

"I see you've found your way to work, Miss Stone. Do you have anything to say for yourself?"

"I'm very sorry for being late, sir," I said. "It won't happen again."

That disarmed him for a moment. But being the odious worm that he was, he found his bearings in short order and resumed his attack with a new salvo.

"Are you aware that I've taken the Darleen Hicks story away from you and given it to George here?"

"Yes, sir. Mr. Reese just told me."

Artie Short didn't like the direction our conversation was going. He was egging me on and wanted a strong reaction, probably so he could fire me on the spot for insubordination. Charlie looked uncomfortable, surely expecting me to rise to the bait, and Norma was green. Even George Walsh tried to shrink from sight.

Short harrumphed. "Well, have you seen George's piece for today's edition?"

I nodded meekly. That seemed to floor Georgie Porgie. He looked alarmed and relieved at the same time, if that's possible. He must have expected me to cry foul and accuse him of having stolen my notes. I'm sure he had some phony defense all prepared, but I held my tongue, and so did he.

"Very well, then," said Short, his bullying petering out without my participation. "I want you to read that article again, young lady. Pay close attention as you do. You'll learn something. That's how a *newspaperman* writes a story."

"Yes, sir."

But he wasn't quite finished yet. He smiled at me with all the self-righteous condescension he could muster and offered this: "Even with the help that Charlie Reese provided for you—an assistant . . ." He leaned backwards to whisper to his son-in-law, "What's her name?"

George whispered back, and Artie Short bellowed, "What'd you say? What's her name?"

"Norma Geary," said George, loud enough for all to hear.

"Yes, Norma Geary," repeated Short, aiming his scorn back at me. "George, here, didn't have an assistant, Miss Stone, and still he bagged the story. What do you have to say about that?"

I said nothing. One word from me, and he would fire me. The humiliation mounted with each passing moment. So many witnesses to my dressing-down. I wanted to kick him in the shins and wring George's neck.

"I didn't think you'd have anything to say," he smirked. "Well, that cozy situation is over, young lady. Mrs. Geary is being transferred back to the steno pool."

I glanced at Norma whose expression told me she'd known about the change when I entered the room. In fact, she'd already gathered her belongings and put them in a box. Though I'd never asked for her, losing her would be a bitter pill to swallow.

"You'll have to make your way without unfair advantages and accommodations for your gender," continued Short. "Men have it tough enough as it is, without us making things easier for women to supplant them in the workplace."

That was the last straw. I had been holding my temper in the hopes of staying on the story, but also because I wanted to keep this job. What were my options if I lost it? A secretary for some lawyer? I didn't want to know what other humiliation Artie Short had in store for me. But I'd had a bellyful. Job or no job, I was going to tell Artie Short and George Walsh what I thought of them. I was going to tell them both where to get off, then quit in triumph. From the corner of my eye, I caught Charlie Reese's terrified expression, practically begging me to shut up. But all went quiet in my head. Dead silence. I was resolved, decided, and ready to accept the consequences of my sharp tongue. My lips parted and squeezed into place for my first syllable. But then, satisfied he'd taken me down a few notches, Artie Short turned and looked to his son-in-law. I hesitated.

"Now, George," he said, "are you all set? All packed? Got your traveler's checks from Millicent? Do you have your ticket?"

Oh, my. I took my finger off the trigger. Was this really happening?

"Now, it'll take you almost three days to get there by bus," continued Short, "so don't go wasting my money phoning in from Peoria or Jefferson City to tell me about the weather. This is costing me enough already. Wire me when you reach Tucson. No long-distance phone calls. You got that?"

"Yes, sir," barked George.

I shifted my mouth to park, my explosive invective holstered safely again, and hung on each word. This really was happening.

"Your bus leaves in an hour," he said. "Billy will drop you at the station. Have a good trip and bring home that story."

I nearly snorted a laugh, and Artie Short took it for a stifled sob. I played along, assuming the best hangdog expression I could manage. I dug my fingernails into the palms of my hands, bit my lower lip, and tried to conjure up my saddest memories to beat back the laughter that wanted to burst out of my chest. It must have been quite convincing; Charlie told me later on that he'd almost stepped up to punch Artie Short in the nose. I'm glad he didn't.

"Something to say, Miss Stone?" asked Short.

"Yes," I said once I'd wrestled my joy into submission. I took a deep breath and stared into George Walsh's eyes. He seemed to flinch. "Have a nice trip, George," I said. "You deserve this."

✸

In spite of the satisfaction I felt at the prospect of the fool's errand Georgie Porgie was about to embark upon—at precisely 2:15 local time, by the way—I was humiliated by the public flogging I'd endured at the hands of the publisher. I sequestered myself for twenty minutes in a stall in the ladies' room before my eyes were dry and white enough to face the world. Charlie and Norma were sure to notice anyway.

I wandered into Charlie's office, curious to know how George Walsh and Artie Short could be so careless not to have contacted Wilbur Burch. Had they done so, they surely would have known that Darleen had never used the bus ticket he'd sent her. I asked Charlie as innocently as I knew how if George had spoken to Wilbur.

"He wired his CO," said Charlie, distracted, as he wrote a note to himself. "It seems Wilbur and his unit are finishing some week-long survival training hike, so George hasn't been able to reach him yet."

"Bad luck for George," I said.

"Listen, Ellie," said my boss, looking up from his desk. "I don't want to do this, but Short is insisting. He wants you to take over the Society Page for a couple of days, just while Mrs. Stevens is visiting her sister in Rochester." (Wow. Artie Short just kept kicking, whether I was down or not.) "Promise me you won't blow your stack and get yourself fired over this. It's just temporary, and I need you."

"Okay," I said calmly, which seemed to upset Charlie even more.

"Are you okay, Ellie?"

"I'm fine. Just tell me what to do."

✸

The Society Page's staples were engagement announcements and wedding photos. January was off-season for weddings, though, so I only had two engagements, three ugly babies, and seven confirmations to report. These were mindless tasks that I performed with my eyes half closed.

Mary Ellen Wikowski and Glenn Stanich were planning a June wedding and honeymoon in the Poconos. They were both twenty-one. Glenn was an electrician's apprentice to Mary Ellen's dad.

Mr. and Mrs. Gordon Dawson were proud to welcome their first child: an eleven-pound, eight-ounce bouncing baby boy named Gordon Jr. Eleven and a half pounds! Good God, that's the size of a bowling ball.

And then there were the confirmations. Little kids dressed in ill-fitting white suits and dresses, with bad haircuts, missing teeth, and hands pressed together in pious prayer. All I needed to do was get their names and churches right, and I was laps ahead of Mrs. Stevens.

"What can I do next?" I asked Charlie as I handed him my piece around four in the afternoon.

"You've finished already? That didn't take two hours."

"It wasn't that hard, Charlie. The wedding of the season, Baby Huey, and a conclave of Catholic kids."

"Okay," said Charlie. "Come with me. I've got to have a smoke, and I don't want to do it here. Doreen will tell my wife."

I followed Charlie downstairs, where we stood in the alleyway between our building and Wolfson's Department Store. It was such a nice evening, so unseasonably warm, that we each smoked a second cigarette as we talked.

"As you can see, Charlie, I'm being a good girl," I said. "What's my next assignment?"

"You've got your pick: there's a PTA bake sale at Clinton Avenue Grammar School . . ."

"Hmm, tempting. What else have you got?"

"Well, there's also the big polka concert at Janakowski Hall. You could interview a big star and enjoy an evening of music at the same time."

"No thanks."

"Come on, Ellie. It's the Al Stoyka Orchestra. They play all over the country."

"Isn't there a pencil-sharpening contest I could cover instead? Next."

"I could make you do it, you know," he mumbled, and he flipped his cigarette butt into the gutter. "Okay, how about the new firehouse they're inaugurating? Or the SPCA? They're holding a fundraiser. And you told me you like cats."

Oh, God, I thought. What sins had I committed in a previous life to deserve this? Then I realized that my present mess could well be punishment for the sins of this life alone.

"I'll take the firehouse," I said. "Maybe I'll meet Mr. Right."

We made our way back upstairs to Charlie's office. I stood there waiting as my boss wrote out the details on the firehouse event for me on a pad of paper. I stared off into space, cursing my life and the bed I'd made for myself. Then something wonderful happened. Charlie's phone rang.

"Reese," he said into the receiver. I watched as his eyes narrowed and his jaw tightened. He ran a hand through his silver hair. "Yes, she's here, but . . . I thought you said . . . All right. I see." He tore away the top sheet of paper from his pad, wadded it in his palm, and tossed it into the wastepaper basket. So much for my firehouse story. He scribbled something new into the pad before him. "Okay, we're on it," he said and hung up the phone.

"What is it?" I asked.

"That was Artie Short," he said. Now I was worried.

"Am I through?" I asked.

"The sheriff just phoned looking for you while we were downstairs," he explained. "No one could find you. He said it was important, so the switchboard tried to find me. Then they put him through to Artie."

"What did he want?" I asked.

"They just found a lunch box near Darleen Hicks's house. Artie wants you to get out to the Metzger farm right now. You're off the bench."

CHAPTER TWELVE

George Walsh was on a Trailways bus, probably just past Syracuse, incommunicado, with "Wonderland by Night" by Bert Kaempfert playing over the bus' speakers for seventy-two hours straight. (Perhaps not, but a girl can dream, can't she?) And he had orders not to waste time or money phoning home, so he would be in Arizona before he realized he was on a wild-goose chase. Artie Short was already painfully aware of that fact.

I pulled to a stop a few yards behind the last of the county cruisers. Up ahead, a diesel generator was roaring, supplying power to the four sets of floodlights the sheriff had aimed at the snow hills at the end of County Highway 58. This was the place where Gus Arnold had turned the school bus around the day I'd hitched a ride to speak with Darleen's friends.

Pauline Blaine, the widow who lived near the Metzger farm, had phoned the authorities when her two boys arrived home from school around four p.m. with a lunch box they'd found in the melting snow while playing in the hills.

"Hiya, Frank," I said, once I'd located the sheriff at the center of the command post.

"There you are," he said. "For a while I thought Artie Short wasn't going to send you. What did you do to get him so riled up?"

"I wore a skirt," I said. "What's the story here?"

"A couple of kids found a lunch box in the hills where Brunello's standing over there," he said, pointing to his deputy about thirty yards away. "Buried pretty deep. The boys were digging and uncovered it."

"Are you sure it's Darleen's?" I asked.

Frank nodded. "Pretty sure."

"Why's that?"

"There was a note inside, addressed 'Dear Darleen.'"

"What's it say?" I asked.

"'I'll meet you near the buses before you go home.'" said Frank in a monotone as he read from a scrap of paper.

"Any idea who wrote it?"

The sheriff folded the paper, secured it in his breast pocket, and motioned for me to come closer. He whispered in my ear, "Ted."

I flushed. The sting was sharp, but I couldn't let on to Frank. "Can I get a picture of it?" I asked, wanting desperately to compare the hand-writing to the love note Frankie had brought to me.

The sheriff shook his head. "This is evidence, Ellie. I can't risk our case by showing it to you. And, by the way, I don't want any news of the note in the press for now. Same as with the bus ticket."

"But, Frank, what am I going to write?" I asked. "You're not leaving me much."

"No mention of the note, okay? You can say we found a lunch box that may or may not belong to Darleen Hicks. There's no name on it, so it could be anyone's."

"Except for the note."

"Right. Which remains a secret for now."

"Okay," I said, wondering when I had stopped working for the *New Holland Republic* and signed on with the sheriff. I distracted myself from my self-recrimination by plotting how I might make Ted Russell pay for his crimes. In a moment of painful honesty, I wondered if I wanted to punish him for having debauched Darleen or for having taken me in. I shook the thought from my head. I still had a job to do.

"Can you tell me what's going on here now?" I asked Frank.

"We're searching as best we can all through this area," he said, indicating the snow hills with a wave of his hand. "So far we haven't turned up anything."

"So what's next?"

Frank pulled his cap off and scratched his head. I could see the perspiration on his scalp. The weather wasn't exactly tropical, but it was still in the low fifties, even with the sun down.

"I've decided to have the county haul this snow out of here starting tomorrow if we don't find anything tonight." He paused, looking out over the tons of snow. "That girl is in there somewhere, and we're going to find her."

I took some pictures of the lunch box. It was one of those plain, dark-gray, workman's lunch boxes, scuffed, with some dents, and a metal buckle to snap it closed. Inside was some crumpled waxed paper, a chilling reminder that the missing girl had used the lunch box just three weeks earlier—that she had eaten from it, and evidence of her last meal remained. I wondered what she had drunk to wash down her lunch. Perhaps a couple of swigs of whiskey on the bus to Canajoharie. But, of course, the whiskey had never left her locker. And there was no thermos found with the lunch box.

I thought about how little separated us in time and space. On December 21, Darleen had been in the very spot I was standing in now. The time of day had been the same as well, give or take an hour. And there was more that we shared, Darleen and I. A penchant for poor judgment and ill-advised adventures with older, slippery men. The same man in this case, I feared. Two similar girls with two very distinct outcomes.

I drove away from the snow hills beyond the Metzger farm, leaving the sheriff and his men to their task. If they didn't recover the body by morning, the trucks would come to cart off the tons of snow. The sheriff intended to scrape the ground clean if necessary until he'd found the remains of a young girl.

The road back to the Metzger farm was crowded with official vehicles and a few gawkers for about a hundred yards. Once I'd negotiated the tight passage, I gained speed as I headed toward the highway. But then I reached the dented mailbox with the black lettering, and I slowed to a stop. "METZGER." I turned into the narrow road and drove to the gray clapboard house, this time determined to have a word with Dick Metzger.

It was almost six thirty when I rapped on the door. The man of the house answered, freezing me in place with his gaze. I stood transfixed, staring up at those pallid blue eyes. He waited there in his coveralls, chewing something that must have been the last of his supper, regarding me with a stony countenance. I thought he would make a fine poker player. From the kitchen, the rich aroma of meat, onions, and frying butter drifted past me and out into the night air.

"Well?" he said, low and hard. "What do you want?"

"I've come with some news," I said.

Irene Metzger appeared from behind her husband and ushered me into the sitting room. I apologized for having interrupted their meal, but she waved me off.

"We already ate," she said, motioning to the lumpy sofa. She took a seat in an armchair opposite me. Her husband just stood there in his boots, smelling of horses and dirt.

"I was wrong about Darleen," I said. I couldn't tell her about the bus ticket without the sheriff's okay, but that's what I was thinking. "I don't believe she ran away after all."

Irene Metzger stiffened, seemed to quell a frisson. "I told you she didn't run off. I know my daughter." Then she sniffed, almost as if she were satisfied.

"Your neighbor Mrs. Blaine telephoned the sheriff earlier this afternoon," I continued, putting her inexplicable gloating to one side. "Her two boys were playing in the snow hills at the end of your road. They uncovered a lunch box a couple of hours ago."

I paused, staring into her unblinking eyes. They sank into their sockets as the sum and substance of my words hit home. I saw the blood drain from her cheeks, and she uttered a soft and hollow "Oh." Her husband flexed his jaw and clenched his right hand hard enough to whiten his knuckles. He noticed me watching him and stoked his smoldering glare.

"You said that Darleen had taken her lunch box the day she disappeared," I said. "Can you describe it?"

She nodded. "It was dark-gray. A little beat up. And she had a red-and-black plaid thermos."

"There was no thermos inside, but that's the lunch box they found. Buried in the snow. Deliberately, it seems." I swallowed hard. "As if to hide it."

"So what does that mean?" asked Dick Metzger.

"Well, I know that Walt Rasmussen saw Darleen on the highway sometime around four that day."

"On Five-S?" he asked. I nodded yes. "What was she doing there? Why wasn't she on her bus?"

I glanced at Irene Metzger, who looked lost in thought. "She was climbing out of a taxi," I said. "We know she'd missed her bus, so it appears she tried to reach home by taxi instead."

"Damn it!" said Metzger through his teeth, tuning me out. "I told that girl if she missed the bus again I'd beat some sense into her with my belt buckle."

He ran a hand through his oiled hair and paced back and forth. The violence of his reaction pushed me back in my seat.

"The taxi dropped Darleen about two and a half miles from here," I continued. "Assuming she walked briskly, it would have taken her about a half hour to get home. But, of course, she never arrived."

"What do you think happened?" asked Irene Metzger. Her husband was still steaming not far off.

"The snow hills are about a mile past here, aren't they?" I asked.

She looked at her husband, and he nodded. "I suppose so."

I thought on it for a moment. "I suppose it's possible Darleen was never near the snow hills, that someone dumped the lunch box later on. But if the presence of Darleen's lunch box in the snow means that she *was* in the hills, then someone must have picked her up in a car and driven her there. She couldn't have reached the hills that day without having been seen."

"How do you figure?" asked Metzger.

"The school bus," I said. "It must have passed down this road around four fifteen. The driver and Darleen's friends would have seen her."

"Unless the girls were already off the bus when the driver reached her," said Dick Metzger. "How do we know he isn't a pervert who likes little girls? What do you know about him?"

I shrugged. (Talk about the pot calling the kettle black.) "I suppose anything's possible," I said. "All I know is that he's a retired garbageman. He lives by himself and drinks rye."

Dick Metzger demanded the driver's name. I could just picture him searching out Gus Arnold, finding him drunk, and beating him to death with a shovel. There was no way I was going to give him the name, even if I harbored my share of doubts about him, as well.

"I don't know his name," I said, and Dick Metzger seemed to accept it.

Irene Metzger asked me what would happen now.

"The sheriff and his men are searching the snow hills, but there are hundreds of tons of snow. If they don't find her tonight, they plan to dig up all the snow and haul it away."

Irene Metzger cast her eyes down to the floor. She sat there, quiet, miserable, but dry-eyed. In fact, I thought, I'd never seen her shed a tear from the moment I met her. I wasn't judging her; I didn't cry when my mother passed away, and I loved her dearly. That hadn't been the moment for me to vent my grief. Not so soon after Elijah. But Irene Metzger was tearless for a very different reason: She was holding it inside. All the devastation, all her sorrow, was dammed up within her, pushing to get out, for sure, but subdued by a conscious sobriety, bordering on stoicism, in the face of her daughter's demise. She was of simple and rugged stock, and her hard life had only taught her to be tougher; weeping was not a luxury she could permit herself.

"Do you think she's in those hills?" she asked softly.

"It's possible," I said. "Likely. What with the lunch box having been found there."

"And we just have to wait?" bellowed Dick Metzger, quite unexpectedly, as if the failure to find Darleen were my fault. "What are we supposed to do in the meantime?"

"Since you ask," I said, "it might help if you answered a few questions about Darleen for me."

Irene Metzger expressed alarm. Her eyes darted to her husband, whose glare, aimed at me, suggested extreme animus.

"What do you want to ask me?" he more or less threatened.

"Well, for starters," I said, retreating even farther into my seat, "where were you that day around five o'clock?"

His eyes opened wide, looking like two tiny blue marbles in a sea of white, and his face constricted, twisted, and flushed red. Almost purple. I thought his scalp was going to blow off his head. His wife jumped to her feet and grabbed his arm.

"You want to know where *I* was?" he hissed at me, incredulous.

"Yes," I said, shrinking ever smaller. "If you don't mind."

"Hell, yes, I mind!" he roared, blasting a spume of saliva off his lips in my direction with his last word.

"I already told you that Dick doesn't know anything about this," said Irene Metzger, pushing herself between her rabid husband and me. "Now why did you have to go and ask him like that?"

I gaped at the two of them. Considering the circumstances, I thought my question was a natural one. Someone should ask him where he'd been, if only to find out if he'd seen or heard anything.

"If you are truly interested in finding out what happened to your daughter," I said, "you should be eager to answer my questions. I'm trying to help, so I need to know who was where, what they did, and what they saw." I turned to Dick Metzger, who was staring daggers at me. "Darleen was seen on Route Five-S around four. How did her lunch box wind up at the end of this road? She would have had to pass this very house to reach the snow hills. Were you here at the farm? Did you see or hear anyone drive past? Walk past?"

He just stood there glaring at me, huffing, but I could see the red starting to drain from his temples. He was struggling to maintain his indignation in the face of my logic.

"At the very least, you should want to help me," I continued. "But instead, you've been avoiding me and stonewalling as if you have something to hide. Do you have something to hide, Mr. Metzger?"

He turned away and stalked to the window and back. I couldn't be sure if he was about to strike me or confess to Darleen's murder. He ran his hand through his oily hair again then stared me down.

"Get your pretty little behind off my sofa and out of my house," he said in an eerily soft voice. He sneered, revealing his long teeth, stained brown from chewing tobacco and coffee. My knees were shaking.

His wife grabbed him from behind and yanked him off to the side, where she scolded him in an excited whisper. He tried to pull away, ranting that he wanted me gone, but she wouldn't let go of his arm.

"No one else will help us, no one else cares," she hissed through her teeth. "Don't chase off our only hope of finding out what happened to our Darleen."

I wanted to leave, but I didn't dare move with the beast blocking my path to the door. He seethed, pouted like a child, but finally quieted down after a long minute. Once his respiration had returned to normal, his wife released his arm from her grip, but not her eyes from his. I could see the silent communication, built on years of living together, passing from one to the other, as she willed him to calm down. He turned and approached me slowly, his hard, cold glare fixed on me. He stopped a few feet away from the sofa, towering over me.

"I did not harm that girl," he said determinedly, slowly, punctuating each word with a jab of his finger. "I have nothing to hide."

I stared up at him, willing myself to appear strong, to show no weakness. He was so close that he could have reached out and wrung my neck without taking a step closer.

"If that's so," I said softly, "you won't mind answering my questions."

He clearly hadn't expected that, but he didn't lay a hand on me. He drew a deep sigh instead and shook his head.

"So go ahead and ask me," he said.

"Where were you that day around five o'clock?"

He nearly blew up again but contained his anger. Had he really expected me not to repeat my question?

"I can't remember exactly," he said. "I was out in the field or in the barn somewhere."

"Did you hear any cars or see anyone on the road?"

"No."

"Were you near the Karl's property line, by any chance? Did you see Bobby Jr.?"

"No. I don't remember when I seen him last, but it wasn't that day." He paused to think. "Besides, it was dark by then. I wouldn't have seen nothing."

I weighed my words carefully, debating whether to ask or not. In the end, I had to. I had to put the question to him.

"Can you describe your relationship with your daughter?"

He looked confused. "My . . . relationship? I'm her father."

"I mean, do you get along with Darleen. Are you affectionate? Stern? Indulgent?"

"I'm her father," he said. "I don't know how else to tell you."

"Are you a doting father? Is Darleen Daddy's little girl?"

He gaped at me. "What?"

If he was too dim to answer delicate questions, I'd have to be blunt: "Did you beat Darleen?"

"No!"

"Didn't you say you would beat her with your belt buckle if she missed the bus again?"

"Well, yeah," he granted. "But that's just discipline. Didn't your father ever beat you for not minding him? He should have."

I ignored his question and opinion. We were talking about him, not me. And now I braced for the big one: "Have you ever kissed Darleen on the lips?" I asked.

I was lucky that Irene Metzger got to me before her husband did. She pushed me to the door, holding Dick Metzger off with a straight arm as she screamed like a harridan. She managed to run interference long enough for me to get out in one piece.

"Don't ever show your face around here again!" he yelled after me, and he meant it. But angry or not, he still managed to steal a long, healthy look at my "pretty little behind" as I hurried to my car.

TUESDAY, JANUARY 10, 1961

At seven thirty the next morning, I was parked on Division Street, opposite the junior high school. A growing stream of kids arrived on foot as the time for the first bell approached. The students milled about on the sidewalk, enjoying the warm weather, chatting and laughing as they awaited the start of another dreary school day. In the alley next to the cigar store, a dozen or so toughs leaned against the brick wall, smoking cigarettes. They were all of fifteen. Then the buses chugged into the parking lot and disgorged their loads. I wasn't looking for children this day. I was waiting for bus number 63 and the man who drove it.

Gus Arnold was not happy when he saw me climb the stairs into the bus. He'd probably wanted to steal a nap or a drink somewhere, and I was a stone in his shoe.

"You?" he asked, positively shaking at the sight of me. "What do you want now?"

"I want to know what you did after you dropped off Carol Liswenski the day Darleen Hicks disappeared."

His large, gray face, jowled and unshaven, froze in place. He didn't know what to say. I helped him out.

"Darleen Hicks's lunch box was found in a snowbank yesterday afternoon," I said. "Right where you turn the bus around on County Highway Fifty-Eight. The sheriff must have missed you by minutes there yesterday, just after you finished your run around four thirty."

He ran his tongue over his lips. "That's right," he said. "Four thirty like always. I drove straight back to the depot."

"But not so on December twenty-first. You made an extra stop that day, didn't you?"

"I already told you. I had a flat tire."

"That's what you told the dispatcher, but not what you told the sheriff."

"What, are you keeping score? Why can't you leave me alone?"

"Let's make a deal," I said. "You show me where you took your nap that day, and I won't tell your dispatcher you punctured the spare to cover for yourself."

He was trapped. He wiped his brow and then his whole face with a yellowed handkerchief.

"I can't drive out there now," he whined. "They keep track of the gas and miles."

"My car's just over there," I said. I had him.

Gus Arnold was no conversationalist. He sat slumped against the passenger door, staring at the mileposts whizzing by. With the bench seat set so far forward, his long legs were bent and touching the dashboard.

We passed the turnoff for County Highway 58, and my passenger grumbled directions. "Take the next right," he said. "Slow down or you'll miss it."

It was a narrow, unpaved track that ducked into the woods, almost invisible if you were driving too fast or not looking out for it. I turned off Route 5 and crunched over the gravel path. Gus Arnold told me to continue straight for about a quarter mile. Then the road came to an end in a large clearing, about fifty yards wide, amid the same high pines that bordered County Highway 58 on the other side of the mountains of snow. I rolled to a stop and pulled the brake.

"You wanted to see it. This is it," said Gus Arnold.

I popped open my door and stepped out. The snow hills rose before me. I calculated in my head without success just how far we were from the spot where Darleen's lunch box had been found on the other side of the snow.

"So you parked here and took a nap?" I asked.

"No," he said, climbing out of the car after me. "Over there, behind that row of trees."

I looked to where he was pointing, about forty yards away, and couldn't see it. It just looked like woods.

"Go take a look," he said. "There's a narrow opening between those trees and the rest of the forest. I park there because no one can see me. It's quiet."

I investigated his claim, and discovered he was indeed telling the truth. The small gap between the line of trees and the woods was just large enough to back a bus into, and it would be quite invisible to anyone at the other end of the clearing.

I returned to my car and approached the snow hills, gazing at the melting mountains, looking for evidence of something out of the ordinary. Through the tall pines, I could hear the roar and rumble of trucks in the distance. They were clearing snow on the other side.

"It must have been dark that day," I said to Gus Arnold. "Did you leave the bus?"

"I just put my feet up and took a snooze. A half hour later, I drove back to the depot."

"You didn't open the door?" I asked.

"What are you driving at?"

I strode over to the edge of the woods and picked up an empty pint bottle from the slush. It was Old Crow, the label slipping off from several days of soaking in the wet.

"I thought you said you parked over there," I said, indicating the line of trees opposite.

"That's not mine," he stammered. "You can't prove it's mine."

"I'm not the police," I said. "I don't care if you were drinking on the job, although the parents of your passengers might have something to say about that. But we're about a hundred yards from where Darleen Hicks's lunch box was found. Now, do you want to tell me the truth or would you rather I have a talk with your dispatcher about the flat tire?"

He thought about it, probably wondering if I might really rat him out. In the end, he chose to play it safe and admitted the bottle was his.

"If I were to dig around here, would I find more empties?"

He hung his head and grunted yes.

I gazed up at the snow hills again, gauging their height. The tallest peaks were easily fifteen or twenty feet high. Could a sixty-year-old drunk scale the hills carrying a girl over his shoulder? I doubted it, but Gus Arnold was a large man. And what about the lunch box? It seemed possible that he could have lost track of it while scrambling over slippery snow.

"Did you climb through the hills that day?" I asked, just to cover my bases.

"Are you crazy? Of course not. I don't have any reason to climb over the hills."

He sounded sincere, but how could I be sure?

I looked back to where I'd found the empty bottle, and I realized I hadn't considered the woods properly. They bordered the hills, with the snow piled right up against the trees. I made my way over to the nearest thicket and waded in a few feet. One could easily weave through the woods and reach the other side, I figured. Sure, the path was tight with sharp, brittle branches to navigate, but it seemed possible. Certainly easier than carrying a body over the snow hills.

"And you didn't go through the woods either?"

"No. I sat in the bus drinking till the bottle was gone. I was here twenty or thirty minutes. Why do you got to ask me such things?"

"It's not an accusation," I said.

"I didn't kill that little girl," he said. "I swear I didn't."

"And you didn't see anyone else here that day? Another car, perhaps?"

He shook his head firmly. "I didn't see no one."

"What can I do for you today, Miss Stone?" asked Arnold Dienst, leaning toward me at his large, oak desk. Some Stravinsky pulsed at a low but distinct volume from a hi-fi in a wooden cabinet behind him. I recognized the "Concerto in D for Strings"; my father was an admirer of Stravinsky's, and I knew this piece well, having heard it countless times since it was first recorded in the late forties. The first movement sounded like the score to a suspense film.

"Do you like Stravinsky, Dr. Dienst?" I asked.

He mugged an expression of mild satisfaction. "I think the better question is how is it that you know Stravinsky?"

I blushed, now wishing I hadn't mentioned it. Yes, I had been showing off a little. "Never mind. I meant to ask if you found this music conducive to your work here. It's not always soothing."

"I find modern music stimulating and inspirational. That creates a peaceful satisfaction in my mind, no matter how frenetic or dissonant the music. I conduct therapy sessions with the boys once a week, always with music playing. Everything from Webern to Schoenberg, Janacek, Hindemith, Ravel. And if I want to pander to the boys' tastes, I play something they'll like. Copland, for instance."

"Really? They go for Copland?"

He pondered my question for a moment, possibly reconsidering his choice of words. Perhaps "like" was an exaggeration.

"Yes," he granted reluctantly, "the boys would probably rather listen to their rock-around-the-clock music."

Dr. Dienst noticed my grin despite my best efforts to swallow it. He smiled awkwardly, covering his large teeth with his stretched lips, but his eyes betrayed a vague awareness that he'd said something wrong.

"Do the boys like the modern music you play?" I asked, wanting to put him back at his ease. I was certain I knew the answer.

"They hate it, of course," he said with a good-natured smile that parted his lips and showed the long teeth he'd been trying to hide moments before. "But the music provokes strong emotional responses in them without the accompanying physical violence. I believe that to be a salubrious exercise."

"What about Joey Figlio? How does he react to Stravinsky?"

Dienst sat back in his chair and rocked, aiming his penetrating stare at me, trying to understand what made me tick. His wasn't a lecherous gaze but a curious one.

"Joey Figlio sticks his fingers into his ears," he said. "And when he's feeling particularly industrious, he plugs his ears with wads of paper."

He watched me a while longer, as the energetic first movement ended and gave way to the lighter second.

"Why are you here, Miss Stone?"

"I'm investigating the disappearance of Darleen Hicks," I said.

"Yes, I get that. But you're talking to me about Stravinsky and beating around the bush. I know you're not in love with Joey Figlio, as he claimed in court. So what exactly do you want, Miss Stone?"

Dienst was a smart man. He'd seen through my circling and stalling, the conversational chairs I'd upended as diversions to trip and delay him while I worked my way around to asking the real questions. A cheap tactic on my part, to be sure, and not particularly clever. Sometimes outright flirting worked better. But with a man like Arnold Dienst, my charms—such as they were—and trickery proved equally ineffective.

"What I really want is to search Joey Figlio's belongings," I said finally. "I think he may have messages or notes from Darleen Hicks in his possession. They may provide clues as to what happened."

"This may be a reformatory, Miss Stone," he said with a gentle smile, "but we try to respect the privacy of our boys to the extent possible. Now, if you were to obtain a warrant from a court of law, we would, of course, comply. But I cannot let you root through Joey Figlio's possessions."

That's the answer I'd expected and why, frankly, I had been beating around the bush. But I hoped Dienst still might provide some kernel of information for me.

"Joey Figlio had a handwritten note, addressed to Darleen from a man named Ted. He was hiding it somewhere here at Fulton, and he gave it to Frankie Ralston to give to me."

Dienst swiveled toward the window and looked off into the distance as the third movement began, buzzing like wasps. He rocked in his chair.

"The last time you were here, Miss Stone, you asked me to search Joey Figlio's belongings as well." I said nothing. It wasn't a question. "When he left the facility without permission and stole your car, I felt it was justified under the circumstances."

"You felt what was justified?" I asked.

He swung his chair around, folded his hands on the desk before him, and looked me in the eye. "I searched his room and locker," he said. "While he was missing and then again when I brought him back here after the hearing. I needed to be sure he wasn't bringing contraband into the school."

"Contraband?" I asked.

"Cigarettes, alcohol, chewing gum, soda pop, weapons. I believe that in order to cure the juvenile delinquent, we must nourish the body and mind. A boy must be provided a nutritious diet, or he will make no progress toward rehabilitation and, in fact, will recidivate. That means no candy or smoking or fizzy soft drinks here. We only allow drinks such as wheatgrass, carrot, and orange juice. Milk, of course, though I'm trying to replace it with yogurt. And distilled water. No chlorination permitted in our diet here. And I believe margarine is superior to butter in every way."

"Not taste," I said.

"No, not taste," he granted with a disapproving look. "I met the violinist Yehudi Menuhin in Switzerland three years ago, and he impressed upon me the benefits of the vegetarian lifestyle and yoga. No meat has passed my lips since that month in Gstaad. Of course, the board of directors here insists that we provide meat to the boys, but I have faith that one day I'll win them over, once the research proves the benefits of a meatless diet."

"And the yoga?" I asked.

"I haven't been able to find a yogi anywhere north of Greenwich Village, I'm afraid. But I'll keep searching."

"I'm sure the boys appreciate these efforts," I said, scolding myself silently for cracking wise with such an earnest man.

"One would think," he said. "But not really. I instituted the new regimen when I arrived two years ago. Meat only on Monday, Wednesday, and Saturday. Fish on Friday—we have our share of Catholic boys," he said in a dramatized whisper, which included cupping his large hand to one side of his equally large mouth. "But I feel that fish is a healthful option, religious edicts aside. And the rest of the week we serve vegetarian fare."

"Did you find anything?"

"I beg your pardon?"

"When you searched Joey Figlio's belongings, did you find anything interesting?"

"No poems, if that's what you're aiming at."

"I'm casting a wide net," I said. "I'm interested in anything that little JD might have squirreled away under his mattress."

"There was nothing written at all," said Dienst. "As I've said before, I'm not entirely convinced he knows how to read and write."

I cocked my head. "But there was something."

"I hate to disappoint you, Miss Stone," he said just as the Stravinsky came to an end. The needle scratched round and round, bumping against the paper label. Dienst stood and switched off the hi-fi. "There was nothing out of the ordinary. Just his dirty clothes, a transistor radio—stolen, surely—twenty-three cents, and his thermos bottle."

"He brought back a thermos, or was it already here?" I asked.

Dr. Dienst looked alarmed. Had he overlooked an important detail? "It was already among his things when he escaped and stole your car," he mumbled. "Just a run-of-the-mill thermos bottle. Red-and-black plaid."

CHAPTER THIRTEEN

D r. Dienst called Frank Olney to give him the news. I watched him silently as he clutched the receiver tightly in his hand, explaining how he had discovered the thermos among Joey's possessions.

"Miss Stone says the girl's mother mentioned a missing thermos from the lunch box you found in the snow," said Dienst. "I thought it wise to inform you immediately in the unlikely event that Joey has the girl's thermos and not his own."

Frank said something on the other end of the line, and Dienst nodded. "Of course. I'll confiscate it immediately and hold it here until you arrive."

He replaced the receiver and gave me a sheepish shrug.

While Dienst's went to recover the thermos, I waited outside his office and reviewed the new information in my head. By his own admission, Joey Figlio had been caught in the Metzger barn by Darleen's stepfather well after dark on the evening she'd disappeared. He was—seemingly—in possession of her missing thermos. A thermos Irene Metzger had filled and placed in her daughter's lunch box that very morning. Did that mean Joey Figlio was a killer? He'd threatened me twice with a knife and left me to die on a frozen stretch of desolate county highway. And he'd definitely tried to murder Ted Russell. He was a deeply disturbed boy, at least by my reckoning, and I had no doubts he could kill. But could he kill Darleen? Did he love her as much as he claimed? And would that even matter? Perhaps his love justified murder in his twisted mind. He had written on the back of his photograph that if he couldn't have Darleen, no one else would. I recalled the envelope in Darleen's locker. The one with the money, the phony driver's license—a good enough forgery to get the underage girl married—and the letter from Wilbur Burch, outlining their plans for a secret and illegal elopement to Arizona. If Joey Figlio had learned of the plan, could he have carried out his threat and killed the girl he loved? I wasn't sure, but the pallor of Dr. Arnold Dienst's large, horselike face told me where his worst fears lay.

"It *is* you!" a voice startled me from behind. "I knew you'd come."

"Frankie," I said. "You nearly scared me to death."

"I could never do that, Ellie. I'm in love with you."

"Stop it, Frankie. You're not in love with me. And I'm not here to see you. I came about Joey."

"You're not in love with him, are you?" he asked. "That's what he's been telling everyone ever since he got back. 'I'm in love with Joey Figlio,'" he said in a falsetto voice and made an accompanying cross-eyed, palsied gesture to indicate some form of besotted infatuation. I couldn't be sure if the pantomime was meant to ape Joey or me.

"I'm not in love with him or you, Frankie," I said, and that appeased him.

"Well, good," he said. "I don't mind if you don't know you love me yet, but if you were in love with him, I'd kill that backstabbing son of bitch, I swear it. I'd kill him for you."

"Cool your jets, space cadet," I said. "And mind your language. You're not killing anybody. Besides, Joey has bigger worries than threats from you just now. The sheriff's on his way, probably to arrest him on suspicion of Darleen Hicks's murder."

"I doubt it," he said, staring into my eyes. "Joey lit out about an hour ago. Said this place wasn't going to stop him from slitting that teacher's throat."

"One of the boys told Joey that Miss Stone was here talking to me," Dienst said to Frank Olney. We were all three sitting in the principal's office, reviewing the events of the past two hours. "That spooked him, the boy said. Joey suspected her visit somehow spelled bad news for him, and he escaped the school grounds."

"Check the backseat of my car," I said, and Frank glowered at me.

"This isn't the time for humor, Ellie," he said.

"Who's joking? Check the backseat of my car. I'm not leaving here until someone assures me he's not lying in wait for me."

"The thermos looks like it was Darleen's," said Frank, ignoring my pleas. "I've sent a deputy over to the Metzger place with it for the mother to confirm, but I think it's the one. Now we're going to have to locate this Joey Figlio. Any idea where he might run?"

Dienst shrugged. "His parents' house, perhaps?"

"He doesn't get along with his father," I volunteered. "Although he is close to his mother. But I doubt he'll go there. Too obvious."

"Then where do you think we should look?" asked Frank.

"I already told you. My car."

"Okay," said Frank, turning back to Dr. Dienst. "We'll inspect Miss Stone's car then we'll go from there. We know he's after the teacher, Russell, so we'll post a deputy at the junior high and at his house in Cranesville. Joey's not the smartest criminal I've come across. Maybe we'll nab him sooner rather than later."

"And you promised to watch my place," I said to admonish him. "Last Sunday, remember?"

"Yes, we'll make sure you're safe," said Frank with impatience. "I've already asked Chief Finn if his boys could help, and he said he'd police his own town."

"That's comforting," I said.

"Take it easy. He might be a goon, but he's not going to put up with trouble in his backyard. He'll gripe about it and make a show about not doing anything, but I guarantee the city police are keeping an eye on you."

Feeling no more confident of my safety, I let it go. Frank called the DA, the Thin Man, Don Czerulniak, to ask for some advice. Don suggested questioning the boy if he was found, but not to arrest him yet.

"Prove to me that she's dead," Don told Frank, "and find this little delinquent. Then we'll talk about an arrest."

WEDNESDAY, JANUARY 11, 1961

The temperatures continued to defy the season, with the mercury reaching fifty-six degrees on the giant thermometer outside the Mohawk Savings Bank. I had an 8:30 meeting with Charlie Reese to review some stories he'd assigned me, including the one on Teddy J. There was a home game Friday night, which I was scheduled to cover, and I promised I'd drop in on a practice before then to finish up the feature.

"There's one more thing I wanted to tell you, Ellie," Charlie said, adjusting himself in his seat. "Artie Short managed to wire George and intercept him at St. Louis. He'll be back late tomorrow night."

"Well, we knew it was too good to last," I said, shrugging my shoulders.

"It sure was a lucky thing that you didn't publish that story on the bus ticket," he said, and I nodded. "Otherwise, it might have been you on that bus to Arizona."

Charlie stared at me for a long while, holding my gaze with his. I think he wanted to accuse me of concealing information, but he didn't dare. I thought about my pact with Frank Olney, that we'd agreed to keep the unused ticket and the love note from Ted Russell secret for the time being. But now I was in danger of missing my own scoop. I wasn't listening to Charlie suddenly but was planning my discussion with the sheriff: the one where I would tell him I needed to publish my story whether he wanted me to or not. I had a job to do, just as he did, and I hoped my decision wouldn't damage our relationship; I needed the sheriff on my side.

"Ellie?" asked Charlie, pulling me back into the room.

"Yes?"

"I said fine. You don't have to cover the Laundromat ribbon-cutting. I'll find someone else. But finish up that Teddy J. story for me. It'll help keep Short off my back." He looked me in the eye again. "And yours."

✦

"I've already blown the entire year's snow budget on this thing," grumbled Frank Olney. "And we haven't towed off even a quarter of the stuff."

I was in his office, a little past ten, sipping a cup of tea across the table from him.

"You haven't found any trace of her there?" I asked.

"We recovered a pair of gloves in the snow last night," he said. "Dark-blue wool gloves. Darleen's mother says they're hers. The father's not sure."

"That's promising, then, isn't it? The lunch box and the gloves in the same place."

"Not exactly," he frowned and rubbed his bald head. "The gloves were all the way over on the other side of the hills. Near the edge of the clearing just inside the woods."

I thought of Gus Arnold. It was one thing to say you hadn't seen anything, but a little hard to believe when the girl's gloves turn up about twenty-five yards from where you tossed your empty bottle of rye.

"Anyways," continued the sheriff, "I'm not convinced the gloves are hers. And maybe she lost them there weeks earlier. There's no way to know if we don't find the body."

"Then you're sure she's dead?" I asked.

He looked at me pointedly. "That girl's not coming home."

I admitted that I thought he was right.

"And that damn Marv Kenner, the county supervisor, is making noise about the money I'm wasting carting away the snow. It's no secret his son Ernie is thinking of running against me next year."

"Sorry, Frank," I shrugged. "Maybe the snow will all melt before you haul it away."

"Not funny," he frowned. "If we don't find that girl, the taxpayers are going to want to know why their roads aren't plowed."

"So what do you think?" I asked. "If Darleen Hicks isn't buried in the snow, where is she?"

"I don't know, but I sure wish she'd run off after all." he said.

"But, of course, the unused bus ticket ruins that hope." I was trying to steer the conversation to my big scoop, but Frank wasn't biting. "Speaking of that," I said. "It's been three days since we found the ticket, hasn't it?"

Frank grunted.

"I've been thinking about what we discussed."

"What's that?"

"Well, since you've found Darleen's lunch box, I thought there's no longer any need to hide the story about the bus ticket. And then there's the note that was inside. And the love letter, too."

"You haven't even seen the note," he said. "You can't publish a story about evidence you haven't seen. And to tell you the truth, I'm keeping the bus ticket in reserve. I've got someone in mind and was hoping to catch him with it."

"But you've got Joey Figlio," I said. "It looks as if he might be the one. He had her thermos, didn't he?"

"He says she gave it to him for his breakfast in the morning *before* she left for school," said Frank. "I thought we had an agreement, Ellie. I really don't want this out before next week."

We stared at each other for several long, uncomfortable beats.

"Frank, I wouldn't ask, but I need this story now. I almost lost my job Monday. And now George Walsh is heading back from his wild-goose chase. He'd like nothing better than to take this story away from me. I have to go to print with this, Frank. This is my career."

He shook his head slowly. "Is your career more important than catching the guy who did this?" he asked.

"Frank, please try to see my side. This means a lot to me."

We'd reached an impasse. Frank folded his hands together and bowed his head. He looked hurt, and I struggled with my remorse for letting down a friend and the conviction that I was the one being sacrificed.

"You're going to do what you want, no matter what I say," he said. "I can't stop you."

I left the sheriff's office without saying goodbye to Pat Halvey, who stared dumbly after me as I rushed by him on the way to my car. Now the rain had started. A heavy, wet rain that washed the melting snow from the edges of the road into a thick slush, clogging the gutters and drenching the sidewalks. Pedestrians braved the rain at their own peril, especially if I drove past them; I wasn't slowing for anyone, and the plumes of sludge I sprayed soaked them head to toe. I even splashed a cyclist then caught sight of him in my rearview mirror losing his balance and plunging face first into a giant puddle. Well, what was he doing riding a bike in that weather anyhow?

My chest tightened as I reran the scene with Frank in my mind. I rubbed my eyes with one hand and steered the car with the other. Then I wiped the foggy windshield, nearly opaque from the muggy rain and my own body heat, smearing streaks of moisture across my view. And I hit a trash can on the side of the road. Not hard enough to damage the car, but the garbage can leapt through the air nonetheless and spat its contents onto someone's slushy lawn. Then the cherry top lit up in my rearview mirror.

"Is everything all right, miss?" asked the New Holland cop as he leaned in the window, dripping rain on my shoulder.

"Yes, officer," I said, recognizing him as one of the heels who'd laughed the hardest when Chief Finn called me a "Jew girl" exactly one week earlier. "I'm afraid I bumped a trash can."

"License, please," he said, standing up and surveying the street as if it belonged to him.

He took my license, retreated to the cover of his patrol car a few feet behind mine, and sat there for at least twenty minutes. I wanted to climb out and ask him to hurry things up, but the rain was really coming down. A group of bystanders collected, standing beneath their umbrellas to watch my humiliation, and I was thankful for the fogged-up windows and the screen they provided.

Finally, there was a tap at my window, and I hurriedly rolled it down. The cop handed me back my driver's license and told me I'd have to come with him to the station.

"What?" I asked. "Why?"

"Suspicion of drunken driving," he said.

"That's absurd. It's eleven in the morning. I haven't been drinking."

"Please come quietly, miss, or I'll arrest you for resisting an officer."

I soon realized that no amount of pleading or tears—which I refused to let fall from my eyes in front of that louse—could have persuaded him to let me go. I knew I wasn't drunk, so he couldn't make that stick, but he could charge me with resisting arrest if I didn't comply. So I did. I grabbed my purse and umbrella and popped open the driver's door, which, thanks to the protracted warm spell, was now unfrozen and functioning as designed. I stood up in the rain, opened my umbrella, and slammed the car door shut. Sergeant Joe Philbin, as I later found out he was called, put me in the back of his squad car and drove me off to the station downtown.

I'd visited the station many times in my capacity as a reporter, but I'd never made it beyond the lobby, where a duty sergeant sat behind a high, wooden desk, scratched and worn from decades of use. The desk, not the cop. This day was different. I was going into the clubhouse.

Philbin escorted me inside and left me in a dingy questioning room. I cooled my heels there for nearly an hour, sitting on a hard wooden chair, before the door opened, and Chief Patrick Finn stepped in.

"You're always turning up somewhere, aren't you?" he said, his red face practically throwing off heat. His was a drinker's red, a flush that comes from within, not from sun- or windburn, and the edges of his nose showed a spiderweb of broken blood vessels. Not the pock-marked schnoz that Gus Arnold sported, but Chief Finn tipped the bottle, that much was obvious.

I cleared my throat. "May I ask why I'm being detained?"

"Detained?" he laughed. "Oh, you're a classy one, aren't you? Big words and a fancy job as a girl reporter."

"I'm not lit, and I ain't nicked nothin' neither," I said for his benefit, and just as sassy as it sounds. "I know my rights. Wait till my mouthpiece gets here."

He smirked. "Real funny, girlie. You got a wise mouth, you know that? Some folks don't appreciate your big-city sense of humor." He pronounced "humor" without the *H*.

"I want to call my lawyer," I said.

"First you're gonna walk a straight line," he said. "Get up."

I said nothing but looked away and crossed my arms over my chest.

"Up," he said, but I wouldn't budge and pretended to be deaf.

Finn took a step toward me, and I grabbed onto the chair with both hands.

"'Police Chief Roughs Up Girl,'" I said.

He stopped. "What? What are you talking about?"

"That will be the headline in tomorrow's paper if you lay one finger on me."

Finn waved a hand at me and chuckled. "I'm not going to touch you, girlie. You got a wild imagination."

"I believe I have the right to make a phone call," I said.

⊚

I phoned Charlie Reese, who wasn't too happy to hear I was in stir. I assured him he couldn't possibly be more upset than I was. He said he'd get me out as soon as he could.

After my phone call, Finn left me alone in the questioning room, door closed, for another forty-five minutes. He had taken my purse with him, so I had no pad, no pencil, no cigarettes. This was solitary confinement. I passed the time working out possible corruption stories I could write about Chief Finn and the NHPD. There was a shady investment that had panned out extremely well for the career cop: some property he'd bought just weeks before General Electric announced plans to build a research facility in nearby Saratoga County. As luck would have it, the land earmarked for the plant had recently been acquired by Finn. The rumor was that the police had hauled a GE executive in on a charge of corruption of a minor two months before Finn bought the land. Somehow, the man was never arrested, and the whole thing went away. I'd heard the story from Pat Halvey. Not the most reliable source, but he claimed he had buddies on the New Holland police force who'd given him the skinny. It would be sweet to serve the crooked cop his comeuppance and nail a pervert at the same time. I was thinking just that when the door sprung open, and Philbin told me I could go.

"What, no blood test?" I asked.

"No. Just a citation for a broken taillight," he said with a smile.

"I don't have a broken taillight."

"You do now," he said, handing me the ticket and my purse.

Outside in the lobby, Charlie was waiting for me with Sol Meshnick, the *Republic's* lead counsel. Bespectacled and befuddled, nearing seventy, Sol tilted his head back on the fulcrum of his neck and inspected me as if looking for damage. He looked me up and down, taking his time and care as his eyes ran over my bust and the curves of my hips.

"I'm fine, Sol," I said, pushing past the old lecher. "Let's get out of here."

Charlie drove me to collect my car, still parked in the slush where I'd left it. We didn't say much to each other. He knew when not to test me, and I was so angry—both at the cops who'd harassed me for their own entertainment and the lawyer who'd ogled me for his—that Charlie kept the conversation to a minimum.

The rain had stopped, but the streets were still a sloppy mess, with puddles and mud everywhere. I examined the left taillight of my Dodge, broken very recently by what looked like a sharp kick from a black shoe. I sighed, climbed in, and drove off toward the *Republic's* office on Main Street.

Norma Geary met me at the City Room door. She gave me a sidelong glance, as if playing it cool in front of potential witnesses, then told me to stop by her desk in the steno pool when I had a chance. I wanted to get my bus-ticket story down and into Composition before another hour had passed, but Norma squeezed my arm and said it was important. I dropped my purse on my desk and picked up an old memo to use as a prop for my visit to the steno pool.

"Why, you're right, Miss Stone," she said, holding my memo out at arm's length, hamming it up for anyone in earshot. "That is quite a bad typo. I'll redo it." Then in a whisper, she told me it wasn't safe to talk near her desk. "Let's go downstairs to the alley for a smoke."

"I didn't know you smoked," I said once we were outside. It was still warm enough to leave my coat unbuttoned.

"I don't. But I know that Mr. Reese comes down here when he wants to sneak a cigarette. He's not fooling anyone, by the way."

"So what's the big secret?" I asked, lighting a cigarette for myself.

"I suppose you already know that Mr. Walsh is on a bus heading back to New Holland," she said. "But what you and he don't know is that he got a telegram from the army base in Arizona today. From the office of the base commander. I was the only one here at lunchtime when the boy from Western Union delivered it, so I signed for the wire. You may recall it was raining quite hard at that hour. Well, the boy said a car barreled past him and knocked him over with a tidal wave of slush. He fell into a great big pothole filled with water and mud."

"How awful!" I said. "And the driver didn't stop?"

"No. Imagine that," said Norma, shaking her head in woe. "Anyhow, that's not the point of my story. When the boy handed me the telegram, it was soaking wet from the dunking he'd just had. The paper was nearly mush, and I could read everything without even opening it."

"What did it say?"

Norma peeked around the corner of the building to make sure no one was listening. Once she was confident we were alone, she turned back to me. "It said Wilbur Burch has gone AWOL."

⁂

Back at my desk, I rolled some paper and carbon into the typewriter and set about writing the story I'd been thinking about since Frank Olney and I had discovered the unused bus ticket in Darleen's locker. There are times when I struggle to string three words together, when distraction short-circuits the connection between what I want to say and the tips of my fingers on the keys. In those moments, I labor to type correctly, mashing keys clumsily and jamming the type bars into a frozen pileup. I disengage the bars, rub out the misspelled words with an eraser, smudging the ink then tearing the paper. But it's all an unconscious manifestation of the reluctance to concentrate on ordering the thoughts in my head.

Then other times, I type like a Horowitz of the steno pool, a virtuosa graduate of secretarial school, fingers and mind in perfect accord, words materializing as if by magic on the page.

I've never considered myself a wordsmith, but I had managed to sand most of the rough edges off my writing during my three years at the *Republic*. Charlie Reese was a good mentor, and I'd had plenty of opportunities to make dull-as-ditchwater stories sound interesting. From school-board meetings to Kiwanis Club Man-of-the-Year banquets to demolition derbies up in Fonda (actually, those are kind of fun), I'd had my share of stinkers to clean up and make presentable for the twelfth page of the second section of the paper. I'd learned to write those with my eyes closed. But when something that mattered to me came along, I pressed to make the piece perfect. It was often a slog. This day was different. With George Walsh's imminent return, I felt the motivation more keenly than usual. I wrote fast and, in less than an hour, I had my story, which I thought, despite my haste, had turned out well—organized, logical, and succinct— and I was confident I'd written one of my best pieces.

I led with a dramatic headline: "Missing Girl No Runaway: Cash and Ticket Found Unused." The public knew already, of course, that a lunch box had been found, but that didn't prove conclusively that she hadn't run off. There was no proof it was hers. And even if it was, perhaps she'd tossed it from a car window as she and an accomplice roared out of town for parts unknown. But the unused ticket—and even more telling—the wad of cash found in her locker, put to bed any reasonable doubts that Darleen Hicks had left town of her own volition.

My story traced the history of the evidence trail. I connected the dots on the timeline, from the December 21 disappearance to the discovery of the receipt in the Metzger home, which had led authorities to hope for the best. But the bus ticket and cash in her locker made it likely that the girl had met with foul play. And then, shortly after, the dramatic reappearance of the lunch box buried in the snow convinced the sheriff of the worst. I found myself painting a positively heroic portrait of Frank Olney, perhaps out of affection for him, but more likely out of guilt. My description, while somewhat embellished, was not far from the truth; the sheriff was carrying out a careful and thorough investigation, even if it hadn't gotten off to the fastest start.

As I tore the final page from the typewriter, I knew it was good, that Charlie, and even Artie Short, would recognize my fine work. I pictured my byline and headline anchoring the front page in the upper right-hand corner. I had a photograph in mind as well: a low-angle shot of Sheriff Frank Olney, looking rugged and in charge under the floodlights at the snow hills. I'd taken it the evening the lunch box was found. But the best thing about the story was the drubbing it would represent for George Walsh. This article would wash him out of my hair for good, or at least for this story. He had a knack for ingratiating himself to the publisher, most probably by serving him toadying helpings of peas and potatoes with meatloaf whenever his wife invited Daddy over for supper.

"Yes?" asked Charlie, looking up when I rapped on the mahogany jamb of his open office door. "Come in, Ellie," he said, waving at me.

"What are you working on?" I asked.

"This thaw," he said, referring to the weather. "There's a lot of snow, and now the big downpour today. I've been putting together a piece on the flood risks, interviewing a couple of engineers and meteorologists down in Albany. Did you know that they're going to start lowering the gates on some of the locks east of town? All the way past Schenectady to Cohoes. That doesn't happen often in winter, but the water is rising and they need to control it."

Charlie loved engineering stories. He'd told me how he'd always wanted to build things, but settled into the newspaper biz after a summer job in the printing room back in the early twenties. Then he got married and had a couple of daughters. It was too late to change careers now, but he made sure that no one but himself ever got to do stories on bridges and highways and building demolitions. I loved listening to how excited he got about these things, even if the subject didn't thrill me personally.

"That's great, Charlie," I said. "Snow melts, makes water."

"Clever girl," he said. "You should be begging me for stories like this one. But if you're too *hep* for this, I've got an idea for a human interest story for tomorrow's edition. Short and easy. You can knock this one out in your sleep."

I rolled my eyes.

"No, really, Ellie," he said. "This one is good. Remember that boy who won the spelling bee last year? What was his name? Gordie Douglas. A little genius, that kid. What if we did a follow-up on it? 'Winning Spells Success for Fifth Grader.' What do you think?"

"I think it S-T-I-N-K-S," I said, and Charlie's face fell. "Why don't you ever ask George Walsh to write that kind of stuff? He'd be a natural. Might even learn to spell."

"Ellie, I can't ask George to write that," said Charlie. "Besides, you don't have anything else for tomorrow's paper, unless you've finished your profile on Teddy Jurczyk."

"That's not fair," I said, taking the seat in front of his desk. "You know I didn't get the chance to work on that today. And I've already done the social calendar for next week and the Rock 'n' Roll Hymnal thing you wanted me to cover at St. Agnello's."

"You actually went to that?"

I thought for a moment. "Well, no," I confessed. "But I phoned Father Francis, and he told me who won. Anna Maria Galderoni, in case you had money on it. But maybe I've got a big story for you. Right here in my hand, perhaps."

Charlie feigned a chuckle. "Very funny. Now do this little genius story, and you've had a great week. I would have liked to print the Teddy J. story before the game, but I guess you didn't have time to do that in the slammer."

Now it was my turn to fake a laugh. Then I realized I hadn't thanked him for getting me out of stir. I was even feeling kindly toward Sol Meshnick. I supposed a leer or two was the least I could grant him for such prompt results.

"I was upset this afternoon," I said. "And it was rude of me not to have thanked you."

"Thank me for what?" asked Charlie.

"For the get-out-of-jail-free card."

Charlie shook his head. "Thanks for the thanks, but it wasn't me."

"Then I'll thank that old pervert, Sol Meshnick," I said.

Charlie scoffed. "It wasn't him either. We got to the station and started making a ruckus, threatening lawsuits and bad press if they didn't spring you pronto. But they wouldn't even let us in to see Chief Finn."

"Then who fished me out of there?" I asked.

"You should call Frank Olney," said Charlie, and I flushed.

"Frank? What for?"

"While Sol and I were yelling and screaming and getting nowhere, Don Czerulniak showed up and zipped inside to have a chat with the chief. Five minutes later you were out."

"So what's that got to do with the sheriff?" I asked, feeling a knot in my stomach.

"The DA was in a hurry, but he stopped to say hello on his way out. He said Frank Olney had phoned him and told him to get you the hell out of jail. He'd heard all about it from that nitwit Pat Halvey, who's got a buddy on the NHPD. A guy he bowls with. Paulie Iavarone, I think he said."

I felt the bus-ticket story burning in my hand. I tried to hide it behind my back, and Charlie noticed.

"So, what's the big story you've got?" he asked. "Is that your Rock 'n' Roll Hymnal story?"

"No," I said, taking a step back. "It's just a memo. It's nothing."

Back at my desk, I swore to myself, stuffed the doomed story inside a drawer, and went home.

CHAPTER FOURTEEN

THURSDAY, JANUARY 12, 1961

At three in the morning, I was still wrestling with my decision to pull back the unused-bus-ticket story. I'd been grinding it through my head since bedding down four hours earlier, having been awakened several times with ever-new, twisted dreams to torture me. One had me getting fired for not producing anything more interesting than a high-school boy could write. Another was my assignment to a new position at the paper: assistant to Luba, the office's ancient, Ukrainian cleaning lady. She swept and mopped, emptied wastepaper bins and trash cans, washed windows and polished brass, always half bent over, with a kerchief tied around her head. A third torture had me leaving the paper altogether and jerking sodas for Fadge at Fiorello's. A nice enough place to spend time, but not my idea of a future.

When I wasn't sleeping and dreaming of my life circling the drain, I lay awake staring at the ceiling, searching for convincing arguments for why I would be justified in printing the bus-ticket story. I had found the ticket, deduced the significance of its presence, and handed it to the sheriff myself. It was true, of course, that he'd invited me along to search the locker, but it had been my idea in the first place. Frank never would have thought of looking there. And then there were the mind-numbing human-interest stories my dear friend and mentor, Charlie Reese, felt were my bailiwick. Not even the success of the Jordan Shaw investigation had shaken me loose from the second string, and I was beginning to think that, despite his affection for me, Charlie shared the same old-school ideas on girls in the workplace. Coffee and shorthand, for sure, but newspapers were a man's game. At best, the fairer sex might be entrusted with the society pages or church news. But even those positions put effeminate men and pious laymen out of work. As for the big stories, leave those to the boys like George Walsh.

Now I'd worked myself into a lather of resentment toward Charlie Reese for things he'd never said and, as far as I knew, didn't even think. My runaway fantasy had my heart racing in my chest and my anger seething. I got out of bed and poured myself a Scotch from the cabinet in the parlor. I spied that damned letter from the Berg and Raphael Statuary sitting on the end table, calling to me. And there was my bag, leaning against the wall, still packed and waiting. I switched on the television without thinking. There was nothing on, of course, but the Indian-head signal, so I put some soothing music on the hi-fi, low, so as not to wake Mrs. Giannetti downstairs. Schubert's "Trout" quintet was jaunty and lighthearted, but the next LP that dropped down the spindle was "Death and the Maiden." Why had I loaded so much Schubert? I switched it off and went back to bed. Despite my best efforts, I still hadn't convinced myself to print the bus-ticket story, nor had I fully resolved to bury it. And that made me even angrier at Charlie Reese, who'd had nothing at all to do with my moral quandary.

⚮

The morning found me in a foul mood. All bile and no mirth make Ellie a dull girl. I shuffled to my desk, placed my purse in the lower right-hand drawer, and opened my agenda: Gordie Douglas at half past ten in the Academy Street School cafeteria. Eat your heart out, Edward R. Murrow. Then nothing until the four o'clock basketball practice at the high-school gym.

"Any news on George Wash?" I asked Norma as I poured myself a cup of coffee from the percolator.

"Nothing," she said. "But I heard from Brenda in the steno pool that his son wets the bed."

"Thanks for trying to cheer me up," I said. "But it didn't work."

⚮

The shrill bell rang, caroming off the bare palazzo floors and glossy paint of the walls, signaling the end of yet another illuminating lesson at the Academy Street School. The children spilled from their classrooms, twittering and twaddling like ... well, schoolchildren. A thin woman in a taffeta dress approached me in the cafeteria, her heels clacking over the hard floors. She was pushing a small towheaded child in a striped shirt and black, high-top PF Flyers before her. She introduced herself as Dorothy Galligan, teacher's aide. The little, blond dingus was Gordon Douglas, boy genius.

"I'll be back in ten minutes to collect him," said Mrs. Galligan. "He has midmorning milk at ten forty-five, followed by arithmetic at eleven." Mrs. Galligan disappeared, leaving me alone with the spelling prodigy.

"How are you, Gordie?" I asked.

"Fine," he said, looking off into the nothingness beyond me.

"So, you're the spelling champ?"

"Yeah, I guess."

"Tell me. Has winning the spelling bee changed your life?"

"No."

"Are you going to enter the spelling bee again this year?" I asked, thinking what a dullard this kid was.

He shrugged. "I guess."

"What word did you spell to win?"

"'Poodle,'" He said, and wiped his nose.

"Really?" I asked. "'Poodle?' P-O-O-D-L-E?" He nodded. "And that won?" Again he nodded.

"The other kid missed 'endomorphic,' so I won."

"Can you spell 'endomorphic'?"

"No."

"May I take a picture of you?" I asked. Interview over.

I drove back to the office, one frame of Gordie Douglas in my camera, regretting even the waste of that much celluloid on the worst story of my career. But I promised myself that I would write the best spelling-bee follow-up profile ever written. No one would know or care if I embellished the lad's personality and intelligence in my article. In fact, I was sure everyone, from Gordie's proud parents to Charlie Reese and Artie Short, would appreciate the snow job I was rehearsing in my mind. I'd be done with my piece before Gordie had managed to snort his midmorning milk through his nose.

Back at my desk, I pounded out the story in eleven minutes and dropped it into Charlie's in-box before heading out to lunch at Wolfson's Department Store next door. Gordie Douglas's eyes were closed in the photo I'd taken.

As I slurped chicken-and-rice soup out of my spoon, I eyed the waitress who'd served me. Consolidating two pots of coffee into one, she stood there in a flowered cotton dress and blue apron, her narrow shoulders sloping gradually into her wide middle and wider behind. Her legs were trunks planted in white orthopedic shoes. Her name tag read Maureen. She was sweet, about thirty, with a blonde beehive and thick glasses.

"Endomorphic," I thought, sipping my soup, recalling the little genius and his moment of triumph. And I'd come across that word somewhere else recently, too.

The New Holland High School gymnasium echoed with shouts and squeaking sneakers. A vague smell of stale sweat hung in the air. I climbed halfway down the bleacher stairs from above and took a seat to watch. The coach was running a half-court drill, working on the offensive schemes with the first and second strings. The plays were designed to get the ball into Teddy J.'s hands to shoot, and he was on the mark this day, sinking six of his first eight shots. Then he caught a glimpse of me taking in the practice from the bleachers, and he lost his touch, missing his next three attempts. A couple of the upperclassmen razzed him—and me in the process—for having his "girlfriend" come to watch him. Teddy sulked. Then Coach Mahoney blew his whistle and told the boys to take a knee. Several players craned their necks to look up into the stands, and the coach took notice of me for the first time. He told the team to run a lay-up drill, while he climbed the stairs to speak to me.

"Hello, Miss Stone," he said. "What can I do for you today?"

"I'm just watching the practice," I said. "Research for the feature I'm doing on Teddy Jurczyk.

He fidgeted and scratched his neck. "I thought we had an agreement that you would leave Teddy alone."

"I'm just finishing my feature on him."

"I'm afraid that's not possible. This practice session is closed. You're going to have to leave."

"But I've got an assignment from the paper. It's all been approved by the principal's office."

"This principal's office?" he asked.

"No, the junior high school's," I said. "Mr. Brossard."

"Look," he said, avoiding my eyes. "You're a nice girl, and I know you don't mean any harm. But you're kind of a jinx to Teddy."

"A jinx?"

"Yeah. He gets all tight when you're around. You make him nervous. I just can't have you upsetting him like that."

I flushed. My mouth went dry, and I didn't know what to say. I was being kicked out of the gym and off my story with one swing of Coach Mahoney's leg.

"It's not personal," he said, but I was dumbstruck. A jinx? "Oh, there's Mr. Brossard now," said Mahoney. "Maybe you can talk to him."

I made my way up the stairs, temples throbbing from the humiliation. Brossard waited for me atop the bleachers and extended a hand to shake mine. I offered it dumbly, and he asked me what was wrong.

"I've just been asked to leave the practice and to stay away from Teddy Jurczyk."

"What? Why?"

"Coach says I'm a jinx. But it's my job to do a story on him. How can I tell my editor that I can't write it because I'm not welcome here?"

"That's rough," he said. "Listen, maybe I can help. I'll have a word with the coach later on. For now, it might be better to do as he asks. Come on. I'll buy you a cup of coffee."

Dean's Coffee House had served sodas and malteds to generations of New Holland high schoolers. Just a few blocks from Walter T. Finch High, Dean's was a friendly spot, open only till about six, when Dean and his wife, Edith, punched out for the day. Out of loyalty to Fadge, I didn't patronize the shop. To tell the truth, he'd threatened to ban me for life if he ever caught me in there. The same went for Mack's Confectionery up the street. Under the present circumstances, I decided to risk the wrath of Ron Fiorello.

"I wanted to have a word with you," said Brossard once we were seated at a table near the window. "It's about Darleen Hicks."

"What about her?" I asked. He had my interest piqued.

"I've been reading the articles in the paper, and I got to thinking. I've come to believe that girl simply ran away with someone. To Arizona."

Wow. What powers of deduction.

"Why do you think that?" I asked.

"Well, there was the receipt they found in her bedroom. The one for the bus ticket. Clearly she used the ticket and motored off to the Southwest. Didn't she have some boyfriend in the army?"

"What about the lunch box they found near her property? Doesn't that point to foul play?"

"I've been thinking that over, too," he said, blowing on his black coffee to cool it. He took a sip then resumed. "There's really no evidence that the lunch box is hers, is there? Didn't you write that the sheriff merely found an average lunch box like so many others? It could belong to anybody. Or, it's possible that she threw it away herself. Young girls behave oddly at times."

I squinted across the table at him. A gap between two houses on the other side of the street let a fierce beam of sunlight through, and it was directly behind Brossard, rendering him a near silhouette before me. I couldn't quite make out his expression, but not for lack of trying.

"Is something wrong with your eyes, Miss Stone?" he asked.

"The sun," I said. "You've given this business a lot of thought, I see."

"Well, when one of my girls disappears, I want to know why."

"Naturally," I said. Then, wondering how often this kind of thing came up, I asked him if it had ever happened before.

"As a matter of fact, yes," he said, shaking his head. "When I was in Hudson, a young girl disappeared. The police never found out what happened to her. It's a sad thing, but it happens every day across the country. I'm afraid our society has lost its way. With filth like *Lolita* passing for literature . . ." He stopped himself and smiled sadly. "I'm a bit old fashioned, Miss Stone. I still believe in God, sin, and judgment. Just an old altar boy with very Catholic ideas. You probably think I'm very unhip."

"Why do you say that?"

"Well, you're a New York City girl, after all."

Huh? I wasn't sure if he was insulting me or admiring my cosmopolitan attitudes. And how did he know that, anyway? "Is that why you wanted to talk to me?" I asked. "To tell me Darleen probably ran away?"

"Yes," he said. "I thought I could be of help to you. You know, get in on the whole investigation thing." The sun shimmered out of sight behind the house across the street, and I could see him clearly again. He smiled awkwardly.

"Can you get me an interview with Teddy Jurczyk?" I asked, flashing my most fetching smile at him. He seemed unmoved.

"I'd like to see the story done, of course," he said. "We're very proud of our Teddy, as you know. And it would be great publicity for him, too. Maybe help get him into a fine college in four years. St. Bonaventure or Siena." He paused, looking at me with indifferent eyes. "But if Coach is against it, I'm not sure I should interfere."

"Just one more meeting, then I'll leave him alone," I said, trying to catch his eyes. But he was focusing on nothing in particular. Certainly not on me.

Brossard shrugged finally and agreed. I'd won the game without scoring any points, and I was ashamed of myself for the flirting. Then Brossard's face lit up as he told me how excited he was to see the game Friday.

"Teddy will be in rare form," he said, beaming.

I returned to the office in time to hand in two more stories for Saturday's edition: one on pothole repairs on the East End, and the other on some complaints about pollution of the river. New HollandCo, a manufacturer of low-cost carpeting and flooring, was the largest employer left in the city. They had taken over one of the Shaw Knitting Mills' larger buildings. Wastewater from the factory poured into the Great Cayunda Creek at the rate of five hundred gallons an hour. The Cayunda carried the polluted water down the hill and vomited it into the Mohawk, just underneath the Mill Street Bridge. A local woman had started making noise two years earlier, protesting outside New HollandCo's offices about the pollution, but most people considered her a crackpot and ignored her. Then she somehow got the ear of a young assistant attorney general for the State of New York, and things began to change quickly. The State commissioned a study of the river in 1959 and pronounced the Mohawk so polluted it was "dead." Public awareness about pollution grew. I had written several articles on the protests over the past two years. The pothole report was also a regular beat of mine.

Charlie didn't seem to care about those stories. He called me into his office to discuss Teddy Jurczyk instead.

"I just spoke to Artie Short," he said, and I recognized his I-hate-this-job frown. "He got a call from Principal Keith at the high school. He says they don't want you hanging around basketball practice anymore. What did you do, Ellie?"

"Why do you assume I did something wrong, Charlie? Why don't you ever assume I'm in the right and then ask questions?"

"Come on, Ellie," he said. "You're always getting under someone's skin. It's your specialty."

"I think it's my skirt," I said. "Anyway, I didn't do anything to Teddy. For some reason, he thinks I'm a jinx to him."

"Well, the principal said you can cover the games, but not the practices."

I smiled.

"What is it?" asked Charlie.

"Just that I don't need access to the high-school gym to finish my story. Louis Brossard said he'd fix things up for me with young Teddy."

"Who's Brossard?"

"Assistant principal of the junior high. And now he fancies himself an amateur detective."

"How do you mean?"

"He told me he's figured out that Darleen Hicks ran off because there was a bus-ticket receipt in her bedroom."

Charlie scoffed. "Hardly discovering penicillin. That bus receipt kind of makes it obvious doesn't it? Now it would be another thing if she hadn't actually used the ticket."

My face must have turned red, because Charlie asked me what was wrong. I shook my head and made up a lie. I left Charlie's office in a funk. That bus ticket needed to come out, but my hands were tied. I wanted to kick a dent into Frank Olney's car door. Instead I wandered back to my desk and slumped into my chair. It was nearly six anyway, so I thought I'd head home to wash the taste of the day away with some whiskey and ice. I grabbed my purse and stood to go. Then Norma Geary appeared.

As the room was empty, we sat down to talk without fear of being overheard. She asked me what progress I'd made on my Teddy J. story, and I gave her the short version.

"Lucky that Mr. Brossard showed up," she said. "He's probably got eyes for you."

I shook my head. "I know when a man is interested, or at least entertains ideas, but there's nothing there. He's strangely detached or bored or indifferent when he talks to me. I noticed it today."

"Is he married?"

"He wasn't wearing a wedding band," I said. "But not all men wear them. He strikes me more as the priestly type anyway."

"I'm sure you're mistaken, Miss Stone," said Norma. "I've seen how men look at you."

Driven by turns sideways and vertical by strong winds, the rain drummed on the roof and ran down the windows in sheets. The snow was gone from the streets and sidewalks, and the slush washed into the gutters then disappeared, flushed away for good by the downpour. Mrs. Giannetti's small rectangle of a lawn was exposed, brown and muddy grass, for the first time since Thanksgiving.

Thursday's television lineup—mostly westerns—didn't interest me. There was *Donna Reed,* but that just reminded me of what a mess my life was compared to hers. So I ignored the television and curled up with several whiskeys on the couch to read Lampedusa's *The Leopard.* I liked history and far-flung places, and it was a bestseller. Sicily and the *Risorgimento* seemed like a tonic to take my mind off the unused bus ticket, and, at the same time, I conjured some peaceful memories of my father reading his beloved Italian literature and history. But alcohol and reading don't mix, at least not for me. I couldn't concentrate, kept losing the thread, and found myself pages ahead without remembering what I'd just read. It was getting late anyhow, and I was thinking about bed, when there was a knock at my kitchen door.

"Who is it?" I asked, a broom cocked behind my head like a baseball bat, in case it was a marauder on the other side of the door. I had received, after all, my share of unwanted visitors in recent days, and it was after eleven thirty. As I stood there, elbows bent, twitching the broom like Mickey Mantle waiting for a pitch, I realized that this attack position meant that the head of the broom, with its relatively soft bristles, would be employed to fend off any and all comers. Effective for chasing mice, perhaps, but against an attacker with nefarious intent, it was a poor choice of weapon.

"It's Irene Metzger," came the voice through the glass panel and sheer curtain.

I opened the door and let her in. She brought the same smell of wet wool as she had the first time I'd met her on New Year's Eve. She was wearing the same transparent rain hat as well. And once she'd sat at my kitchen table, I served her the same whiskey we'd drunk that night.

"I haven't seen you in a few days," she said, settling in with a cigarette between her fingers.

"Your husband threw me out," I said. "He threatened me."

She waved her hand and drew a deep drag on her cigarette. "He's sorry about that."

"I didn't get the flowers and chocolates."

"He's a good man, miss," she said, ignoring my remark. "Give him a second chance. We just have to find out what happened to Darleen."

"The sheriff's your man. He's on the case, isn't he?"

She nodded. "Sure, but he keeps things to himself. He doesn't tell us what's going on. And we haven't seen any articles in your paper since the lunch box was found. Have you given up on Darleen?"

I thought about the bus ticket yet again. How I wanted to tell Irene Metzger that I was still hot on the story of her daughter's disappearance and had even written a significant piece for the paper just the day before. I wanted to tell her that my hands were tied, but that would have been a coward's way out. I could publish the story if I wanted. I was just angry with myself for putting my loyalty to Frank Olney ahead of my own interests. The small bit of consolation I felt was that I actually had come around to Frank's way of thinking: namely that withholding the evidence of the unused bus ticket was surely the wiser way to proceed. After all, if Louis Brossard had formed his conclusion on Darleen's fate based on his ignorance of the unused ticket, perhaps others would as well. That could work in the sheriff's favor.

"I have not given up on your daughter, Mrs. Metzger," I said, and we both took a sip of Scotch. "The trail is cold, but there's the lunch box and the note inside."

"Yes, the sheriff told me about that. He thinks the note could have been written some time ago, and the lunch box might have been lost earlier, too. But I know Darleen took it that morning."

"Perhaps the sheriff just doesn't want you to get your hopes up."

"Hopes?" she snorted. "Are you kidding? I ain't got no hopes, except to find my little girl and give her a proper burial. Reverend Holman at the Presbyterian church in Tribes Hill tells me that a funeral gives a person solace. I sure hope so, 'cause that's all I've got to look forward to." She paused, took a gulp of whiskey, then added that she and Dick Metzger weren't Presbyterians at all. "We just go to that one 'cause the closest Lutheran church is in New Holland. What church do you go to?"

"Saint John the Mattress," I mumbled, repeating one of Fadge's oft-told jokes.

"I see," she said. "Catholic."

"Why did you come here tonight?" I asked, pouring us each another drink. "Surely not to scold me."

"I got some information to tell you that might help." She had my ear. "We have a party line at our place, so we have to share with the neighbors. Mrs. Norquist hogs the line in the evenings when she does her telephoning."

"Yes, I've had the pleasure of waiting for Mrs. Norquist to take a breath."

"Beg your pardon?"

I explained about my evening at the Karls' place.

"Well, I had to break into her conversation the other night, and she said she heard about Darleen. Thought it was a terrible thing. And then she said she overheard a strange phone call between Darleen and a man about a month ago."

"A man? Did she know who it was?"

Irene Metzger shook her head. "No, she just heard a part of what they were saying."

"And what did she hear?"

Irene clamped her lips down on a fresh cigarette, struck a match, and lit it, sucking its smoke into her lungs as if trying to prime a siphon.

"Mrs. Norquist said the man was older," she said finally. "He was talking sweet to her. He wanted to meet her after school, but Darleen said no."

"An older man," I said, half to myself, the specter of Ted Russell raising its ugly head in my mind. "And you say Mrs. Norquist didn't hear any names?"

Irene Metzger began to answer, but stopped mid-word. There was a creaking on my back staircase and the sound of footsteps climbing.

"You expecting someone?" she asked.

I shook my head no, eyes fixed on the kitchen door. The steps climbed higher, softly, carefully, as if whoever was out there wanted to be quiet. It might have been someone not wanting to disturb Mrs. Giannetti downstairs. Heck, it might have been Mrs. Giannetti herself, having heard noises upstairs and wanting to catch me *in flagrante*. I doubted it was Fadge. He'd closed up the store about an hour earlier and asked if I was interested in a late-night cheeseburger and fries at Whitey's. I told him I had retired for the evening and wasn't putting my face on again for a cheeseburger. Besides, Fadge made more noise climbing the stairs than the Rough Riders charging up San Juan Hill. And he wouldn't have troubled himself about disturbing Mrs. Giannetti's sleep. (Fadge enjoyed an antagonistic relationship with her, having once emptied his garbage can on her lawn after she'd complained he wasn't keeping the store's stoop clean enough for her liking.) In any case, I was alarmed. I was certain it wasn't Fadge and couldn't imagine who else would be creeping up my stairs in the middle of the night.

"Dick?" called Irene Metzger, startling me with the volume and coarseness of her voice. The creaking on the stairs stopped. "Dick, come on up so you can say your apologies to Miss Stone properly."

There was no answer from the stairs, and Irene Metzger looked puzzled. "Dick!" she roared.

The only answer she got was the sound of retreating steps scrambling back down the staircase. Irene Metzger and I both leapt up from the kitchen table. I grabbed my trusty broom and committed the same blunder as the first time, holding the hard end, ready to attack with the soft. Irene Metzger lunged for the back door and didn't hesitate to follow the visitor down the stairs. I made my way down more cautiously; I'd had a few more drinks than she.

Outside, I stood on the porch, looking up and down Lincoln Avenue through the rain, seeing no one except Irene Metzger crossing the street to her husband's green pickup, parked directly in front of Fiorello's.

"Dick?" I heard her call. "Dick, what did you run away for?"

Braving the wind and rain, I joined them across the street. Irene Metzger now wore an expression of distress. She squinted into the darkness and rain in both directions, trying to see something.

"What is it?" I asked, still clutching the now-wet broom.

Dick Metzger echoed my question. "What the hell's wrong, Irene?" he demanded.

She turned to me, ignoring her husband for the moment. "Dick was fast asleep in the truck just now."

CHAPTER FIFTEEN

The city police arrived ten minutes later. I doubted the utility of asking for their help after the treatment I'd received the day before, but Irene Metzger had insisted. I breathed more easily when I saw the responding officer climb out of his patrol car. Vic Mature had come to my rescue. Over a cup of coffee at my kitchen table, Officer Palumbo listened patiently as I described the eerie visit. Irene Metzger nodded and embellished, peppering my account with her details as well. Dick Metzger leaned against my icebox and said nothing.

"Well, it's not a lot to go on," said Palumbo in his deep baritone. "No breaking and entering, no assault. You didn't even see him to give a description."

I stared at him, knowing full well that there was nothing he could do. Still, I wanted him to say something useful to help me make it through the night. My flimsy kitchen door had been breached before, just a month earlier when I'd made the wrong person nervous investigating the Jordan Shaw murder.

"I can ask the duty sergeant to put a patrol in the neighborhood," he offered.

"Who's on duty tonight?" I asked, afraid of the answer.

Palumbo cleared his throat. "Joe Philbin."

My head fell into my hands. I could call Frank Olney, but what kind of person would that make me? Ready to ignore his wishes one minute, then begging him to fight my battles the next. There was Fadge, of course. But I didn't want to give him the wrong idea. And Steve Herbert? No thanks. Why did I need to run to a man anyhow? Because I was terrified, that's why. It could have been Joey Figlio on my stair, a bully of a city cop, Ted Russell, Bobby Karl Jr., or someone worse. I didn't know who was responsible for Darleen Hicks's disappearance, which made my sense of security even shakier. In fact, one of the men I suspected most of all was standing in my kitchen at that very moment, preventing my icebox from falling over, glowering at me the whole time. And he still hadn't apologized or offered flowers or chocolates.

"Thank you just the same," I said to Officer Palumbo. "I'll take my chances with the thugs and murderers prowling about."

Palumbo smiled softly. I love it when big, tough guys smile like that. And when they're cops, well, doubly so.

"I'm on duty till morning, miss," he said. "I'll circle around Lincoln Avenue a few times and keep an eye on things."

I'd have preferred he just spend the night, but thought better of suggesting that. I nodded and thanked him instead.

Irene Metzger asked me to keep her informed of my progress, then she and her husband took their leave. As they stepped through the kitchen door, Dick Metzger turned and regarded me uneasily. Still no apology. We stared at each other for a long moment as I considered my options. He was very close, but Officer Palumbo was just behind me. That was no guarantee of my safety, but I thought I'd never have this kind of protection again. So I asked him. Slow and measured: "Did you ever kiss your daughter on the lips?"

He blanched. His wife grabbed his forearm to still him, and his eyes bulged the same way they had the last time I'd asked that question. But then they darted to my left, over my shoulder, just for a split second. He pinched his lips together, holding back his rage. I didn't move or breathe. I just stared deep into his eyes, trying to read his thoughts, waiting to see what secrets they might betray if he finally consented to answer my question.

"Yes," he said, quiet but hard. "It's our way to kiss our loved ones, including children." He drew a difficult breath through his flaring nostrils. We stood so close that I could smell the hatred in his words, which passed over my face, almost strong enough to move the ringlets of stray hair around my temples. "My mother kissed me that way," he continued. "I kissed my daughter that way. And no pretty, little city girl with a dirty mind is going to tell me that it's wrong."

He turned and followed his wife down the stairs, and I finally drew a breath. Palumbo had turned white. He stood there big and tall, filling up my kitchen. Then he cleared his throat again, like a shy suitor, and told me he would watch the street that night.

And with that, my only protection—besides the soggy broom—left me in my kitchen to face the rest of the night alone.

FRIDAY, JANUARY 13, 1961

I was slow out of the gate on Friday, due to a sleepless night. As tired as I was, though, there was no question of phoning in sick. For one thing, I didn't want to add to Artie Short's Friday absenteeism ammunition, and, for another, I wanted to get out of that house. I felt like a sitting duck, waiting for someone to come for me. On my way out the door, Mrs. Giannetti caught me and questioned me about the night before.

"I heard a party going on," she said. "I thought I was clear about entertaining during the week."

"There was no party," I said. "Just the police."

"Oh, my!" she gasped. "What have you done now, Eleonora?"

"I didn't do anything," I said. "Someone was prowling around last night, so I called the police."

"A prowler? Again? That's twice in a month. What's this town coming to?"

I stopped myself from pointing out that both intrusions, actual and attempted, were not part of a greater crime wave or loss of civility in New Holland. They were the direct result of my poking around on murder stories: Darleen Hicks's and Jordan Shaw's. If I minded my own business, Lincoln Avenue could retake its rightful spot in a Norman Rockwell painting.

"Did they catch him?" asked Mrs. Giannetti.

"Who?"

"The burglar. I won't be able to sleep if they didn't catch him."

I churned through my purse, searching for the car keys. "Don't worry, Mrs. Giannetti," I said, climbing into my car. "He wasn't after you."

The rain had started again. I wrestled my umbrella open then made a dash for the office from my parking spot down the street. The wind was strong enough to blow me off course a couple of times. I arrived at the brass-and-glass door of the *Republic* offices at the same time as George Walsh, and we nearly bumped into each other as we tried to squeeze through the entrance with our dripping umbrellas. Inside, we exchanged stiff good mornings then had to make our way up the stairs together in awkward silence. Finally, I broke the ice.

"Nice tan you got in Arizona," I said as we reached the second floor.

I spent the morning preparing my feature on Teddy Jurczyk. All I needed was ten minutes of his time and a couple of nice action shots from the game that evening. Louis Brossard called mid-morning to let me know I could meet Teddy at three after his last class ended.

To confirm what Irene Metzger had told me, I telephoned Alma Norquist, the neighbor who shared the party line with the Metzgers. Of course, this wasn't the first time I'd spoken to her. The evening I got stranded at the Karl farm, I had interrupted Mrs. Norquist on the phone and told her we were under nuclear attack. I thought the odds were long that she would recognize my voice, but even if she did, at least she couldn't complain about how Armageddon had turned out.

Her version of Darleen's adult-male caller matched Irene Metzger's in the main, but I had a couple of questions of my own for her. I wanted her to describe the man's voice. Deep? Did he speak slowly? Did he have an accent? Did he sound like a young man or middle-aged? No, no, no, and hard to say. His voice, it seems, was quite unremarkable.

"And you're positive you'd never heard the voice before?" I asked. "Could it have been a neighbor? Bobby Karl, perhaps? Or Mr. Rasmussen?"

"Oh, no," she said. "I know those two. It wasn't them. Besides, Bobby Karl is tongue-tied in front of girls. And the man asked to meet her at the school."

"Do you know if Darleen ever got other calls?" I asked. "From friends or boyfriends her own age?"

"Of course. That girl was always on the phone. Used to hog the line."

"Any boyfriends?"

"Two or three," she said. "Let's see. There was Wilbur, of course. But that was months ago. What a dullard that boy was," and she laughed. "And there were two others she spoke with more recently."

"Was one named Joey?" I asked, wondering if Alma Norquist had a television—or was the party line her own personal soap opera?

"Oh, yes, I remember him. The little snot called me 'Grandma' when I told him it was my time to do my telephoning. 'Keep your shirt on, Grandma,' he said. Of all the nerve."

"Who was the other boy?"

She searched her memory but couldn't retrieve the name. "It's on the tip of my tongue," she said. "A polite boy."

My skin tingled, as I remembered a series of notes I'd come across.

"Was it Ted, by any chance?" I asked.

"That's it! Smart boy. And polite. Never called me 'Grandma.'"

I'd had a feeling itching the back of my brain since my interview with little Gordie Douglas. The boy wonder said "endomorphic" was the word his opponent had missed when he'd won his crown. (I still couldn't believe they'd asked one kid to spell "endomorphic" and then given Gordie "poodle" for the win.) And that had reminded me of the note I'd found in Darleen's room, the one from Edward, who, according to Irene Metzger, had been in love with Darleen since seventh grade. He'd referred to a Mr. Bellows as an "endomorphic walrus." Then there was the note in Darleen's lunch box, signed "Ted." And the love note smuggled out of Fulton to me by Frankie Ralston, also signed Ted. What if Ted and Edward were one and the same? Ted was a common nickname for Edward, after all. I asked myself if a grown man like Ted Russell would sign his name so blithely on love notes to a fifteen-year-old girl. Possibly, but I pegged him as savvier than that. He still might be a child molester, but he wasn't a fool.

So, back to my question: What if, by some chance, Edward and Ted were one and the same? Teachers don't often mock each other in signed notes to students, so I doubted Edward's note had been written by Ted Russell. Despite the advanced vocabulary and good punctuation, I was sure that note had come from a student. And if Edward was Ted, what did that say about the love note Joey Figlio had smuggled out to me via Frankie Ralston? And the last note from Ted found in Darleen's lunch box?

Why would Edward change his name to Ted? Who knew what ideas got into kids' heads? Maybe he'd been given a new name against his will, a name he didn't like. Whatever the reason, I was sure Teddy Jurczyk was in love with Darleen Hicks up until the day she vanished. And it appeared he may have slipped a note into her lunch box asking her to get off the bus to speak to him just moments before it rumbled off without her.

Brossard held the door for me, and I entered his office. Teddy Jurczyk was sitting in a ladder-back chair before the assistant principal's desk, fidgeting and sweating in his checkered shirt and blue cardigan. I said hello, and Teddy cracked a smile. His Adam's apple bobbed as he swallowed hard, and I took a seat in the chair next to him.

"Now, Teddy, there's nothing to be nervous about," said Brossard, taking his place behind his desk. "Miss Stone is writing a nice little feature on you and your basketball success. Just a few questions for you. It'll only sting a bit," and he chuckled. When he saw that Teddy wasn't laughing, he went all serious again and cleared his throat. "Miss Stone, please proceed."

I smiled as genial a smile as I could muster, but Teddy looked white. Even whiter than usual. "When did you first start playing basketball?" I asked, hoping such an innocuous question would assuage his fears. He didn't answer, so I dumbed it down even more: "How old were you?"

He gulped again and said, "Six." Then he smiled awkwardly and drew a deep breath. With the first word out of the way, he relaxed a bit.

"Good boy," said Brossard, positively drinking in Teddy with his adoring eyes.

"Did your dad play basketball?" I continued.

He nodded. "Yes, he liked to play. Played in the CYO when he was my age."

"He didn't play for New Holland?"

"No." For the most part, Teddy avoided my eyes, but at least he had found speech. God, this kid was going to have a hard time asking a girl to a dance. "Pop didn't finish high school. He went to work in the mill and then came the war. He had to stop."

"Okay, now here's a tough question," I said. "You're just a freshman, playing with boys much older than you. Were you nervous the first time Coach put you in the game?"

Teddy straightened up in his chair and looked me in the eye. "Before the game, yes, I sure was. Coach told me Dickie was too sick to play, and I was in. I threw up twice in the locker room. But then," his eyes actually sparkled at this point, "as soon as the referee tossed up the jump ball, my butterflies disappeared. It was a very peaceful feeling. Phil Carbone got the ball and passed it to me. I scored on a layup on the first play."

I smiled at him, and he gave me a big grin back. "Do you want to pursue basketball in college?" I asked.

He shrugged. "I don't know about college. My pop says if I get a scholarship somewhere, maybe I can play. Otherwise, I'll probably go to work in one of the mills."

If there are any mills left by the time he graduates high school, I thought.

"Your pop must be very proud of you. Does he come to your games?"

"He hasn't missed one yet," said Teddy. "He sits in the middle row at center court with my little sister, Patricia."

"The boy's mother passed away a few years ago," said Brossard to me as an aside. Teddy said nothing.

"That's nice that your sister comes to root you on," I said, and I meant it. He blushed.

"Now, what about girls?" I asked. "Are you going steady with anyone?"

"Perhaps you have enough now, Miss Stone," interrupted Brossard. "Teddy has to eat something and get up to the high school for tonight's game."

"Almost finished," I said. "Just one more question?" Brossard consulted his watch and nodded. "Is Edward your full name?" I asked Teddy.

His face darkened, and Brossard choked on something across the desk. Teddy hesitated, almost as if weighing his answer. I noticed a sparkle in his eyes, but not the happy glittering I'd seen just a few moments before. Finally he uttered a simple "Yes."

"Why don't you like the name 'Teddy'?" I asked.

He fidgeted again, as if he just wanted to get out of there. "No one ever called me 'Teddy' until recently. Since basketball season started. It makes me feel like a kid."

The explanation seemed sound to me, so I nodded. "Would you like me to refer to you as Ted Jurczyk in the papers?" I asked.

His smile returned, broad and beaming. "That would be swell," he said.

"Did your mother call you Ted?" He didn't answer. "I lost my mother, too. She called me Ellie when my father named me Eleonora."

"What was all that business about his name?" Brossard asked me once the boy had left. He seemed miffed. "I think Teddy J. is a fine name. It'll make him famous."

"He told me he hated that name," I said as a matter of fact. "At the game last week."

Brossard huffed and shook his head. "But I came up with that name," he said.

"It's all right, Mr. Brossard," I said, patting him on the shoulder. "There'll be other boys to name."

✦

Back at the office, I had a couple of hours to work on my profile of Ted Jurczyk and grab a bite at the lunch counter next door. I selected three shots of the freshman for the article: a graceful layup, a defensive pose, and his team portrait. He stood there in his satin uniform, holding a basketball on his hip, as he smiled at the camera. I entered the caption: Ted Jurczyk, freshman guard. I was working on a paragraph describing his stellar academic record when George Walsh rushed into the room.

"Whaddya know, Georgie Porgie?" I said, not even looking up from my typewriter and certainly not expecting an answer.

He stuffed his arms into his coat, grabbed his umbrella and hat, then headed for the door. He paused over my desk and said with a sarcastic grin, "Read the papers, Eleonora."

✦

By halftime, the New Holland Bucks were leading the Flying Horses of Troy by fifteen. (*Flying* Horses? Who named these teams?) Ted Jurczyk had scored sixteen points on seven-for-twelve shooting and two-for-two from the foul line. I turned in my seat behind the scorer to see his father beaming in the middle row at center court. Beside him was a little blonde girl of about nine. She laughed and chatted with her father's friends, who treated her like a little princess. When the teams took the court to warm up for the second half, I turned again to snap a picture of the little girl watching her big brother. I focused my zoom on her bright face. That's when I saw the little crutches leaning against the bench next to her. She hadn't stood the whole time I'd been watching her. Then, through my lens, I saw the flash of metal on the poor little thing's legs. I lowered my Leica without squeezing the shutter release.

Ted Jurczyk cooled off a bit in the second half, scoring only eight points. But he managed the last six for New Holland, who eked out a win 52–50 and reclaimed a share of first place in the Class A League.

I was packing away my camera and pulling on my coat when Frank Olney sidled up to me.

"Good game," he said.

I mumbled something like yes.

"I haven't seen you since our little talk at the jail."

"I've been busy," I said, avoiding his eyes. "Work keeps me on the run."

He nodded. "And late-night intruders?"

I jerked my head to look up at him. "What do you know about that?"

"I know a lot of what goes on in this town," he said. "Ellie, why didn't you just call me? I would have put a man on your house."

"I'm all right," I said.

A long pause ensued. It was getting to the point where someone had to say something, so I obliged.

"I wanted to thank you for sending Don to get me out of jail," I said. "You didn't have to do that."

Frank dismissed my thank you with an uncomfortable pshaw.

"Really, Frank," I said. "And after our ... little chat, you still came through for me."

He shuffled his feet a bit and looked around at the emptying crowd. He coughed once or twice then said it was nothing. "I wasn't about to let you rot in Pat Finn's jail."

"Even after I said I was going to publish that story?"

"What do you take me for?" he said.

"Well, you don't have to worry. I'm not going to print it."

Frank sighed. He looked as if I'd pierced his heart. "Ellie, whether you print your story or not, I'm not going let the New Holland cops bully you."

I was a little overcome. I wiped my eyes, tried to compose myself, then looked up at the big guy. A warm tear rolled down my cheek. "Did you know Ted Jurczyk's little sister had polio?"

After the game, I dropped in at the office and wrote out my story on the game. That took about forty-five minutes. I dropped it off in Composition then found my way to Fiorello's, where the kids had descended to celebrate the victory. I felt safe in the crowd, but was dreading returning home where intruders had no qualms about entering uninvited.

Fadge was too busy to pay any attention to me, but Bill, the dishwasher, was only too happy to chat. He listed the catalogue of products he'd bought that day entirely with coupons at Louie's Market on the East End. His haul included wilted, unwanted produce, dented canned goods, remainders, and bargains of every description. Bill packed groceries for tips at Louie's by day and washed dishes at Fiorello's by night. He was known far and wide for his frugality and refusal ever to throw anything out. Fadge called him the third, retarded Collyer brother. Bill also liked to share embarrassing information.

"Do you know why they wouldn't take me in the army?" he asked me, apropos of nothing, the first day we met.

"Flat feet?" I asked, dreading the answer.

"Breasts like a woman," he announced proudly.

There were no seats free in any of the booths, and the counter was full. I leafed through a *Look* magazine and waited for someone to leave. A girl had the same idea, stationing herself next to me and grabbing a copy of *16 Magazine*. I wouldn't have given her a second thought, but Fadge looked up from the egg cream he was stirring to bark at us.

"Hey, you two. This isn't a library," he said. "Buy something or get out."

I stuck my magazine back onto the rack and reeled around to look at him, blushing from the public censure, and saw that it was Carol Liswenski standing next to me. We exchanged embarrassed glances. Then, upon recognizing me, Fadge turned white.

"Ellie, sorry," he stammered. "I didn't see you there." He scanned the counter and zeroed in on Zeke, a fifteen-year-old regular who was always begging Fadge for a job. "Over here, Ellie," said Fadge, snatching a half-drunk cherry Coke from the boy. "Zeke was just leaving."

"Hey," protested Zeke, but his time was up. He slid off the stool and, head down, shuffled out of the store.

I took his seat at the counter, feeling vaguely guilty and ordered a cup of coffee. Fearing he was next in Fadge's sights, the young man next to me downed his drink, wiped his lips on his sleeve, then slipped away.

"Carol," I called to the girl, still standing near the magazines but now too afraid to touch them. "Carol, there's a seat here," and I patted the red Naugahyde to my left.

She accepted my invitation warily and climbed up onto the stool.

"I'll stand you a Coke," I said. "What would you like?"

"A hot-fudge sundae," she said softly.

"Okay," I said, eyeing Fadge. I'd offered a Coke, but never mind . . .

Carol was alone, and I asked her where her friends had gone.

"Susan is with her new boyfriend, Rick Stafford," she said. "And Linda always has family dinner at Johnnie's Seafood on Fridays."

"You're a long way from the Town of Florida," I said. "How are you getting home?"

"I'll get a ride from one of the girls, I guess. If not, I have enough for a taxi."

"That's not a good idea," I said. "I'll drive you home if you need a ride." She nodded okay.

"I wanted to ask you something, Carol."

"Okay," she said, a little doubtful.

"The day Darleen disappeared from the bus," I began in a low voice. The chatter surrounding us drowned out our conversation, rendering us inaudible in the middle of a crowd. "You said she got off the bus to see someone. And you said you didn't see who it was."

She nodded just as Fadge put a hot-fudge sundae and a glass of water down in front of her. She lit up and dug in.

"I think you or Susan or Linda *did* see who it was," I said, and Carol chewed more slowly, her mind working on an escape or an excuse. "And you three must have discussed it a hundred times since Darleen vanished. Now, I'm going to say a name, and you're going to tell me if I'm right."

Carol looked up at me, a smear of melting ice cream on her lower lip. She looked like a child; she was only fourteen after all.

"It was Ted Jurczyk, wasn't it?"

Carol choked, wiped her chin with a napkin, and took a sip of her water. "How did you know that?" she hissed in a whisper. Her eyes darted from side to side to ensure no one was listening. Then she leaned in closer to me. "Darleen made us swear not to tell, and Susan would kill me if I did."

"So Darleen took the time to swear you three girls to silence before she got off the bus to talk to Teddy?"

Carol looked confused by my question, but nodded finally. "Yeah, I guess. She didn't want Joey to find out because he was so crazy jealous."

"I thought you said she was over Joey."

"Well, yeah, she was. But he was still in the picture. You know, when Darleen had nothing else going on, there was always Joey."

"Joey had quite a different idea about their relationship. He said they were going to run away together to get married."

Carol shrugged and turned back to her sundae. She stirred the ice cream and hot fudge absently. The spoon clinked against the bowl, and there was another tinkling as well. A charm bracelet on her wrist.

"Nice sweater you've got there, Carol," I said. "And you've changed your hair, haven't you?"

"I guess."

"That's a swell charm bracelet, too. It looks new."

⌀

SATURDAY, JANUARY 14, 1961

The rain had moved on during the night and so had the unseasonably warm temperatures. By Saturday morning, we were back into the upper thirties, with sun and blue skies. I had retired late the night before, looking for any excuse to stay away from my apartment as long as possible. First, I drove Carol Liswenski home to the Town of Florida, but it wasn't yet eleven when I returned to Lincoln Avenue. I talked Fadge into joining me for a late-night pizza at Tedesco's. In truth, it didn't take much convincing, and the big lug insisted on picking up the bill. By the time we'd finished, it was after one, and the moment of truth was upon me. I had to go face the night alone in my place.

I didn't want Fadge to know what was bothering me. That would just worry him. But I had no intention of entering that apartment by myself at one thirty in the morning. I invited him up for a nightcap, but he begged off. He whined that he was tired and the pizza and beer weren't agreeing with him.

"Maybe next time don't eat so much," I lectured. "Come on up, and I'll give you a Bromo-Seltzer."

Thank God he agreed. I made sure to make as much noise as possible climbing the stairs, asking Fadge loud questions to alert anyone who might be inside that I was not alone. Fadge thought it strange that I went from room to room, switching on the lights and peering behind doors before I fetched him his Bromo-Seltzer, but it satisfied me that we were alone.

"Here you go," I said, handing him the fizzing glass.

Once he'd left, I barricaded the kitchen door with a dresser and left all the lights on before retiring for the night. Despite my fears, I managed to sleep for seven hours. It was a luxury to rise at almost ten, and one glance out the window proved that Fadge had done the same. The store was locked, "Closed" sign hanging in the window, and the newspaper bundles left on the stoop had already been opened and thinned by early patrons.

I took a second look out the window an hour later to see if Fadge had arrived. He hadn't but the *New Holland Republic* delivery truck was just pulling away from the curb, having left two bundles of papers on the stoop. That was odd, I thought, since the *Republic* was an evening paper.

I showered and dressed, still thinking about the special early edition. Surely Charlie would have told me about it. But then I remembered he'd left for Utica the previous afternoon for a weekend with his in-laws.

Fadge was just tying on his filthy apron when I walked in. He grunted good morning, and I reached for the *Republic* from the stand near the door.

"Good morning," he repeated.

"Sorry," I said, unfolding the paper to scan the headlines. "Good mor—"

I froze. There, in the upper right-hand corner of the front page was the headline: "Missing Girl No Runaway." And the byline read "George Walsh, senior reporter."

My heart sank, and no amount of sympathy from Fadge helped. I read it over and over again. Nearly verbatim, my story had been stolen by George Walsh yet again. I had forgotten having left it in my desk, and, especially while George was out of town, I hadn't been worried about a repeated theft. Now my story was gone, and the sheriff would be furious. Darleen's killer now knew what the authorities knew.

"He comes in here from time to time," said Fadge. "I'll make sure he gets something extra in his next sundae."

"Thanks," I said, staring at the special edition in disbelief. "You're a good friend, Fadge, but that won't help. Please, by all means, go ahead and do it. But it won't help."

∂⊃

I wasn't willing to let Georgie Porgie off the hook this time for stealing my work. It was Saturday, with a special edition already on the streets, so there was no one in the office except Luba when I stormed in, ready to make my *J'accuse* speech. My frustration mounted. Charlie Reese was out of town, George Walsh was basking in glory that was rightfully mine, Artie Short was probably counting beans somewhere, and the offices were empty. I rifled through George Walsh's desk drawers, hoping to find something I could use against him: my original story, perhaps, or pictures of him in ladies' lingerie. But there was nothing. I would have to be content with the hope that he'd visit Fiorello's very soon.

Then the City Desk phone rang. I didn't want to answer it, for fear of barking at the person on the other end. But Luba was there, looking at me with hands turned upward, as if to ask what her broken English couldn't: "Why don't you answer it?"

I picked up the phone.

"Is this the *Republic*?" came an excited voice over the line. I said it was. "You got to get someone over to Cranesville right away," the man said. "They just found a body stuck in the lock on the river."

CHAPTER SIXTEEN

I roared down Route 5, speeding toward Schenectady. To my right, the swollen Mohawk roiled and churned, a brown sludge coursing east, washing huge chunks of dislodged, melting ice down its throat. The river was running as high and fast as I'd ever seen it. I tried to outdrive it in my rush to reach Lock 10 at Cranesville.

Five county prowlers crouched on the side of the highway, just beside the railroad tracks and the huge, arching trestles that formed the lock and spanned the river. The gates were down, submerged into the rushing Mohawk, holding it back to the west, while releasing rockets of water out on the other side. The river was at least fifteen feet lower beyond the lock heading toward Schenectady. I marveled at the ferocity of the pitched battle between man and river, as if both had agreed to meet at this site to settle which would hold dominion over the Mohawk.

A big Packard Henney hearse sat behind the line of county cars facing the river, its back door swung open to the side, as the coroner, Fred Peruso, stood by with two uniformed crewmen and several county deputies. Bob Franklin, the police crime scene photographer, leaned against the hearse, his camera hanging from his hand. The Cranesville fire truck, a relic from the thirties, had made the quarter-mile trip across Route 5 from its station, ostensibly to put out any fires that might break out. Four volunteer firemen lounged about, smoking and chatting. Besides a couple of onlookers who had pulled off the highway to watch the scene, I was the only civilian present.

I called to Stan Pulaski, who was guarding the perimeter, and caught his attention. He waved for me to join him.

"The sheriff's over there," he said, indicating the concrete deck of the lock near the edge of the river. The water roared over the gate just a few yards below his feet. Frank Olney and a man in a brown overcoat and fedora talked and pointed as they examined alternately the west and then the east side of the lock.

"What's the scoop, Stan?" I asked, breathless, trying to see past him to the hearse.

"A state inspector came out here about an hour ago to check on the lock. To make sure it was working properly and not damaged by the fast water and ice. He found a little girl jammed in the gate. Stone cold dead."

"Oh, God," I choked. "Is it Darleen Hicks?"

Stan pursed his lips and nodded sadly. "That's what the sheriff thinks. No positive ID yet."

"Oh, God, oh, God," I found myself repeating, feeling as if I'd been kicked in the stomach. Although I'd known in my heart she was dead since we found the unused bus ticket, this news hit me harder than I'd expected. This was the confirmation, the finality, the end. The girl who'd helped me when I was sick in the bathroom, the one whose risks mirrored mine at her age, that one: she was dead, dashed and buffeted against the cold steel of a mechanical lock by a raging river. "That poor girl," I said, wiping the tears from my cheeks with my gloves.

"Take it easy, Ellie," said Stan, handing me a handkerchief. "Come on over here and have a seat in the car."

"No, I'm all right," I said, pushing past him. "I want to talk to Frank."

Stan tried to stop me, but Fred Peruso saw me and signaled it was okay. I reached him, and we stepped away from the others to speak privately.

"You always seem to appear when a body turns up," said Fred, puffing on his pipe.

"I've been following this one," I said. "I was at the paper when someone called with the tip. What can you tell me?"

"Looks like it's the Hicks girl. Adolescent female, between thirteen and sixteen, I'd say."

"Braces on her teeth?" I asked.

Fred nodded solemnly.

"Can I have a look at the body?"

"You don't want to see it. Trust me. This isn't like Jordan Shaw," he said. "She was badly beaten up by the water. It's not a pretty sight."

I looked over Fred's shoulder to the hearse, its back door still open, but the contents dark and invisible from my position.

"The body is remarkably well preserved," he continued. "That tells me she's been in the river since shortly after she died. Very little decomposition. Temperatures under forty degrees prevent most decay for extended periods. Imagine meat in your refrigerator. This is about the same thing."

"But the weather's been so warm," I said, still trying to see inside the hearse.

"The river was frozen over until a couple of days ago. She was surely trapped in the cold water near the bottom for three or four weeks. Then when the ice began to melt and move, the fast currents must have dislodged her and carried her here."

"Unless she was here all along," came a voice behind us. Frank Olney. "Ellie," he nodded to me.

"How do you mean, she was here all along?" asked Peruso.

"Just that," said Frank, looking back west past the lock. "The most logical conclusion is that whoever killed her dumped her in the river somewhere back there. Not too far, I'd say."

"Why's that?" I asked.

"Remember I asked you to keep that information about the bus ticket quiet?"

I frowned. "Yes. Too bad you didn't ask the same of George Walsh."

"What do you mean?" asked Frank.

"Georgie Porgie stole my story and printed it. There's a special edition of the *Republic* this morning. Front page."

Frank swore.

"What's the difference now anyway?" I said. "Tomorrow the whole world will know Darleen Hicks was pulled out of the river dead. No need to keep it quiet anymore."

I stewed, while Fred Peruso packed his pipe with tobacco and lit it. The sheriff glowered at the ground, then the river, then me.

"What makes you so sure the body went into the river near here?" asked Peruso, breaking the silence.

"Like I was saying," began Frank. "I asked Ellie not to print some information that made it clear Darleen Hicks never left town when she disappeared. We found her bus ticket in her school locker. Unused."

Peruso nodded.

"Well, I didn't want her to print the story and tip our hand to whoever killed her."

"What did you hope to gain by that?" asked the doctor.

"You never know," said Frank. "Maybe nothing at all. But sometimes the killer will do something to reveal himself. No need to arm him with everything we know."

"So, again," pushed Peruso. "What makes you think Darleen Hicks went into the river here and not upstream somewhere?"

Frank turned and pointed to the hills to the north, just on the other side of Route 5.

"The guy I've had my eye on just so happens to live three hundred yards over there."

"Ted Russell?" I asked, nearly gasping. The proximity was indeed compelling. I'd been in such a rush to reach the scene, I hadn't even thought that Ted Russell's house was so close. If not for the thick trees on the hill, it would have been clearly visible from our position near the river.

Frank nodded. "We're looking for him right now. He wasn't home when we went visiting a while back. We'll get him."

"So how do you think he did it?" I asked. "Just dumped the body in the river three and a half weeks ago?"

"Maybe. Or maybe more recently than that. We found her lunch box and gloves in the snow hills out near her house in the Town of Florida. I think he buried her there, then went back to dig her out later on."

I considered Frank's scenario. It seemed solid. The presence of the lunch box and the gloves in the snow hills, together with Walt Rasmussen's sighting of Darleen around four p.m. on Route 5S on December 21, proved that she had been alive in the vicinity of her home that afternoon. The sheriff's theory that she'd been buried for some time also made sense. And it would explain the preservation of the body after twenty-four days. It was impossible to say how long the body might have been in the snow, but even if it had only been for a day or two, Fred Peruso said that interment in a snow bank would retard decomposition just as well as three weeks at the bottom of the river. Probably better.

In addition to this physical evidence, the sheriff had a handwritten love letter signed "Ted," as well as a note signed with the same name discovered in Darleen's lunch box. I hadn't actually seen the latter, but Frank had described it well enough. Of course, I was convinced Ted Jurczyk had written those, but what if I was wrong? Standing on the banks of the raging Mohawk River, I had to concur with the sheriff. Things looked mighty bad for Ted Russell, dreamy music teacher, unprincipled Lothario, and seducer of little and not-so-little girls. That wasn't exactly fair; Ted Russell hadn't seduced me. I had known exactly what I was doing and could blame no one but myself for my poor judgment. I kicked myself—figuratively—yet again for having been so foolish. Why had I gone back to his place that night?

"Ellie, are you all right?" asked Frank, rousing me from my nightmares.

Before leaving the scene, I begged Fred Peruso to let me have a look at the body, but he refused. He finally agreed to meet with me after the autopsy at New Holland City Hospital Sunday morning.

"It's not for kicks that I want to see her, Fred," I said one last time. "It's something very personal. Please."

"Think it over," he said. "If you still want to see her tomorrow, we'll talk. But take my advice: You'll regret it if you do."

Frank Olney called his men together to dispense final marching orders. It was after four, and the light was falling fast. The hearse drove off with the body in the back, and I watched it disappear down Route 5, heading to New Holland. The wind was whipping cold from the west just as another county cruiser skidded to a stop on the shoulder of the road. Pat Halvey jumped out and ran to deliver an urgent message to Frank. I was just a few feet away.

"Sheriff," he called, his breath puffing in the cold air. "I just heard that Joey Figlio attacked Ted Russell in the casual wear department of Mertens. He stabbed him in the neck with a knife."

"Holy hell," said Frank. "Where's Russell now?"

"St. Joseph's Hospital."

"What about Figlio?"

Pat shook his head.

"Don't tell me he got away again."

"City police said he ran down Mohawk Place and disappeared over the railroad tracks by the river. They haven't found him."

The sheriff dispatched a car with two men to the hospital and ordered them to keep him apprised and to await instructions. Then he sent the rest of his deputies back to duty. Before he left, he sauntered over to talk to me.

"What's first on your agenda?" I asked, wearing my reporter's hat again.

He frowned and looked off into the distance. "I've got to go visit the Metzgers," he said. "That'll be a treat. I need one of them to ID the body."

"Can I come with you? To break the news, I mean."

"You actually *want* to do that?" he asked.

I shook my head. "Of course not. But I promised Irene Metzger I'd see this through to the end."

"Let me take a rain check on that," said Frank. "It wouldn't look right. You'll have to visit the family on your own."

"I understand."

"Ellie . . ." he began after a short pause. "About that story of yours."

"Never mind, Frank," I said. "You were right to ask me not to print it. It's not your fault that George Walsh is a thief."

His eyes expressed relief, even if he said nothing.

Long after the hearse had driven away with Darleen Hicks's remains inside, and long after Fred Peruso and the sheriff had closed shop and decamped, I sat at the wheel of my Dodge Royal Lancer, scribbling notes for my story. A little after five, I pulled away from the shoulder and gained speed traveling east toward Schenectady, looking for a spot to make a U-turn. A few hundred feet along, I turned onto Cranes Hollow Road—the scene of my disgrace with Ted Russell—and wheeled around toward New Holland. My headlamps lit up a square signpost that read, "Congregation of Israel Cemetery." It pointed off to the right. I veered up the narrow road that led to Ted Russell's house but pulled over well short of it, cut the motor, and stepped out into the cool night air.

The cemetery gate opened with a simple lift of the latch. Walking along the dark path, I could see large stone mausolea to my right with names like Gold, Lipshitz, and Stein. Smaller markers followed as I made my way through the tombs. Family plots: Alpert, Singer, Olender, Horowitz, and Levy. I stopped to read some inscriptions. I was struck by the short lifespans on the older stones. An unscientific study convinced me that fifty must have been a ripe old age for the previous generation. More families ensued: Dorfman, Gluck, Suskind, and Salmon. I needed to strike a match to read some of the names and the years. I wandered to the front of the cemetery, up to the black wrought-iron fence that bordered Route 5 and looked out on the Mohawk. I could see the dark shade of Lock 10 in the moonlight. It was time to go. I turned to head back, and I stumbled on the footpath. Steadying myself, I glanced down. There in the ground before me, a small rectangular marker read, "Stone." I fell to my knees and dissolved into tears.

I had my head start over George Walsh, but I doubted that would last for long. And even if I maintained my lead over him, what assurances did I have that he wouldn't steal my story when I was done? Besides George Walsh, I had the Capital District papers to worry about. The *Schenectady Gazette*, *Albany Times-Union*, and *Knickerbocker News* might well be muscling in on the story in time for their Sunday morning editions. I needed to shift into high gear.

My first stop took no small measure of courage: the New Holland Police Department. Just three days before, Chief Patrick Finn had been ready to slap me in irons on a trumped-up charge. I was about as confident of walking back out of the station as I was of winning Miss Montgomery County at the next 4-H fair. Despite my fears, I marched up to the duty sergeant and smiled. He didn't smile back.

"Eleonora Stone from the *New Holland Republic*," I announced to little effect. He didn't know who I was and didn't care. "I understand there was a stabbing at Mertens Men's Store a while ago. I was hoping to get a statement for the press."

"I just came on duty," he said. "Why don't you ask Iavarone. He makes it a habit to know everyone's business."

The name sounded familiar. Then I remembered him as Pat Halvey's bowling pal. The desk sergeant waved me past, and two minutes later I was in conference with Officer Paulie Iavarone in a small private room. Iavarone was a short, thin man, with a friendly face and a thick mop of dark hair slicked down with oil. His black uniform was pressed and creased, and his badge sparkled silver on his chest.

I repeated my name and affiliation for the officer's benefit then asked if he had any information on Ted Russell's condition or Joey Figlio's whereabouts.

"No, miss. The assailant eluded capture and is presently at large," said Iavarone in his most official tone. "I don't have any word on the victim's condition either. He's at St. Joseph's. They'll be able to provide you with that information."

"Can you tell me what happened?" I asked.

Officer Iavarone demurred politely, saying he wasn't sure if he was authorized to speak to the press.

"Chief Finn is having dinner with his family and doesn't like to be disturbed on Saturdays. He was annoyed enough as it was when we called about the fracas."

"Aren't you a friend of Pat Halvey's?" I asked, changing tactics. "He said you two bowl together and told me how much he admires your grip."

"My grip? There's three holes in the ball. Everyone has the same grip," he said. When engaged on the topic of bowling, his policespeak melted away.

"I mean your technique." Damn, I knew almost nothing about bowling. Why couldn't he have been a softball or tennis player? "Anyway, he said you were an ace."

Iavarone was taken aback for a moment, then a mushy grin spread slowly across his face. "Well, I did bowl a 167 last Saturday night."

"I understand it all happened at Mertens in the menswear section." I said.

"No," he answered, confused. "It was at Windmill Lanes."

"I meant the stabbing. Joey Figlio."

"Oh, right. Yeah. Well, casual wear, actually."

"He just jumped out and stabbed him?" I asked. "Did he say anything? *Sic semper tyrannis* or anything like that?"

"I don't know if he said anything in Spanish," said Iavarone guardedly. "But it looks like he followed Mr. Russell down Main Street into Mertens. Then he ambushed him in the casual wear department. Got him pretty good in the neck but missed the artery."

"Did Joey say anything at all that you know?"

"Well, I responded to the call at Mertens along with two other patrolmen. Mike Palumbo and Denny Kerry. The tailor saw everything and said the kid was swearing and yelling that he would kill the SOB if it was the last thing he did."

Mike Palumbo. So that was his first name. I still thought of him as Vic Mature.

"Anything else?" I asked.

"He said, 'She will always be mine!' Then he ran out into the alley and disappeared down Mohawk Place."

"Can't anyone catch that kid?" I asked. "He's slipperier than an eel."

"When we find him, we'll book him for assault with a deadly weapon and attempted murder. Of course he is a minor, so he'll probably just get sent back to Fulton."

I agreed. "Yeah, he's got a good lawyer."

On the station's front stairs, I bumped into the handsome Officer

Mike Palumbo. He tipped his hat and told me he was just going out after his dinner break. I asked if he'd heard anything new about Joey Figlio.

"No, miss. Nothing yet."

"To tell you the truth, Officer, I'm worried he'll come after me. I think that might have been him the other night at my place."

"I'm on duty until midnight," he said. "I'll circle your block every hour like last time, if you'd like."

"I'd appreciate that," I said, my eyes surely sparkling at him; he was blushing. "I'll leave my front lights on if everything is fine. If there's trouble, the room will be dark."

"All right," he said, smiling. "If I don't see the light, I'll come up those stairs with guns blazing."

I chuckled and wondered if he'd be annoyed or pleased if I turned off the lights for no reason ... Put a stopper in it, Eleonora. I took a quick breath of cool evening air and skipped down the steps to the street.

I returned to the office to write stories on the discovery of the body and the attack on Ted Russell. I still needed official confirmation of the ID of the body from the sheriff's office, but I expected to have that before the evening was out.

Of the three rolls of film I'd shot at the lock, I recalled several shots that would do nicely for the front page: the brown water roaring over the spillway, the sheriff consulting with the State engineer, and the tragic open door of the Packard Henney hearse. My only concern was whether I had used the correct shutter speed and aperture settings in the falling light. I left the film for Bobby Thompson to develop on Monday morning. Then I tucked my article into an envelope and slid it into my purse to take with me when I left the office. George Walsh wasn't getting his mitts on this story.

I called St. Joseph's Hospital before writing my Ted Russell-Joey Figlio piece, thinking that the lustful music teacher's condition might well change my headline from "Manhunt for Vengeful Teen Who Stabbed Teacher" to "Manhunt for Vengeful Teen Who Stabbed Teacher to Death." I spoke to Sam Belson, an emergency room doctor I knew casually from previous scrapes and bruises. Sam confirmed that Ted Russell's wounds were quite superficial and had been repaired with a pair of stitches, after which two sheriff's deputies trundled him off to the county jail on suspicion of murder.

I telephoned the DA for comment, but his service said he was unreachable. The sheriff was next on my list. He answered the phone at the jail and told me Don Czerulniak was sitting in front of him at that very moment.

"The mother ID'd the body," he said. "No surprise, except that she flat out fell apart. Wept for an hour until she'd exhausted herself. Real sad scene."

I felt a knot tighten in my chest and a mounting pressure in my throat that took my voice away. I struggled to draw a breath and dabbed my eyes with my handkerchief. Irene Metzger's self-possessed calm had crumbled with the presentation of her little girl's dead body, mangled and torn, having been battered against the cold steel of a canal lock by the roaring waters of the Mohawk. The unspeakable hope she'd expressed to me—to recover her daughter for a proper burial—had sustained her in her quest until this moment. Now her work was done. She no longer needed to be strong. Now she, too, could weep and abandon herself to her unfathomable grief. Darleen was gone, but she was home again. Irene Metzger's motherly charge to safeguard her child was over. For good.

"Ellie, are you still there?" asked Frank from the other end of the line.

"I can't talk now," I choked and dropped the receiver into its cradle.

Later, having splashed water on my face and stared at my wan reflection in the ladies' room mirror long enough to rebuild my composure, I returned to my desk and finished my article. I had no photographs to illustrate the Joey Figlio-Ted Russell story, but I thought we probably had a picture of Russell in the school-district photo file. I left a note for Maggie in Research to dig one up.

As I was hurrying out, I stopped at George Walsh's desk, the emotional hangover from my breakdown still tingling in my head. I considered the order. Everything in its place. A pad of ruled paper, three number 2 Ticonderoga pencils, a rotary sharpener (emptied daily of its shavings by its master) screwed down to the edge of the desk, and a fancy IBM Executive Typewriter on top of the green blotter. I eyed the cloth cover and its smug little IBM logo, comparing it to my sturdy, serviceable Underwood manual machine. Tucked neatly around the sleek lines of the IBM, the gray cover mocked me silently.

George Walsh was a pitiful typist. Shortsighted and lacking hand-eye coordination, he had to lean in so close to the keyboard that the swinging type bars practically clipped his nose as he typed. He had never memorized the arrangement of the keys, so he couldn't touch-type. Georgie Porgie was the classic hunter and pecker, a two-finger man, slow and methodical.

I cast a glance behind me to see if Luba was on the prowl. She had the habit of materializing out of nowhere like a ghost and scaring the wits out of you. It didn't help matters that her hair was a wiry, gray rat's nest and that her chin nearly reached the tip of her nose, giving her an eerie resemblance to a caricature of a witch. Having spotted no Lubas in the vicinity, I peeled the cover off the typewriter and retrieved a nail file from my purse, ready to operate. Placing the point of the file under the edge of the *W* key, I pried the plastic key top off with little trouble. I did the same to the *E* key. Then I pushed the *E* down onto the *W*'s type lever until it clicked smartly into place and put the *W* where *E* should have been. Then I did the same with three more pairs of keys. With his nose so close to the grindstone, George might well type an entire page before realizing he'd written gibberish. Then he would surely try again with the same results. It would take him an hour to figure it out.

I realized that my sabotage would only be temporary, but it served as a tonic for my frustration. I had toiled and sweated and frozen for the story that Georgie Porgie stole from my desk. If he wanted another scoop, he'd have to write it himself and learn to type all over again.

Satisfied with my work, I replaced the cover carefully, smoothed its wrinkles, and made good my escape undetected.

After my meltdown, I had to visit the sheriff without delay or never be able to show my face there again. I walked in, clearheaded and composed, as if nothing had happened, to speak to him and the district attorney.

"The jailbird herself," said the DA.

"Thanks for getting me out, Don," I said.

"Yeah, those morals charges are tough to beat."

Frank didn't appreciate that kind of humor in general. In particular, when it involved me, it seemed to pain him.

"Any word on Baby Face Nelson?" I asked.

Frank shook his head. "Last seen downtown, heading toward the river. If he fell in, he's a goner."

"What'll happen when you find him?"

Frank smirked and nodded in the DA's direction. "I'll let the honorable district attorney break it to you."

The Thin Man took a long, slow breath, then groaned in his typical manner. "The kid's got to go back to Fulton," he said. "Nothing we can do about it. He's a minor."

"Can't you forget where you set him down until he's eighteen?" I asked. "I'm afraid of that kid."

"He won't bother you," said Don. "He's got bigger worries now."

I shook my head in disagreement. "Joey Figlio has exactly one worry: how to kill Ted Russell. Now that it's certain that Darleen is dead, he has nothing else to live for."

"Well, I've got Ted Russell now, and Joey Figlio ain't getting near him," said the sheriff.

"How about me?" I asked, aiming my best smile at him. "Can I get near him?"

Frank wasn't keen on the idea.

"What about his lawyer?" I asked. "Who's representing him?"

"Public defender," said Don. "Some kid who just passed the bar. But I called the superintendent and the teacher's union and told them to get on their horse and hire him a real lawyer."

"How magnanimous of you," I said. "Itching for a fair fight?"

"Not really," said the DA. "If I think a guy's guilty, I don't care if he's got a trained monkey for counsel. In fact, I prefer it. But I'm not convinced yet. There's some circumstantial evidence, but this doesn't look open and shut to me."

"It does to me," said Frank. "I got the girl's dead body not four hundred yards from the guy's house, plus a signed love letter and another handwritten note from him to the victim."

"But why did he kill her?" I asked. "What was his motive?"

"I got a theory," he said, and the DA and I waited for it. "She was planning to run off with another guy—that Wilbur Burch out in Arizona. Russell didn't like the idea. Maybe he couldn't stomach losing her."

I exchanged a glance with the DA. "Seems pretty thin to me," said Don to the sheriff. "But we'll go slow on this and see. Maybe he'll say something stupid to Ellie."

I had one more nit to pick with the sheriff.

"Have you checked Ted Russell's handwriting against the love letter and the note you found in the lunch box?" I asked.

"Yes, I have," said Frank. "And they match. Both letters were written by the same hand."

"No, I meant did you check them against a writing sample from Ted Russell?"

"Not yet," he said. "But what are you driving at anyway? You don't think he wrote those?"

I shook my head. "I'm positive he didn't."

"Then who did?"

"You're not going to like it," I said. "And neither will the adoring public."

"Just tell me who you think wrote those letters to Darleen."

"Teddy Jurczyk."

"Holy hell," said Frank, sitting up straight in his seat. The DA whistled through his teeth. "Are you saying that an All-American, straight-A, basketball hero murdered Darleen Hicks?"

"Of course not. But I believe he wrote the notes. According to Irene Metzger, he's been in love with Darleen for years."

"But the letter and the note were signed 'Ted,' not 'Teddy,'" said Don.

"He told me he hates the name Teddy," I said. "So he wouldn't have signed the letters that way."

Frank consulted a page from the open file on his desk, picked up the phone, and dialed. After a couple of rings, he asked for Leonard Platt, Ted Russell's attorney.

"This is Sheriff Olney," he said once he'd reached his party. "I'd like you to come over to the jail, if you don't mind." The man at the other end of the line said something, and Frank explained. "I need a handwriting sample from your client, and I want the whole thing to be done above board." Another pause. "Well, I understand it's Saturday, Mr. Platt, but I think this is a reasonable request." Frank waited some more, frowned, then tried again. "*Gunsmoke* isn't on till ten. You'll be home long before that." Another pause. "Don't tell me you're watching Lawrence Welk." He listened a bit more then lost his temper. "Of course you're not getting paid enough to come over on a Saturday night. You're a public servant, you jackass. Just forget it. We've already impounded his car. We'll check the briefcase he had inside. Good night, counselor," and he slammed down the receiver.

At times like these, I truly admired Frank Olney.

"What?" he asked, noticing my adoring stare. "The guy deserves a better lawyer than that."

"So do I get to talk to Ted Russell or not?"

I met the prisoner in a room reserved for interrogations and meetings with counsel. He entered the room in a gray county jail shirt and trousers. No stripes, but "Montgomery County Jail" was stenciled across the front and back of the oversized shirt. His hands were shackled before him. A precaution to protect me, I figured, just in case he really was a murderer. He was also sporting a large, white bandage on the right side of his neck. He looked scared.

"How are you, Ted?" I asked once he'd sat down.

He shrugged and said he was okay. "I agreed to meet with you, Ellie, because I want you to tell the world I'm innocent. I want you to print a story about me in the paper right away explaining that I did not kill Darleen Hicks."

"How about you convince me first?" I said.

"I just can't believe this is happening. It's all one giant mistake."

"How well did you really know Darleen Hicks?" I asked. "Is it true that you wrote her love letters and notes to arrange secret meetings after school and on the weekends?" Of course, I knew he hadn't, but I wanted to get him talking.

"What? No! Never. I swear to you that I only knew that girl because she was in my music class. I never wrote her any notes or letters." His eyes blurred just a touch with his last pronouncement, as if he'd just remembered something significant.

"This is the time to tell me everything, Ted," I said. "If you want me to make your case, I have to believe you. Even if it looks bad, tell me now. It will only look worse later when it comes out." I paused. "And it will come out."

"There was nothing," he said. "Yes, I wrote one note to her, but it was perfectly innocent. I even signed it 'Mr. Russell.'"

"What was in the note?"

Ted chewed on my question for a good while, squirming in his seat and taking several long, deep breaths. I waited. I don't like to fill dead air when I'm interviewing a subject. Eventually, people start talking, and if the hole in the conversation is large enough, they try to fill it.

"It sounds bad, but it really was innocent, I swear," he said finally. "Look, she'd asked me to do her a favor, and the note I wrote to her was to tell her that I would do it."

I stared deep into his eyes, almost gazing, not judging, but blank, inviting him to go on. He was sweating.

"She asked me for money," he blurted out. "I said no, of course. At first. Then she said it was important and she really needed it."

"How much money did she want?" I asked, feeling the impasse had been broken.

"Oh, she wanted a bundle," he said, chuckling nervously. "She asked me for a hundred dollars. I don't have that kind of money. I'm just a high-school music teacher."

"But you relented and gave it to her?" I asked, thinking of the ninety-seven dollars the sheriff and I had found in Darleen's locker.

"Not a hundred dollars, I didn't," he said with as much indignation as he could summon. "I gave her twenty dollars, and that was all I could spare."

"What did she say the money was for?"

"She didn't."

Again the look in his eye. I waited and gazed.

"Okay, she told me."

"So what did she say the money was for?"

Ted looked down at his hands, turning them over, buying time or steeling his nerve. He couldn't look at me when he said it. And I shook when he did.

"She said she needed the money for an abortion," he said softly.

I wrestled with that word. Probably harder than Ted Russell had struggled just to say it. A rush of memories buried deep and far almost took my breath away. I didn't want Ted to see my reaction, but I was too stunned to do anything to conceal it. Enough surprises from this girl, I thought. Our meeting in the high-school girls' room during a basketball game; my bottle of whiskey in her locker; the risks chanced; and now this. Darleen Hicks had crawled under my skin or at least wormed her way into my mind. There was something obsessive and compelling in her behavior, and too much of it dovetailed with my own life. This was nothing akin to my reaction to Jordan Shaw's murder. I had felt sympathy for her, a connection of sorts, too. But it was cursory, perhaps even wished for by me. Darleen Hicks was different. Of course I felt sadness for Darleen, who had treated me kindly even while stealing my bottle of Scotch. But I felt more for her mother. And somewhere deep inside me, I felt remorse and bitterness and sorrow for myself. I couldn't explain it without an overly simplistic solipsism that Darleen was me. The dead me.

I chased away the thoughts of my own abortion at the age of sixteen, the event that battered and choked my relationship with my father until the last breath of his life. Enough, I thought. That rotten corner of my memory had festered too long. It was over, and I wanted to get over it. I was going to get over it, put it behind me once and for all. Just as soon as I finished with Darleen Hicks. Just one more reason to solve the case and feel sorrow for a murdered girl, instead of for myself.

"Why would she ask you for money?" I resumed. Ted Russell was still looking at his hands. "It makes me suspicious that she went to you, almost as if you had a stake in the situation."

"It's not true, Ellie. I never laid a hand on that girl, never even smiled at her. And I wasn't the only one she asked."

"Then why did you agree to give her anything at all, even if it was only twenty dollars."

"Because she threatened to say the baby was mine. I'd be ruined, don't you see?"

Ted Russell stood up from his chair and paced the room, wringing his shackled hands as he went. I watched him carefully. He was frightened and desperate.

"Let's change course," I said. "You know Darleen's body was found a quarter mile from your house. That looks very bad to the sheriff and the district attorney. They think you might have dumped her body in the river when the thaw started, or maybe even before, when the river was frozen."

"That's baloney," he said, stopping his pacing to point his two hands at me in an attempt to emphasize his point. "There are signs posted along the river to the west of the locks. Do you know what they say? 'Danger. Thin ice.' The river was running down the middle of the channel even at the height of the freeze. I couldn't have walked out there and thrown her body in. I would have broken through the ice."

I raised an eyebrow and nodded. He had a good point. "But you could have climbed up on the concrete pier at the river's edge and tossed her in."

He thought for a second, tried to rearrange some facts in his head, then gave up in frustration.

Now it was my turn to rearrange some facts. If Ted Russell had dragged the dead girl up onto the pier to dispose of her body, why would he throw her in on the west side? Even with the gates up, she would still have to pass through the lock and risk getting snagged on some piece of metal. Why not just dump her on the opposite side, past the lock altogether, and send her floating off toward Scotia to the east?

I didn't mention this defense to Ted Russell.

"You said Darleen asked someone else for money, too. Can you tell me who?"

He looked terrified and shook his head violently. "No. Besides, it wasn't his fault she asked him. He was a victim just like me."

"Do you know if he gave her any money?"

"No. At least, I don't believe so."

I stood up and approached him on the other side of the table. "Who was it, Ted?"

He shook his head.

"I can't help you, Ted," I said. "You just keep lying. I can't be sure anything you've told me is true."

"I've told you the truth," he said.

I was inclined to believe his story. He was convincing in his denials and, let's face it, for my own selfish reasons, I was hoping against hope that he hadn't bedded or murdered Darleen Hicks. I had, after all, spent an ill-advised evening with him. Well, a small fraction of an evening to be precise, but that somehow made the shame worse.

"I just can't tell you his name, Ellie," he said. "Don't ask me to do that. He's a friend."

I gathered my things and told him it could mean that he'd rot in jail. That hit home. He actually started to cry.

"Is there anything you can tell me, Ted? Anything that might prove your innocence?"

He sobbed then composed himself. "Louis Brossard."

"What's that?" I asked, startled and not sure I'd heard correctly.

"Brossard," he repeated. "Darleen asked him for money, too."

⁂

When I returned to Frank's office upstairs, he and the DA were poring over some papers they'd retrieved from Ted Russell's car. They compared several to a scrap of crumpled paper that looked like the one Frank had read out to me that afternoon in the snow hills, the day the kids discovered Darleen's lunch box in the melting snow.

"Well, what's the verdict?" I asked.

Frank shook his head, and the DA took a seat. "Different hand," said the sheriff. "Ted Russell didn't write those notes to Darleen."

CHAPTER SEVENTEEN

I left the county jail at nine forty-five, convinced that Ted Russell was probably innocent of Darleen Hicks's murder. He clearly hadn't written any love notes to her. At least not any that had been found. And by my own logic, he wouldn't have been so foolish to dump the body into the river on the wrong side of the lock.

And what about the Louis Brossard revelation? Did that make him a suspect? More of a suspect than Ted Russell, who'd actually been accused of improper behavior with the underage girl? Brossard certainly knew the victim; he'd carried out the investigation, interviewed both subjects, and delivered the verdict. But other than that, I knew of no other contact with Darleen Hicks. He seemed to have an alibi for part of the evening of the murder. He'd been at the superintendent's Christmas banquet at Isobel's Restaurant on Division Street on the West End from seven till after ten. Still, he couldn't account for a large block of time, and I would have to ask him about that.

Sorting out these details in my head cleared room for more ideas. When I spotted a telephone booth on the side of Route 40, near the shopping center north of town, I hit the brakes, slowed to a stop, and climbed out to make a call.

I thumbed through the weathered phone directory chained to the shelf inside the booth, finding Brossard, L. at VIctor 2-1650 at the Northampton Court Apartments. I dropped a dime into the slot and dialed the number. Brossard answered after two rings.

"Mr. Brossard, this is Ellie Stone from the newspaper. I'm sorry to interrupt your evening, but I need to ask you a few questions."

"Questions? What about?"

"Darleen Hicks."

"Can't this wait until Monday? It's nearly ten on a Saturday night."

"I know, and I apologize, sir. It's urgent and will only take a few minutes."

He grumbled some more before finally agreeing.

"You may have heard that Darleen's body was found in the river this afternoon," I began.

"My God, no," he said. "She's dead? Where?"

"Her body was found at the Cranesville lock. She was caught in the dam gate."

Silence down the line. I waited for him to compose himself and find something to say or ask.

"I'm shocked," he said finally. "I was convinced that she'd run away. This is terrible, terrible news."

"Have you been following the story in the paper?" I asked.

"Of course. That's why I was sure she was alive."

"Then I guess you didn't see the front page of the *Republic* this morning. There was a big story about Darleen's bus ticket."

"No, I didn't see the paper today," he said. "The paperboy must have missed my house. What did it say?"

"That the bus ticket was found unused," I told him. "Actually, it was found a while ago in Darleen's locker. Last Monday."

Now the silence was electric. Perhaps he was doing the math in his head. Or maybe he was simply trying to make sense of the discovery.

"Are you still there?" I asked.

"Yes," he said. "Last Monday? Wasn't Monday the day you and the sheriff searched the girl's locker?" I said that it was. "Then why didn't you or the sheriff mention it? You've known about it for nearly a week, and only now you report it?"

"The sheriff asked me to hold off on the story. He thought Darleen's killer might benefit from knowing what he knew."

"So, does the sheriff have any suspects?"

"Just one. Ted Russell. He's under arrest for suspicion of murder."

"Ted? Oh, God, no. This is even worse. Why does he suspect him?"

"Well, there was that mess about improprieties with Darleen Hicks," I said. "That didn't look good for him."

"But he was completely innocent of that. Even the girl said so."

"Perhaps," I said. "And, of course, the body turned up right in front of his house."

"That must be a coincidence," insisted Brossard. "Ted is a good man. I can't believe he's capable of such an abomination. I must pray for him."

"It might be a coincidence, but there's one more thing."

"What's that?"

"He admitted that he gave Darleen money."

A short pause from Brossard. "Well, that doesn't prove anything. Maybe she needed lunch money."

"She asked him for a hundred dollars."

"He gave her a hundred dollars?" asked Brossard, alarmed.

"No, but he did give her money. More than lunch money." I paused. "It seems Darleen was trying to accumulate a certain sum. Do you know if she asked anyone else for money?"

"Of course not," he huffed. "What did she want the money for anyway?"

"She told Ted Russell that it was for an abortion," I said.

"My God," groaned Brossard. "I can't believe it. Abortion is a sin, Miss Stone. A cardinal sin. Are you telling me that a fourteen-year-old girl was pregnant and considering an abortion?"

"Fifteen," I said. "And, yes."

He seemed genuinely distressed. I could almost hear the rosary beads clicking in his hand as he recited one *Ave Maria* after another. My interview wasn't going anywhere fast. He'd missed his chance to admit that Darleen had asked him for money.

"Mr. Brossard," I said at length. "Did Darleen Hicks ever ask *you* for money?"

"Of course not," he said. "Do you think I would have anything to do with a wretched abortion? Do you think I would risk my soul for a girl in braces? For anything in the world?"

"I really don't know," I said.

"That's enough for one night," he said curtly. "Good night, Miss Stone."

I replaced the receiver and fished for some more change in my purse. In my time in New Holland, I had built up a fair list of contacts and phone numbers. Fred Peruso, county coroner, was one of them. I slipped another dime into the slot and dialed his number, reading it from my address book in the pale light of the phone booth.

"Sorry to bother you at this hour, Fred," I said once I'd identified myself. "I know it's late."

"It's only ten," he said. "I was just having a drink and a cigar. What do you take me for? Your grandmother?"

"Okay, sorry to interrupt your post-prandial indulgences," I said. "Listen, I need you to check for something in the autopsy tomorrow."

There was a pause down the line. "Really? Like what?"

"I think Darleen Hicks was pregnant. Can you check for that?"

Fred laughed. "That's pretty routine," he said. "I thought you were going to ask me to look for something I might miss, like a bullet hole in her head or a knife wound in her chest."

I blushed. Was a pregnancy obvious to see in a postmortem? But I didn't have time to be embarrassed about my ignorance. I just thanked him and made a date to meet him at the hospital the following morning at eleven.

"Say, what makes you think a fifteen-year-old girl was pregnant?" he asked before I could hang up.

"Just covering the bases," I said.

❧

It was a little past ten when I arrived home. The street was filled with loitering teens, and Fiorello's was jammed as usual on a Saturday night. I headed straight upstairs to jot down some notes that had occurred to me in the car. After that, I made a sandwich under the broiler: baked beans from a half-empty can with a slice of cheese on top. I burned it a little black, but I like it that way. I added a pickle and a couple of gin-soaked olives that I kept in a jar in the icebox. I liked the taste of olives and gin, but didn't trust myself drinking Martinis anymore; one too many mornings with no recollection of the night before. My gentlemanly Dewar's has never taken advantage of me that way.

I carried my dinner into the parlor, kicked off my heels, and sank into the sofa. I switched on the television in time to see the sign-off of the fights, and bowling was up next. Not interested in that. No wonder I hadn't been able to snow Paulie Iavarone earlier in the day.

I switched off the set and put on some music instead. I was in the mood for Brahms and put on his second piano concerto, enjoyed my burnt remains and olives, and rinsed it all down with a glass of whiskey.

I got up to pour a second drink then remembered I needed to wash some underthings in the bathroom sink if I wanted to dress fully come morning. Five minutes later, I retrieved my drink from the kitchen table, uttered a brief scream, and dropped my glass, which bounced and pitched its contents across the room, but somehow didn't shatter. There before me, looking cold, miserable, and starving, stood Joey Figlio. He was breathing hard, staring daggers into my eyes, and holding one in his hand. Or quite nearly. While I was otherwise occupied in the bathroom washing my unmentionables, he had broken in and armed himself with one of my longer carving knives.

"What are you doing here?" I demanded. "Get out now."

"I can't go," he said, and wiped his nose with the back of his hand. "The cops are looking for me. Almost caught me this afternoon."

"Too bad they didn't shoot you."

"I need a place to sleep tonight. I'll stay here."

"You will not stay here," I said.

"Can you make me something to eat? I smell something good."

"You're not staying here. Get out."

"Is that liquor good? I want to try some," he said, pointing with the carving knife to the bottle of Dewar's on the table.

"It's very mild," I said, changing my tune. Was I too obvious? "Let me make you a drink."

I grabbed a tumbler and a couple of ice cubes from the freezer. Then I filled the glass to the brim with whiskey.

"I'm real hungry," he said, taking the glass from me. "Cook me something quick, will you?"

"Okay," I said. "I'll give you something to eat, and then you'll leave, right?"

Joey didn't answer. Still holding on to the knife, he pulled one of the chairs away from the table and positioned it for an optimal view of the stove. Clearly he didn't trust me. I pulled bacon and eggs and butter from the icebox, and Joey sat down. He took a sip of the whiskey and grimaced. Then noticing that I was watching him, he steeled himself and took a large gulp that nearly made him vomit. He coughed a bit but held it down. I lit the stove.

A few minutes later, the bacon was sizzling in the skillet, and Joey looked ready to nod off. He hadn't finished his drink, and I was afraid he had no intention of doing so. I asked if he minded if I poured myself a new one.

"I don't know how you can drink this stuff, but go ahead," he said. "And you should mop up the one you spilled, too."

I muttered under my breath, but ended up on my hands and knees with a sponge and rag, wiping up the whiskey. Once I'd finished, I poured myself a drink and cheered my guest.

"Bottoms up," I said, raising my glass and taking a long pull. Would he take the bait? He did, but only sipped this time.

"Tastes a little better now," he said. "The melting ice helps."

I put the eggs on to fry, thinking he would only last a couple more minutes. But somehow he was resisting the effects of fatigue and alcohol. A few minutes later, he was wide awake and coherent as he wolfed down the eggs and bacon I served him. Then he patted his stomach, yawned, and downed the rest of his drink. He didn't need to ask me for a refill.

"Let's sit in there," he said, grabbing his glass, and teetering a bit as he rose from the chair. "The couch looks comfortable."

"Sure," I said. "If you're intent on spending the night, I should get you a blanket."

Joey plopped himself down on the sofa, and I ducked into my bedroom for the blanket.

"Hey, where are you going?" he slurred. "Get back in here."

"Coming," I said and switched off the bedroom light. I tossed the blanket to him. "Here, in case you get cold."

"I'm going to kill him, you know," said Joey.

"I beg your pardon."

"Mr. Russell. I'm going to get him eventually. I just needed a better weapon. I've got that now," and he twitched the carving knife to show me.

"But why do you want to kill him?" I asked, willing him silently to take another gulp. I took one myself and shamelessly licked my lips to prompt him.

"He killed Darleen," said Joey.

"I don't believe he did. What reason would he have to do so? He barely knew her."

"Didn't Frankie give you that letter like I told him?"

"He did."

"So, that proves Mr. Russell was in love with her. And when she told him no, that she loved me and was going to run off with me, he murdered her."

"So you two were really planning on eloping?" I asked, marveling at how well this kid held his liquor.

"Of course. We were just trying to save up the money. Maybe a hundred dollars. Two hundred, and we'd have been all set. We were going to go to Florida."

"And you're sure she wanted to go with you?"

"What do you mean by that?" he said.

"Just that certain evidence has come to light. Darleen had a bus ticket for Arizona, you know."

Joey's doubt evaporated, and he smiled, showing his grayish teeth. "That was my idea," he said. "That clown Wilbur Burch was in love with Darleen, so I told her to ask him for money and a bus ticket."

"Your idea?" I asked.

"Yeah. He was going to send money and a bus ticket. She even got him to send the receipt with the ticket so we could exchange it for a refund. Then we were going to go to Florida." He laughed and took a drink.

"And did he ever send the money?"

Joey leaned forward and snatched a handful of cigarettes from a wooden box on the coffee table. He lit one and stuffed the rest into his breast pocket.

"He sure did," he said.

"And was she trying to get money elsewhere?" I asked.

Joey shrugged and took another sip of whiskey. "This is pretty good," he said. "Makes you a little sleepy, though."

I stood and offered to top off his drink. "More ice?"

"Yeah, sure," he said, holding out his glass.

I went to the kitchen, emptied the watery Scotch at the bottom of his glass, and refilled it to the top with only one ice cube.

"Did Darleen go to Mr. Russell for money?" I asked as I put his drink down on the table. He started. Damn, he'd been asleep and I'd roused him.

"Huh?" he asked.

"Did Darleen go to Mr. Russell for money?" I repeated.

He shook his head. "No. She wanted to after Wilbur was so easy to fool, but I told her I didn't want her to talk to him."

I kept quiet. It seemed Darleen made some decisions on her own. I still wasn't convinced that Darleen had any intention of running off with Joey. She had amassed a hundred dollars without even cashing in the bus ticket. And there was twenty dollars from Ted Russell that Joey didn't know about. And who knew if she'd stashed any other funds? I had my sus-

picions about how Carol Liswenski had managed to save enough money to
buy a new sweater, a charm bracelet, and a new hairstyle. Could it be that
she'd gotten the cash from Darleen? I'd tried to get that information out of
her the previous evening at Fiorello's, but she'd clammed up. And she had
lied to me about Susan Dobbs and her boyfriend at the basketball game.
Clearly Carol was on the outs with Susan and Linda, and I wondered if
it didn't have something to do with Darleen's money. I wanted another
chance to make her crack, but I had to get Joey Figlio to pass out before I
could even think about that.

"Anyway," I said, returning to the plan to elope, "two hundred dollars
is a lot of money, but not so much that you could live on it for very long."

"I was going to get a job," he said. "We were going to be on Easy Street.
Then Mr. Russell ruined everything."

"I happen to know for sure that he didn't write that letter, Joey," I said.
"They compared the handwriting to his, and they don't match."

Joey sat up in his seat and folded his black shoe beneath him on the
cushion. Now I'd need to send it to the dry cleaners, as I have a horror of
people putting their shoes on furniture.

"He signed his name," said Joey, and he took another swig of whiskey.

"No. It was someone else," reluctant to say more for fear of putting
Ted Jurczyk in Joey's sights. "Maybe someone wanted to cast doubt on Ted
Russell, so they signed his name."

Joey looked away in thought, searching through the wooly-headed-
ness of fatigue and strong drink, swaying in his seat, at the point of falling
over. Then he slumped backward into the sofa, and the knife fell from his
hand to the floor. I snatched it up before he could awaken.

Then there was a noise from the door. I rushed to the kitchen, still carrying the knife, and glanced at the clock on the stove. I wasn't sure if I had
adjusted the time since Daylight Savings ended the previous October. I
also didn't know if the clock was accurate anyway. I had removed my wristwatch to wash my underthings, and it was in the bathroom. Still, I knew
it must be close to midnight, which meant Officer Mike Palumbo, having
seen my signal, must be on the other side of the door.

I yanked open the door, realized my error immediately, and tried to
slam it shut. The man standing there in the semidarkness was not Officer
Palumbo, but someone I'd never seen before. He lunged forward and stuck
his foot into the doorframe, blocking my one chance to close him out, then

he put his shoulder to the door and forced his way in. I backed off, brandishing the carving knife I'd just taken from Joey. He saw it and kept his distance. A silent standoff ensued.

The man was about twenty, of average height and weight, with a crew cut, a scruffy, week-old beard, and a mad look in his eye. He hadn't bathed in at least a few days, and his hide was throwing off a ripe stench.

"Who are you?" I demanded.

"I'm looking for Joey Figlio," he said. "You can put down the knife. I don't mean you no harm."

"That doesn't answer my question," I said, refusing to sheathe my weapon.

"I'm Wilbur Burch," he said.

"What are you doing here?"

"I told you," he said, holding up his hands to indicate friendly intentions. "I'm looking for Joey Figlio. I've been following him since I seen him this afternoon downstreet. I followed him here."

"Why are you looking for Joey?"

"Because I got word Darleen was missing. So I lit out and hitchhiked across the country to find out what happened to her. And when I get here, I find out that she's dead. I want to get the guy who killed my Darleen."

"And you think Joey Figlio did it?"

He nodded. "He found out about Darleen and me, that I sent her a bus ticket, and she was coming to meet me in Arizona to get married. So he killed her."

"How do you know he found out about you two?" I asked, lowering the knife a touch.

"She wrote to me that we had to keep the whole thing secret because of him," he said. "That's why I had to buy the bus ticket and not her. She said it would be safer that way. Then I wired her a hundred dollars. It was every penny I could borrow on the base."

"Joey says Darleen was going to marry *him*," I said cautiously.

"I got the proof here," he said, reaching into his pocket and pulling out a well-traveled, wrinkled letter. "It says so right here in her own handwriting. She's coming to marry me, and she's through with Joey. See for yourself if you don't believe me."

He extended the letter to me. I took it from him, holding tight to the carving knife.

"I'm sorry I gave you a fright, miss," he said. "But you have nothing to worry about from me."

The letter indeed said everything Wilbur had claimed. It was dated November 2, 1960. Darleen instructed Wilbur to get the money and bus ticket as soon as possible. She also wrote that she knew how to get a fake ID, so there would be no reason they couldn't get married as soon as she arrived in Arizona. And she described how they had to keep it from Joey, or he would ruin everything. I was reading quickly, my eyes darting up and down, from the sheet of paper in my hand to the man I was holding at bay with my large knife. One line in particular caught my eye:

"He's crazy, you know. He said he'll kill me and put the blame on someone else if I try to leave him."

I stared at the letter, reading that line over and over, trying to decide if Darleen was playing Wilbur or Joey or both for the fool. Was it possible that she wasn't interested in either of them? That there was a third man in her life? Perhaps even Ted Russell? Why not, I thought. He was smarter by half than Joey and Wilbur put together. What if he and Darleen had cooked up the scheme to run off, and it was Joey Figlio who'd thrown a wrench in the works by killing her? Ted Russell certainly wouldn't admit to anything after Darleen's death. That could only attract suspicion to him. I was just thinking that my newfound doubts about Ted Russell were a long shot at best when Wilbur Burch snatched my arm and twisted it until I dropped the knife. It clattered on the floor, and Wilbur picked it up with his left hand then hit me hard across the face with a backhand from his right.

"You little tramp," he sneered. And he struck me again, this time knocking me to the floor and into the cupboard, loosing a loud thud and a clanging of pots and pans. In my pain I comforted myself with the certainty that Mrs. Giannetti would be running up the stairs at any moment to investigate. But then I wondered if I'd still be alive to see her arrive.

Wilbur grabbed me by my hair and lifted me back off the floor. "Pull a knife on me, will you?" he said through gritted teeth, his face up against mine, blowing his awful breath against my skin.

"Hey!" came a voice from behind us. "What the hell are you doing? Let go of her!"

Wilbur pushed me away and turned to Joey, standing in the doorway between kitchen and parlor.

"There you are," said Wilbur.

"Who are you?"

"I'm Wilbur Burch," he said, and Joey coughed a short laugh.

Wilbur took a step toward him. "You think it's funny? I'm here to kill you for what you did to Darleen."

Joey didn't flinch, didn't move, didn't do anything. Except to pull a small pistol from his coat pocket and aim it at Wilbur's chest. Despite my fear and the stinging of my cheeks, I couldn't help wondering why he hadn't used the gun before, to threaten me or to shoot Ted Russell. You wouldn't think these things would course through your head in such life-threatening moments, but they do.

And then there was a rumbling on the stairs. Joey looked at me, the gun still pointing at Wilbur, who was backing up slowly toward the door. I figured there were three possibilities: (1) Mrs. Giannetti. I doubted she would make so much noise, which left me with two other choices. (2) Fadge. He was so big and made such a racket when he came up the stairs, you would almost swear it was someone falling down instead. And (3) Officer Palumbo. He'd promised that if he saw my distress signal in the window, he would storm up the stairs with guns blazing.

I was wrong. The man who burst through my kitchen door was Dr. Arnold Dienst, huffing and sweating like a buffalo after a summer rampage across the plains.

"Grab him!" I screamed, pointing to Wilbur Burch, who chose Dienst's arrival as the moment to make good his escape. Dienst was certainly large enough to handle Wilbur, but he was slow, like a lummox, and watched him whiz by. I thanked my lucky stars that Joey hadn't fired the pistol, and then Wilbur tripped on the stairs and tumbled all the way down to the street, crashing through the glass storm door at the bottom. Chaos reigned. I heard Mrs. Giannetti screaming bloody murder downstairs, and then another set of footsteps mounted the stairs. Palumbo. Finally.

On the porch, a second cop handcuffed Wilbur Burch, who had knocked himself unconscious with his half gainer down a flight of stairs. Dr. Dienst tried to talk Palumbo into letting him take charge of Joey, but Vic Mature would hear none of it.

"What were you doing here, anyway?" the cop asked him.

"I've been trying to find Joseph for days," said Dienst. "I finally had a brainwave this evening, and I thought he just might try to bother Miss Stone again. It's not the first time, after all."

"Officer," I said, interrupting. "He's got a gun in his jacket," and I pointed to Joey, who offered it up sheepishly.

"It's not real," he said. "From wood shop. Plus some shoe polish."

Palumbo took it and turned it over and over in his hand, admiring the workmanship.

"This is amazing," he said in his deep baritone, positively aglow. "The best I've ever seen. You made this?"

"Yeah," said Joey, shrugging his shoulders.

Palumbo looked to Dr. Dienst, holding out the fake pistol.

"Now, Joseph," said Dienst, "if you applied yourself to other endeavors in the same manner, think what you might accomplish."

More police arrived, as well as half the neighborhood who'd seen the cherry tops spinning. Wilbur Burch came to and claimed I'd pushed him down the stairs. When asked what he had been doing in my apartment after midnight, he couldn't think of anything and asked for his lawyer instead. The police were willing to oblige him but soon discovered that Wilbur didn't have a lawyer or even a dime to phone one.

"At least you can sleep soundly now that we know who tried to break in the other night," said Palumbo.

"Was it you the other night, Joey?" I asked. He shook his head. "Dr. Dienst?"

"Certainly not, Miss Stone."

"Then it must have been Burch," said the cop.

I shivered. "No, I'm afraid not," I said. "Wilbur told me he got into town this afternoon."

"Then who was it?" asked Palumbo.

"I don't know."

"Now I bet you wish it was me," said Joey. "I always knew you had a thing for me."

Palumbo finished with the legalities and cuffed Joey. As he led him to the door, I reached out and touched Joey's hand. He stopped and looked at me, nothing in his dark eyes.

"Thank you, Joey," I said. "You were very brave."

He shrugged it off and said it was no big deal. "Thanks for the bacon and eggs," he said. "And the booze."

"You served him liquor?" asked Dr. Dienst. "And bacon?"

"Can you do me one favor, Ellie?" asked Joey.

"Of course. What?"

"Take a picture of me and print it in the paper. I've never been in the paper before, and I think it would be cool."

Palumbo had no objections. Dienst just stared. So I fetched my Leica from the other room, focused it on Joey and the arresting officer, Mike Palumbo, and clicked off five quick shots. Joey was pokerfaced in all of them. No expression on his lips or in his eyes. Perhaps a little sorrow, but nothing else.

Once he and Wilbur had been taken away to the station, Officer Palumbo came back upstairs and smiled apologetically.

"I got a call for a break-in on Prospect Street," he said. "Otherwise I would have been here earlier."

"All's well that ends well," I said.

"Are you okay?" he asked, squinting at my red cheeks.

I made a move to cover my face then blushed. "I'm fine. He just slapped me around a bit. Open hand."

"Only a very small man strikes a woman," he pronounced.

We stood in awkward silence for a moment. Then he asked if I might be free for dinner sometime.

I smiled. "Like when?"

He cleared his throat and coughed out an invitation for the following evening.

"Tomorrow night?" I asked. "Sunday?"

"Sunday and Monday are my days off," he said. "If you'd rather not, I understand."

"I've got to eat on Sundays too," I said. "Sure, I'd love to."

"I'll pick you up at eight."

SUNDAY, JANUARY 15, 1961

I read the Sunday papers over a hard roll and coffee in a booth at Fiorello's. The University of Georgia had been ordered to admit two Negro students. President-elect Kennedy was preparing for the upcoming inauguration, while President Eisenhower was packing his bags.

"How's your story coming along?" asked Fadge, who joined me in the booth during a lull in business.

"Things are heating up. I seem to have a target on my back."

"I heard about your exciting night from Mrs. Giannetti," said Fadge. "Sounds like you had every guy in town up in your apartment except me."

"We had a party," I said. "Joey Figlio and Wilbur Burch were going to fight to the death until the cops showed up."

"Who's Wilbur Burch?"

"Darleen Hicks's betrothed. He's AWOL from the army. Thinks Joey Figlio killed Darleen."

"What's Joey Figlio think?"

"He thinks the music teacher, Ted Russell, did it."

"And what does Ellie Stone think?"

I considered his question. Quite legitimate at this stage of my investigation. Who did I think killed Darleen Hicks? There was no dearth of potentials, from Darleen's own household to the neighbors to her various suitors. There was even the taxi driver, whom I had yet to locate. I couldn't eliminate anyone yet, even if I felt the odds were longer for some.

The man currently under arrest in the county jail, Ted Russell, was slippery enough in my mind to be the killer, but the appearance of the corpse so close to his house made him look either very guilty (and stupid) or incredibly unlucky. The Mohawk had been running west to east—presumably—for millennia. No matter where Darleen Hicks had been dumped into the river upstream, she would certainly have had to pass Lock 10 eventually. It was Ted Russell's bad luck that she got caught in the dam gate at Cranesville. He had admitted to giving Darleen money for an abortion. That confession wasn't going to win anyone's sympathy on a jury, even if he was innocent as he claimed. The stink of suspicion would cling to him for a long time.

Joey Figlio's single-minded sense of purpose was remarkable. It pointed to his innocence, at least in my mind. But who knew how a damaged mind might behave? He was certainly jealous enough to kill for Darleen. What I didn't know was whether he was jealous enough to kill Darleen herself. She had written to Wilbur, after all, that he had threatened to kill her if she left him for another. I was on the fence as to whether that letter was part of Darleen and Joey's plan to raise money for their escape. But I couldn't be sure either if Darleen had indeed intended to leave with Joey or use the money for some other unknown purpose. If that were the case, Joey might well have carried out the threat Darleen had described to Wilbur in her letter.

Louis Brossard. Just on the periphery of Darleen Hicks's world, he, nevertheless, had been involved up to his elbows in the investigation of the alleged impropriety between the schoolgirl and the music teacher. Furthermore, a girl had disappeared from the school where he'd worked in Hudson. And there was the question of whether Darleen had ever asked him for money, as Ted Russell maintained and Brossard denied. Unlike Ted Russell and Joey Figlio and her own stepfather Dick Metzger, there were no clues to point to Louis Brossard beyond his general creepiness and the suggestion that he had been approached by the victim for money. By all accounts, even if Darleen had asked him for money, he'd refused. And he had an alibi for December 21. He had been at the superintendent's Christmas banquet, and there was photographic evidence to prove it. I had found no other proof to clear any of the other men on my list. Finally, he just didn't seem interested in girls, at least if I qualified as suitable bait. I confess that I suspected young Ted Jurczyk was more his speed.

Bobby Karl? Strange enough and interested in Darleen in an unhealthy way, but I hadn't unearthed anything more to implicate him. He had no car or truck to transport the body from the Town of Florida to the river, where Darleen had ended up.

I had all but crossed Walt Rasmussen off my list. But he had admitted that he'd seen her just an hour or so before she was killed. I couldn't ignore the overwhelming evidence that Darleen had met her end near or in the snow hills at the end of her road. Her lunch box and gloves had both turned up in the search. That pointed most probably to a quick end between four thirty and five fifteen or so. Walt Rasmussen lived within five minutes of the putative murder scene.

Ted Jurczyk was the all-American boy. A basketball star and smart, polite kid. He seemed to be too sweet and good to be mixed up in any of this sordid affair. And yet he was the one who had lured Darleen off the bus the day she died. He was surely one of the very last people to have seen her alive. Could I cross him off my list?

Then came the two men I suspected most of all.

Gus Arnold, the surly, old bus driver. He had changed his story about Darleen's presence on his bus the day she disappeared. It seemed possible, even likely, that he had come across her along County Highway 58 as he finished his route. Furthermore, he had lied about having returned his bus to the depot, claiming he'd had a flat tire. Finally, and most damning, he had spent as much as an hour parked behind the snow hills, not far from where Darleen's frozen gloves were recovered by the sheriff's deputies. He was old, but looked strong enough to carry a body through the bordering woods to the other side where her lunch box was discovered.

Which brought me to Dick Metzger. His denials of impure intentions while kissing Darleen on the lips, and the suggestion that he may have spied on her in her bath, had done nothing to convince me of the propriety of his relationship with his stepdaughter. He had threatened to beat her if she disobeyed him, and I had endured his wonton, lascivious gazes at my posterior. This man lusted after young women, that much I knew. I didn't like him. He gave me the creeps in spades.

Darleen was one of those girls who attracted older men as well as boys her own age. Unwittingly, unintentionally, she radiated something that the male of the species detected and thought he could exploit, like a pickpocket who sizes up a vulnerable target. I believed her stepfather was one of those men. And if he wasn't the killer, then there was at least one other of that breed somewhere on my list. I just wasn't sure who.

"Ellie," prompted Fadge, bringing me back to the present. "I asked what you thought? Who do you think killed her?"

"Sorry about that," I said. "I have no idea."

✺

Fred Peruso was waiting for me in the doctors' lounge at City Hospital when I arrived at eleven. He told me the autopsy was straightforward: death by strangulation. Darleen Hicks had been dead before she went into the water, which had preserved the body and, thus, much of the evidence.

"What evidence is that?" I asked.

"Her tissues and organs are intact," he said. "It made determining the cause of death a lot easier. No guesswork."

"And?" I asked. "What about the pregnancy?"

Fred paused to light a green cigar. "You were pretty sure about that," he said. "Who told you she was pregnant anyhow?"

I didn't want to say and deflected the question. "Why?"

"Well, you should let whoever told you know that it's pretty hard to get pregnant when you're a virgin."

"A virgin?" I asked. "Are you sure?"

"Shall I draw a picture for you?" he said, puffing billows of blue smoke.

That came from left field. It changed materially the portrait of Darleen that I'd been forming in my head. The rumors and innuendo about her and men and boys. I felt no one was a reliable witness. And what of her quest for money? Perhaps she truly was planning to run off with Joey, and the abortion story was just a ruse. Or maybe she was a ruthless manipulator without scruples or concern for the boys who loved her. I hated myself for thinking ill of the dead, the victim, and a little girl at that, but I just wasn't sure about her. This was the teenager who had been so kind to me in my moment of need. But even then, her kindness may have been a feint, perhaps no different from the scheme she'd hatched with Joey Figlio. Just a ploy to get what she wanted and nothing more.

"Was there any other physical evidence that might suggest what happened?" I asked Fred.

"Pretty simple," he said, shrugging his shoulders. "Two hands around her neck, trachea crushed by intense pressure right about here," and he indicated the location by touching his right index finger to my neck. I gulped.

"Nothing on her clothes? Nothing elsewhere on her body?"

Peruso shook his head. "Clothes? Everything had been torn away by the current. Everything except a belt around her midsection."

I cringed. "Fred, I want to see the body."

※

Peruso finally relented. He only allowed me to see her head, as her neck and thorax had been dissected during the autopsy. He promised me that I did not want to see that. In fact he promised me I didn't want to see any of it.

I had expected a gruesome sight. I had expected to vomit and run from the room. But what I saw affected me in quite a different way. I was serene in my horror, gazing unflinchingly at the cyanotic blotches that swirled over her bloated face, parts of which had been gashed and gouged by underwater collisions and the violent currents of her watery grave. The nose was partly missing, and a piece of the cheek as well. Fred Peruso theorized that ice chunks or the dam gate had scraped the tissue away. He explained that the body floats through or on top of water face down, with the head slightly lower than the trunk of the body. In fast moving water, the bloated skin puckers, swells, and wrinkles. He called it "maceration" of the skin.

I stared at the face before me. Her hair clung together in bunches, like seaweed tangled and twisted on itself. The last thing I focused on was her lips. Swollen and hardened permanently in a grotesque death grimace, her open mouth revealed the white teeth and silver-gray braces. Peruso gently pulled the sheet back over her face, and I left the room.

"You held up better than I thought you would," said Fred who rejoined me in the corridor outside. "Why was it so important for you to see the body?"

I drew a deep breath. Then another. "I want to remember what she looked like when I nail the monster who did this to her."

∂ᴑ

I reached the Metzger farm at half past noon. An old Chevy sedan and a weathered pickup sat parked next to Dick Metzger's green truck and the porch. I knocked on the storm door, and a plump woman in her fifties answered. I told her I had come to offer my condolences to the family. She opened the door, and I stepped inside.

"I'm Winnie Terwilliger," she said in a low voice in my ear. "I live over in Palatine Bridge, but I've known Irene for many years. That's Mr. Sloan and his wife over there. I'm afraid I don't recall their first names. They brought a couple of casseroles and some punch."

I found Irene Metzger in the armchair across the room, staring down at the floor. Mrs. Sloan was holding her hand, patting it from time to time and whispering comfort in her ear. Dick Metzger was nowhere in sight.

I knelt down before Irene, took her hand from Mrs. Sloan, and looked up into her bleary eyes. I told her how sorry I was. She stared back at me in misery, her cheeks fallen, hollow, and ashen. Her lips quivered and tears overflowed her eyelids. She began to sob, her entire body convulsing with each breath she drew and expelled. I squeezed her hand gently and, bowing my head in grief, wept with her. Mrs. Sloan continued her whispering, soothing Irene with her warm, rhythmic voice. Then I felt a hand on my head. I lifted my eyes to see Irene gazing down upon me, patting my head so lovingly, so maternally, that I pressed her other hand to my cheek and held it fast. I muttered over and again how sorry I was, and we remained that way: I, at her knee, she, stroking my hair, for several minutes. Finally, Mrs. Sloan offered me something to eat, but I declined, rising from the floor and wiping my sloppy face with the back of my hand. I touched Irene on the shoulder, my weepy eyes holding hers for one more moment.

I left the house in a rush and ran into Dick Metzger as he came up the porch steps. He caught me briefly in his arms, and I nearly fell, his rough hands groping my waist and my breast. I was sure it was an accident, a mistake caused by our collision and my subsequent loss of balance. But then, for just a split second, as I found my legs beneath me and no longer feared a fall, I felt his right hand slide down my back and take a firm grip of my behind. My body was pressed against him, my face inches from his. I saw his dead, lizard eyes staring at me. No expression, no embarrassment, no apology for his straying hands. I wriggled free and ran. He called after me, but I was gone. Moments later, I roared away in my car, barely able to see through the windshield.

The Figlio house was a brick duplex on the west end of town, a few blocks from the railroad tracks and St. Joseph's Hospital. I had been neglecting my planned interview with Joey's parents. I particularly wanted to talk to his mother. The weather was dry and cold as I climbed out of my car and onto the stoop. Orlando Figlio answered my knocking in a flannel shirt and gray trousers.

"Miss Stone," he said through the storm door. "What are you doing here?"

"You told me I could talk to your wife. Remember?"

"Today's not a good day. She's very upset about last night. Wouldn't even go to church this morning. And now I have to apologize to you again for that no-good, little crook bothering you."

"It's all right, Mr. Figlio," I said. "Actually, Joey kind of saved my life last night. I think we're over the worst, he and I," and I smiled.

"Saved your life? The cops said he busted in and held you hostage or something."

"We had supper," I said. "That was all."

"Chief Finn says he killed that girl. Darleen. He says he's asking the DA to file murder charges against him."

I was shivering on the porch. "May I come in, Mr. Figlio? Can we talk inside?"

He nodded and stood aside to let me in. The place was dark and smelled of tomato sauce, meat, onions, and garlic, all fused together and absorbed by the fabrics and rugs. There was a human smell as well, trapped in clothing and drapes, like when a place smells of dog. Not that the Figlio home smelled bad or dirty or in any way like a dog, but the clinging odor betrayed the presence of people living inside.

"You're welcome to stay a few minutes, Miss Stone," he said, motioning to the roll-arm sofa, upholstered in a faded, worn tapestry. "I could offer you a coffee if you like."

I declined.

"I just don't know what to do about that boy," he said. "The day he was born, his mother's only prayer was for him to stay out of prison. Then, when he started getting into trouble with the law, she prayed to all the saints that he not end up in the electric chair. Now look. Murder."

"I don't believe Joey murdered Darleen," I said.

"Maybe not. But he sure tried to murder that Mr. Russell. Twice."

He had me there.

"I don't know where we went wrong with him," he continued. "Maybe he was just born bad."

"Perhaps if I could speak to his mother," I said.

Orlando Figlio frowned and shook his head. "I don't know. Like I said, this is a bad day."

"It's okay, Lando," came a voice from the hallway. I looked to see a thin, gray woman of about fifty, dressed in a housecoat, her hair disheveled and eyes pink. A smoldering cigarette dangled from her right hand.

"My name is Eleonora Stone," I said, rising to extend a hand to her. She waved me off and took a seat in the armchair next to the sofa.

"You're the girl the police say Joey tried to kill last night, aren't you?" she said.

"Oh, no, Mrs. Figlio. I was just telling your husband that Joey actually saved me from an attack last night."

"Then why do the police say he killed Darleen and tried to kill you?"

"They're looking for a simple conclusion," I said.

"A scapegoat, you mean. Lando," she called, leaning back and craning her neck to make eye contact with her husband, "it's Sacco and Vanzetti all over again."

"He did try to kill that teacher," her husband pointed out gently.

"He's a good boy," insisted Mrs. Figlio. Then turning back to me, she asked what would happen to Joey.

"Since he's a minor, he won't go to prison for the attack on Mr. Russell," I said. "As for Darleen Hicks, I don't believe he murdered her."

"I know he didn't harm her," said the mother with sudden vigor.

This seemed a good opening to make the case for the true motive of my visit. I told her that I wanted to help Joey and was sure I could if she would help me.

"What can a young girl like you do?" she asked. "Cook him a nice meal. That, he would like."

I drew a breath of resolve and resisted the temptation to answer in kind. "I'd like to have a look at Joey's things," I said. "In his room."

"What? What do you think you'll find?"

"They've searched his possessions at Fulton, twice, and I've personally gone through Darleen's room very carefully. No one has found anything to prove that Darleen returned Joey's affections and was actually planning to elope with him. Without that, the police will try to show that Joey was pursuing her against her wishes. That will make the case against him stronger."

"He never said anything about running away," said Mrs. Figlio. "In fact, he hardly mentioned her to me. A couple of times many months ago."

"Did he ask you for money recently? In the past two months?"

Her mien darkened. "As a matter of fact, he did. In November. Before he got sent up to Fulton. I cashed in two savings bonds and gave him forty-two dollars. Lost some value by cashing them in early."

"May I have a look at his room?"

Orlando Figlio said he didn't care either way. The boy was no good, and my rummaging through his things wouldn't do anything to change that. Mrs. Figlio shrugged and pushed herself out of her seat.

"Okay," she said, stubbing out her cigarette in the standing ashtray next to the chair. She didn't quite smother it, and the butt continued to hiss smoke into the air. "If you think it might help my Joey."

Mrs. Figlio led me down the dark hallway, walls papered with an old damask design, past reproductions of lithographic vistas of Naples and the Amalfi Coast and photographs of ancestors posing stiffly in their wedding finery. Of the three doors that squared off the end of the corridor—two bedrooms and one bathroom—Joey's was on the left. Mrs. Figlio pushed open the door and motioned for me to go on in.

The bedroom was dim, close, and stale-smelling, like a cave, as if it had been moist and dark for too long. A small bed, its lumpy mattress covered by an old, blue, wool blanket and a single flat pillow, occupied the wall on the left, and a wooden dresser slouched nearby. On the next wall was the room's only window, its roll-down shade shutting out almost all light from the outside. Across from the bed, a large banded trunk sat against the wall. That's where I would start.

I found comic books, old clothes, newspapers saved for no reason that I could discern, and some scratched forty-fives and older seventy-eights. There was an empty pack of firecrackers, a collection of motor-oil decals, and matchbooks, empty, half used. Near the bottom, I dug out a box of old photographs, but those must have belonged to his parents or grand-parents, as the newest picture of the bunch was at least thirty years old. Finally, stuffed into a corner, I uncovered a crumpled stack of papers that represented the sum of Joey Figlio's literary output.

His poems, like the ones I'd found in Darleen's room, appeared to have been spelled by a troll. The difference was that these were the filthiest verses I'd ever read. But aside from the spelling, punctuation, and dirty words, they weren't badly written. Joey was a raw, undisciplined poet, to be sure, but he had a way with words. Foul, suggestive, forbidden words, especially so when you consider that a fifteen-year-old girl was the subject. And how could he write about Darleen's most private places with such convincing detail if she was a virgin as Fred Peruso had assured me. I supposed the two might have engaged in some heavy petting, but this was clinical and suggested formi-dable experience and familiarity. A perverted collection of bad intentions and mad love for a dead girl. And yet, somehow, I was seized by the fantasy of some beau writing such shameless obscenities for me, about me.

Mrs. Figlio asked me what I was reading, and I blushed crimson. I had forgotten she was there, looking over my shoulder.

"Just some old school work," I said, shoving the papers back inside the trunk.

Joey's dresser was crammed with clothes: shirts, trousers, and socks, most probably too old and small for him to wear. Nothing at all to illuminate Darleen's feelings for the crazy boy.

Then I moved the bed, searched behind and beneath it, finding nothing but a worn, empty valise. I tapped the floorboards for hollow spots, surely giving Mrs. Figlio cause to be suspicious of my sanity. Still nothing. With nothing to show that Darleen had any true feelings for Joey, I feared that, despite his having saved my life the night before, he might well have been delusional. He might well have murdered Darleen Hicks and convinced himself he hadn't. Or perhaps he knew all too well that he had killed her and didn't care. I'd run out of places to search.

I pushed the bed back into place. That's when I noticed that the large, round finial atop the headboard's post was loose. I nudged it then carefully twisted it. It spun effortlessly. I pulled it off and turned it over in my hand to examine it. About the size and shape of a softball, the finial sported a hole two inches deep, drilled to fit the post atop the headboard. The glue must have dried out. One look into the hole solved the mystery. There was a wad of tightly folded paper wedged inside.

Retrieving a pencil from my purse, I dug the paper out with great care. Unfolding it on the bed, I smoothed the wrinkles to find a long note addressed to Joey.

Dear Joey,

It won't be long now. Soon we can leave and get married like we said. You will write me poems and make money from them. Maybe sell them to Brenda Lee or Roy Orbison. We'll be rich.

So far I have $7.50 that I saved from chores and sneaking money from my dad's jar. But I'll get more, just like we planned it.

I know you're no good at math, so I figured it all up at the bottom of the page.

There followed a list of figures. Dollar amounts with projected dates, tallied carefully with remainders carried over. And there were names. Wilbur Burch: $100. Joey's mother: $42. Mr. Brossard: $15. Darleen's savings: $7.50. Ted Jurczyk: $2. There was a question mark after Brossard's name, as if it was a maybe. It all added up to $166.50. At the very bottom, next to a heart pierced by an arrow, appeared Darleen's signature, as clear and as big as day.

"I need to give this to the police," I told Mrs. Figlio. "It will help Joey for sure."

"What if they tear it up and say it never existed?" she asked.

"I'll take a photograph of it now," I said. "We'll put yesterday's newspaper in the picture for proof of the date. And I'll hand it over to the DA instead. It will be safe that way."

Mrs. Figlio agreed and found me her husband's copy of the previous day's *Republic*. Instead of photographing the front page with George Walsh's stolen article, I turned to the funny pages. With the date visible, I placed Darleen's letter on the page and shot ten frames to be sure I'd have a good one.

⟋⟍

My feet were tired, and it was only just after three thirty. No rest for the wicked this day, as I stopped by the *Republic* offices on Main Street to drop off two rolls of film: the one I'd just shot of Darleen's letter and the one with Joey Figlio's arrest in my apartment. I left a note asking Bobby Thompson to develop them for me first thing Monday morning.

Since the district attorney's office was across the street, I left an envelope for Don Czerulniak in the mail slot. Inside was Darleen's letter to Joey, along with a page of hastily scribbled instructions for the prosecutor to keep the original away from Chief Finn, who would most likely make it disappear.

Then there was an errand I had neglected even longer than my visit to the Figlios. I was fairly certain that only two or three people had seen Darleen after she left the bus in the junior-high-school parking lot on December 21. Four, if you counted Walt Rasmussen. I knew Ted Jurczyk was one, and the taxi driver who took her part way home was another. Then, if neither of them was the last to see her, there was a third man. Her killer. On this day, I was looking for the man who had left her on the side of Route 5S moments before she died.

Sitting in my car, idling outside the junior-high parking lot, I asked myself what route Darleen would have taken that day. Whether she exited the parking lot on the north or south side, she still had to turn east to head toward the Mill Street Bridge, the only river crossing in New Holland. Three city blocks separated the junior high from Mill Street, which ran down from the top of Market Hill on the north bank of the Mohawk, over the bridge, and back up the steep incline to Route 5S on the South Side.

I left my car on Division Street, in front of the school, and walked east to Mill Street. There, I turned right and could see the bridge looming several blocks ahead. I passed a florist, a shoeshine shop, and two barbershops before crossing Canal Street. As I waited at the light, I noticed the taxi stand in front of the Nederlander Hotel, an inn that had closed and now housed only a bar on the ground floor: The Keg Room. This must have been where Darleen found her cab.

At the head of the stand, a big, green-and-red Plymouth taxicab marked time, its driver leaning against the fender jawing with two other hacks about the numbers.

"Can you help me?" I asked. The driver looked me up and down, a hint of a smile on his stubbled face.

"Sure, sweetheart. Where you going?"

"Nowhere, I'm afraid. I was hoping one of you gentlemen could tell me if you remember a teenage girl who hailed a taxi here a few weeks ago."

The hack pushed off his fender, and the other two men took a step forward. The three formed a loose semicircle in front of me.

"A few weeks?" he asked, rubbing his chin. "That's a lot of fares ago."

"How about you fellows?" I asked the other two. They shook their heads no. "Come on, how many teenage girls take a cab by themselves? Surely you'd remember that."

"I didn't see no one," said the first hack. Then whistling through his thumb and forefinger, he called out down the line of cabs. "Hey, anybody remember picking up a teenage girl a couple of weeks ago?"

"Four weeks," I prompted. "December twenty-first."

"Four weeks ago!" he yelled.

The other cabbies frowned, shrugged, and shook their heads. All except one. A small, pudgy man in a black stocking cap shuffled forward.

"I used to get fares from a girl. Regularly. Ain't seen her in a while."

"Excuse me," I said. "May I have your name?"

He looked up at me with suspicion. His fat cheeks pushed his mouth into a permanent pout.

"Benny Colonna," he said, as if uncertain. "Who are you?"

"My name is Eleonora Stone. I'm a reporter with the *Republic*."

"So what do you want with me?"

"I'd like to know if this is the girl you picked up on December twenty-first." I produced Darleen's school picture. "She was going to the farmlands out in the Town of Florida."

He tilted his head to see. "Yeah, that's her."

"Can you tell me if she was calm or nervous or normal that day? Was she upset about missing her bus?"

Benny Colonna shrugged. "I don't know. She seemed normal, I guess."

"Did she say anything at all to you?" I asked, and he shook his head. "One last question, Mr. Colonna."

"Sure," he smiled.

"Why did you let her out on the highway? It was about two and half miles from her house."

"Well, she got in the cab right here," he began. "And I recognized her because the last time I picked her up, she was short thirty-five cents on the fare. So this time I didn't trust her. I asked for the money up front. She only had a dollar ten. So when the meter hit seventy-five cents I pulled over and said if she didn't have any more money, that was as far as I was going. A dollar ten minus thirty-five is seventy-five, see?"

The image of Darleen's bluish face, swollen and battered, flashed before my eyes, and I nearly slapped the man. I wanted to do even worse.

"You just left her on the side of the highway in near-zero temperatures?" I stammered.

"Yeah. I mean, she didn't have enough to go any farther. Anyways, she had a winter coat on."

I took a step closer to him, my nostrils flaring, eyes burning. I sensed my hack—the first driver—tensing next to me as I grabbed the fat, little man by his lapels and drew him close to my face.

"I want you to know that you sent that little girl to her death that day."

Benny Colonna's lower lip quivered. He didn't resist, didn't try to push me away or free himself. He just shook. Then he managed to speak and asked me what I meant by that. I shoved him away.

"That girl was murdered that day. The man who killed her picked her up after you threw her out. You might just as well have put a gun to her head and pulled the trigger."

His eyes grew, betraying the dawning of the horrible truth. "Was she that girl that disappeared?" he asked. "I had no idea. My God . . ."

"You killed her," I said with a shrug of my shoulders. Then I reached into my handbag, hands trembling, and fumbled with my change purse. I retrieved a quarter and a dime. "Here's your tip," I said, folding the thirty-five cents into his hand.

Benny Colonna staggered back a step and steadied himself on the cab behind him. His expression of horror told the story. I glanced at my hack standing a few feet away and thanked him for his help. He nodded solemnly, and I strode off back the way I'd come.

By five, I was back home. I spent two hours writing up several pieces for Monday's edition, including one about the cab driver who, for thirty-five cents, had abandoned a young girl on the side of the highway in the freezing dark. I rapped out another article on Joey Figlio's and Wilbur Burch's arrests. And I wrote a third on the discovery of the body at Lock 10. Finally, I put together a timeline for the murder and the dumping of the body in the river. Basing my calculations on what I knew of Darleen's cab ride and Gus Arnold's account of his route that day, I figured the murder had most likely taken place between four thirty and five thirty that afternoon. It was cold that day, so Darleen must have been walking fast to get home as soon as possible. I estimated a walking speed of about five miles an hour. At that rate, she would have reached home in about thirty minutes. But if Gus Arnold had made his last drop at four twenty as he said, then Darleen and her murderer crossed paths along County Highway 58 sometime between four and four fifteen. I was assuming a man in a car stopped and offered her a ride the rest of the way home. Furthermore, I believed that she knew the man, even though she had been known to take rides from strangers. And if she knew the man, I could narrow the field of suspects. But what if someone had been on foot along the road, waiting? That list could include Bobby Karl, Joey Figlio, Walt Rasmussen, and Dick Metzger. I felt sure that Ted Jurczyk had no opportunity to find himself on that road at that time on that day. I made a note to check with Coach Mahoney, just the same, but Ted must have been at basketball practice.

Next, I wanted to establish exactly where Darleen had been murdered and how her body had ended up in the river. I was confident she'd been killed in or near the snow hills at the end of her road. But to be sure, I needed to prove how the body had traveled from there to the lock at Cranesville.

I worked backwards from the river. The Mohawk flowed west to east, of course, meaning that the easternmost spot Darleen could have entered the river was at Lock 10 in Cranesville. I doubted that. For one thing, her body would surely have surfaced earlier, as the water had never completely frozen in Cranesville. That meant the body probably entered the river somewhere to the west. I kept a street map of New Holland and the surrounding area in my car; I often used it to find my way around when working on assignments for the paper. Now, I spread it out before me on the kitchen table and studied the area map on the reverse side. The river bisected the page from left to right, and I could see all the crossings at once. Starting in Canajoharie, there were locks on the river at regular intervals, all part of the Erie Canal system. From the article I'd read in the *Canajoharie Courier Standard* earlier, I knew that the river had been frozen solid at Lock 12 in Tribes Hill on December 21, so Darleen could not have entered the water there or anywhere west of there. Next came Lock 11 to the west of New Holland, just opposite Tedesco's. I wasn't sure if that had been frozen on December 21, but I knew who would: Jimmy Tedesco. He kept an eye on the river and could tell you all you wanted to know about it and then some. I was due to have dinner at Tedesco's with Officer Mike Palumbo in little less than an hour's time.

So, if the river had been flowing at Lock 11, someone could have thrown Darleen's body into the river there. In fact, it was the closest span to the snow hills where I assumed Darleen had met her end: about four miles as the crow flies. Dumping a body off the lock would surely take great care, especially in extreme weather conditions, but one could climb up to the maintenance walkway and reach the middle of the lock and running water. That is, if the water had been running on that day.

꩜

The time had gotten away from me. I would have to finish the timeline later, after I'd spoken to Jimmy Tedesco. Rushing to freshen up and change my clothes, I stepped into my finest underwear and a new pair of nylons. I selected a navy, wool suspender skirt and a pearl-colored blouse I hadn't worn for a while, figuring the look was flattering and would keep me warm. Finally, I touched up my lips and eye makeup just before the doorbell rang. No more unannounced visitors letting themselves in downstairs; Mrs. Giannetti had replaced the entry door with a sturdy model and a dead bolt. She told me she'd had it installed more for her own sleep than my safety. Then, unable to resist, she added the dig I'd been expecting:

"The men climbing up your stairs are usually invited anyway, aren't they, dear?"

I raked a comb through my hair and tamed it with a black hair band. Hopping into my shoes and coat, I grabbed my purse, with my stories folded carefully inside along with my camera, billfold, and various compacts and lipsticks. I made sure I had enough money for carfare in case Vic Mature turned out to be a louse. Then I headed down the stairs.

I opened the door to find Mike Palumbo standing as large as a house, a bunch of flowers in his hand. I smiled and took them from him, wondering where I was going to put them. In the end, I trudged back up the stairs and threw them into a vase of water.

Beneath his overcoat, Mike—as I now addressed Officer Palumbo—looked stylish and handsome in a checked blazer and open-collar shirt. He'd made sure to park facing east, passenger door lined up perfectly with the sidewalk for my convenience. He held the door for me.

Inside the car, which was spanking clean, I noticed the smell of his pomade and aftershave. A mite potent, I thought, but I'd been subjected to worse. His conversation was polite, and he talked about me, not himself. When he smiled, I noticed a row of perfect, bright, white teeth and big, twinkling, brown eyes.

It was eight. I hadn't eaten since morning, so when we arrived at Tedesco's my stomach was growling. I jiggled my purse to cover the noise, but I'm not sure I fooled anyone. As I waited for Mike to open my door, I caught sight of Lock 11 spanning the river in the dark, and a chill went up my spine. I thought of Darleen.

The light was low as usual inside Tedesco's, which was slow—also as usual—on a Sunday night in winter. We had our pick of where to sit, and Mike suggested a quiet booth near the back. The growing emptiness in my stomach was giving me that low-blood-sugar feeling, and I began to sweat and shake with chills. The waitress—Amy, I believe her name was—took our order. Normally, I would have asked for something light, but I was starving. I ordered a hot-meatball sandwich with fries and gravy. I knew I would never finish them, but when your blood sugar's low you can't reason with yourself. Mike looked quizzical, but not so much to suggest that I'd lost him right out of the gate.

"Sorry," I said, shrugging my shoulders. "I haven't eaten since morning." That sounded stupid. What was I doing, saving up to gorge myself on my date's dime? "I had a busy day," I elaborated. "No time to stop for anything."

"That's fine, Ellie," he said and nodded from across the table.

"And your usual to drink?" asked the waitress.

I wasn't aware she knew what I drank, but perhaps my sense of anonymity was exaggerated. I blushed and said yes. A double.

"That is your usual," she said. "And for you, sir?" she asked Mike.

He ordered the veal Parmesan and a glass of Chianti. A few moments later, the waitress returned with a basket of bread and butter, and I fell on it like a lion on a wildebeest. That did the trick. Then our drinks arrived. After the first one I felt better. Soon, I could feel my heartbeat slowing, and my temperature stabilized. Control restored, I stopped shaking, patted the shine off my nose, and smiled at Mike. By the time I'd settled into my second drink, the crisis had passed, and I was my old self, though no longer hungry.

When a lady is invited to a first dinner date, she is acutely aware of the attention she will receive from her escort. He's bound to observe, ask himself questions, and form judgments about her. Why is she drinking so much? Why isn't she married? A steady boyfriend, at least? And look how she's stuffing her face. Very unladylike. So whenever I'm out with a fellow, I'm careful to cut my food into small, delicate pieces that I lift to my mouth slowly and daintily. I chew in a leisurely manner, as if I could take or leave the dish before me, and I make certain to dab my lips with my napkin after each bite.

That evening, there was no need to pretend to eat like a bird; I was full from the bread and drinks. I toyed with my food, spreading it around the plate to give the appearance that I'd eaten more than I had, but there was so much of it. Mike noticed, I'm sure, but he kept it to himself. Good thing, too, as I have a horror of men who comment on how much or how little I eat.

"So, how's your story coming along?" he asked between forkfuls of veal.

"You'd think with the discovery of the body and all the arrests, there would be more clarity in this case," I said, just as the waitress arrived with my third drink. I blushed at Mike.

"The chief says it was the Figlio kid," said Mike.

"I doubt the DA will go along with that. He's got a letter from the victim to Joey Figlio, outlining their plans to run off together. It would seem that Joey and Darleen were in love."

"But they're just teenagers," said Mike. "What do kids know about being in love?"

"Are you joking?" I asked. "Kids know better than anyone the passion, the frustration, the hopelessness of love. Weren't you ever in love?"

Mike blushed but didn't answer. Just then Jimmy Tedesco appeared at our table.

"You don't like my food, Ellie?" he said to me, hands on hips.

"I'm afraid I had a big lunch," I answered, immediately regretting the lie. What was Mike going to think of me now? "It's delicious, Jimmy. Can you wrap it for me to take home?"

He smiled and said sure. "I can't stay mad at you, Ellie. I can't afford to lose a customer who drinks so much."

Now I blushed, but Mike was still wearing his poker face.

"Hey, Mikey," said Jimmy, slapping my date on the shoulder. "How's your old man doing?"

"A little better," said *Mikey*. "He has difficulty speaking since the stroke, but he's moving around now."

"Give him my best," said Jimmy and he started back for the bar.

I called him back to ask a question. "I need to know if the river out there by the lock was frozen on December twenty-first. Any chance you remember?"

"Why do you need to know that?"

"It's a bet I have with my editor," I said.

"Well, the river was definitely frozen at some point in December. I know who'll remember," and he went to the bar and returned moments later with Billy Valicki, one of the pickled regulars who kept Tedesco's in business.

"Billy, what day did you and Tony have that bet about the river?"

"Which one?" asked Billy.

"You know, the one where he bet you couldn't walk across to the other side."

"Oh, yeah, that one. That was about a week before Christmas. I remember because I got my wife a present with the two dollars I won."

"It was a Saturday, right?" asked Jimmy. "I made book on whether you'd make it or not. The house never loses."

Billy glared at Jimmy. "You were taking bets against me? What were you going to do if I fell through the ice?"

"The important thing is that you made it." Jimmy shoved Billy back toward the bar, then turned to me. "So the river was frozen on the seventeenth, and the temperature didn't rise above twenty for a couple of weeks after that. Does that help you?"

"Yeah, thanks," I said, my theory sunk. Darleen's body could not have been thrown into the river at Lock 11. If it had been, it would have lain in plain sight on the ice for three weeks.

"Something wrong, Ellie?" asked Mike.

"It's just this one sticking point in my story," I said. "I think Darleen Hicks was murdered near her home in those snow hills. But if so, how did her body get to Lock 10 in Cranesville?"

"Someone dumped her in the river, of course," said Mike.

"Yes, but where? The closest lock to her farm is that one right outside. Number 11. But the river was frozen over on December twenty-first."

"I see," he said. "I'll tell you where the river wasn't frozen on December twenty-first."

I squinted at him in the dark. "Where?"

"The Mill Street Bridge. The water was still flowing underneath."

The Mill Street Bridge? Right in the center of town. Who would be so bold, or stupid enough, to toss a body into the river there? I really hadn't considered it, perhaps because it was so obvious and risky. But Mike said the river had been flowing on the 21st of December.

"How much water was flowing?" I asked.

Mike took a moment to recollect properly. Then he said it was a steady stream, at least twenty feet wide, down the middle channel of the river. Right down the middle.

"How can you be so sure it was December twenty-first?" I asked.

"That's easy," he said. "I remember because I made a traffic stop on the bridge after one a.m. that day."

"Was it the twenty-first or the twenty-second?" I asked, my skin beginning to tingle, the sensation traveling from my shoulders up through my neck to the top of my head.

"The twenty-second morning," he said.

"And who did you stop on the bridge?"

"I didn't actually *stop* him. He was already stopped on the bridge. Right there half way between the South Side and downtown." He shook his head. "The guy was so drunk, he was crying and pleading with me not to arrest him. He said he'd lose his job."

"Mike, who was it?" I demanded.

"It was the assistant principal," he said, taken aback by my tone. "What's his name? Brossard."

CHAPTER EIGHTEEN

I grilled Mike for the next half hour about the night of December 21. He said that he'd been cruising the South Side, trying to stay warm by keeping the squad car moving. It was nearly time for his shift to end, so he was heading back to the station on the north side of the river. That's when he came across a sedan idling in the northbound lane of the bridge. Just sitting there chugging exhaust into the frigid night air. Grabbing his flashlight, Mike approached the car on foot and tapped on the driver's window. After a second tap, the driver rolled down the window, releasing a draft of warm air along with the strong odor of alcohol. Mike invited the driver to get out of the car and walk a straight line. But the driver confessed straightaway that he'd drunk too much at the superintendent's Christmas banquet. He broke down and wept, begged the officer not to arrest him, even offered a bribe. And, in the end, Mike Palumbo gave him a stern lecture and a warning. He followed the driver home, just to be sure he made it without incident.

"But why didn't you arrest him?" I asked.

Mike shrugged, by now uncomfortable with my interrogation. "I felt sorry for the guy," he said. "And he was the assistant principal, so I didn't want to see him in hot water."

"And you say he was heading north over the bridge? Where was he coming from? Where was he going?"

"I don't know, Ellie," he said.

"Sorry, Mike," I said, realizing I had come on a little strong.

"Sure," he said. "Maybe it's time to call it a night. Tomorrow's Monday, after all."

When Mike dropped me off, he followed me up onto the porch. Nothing to get excited about. If my oddball behavior, heavy drinking, wasted food, and lying hadn't driven him off, the third-degree questioning surely had. He was just being polite or just being a cop.

"I want to make sure your place is safe," he said. "You've had quite a few unwanted visitors lately."

We climbed the stairs quietly, and I turned the key in the kitchen door. Mike entered first, switched on the lights, and checked each room, one by one, for intruders. The last room was my bedroom. I thought he'd played it quite cool and still managed to make it into my bedroom. But then he walked back out and pronounced the place clear. My heart sank.

I accompanied him to the door, resigned to writing the evening off as a bust. But before he left, he asked if I was free Friday.

"I've got a high-school basketball game to cover," I said.

"What about Saturday?"

"I'll check my calendar," I said. "I might have to fend off a pack of juvenile delinquents and murderers."

"I'll pick you up at seven," he said. "And eat something this time. You don't want to fill up on bread."

MONDAY, JANUARY 16, 1961

My week got off to an early start. Arriving at the office at seven, I sat down to rewrite my murder timeline. I was now sure that the body had been tossed off the Mill Street Bridge; it was the only possibility. And before I could convict Louis Brossard of murder in my mind, I reviewed what I knew and didn't know. What had he been doing on the Mill Street Bridge at such a late hour? Why had he been on the south side of the river? He lived in Northampton Court, after all, which was near the northern limits of the city. I knew he'd attended the Christmas banquet earlier that evening, but that had ended before ten thirty. And besides, Isobel's Restaurant was on the north side of the river, on the West End. What had happened to Louis Brossard between ten thirty and one thirty in the morning? Had he been drunk at the banquet or had he fueled up somewhere else? There were plenty of taverns on the South Side, of course, so it was possible he'd tied one on over there. Or maybe he'd returned to the snow hills after the banquet to dig out Darleen's body and deposit it in the river.

I wrote a note to Norma Geary, asking her to make some inquiries for me while I was tied up in editorial meetings later that morning. I slipped the envelope under her typewriter cover, where she would find it first thing upon her arrival.

Georgie Porgie was seated in the City Room for the Monday morning meeting, a large envelope on his lap and a smug grin on his lips. The meeting began as usual with a recap of the weekend's breaking news. Charlie had a bone to pick with the entire staff.

"On Saturday, we put out a special early edition," he began. "George, here, broke a big story on the Hicks girl and her unused bus ticket." George beamed and sat up in his chair. "But then what happened?" asked Charlie. "We all took the rest of the weekend off to rest on our laurels while I was out of town. Does anyone know that they found the girl's body on Saturday? And arrested three suspects?"

There was silence in the room.

"I know that," I volunteered.

"Of course you do," barked Charlie. "Everyone knows it now. What we needed was someone to get on it Saturday. Artie Short just chewed my head off because we missed the biggest break on this story. Now we have nothing for this afternoon's edition."

I waited for the echo of Charlie's voice to fade before serving him his crow with a knife and fork. But Georgie Porgie beat me to the punch.

"I have here a photo of the Figlio boy," he said. "It's a school picture."

"And what am I going to do with that?" snapped Charlie. "We don't have any of the details of what happened, no pictures of the lock where the body was found, nothing to excite readers."

"How about a photograph of Joey Figlio being arrested?" I asked. Everyone turned to look at me. "And two rolls of film of the sheriff and the hearse at Lock 10 on Saturday afternoon? Oh, and I have four articles for you. If you review them right away, all four should make the front page of today's edition, this time with my byline," and I threw a glance at George Walsh.

Charlie stared open-mouthed at me. The room was silent.

"I was here on Saturday afternoon when a tip came in about the body," I explained. "I was on the scene minutes after they fished the body out of the dam gate."

"This meeting is over," said Charlie, a huge smile spreading over his lips. "Ellie, come with me."

Once we were in Charlie's office, I told him about George Walsh having stolen my story for his big scoop.

"That's a pretty serious accusation," he said. "You want to be careful about saying things like that."

"Just ask Frank Olney who discovered the bus ticket in Darleen's locker. I did."

"Really?" he said. "Then why didn't you print the story?"

"The sheriff asked me to wait, and I did."

Charlie almost blew a gasket. "If Artie Short ever heard that, he'd fire you on the spot. Hell, I should fire you for it right now. The press has to be independent, Ellie. You know that. How could you do such a thing?"

"I know," I said. "You don't have to tell me. I feel bad enough already."

"I'm telling you now if you ever do anything like that again, I will fire you."

"I'm sorry," I said. "It won't happen again."

Charlie was steamed. He wanted to toss me out of his office, but we had to discuss the stories I'd done over the weekend. He glowered at me as I produced the four stories from my purse. He read them quickly and softened. Then he congratulated me on my excellent work.

"Okay, Charlie," I said, ready to bring out the big guns. "I've got more news, and I need your advice. I know who killed Darleen Hicks."

He stared dumbly at me.

"I know who killed her," I repeated.

"Who?"

I took a seat in front of his desk and smoothed my skirt. Charlie waited.

"Louis Brossard," I announced.

"Brossard," he mumbled. "I know that name from somewhere. Who is he?"

"Assistant principal of the junior high school."

Charlie choked. "And you say he killed this girl? Why do you think an upstanding school administrator would murder a teenage girl?"

"At this point, all I have is circumstantial evidence. Not enough to nail him."

"Like what?"

"He was collared by the New Holland police on the Mill Street Bridge in the middle of the night after Darleen Hicks disappeared. Drunk and weeping."

"So? What's the bridge have to do with this?"

"You're always telling me you like good science stories, Charlie," I said. "On December twenty-first, the Mohawk River was frozen over completely from Canajoharie past Lock 11 on the West End of New Holland."

"Yes, I remember. It was a rare sight. What of it?"

"Well, the river was not frozen under the Mill Street Bridge."

The penny dropped. "So that's where the body must been thrown into the river," he said, smiling broadly. "Ellie, that's brilliant. How did you come up with that?"

"Just trying to retrace the journey the body must have taken."

Charlie sat down and scribbled some notes into his pad. "I see your point, though," he said as he wrote. "There's no proof that this Brossard fellow is guilty, but his presence on the bridge certainly looks bad for him. Does he live anywhere near there?"

I shook my head. "Northampton Court. And his car was traveling south to north over the bridge. What was he doing on the South Side at that hour?"

"Any other circumstantial evidence to support your theory?"

"Just that Brossard was deputy headmaster at St. Winifred's Academy in Hudson before he came to New Holland."

"And? What's the school have to do with this?"

"A girl disappeared from St. Winifred's at the time Brossard was there. They never found her."

"Okay," said Charlie, looking up at me. "I'm with you. I think you've got the right guy. Now, how do we prove it?"

"That's just it, Charlie," I said. "I don't know. If there were some physical evidence in his car, maybe that would do it. But it's been four weeks. Surely he's had ample opportunity to clean out the trunk of his car."

"Still, we could ask the city police to take this on. They'll get a warrant and scour his car and his house while they're at it."

"I'd rather go to the sheriff for that," I said. "The city police think Joey Figlio killed Darleen. Besides, she was from the Town of Florida and was found in Cranesville. This isn't the city police's jurisdiction."

"Good point," said Charlie. "And it won't hurt that Frank Olney is a good pal of yours. Okay, so you go to the sheriff. Any other ideas?"

"I'm going to talk to Brossard this morning," I said. "And I've asked Norma Geary to contact St. Winifred's."

Charlie whistled. "Great. Okay, you're on this exclusively. Forget about your other stories. I'll take care of them. You get on this Brossard guy. Just be careful, Ellie. You never know how he might react."

"Okay, Chief," I said and stood to leave.

"What about your film?" he asked.

"In the lab with Bobby. Should be ready by now."

"Great work, Ellie," he said, all smiles, as he walked me out the door. "Where can I get ten more like you?"

I thought about reminding him that he'd nearly fired me five minutes earlier, but thought better of it. I would surely need his good will again, and men, like dogs, don't appreciate having their noses rubbed in their mistakes.

Norma Geary strolled by my desk as I was grabbing my coat and purse. She made a subtle hand gesture for me to follow her. She took me to the break room beyond the steno pool. There were some tables, a coffee pot, and a cigarette machine. The room was empty at ten past ten.

"I telephoned St. Winifred's as soon as I got your message," she whispered. "They weren't too helpful, but they confirmed that Mr. Brossard used to work there. He was the assistant headmaster from August 1954 to June 1957. I also called the junior high and confirmed that he was hired as assistant principal in the summer of '57."

"How did you manage to get all that information?"

"I said I was with the New Holland Savings Bank. Routine check for a car loan," she smiled. "Everyone likes to help a person buy a new car."

"What about the girl who disappeared from St. Winifred's?" I asked.

"Well, I couldn't very well ask the school about that. Not if I was calling from a bank. So I called the *Register-Star* in Hudson. That's the local daily. The woman I spoke to remembered the case very well and said that it was never solved. The poor girl just disappeared from the school one day and was never seen again."

"Any other details?"

"She said there was plenty written about it in the paper. Some articles were even picked up by the AP."

I thought it was a long shot to pursue that angle at that moment. If Brossard had been involved in the St. Winifred's girl's disappearance, there would always be time to comb through old newspapers later on. For now, I wanted to know about Darleen Hicks, and Louis Brossard was the man I wanted to ask about her.

"Nice work, Norma," I said, standing to leave.

"But Miss Stone," she said. "Don't you want to see the article?"

"I beg your pardon."

"The article on the St. Winifred's girl. I've got it right here," and she produced a yellowing page from an October 1956 edition of the *New Holland Republic*.

"How did you . . . ? Where did you get this?"

"From the archives in the basement," she said. "The lady at the *Register-Star* gave me the date of the girl's disappearance, and since she said the AP had picked up the story, I thought we might have run it." She smiled. "We did."

Why was Norma Geary marooned in the steno pool? And the far end of the steno pool, for that matter. This woman was a dynamo. Charlie might not find ten more of me, but I was going to tell him about Norma Geary.

The AP article gave the details of the case. A thirteen-year-old girl, Geraldine Duffy, a boarded student at St. Winifred's Academy, had gone missing from school grounds after hours on Thursday, October 25. Local police interviewed school officials, students, and local witnesses, but no trace of the girl was found. A Wirephoto accompanied the brief article: a rough, grainy picture of a beautiful girl smiling in her school portrait. I bowed my head and rubbed the bridge of my nose, drawing a deep breath. Geraldine Duffy was wearing braces and an all-too-familiar mischievous grin.

"Good morning, Mrs. Worth," I said, presenting myself to the secretary at the junior high.

"Miss Stone," she smiled. "What brings you here today?"

"I'd like to see Mr. Brossard."

"May I tell him what this is about?"

"Just a couple of questions about Darleen Hicks," I said.

"What an awful end to the story," she said. "I heard they found her body in the woods."

"You did? From whom?"

"My friend, Helen Semple told me. But it's all over the school today. Buried in the woods!"

I always like to correct misinformation when I hear it, but in this case, I thought it better not to. Just taking a page from Frank Olney. The whole town would know the real story in a couple of hours anyway. As soon as the afternoon edition came out.

Mrs. Worth announced me, and soon I was seated in my usual chair before Louis Brossard. I studied his features as he wished me good morning. Nothing to betray a psychopathic killer of young girls. His broad face was inviting; his smile, genuine; his eyes, sincere. But that's just what a psychopathic killer would want you to believe about him.

"Is something wrong, Miss Stone?" he asked finally, rousing me from my thoughts. "You look confused."

"I have a couple of questions for you, Mr. Brossard," I said.

"Of course," he said. "Anything you want."

I drew a deep breath. Here goes. "Where were you on the night of December twenty-first of last year?"

His smile wilted into a fretful glower. He squirmed in his seat and rearranged the pencil before him on the desk.

"I've already told you where I was that evening," he said. "There was the superintendent's banquet at Isobel's."

"Yes," I said. "Ziti and meatballs. I even saw the photograph in the paper. You were sitting with Mrs. Worth."

"That's correct. Then why the question?" He was trying to build a smile, but it looked ready to collapse.

"Where were you before the banquet?" I asked. There went the smile.

"I was here in my office," he said. "It was a normal school day."

"The school day ends at three thirty, and the banquet didn't start until seven."

"I have plenty of work on my desk beyond normal school hours," he said, managing some indignation.

"So you didn't leave your office? Or the school until you went to Isobel's?"

"Precisely."

"Was there anyone here in the office who might be able to confirm that?"

"I don't know," he said.

"Isn't it true that Darleen Hicks asked you for money, just as she asked Ted Russell?" I said, switching gears to keep him off balance. But I hadn't forgotten my previous question; I intended to ask everyone—Mrs. Worth, Principal Endicott, and the janitor—if Louis Brossard had happened to leave early after school on December 21.

"That's preposterous," he said. "Who told you that?"

"Ted Russell."

"Well, it's a lie. And I certainly did not give her any money like that fool Ted did."

"I think she did ask you," I said.

"Too bad you can't prove it," he said with a forced laugh.

"But I can prove it. I have a handwritten letter from Darleen to Joey Figlio. She noted down everyone she'd hoped to get money from. And your name is on the list. Fifteen dollars' worth."

I'd cornered him. "That proves nothing. Just her word against mine. I swear I did not give her any money. And Ted Russell gave her twenty dollars. He told me so himself. And he admitted it to you. Why aren't you asking him where he was on December twenty-first?"

"I'm talking to you right now," I said.

"Well, this interview is over," he announced, rising from his chair to indicate that I should leave.

"I can go," I said. "But are you sure you want to send me packing with the information you've given so far? That you lied about Darleen Hicks asking you for money? That you can't account for your whereabouts on the night she disappeared?"

"Why do you suspect me, Miss Stone?" he asked. "What have I done to make you think I am capable of such a thing?"

I was ready to play one of my trumps, and I intended to study his reaction very carefully.

"Geraldine Duffy," I said slow and plain.

Brossard's eyes actually grew, and his mouth dropped open just a bit before he caught himself. He couldn't very well deny that he knew who she was, though, so he made the best of it.

"That poor girl," he said. "I certainly had nothing to do with her disappearance."

"Then why did you leave St. Winifred's?"

"I already told you. Better prospects. A man has a right to build his career, doesn't he?"

"The timing is curious," I said. "Just months after Geraldine Duffy disappeared, you left for greener pastures."

"That's a coincidence. One had nothing to do with the other. Now, you've made some heinous accusations here, Miss Stone, and I'm trying to hold my temper. But—"

"I haven't made any accusations, Mr. Brossard," I interrupted. "I've merely asked you questions that you have answered, some truthfully, others not."

"I did not kill those girls!" he yelled, and pounded his fist on the table, causing his pencil and glass of water to jump into the air. "Now I'll ask you to leave."

"What were you doing on the Mill Street Bridge at one thirty in the morning after Darleen Hicks disappeared?"

Just then Mrs. Worth burst through the door. "What was that noise?" she asked. "We heard shouting."

"Sorry about that," said Brossard, forcing another smile. He could do nothing to the hide the red in his face, though. "I dropped a book on the floor. Miss Stone and I are just talking here. Everything's fine."

Mrs. Worth withdrew, casting a severe look my way. I nodded that it was okay. Once the door was closed, Brossard started to pace.

"Look," he said. "I apologize for losing my temper there. But you must understand that I'm innocent, Miss Stone. It's very disturbing to be asked such questions."

"You don't have to answer them," I said.

"But how would that look? You'll print it in your paper, make me appear guilty for the whole town to see."

"What were you doing on the Mill Street Bridge at one thirty in the morning?" I repeated.

He retook his seat, his mind working furiously to find an escape. He wiped his perspired brow, smoothed his oiled hair, and took several deep breaths. I waited.

"I have ... a problem," he began, his face burning fuchsia, nearly purple. I didn't enjoy this, but I was damned if I would let him off the hook. In contrast to his red face, I couldn't shake the blue of Darleen's dead skin from my thoughts. "It's something my father struggled with as well," he continued. "I'm a dipsomaniac. It's a terrible curse, and I pray to Jesus and all the saints for deliverance each day. But there are times when I relapse. I'm weak."

I watched him, his shaking hands, the sweat on his forehead, the licking of his lips. He wasn't looking at me. He just stared at the floor, ashamed, as if he were cataloguing his sins to an invisible priest in a confessional.

"December twenty-first was one of those days when I succumbed. I drank and drank at that banquet. First wine, then a Manhattan. Then three more. Manhattans have always been my weakness. And that day I was thirsty. So thirsty. I couldn't stop, I tell you. Even when Mr. Endicott pulled me aside and told me to get a grip on myself, I still snuck into the bar and downed a shot of rye."

I listened intently, my mouth clamped shut, even though I wanted to scream bloody murder at him. All I could think of was substituting *child molester* for *dipsomaniac* in his confession.

I'm a child molester, a child killer. It's a terrible curse, and I pray to Jesus and all the saints for deliverance every day. But there are times when I relapse. I'm weak.

"So that's how I ended up on the bridge at that hour. I was drunk, Miss Stone," he said, looking to me for pity or forgiveness. But all he got in return was another question he couldn't answer.

"Why were you coming from the South Side? Where had you been?"

The intercom on Brossard's desk buzzed. It was Mrs. Worth again. She said Mr. Endicott wanted to speak to him urgently. Brossard's head fell into his hands, but then he must have seen his chance to escape. He wiped his eyes and brow with a handkerchief and excused himself. I was sure he wasn't coming back.

If I had harbored any doubts about Louis Brossard's guilt before my interview with him, they were gone now. The man seemed a tortured pervert to me. Remorseful, perhaps, deep down, and ashamed of his base urges and his inability to control them, but he knew what he had done was wrong and would condemn him to hell until Judgment Day. Make no mistake, Louis Brossard was a strict Catholic in anguish. I felt some pity for him. But not enough to take my foot off the gas until he'd admitted what he'd done.

CHAPTER NINETEEN

"I'm not going to release Ted Russell, Ellie" said Frank Olney. "The DA says he can't make a case, but I still think he's my best bet. It won't hurt to hold him a little longer."

"Come on, Frank," I said. "He's innocent."

"What do you know about it?"

"Well, I can tell you who killed Darleen Hicks. And, in case you want to score some points with some of your fellow cops downstate, I'll give you the name of the man who murdered a thirteen-year-old girl named Geraldine Duffy in Hudson three years ago."

"What are you on about?" he asked, eyeing me as he rocked in his chair.

"Louis Brossard murdered Darleen Hicks."

He stopped rocking and leaned forward, placing his elbows on his desk. "The assistant principal?"

I nodded. "I know he was on the Mill Street Bridge at one thirty in the early morning hours of December twenty-second."

Frank stared at me. "And?"

"And the river was frozen from Canajoharie to Lock 11 on the west end of town on December twenty-first. The only place the body could have been dropped into the water was from the Mill Street Bridge."

"How do you know he was there?"

I cleared my throat. "A city cop told me he found him there, right in the middle of the bridge, dead drunk at one thirty in the morning on the twenty-second. He was weeping in his car. He had no business being there at that hour unless it was to throw Darleen Hicks into the water."

Frank thought it over. He liked the idea, but wanted to know more. What other evidence, for example, did I have to point the finger at Brossard?

"Darleen asked him for money," I said. "And he lied to me about that."

"She asked Russell, too," he pointed out.

"But she wasn't pregnant."

"Sure, but Ted Russell wouldn't have known that. He still might have wanted to keep her from talking."

"Except that she was a virgin."

Frank threw me an incredulous look. "Where did you come up with that?"

"The autopsy," I said. "So that proves that Ted Russell is telling the truth when he says he never had his way with Darleen Hicks."

Frank mulled it over. "The girl still could have lied about having an affair with her teacher, but if she was a virgin like you say . . ."

"I think she was all bark and no bite. Brossard swears he didn't give her money, and he would have been under the same threat as Ted Russell. And as far as I've heard, Darleen never told anyone that she was sleeping with Louis Brossard."

"So tell me your theory, Ellie," he said. "How did this happen?"

"I think Brossard followed Darleen from school that day. Maybe he saw her leaving the parking lot after her bus drove off. Then she hailed a taxi on Mill Street."

"Then isn't that the end of it for Brossard?"

"No, I believe Brossard became obsessed with Darleen during his investigation of the Ted Russell scandal. This looked like the best chance he'd ever get: Darleen had missed the bus, there were no witnesses. Maybe he could get her alone. So he followed the cab, which dropped her about two and half miles from her home. She was alone on the side of the highway, and it was nearly dark."

"So he just rolled up, and she got in?"

"Why not? Maybe he lured her with a promise of the money she'd asked for. Or maybe it was just cold enough to accept. He was the assistant principal, after all. Must have seemed safe enough."

"Then what?"

"He drove her to the snow hills, where things got messy."

"Wait a minute," said Frank, raising a hand. "You think he drove right past her house and didn't let her out?"

I thought it over. Frank made a good point. Driving her past her own farm posed a huge risk. She could have easily jumped from the car, given the slow speeds cars traveled on that road. And if Dick Metzger had been in the fields near the road, he might have seen.

"You're right," I said. He must have taken her to the next turnoff on 5S. There's a little road on the other side of the snow hills. I visited it with

Gus Arnold. He drank a pint of rye in that very spot after finishing his route that day."

Frank's ears perked up. "He was there? And you don't suspect him?"

"I do. He certainly was in the right place. But there's too much smoke with Brossard."

"So what do you think I should do? Arrest Brossard? Arrest the bus driver?"

I shook my head. "There's no proof. Maybe you could search his place. His car for sure."

"I'm going to talk to the cops down in Hudson. I want to know if this Brossard fellow was ever on their radar. What about you, Ellie?"

"I'm waiting for you to get a warrant."

There was quite a stir when the afternoon edition came out. All four of my stories made the front page, as the Darleen Hicks case was now big news. The discovery of the body made it hard to ignore. And there was salacious interest all around, what with the taxi driver's role and the two men arrested in my apartment. George Walsh also had a piece in the paper that afternoon: "Walsh's Witticisms," five jokes, three riddles, and a caricature of the author. I was already planning to have the cartoon image enlarged and framed for display on my desk. As a bonus, Charlie told me that George's copy had been riddled with typographic errors.

"More than the usual misspellings," he said with annoyance as I tried not to laugh. "It's as if he typed it with boxing gloves on. What's wrong with that man?"

I was sipping some coffee in the back booth at Fiorello's at about six. Fadge and I had been discussing the case, and I was making notes for an article linking the Hudson girl's disappearance to Brossard and Darleen Hicks. I wasn't ready to go to press with it, of course, just outlining the research I would carry out. Fadge wasn't convinced about the assistant principal and was more interested in the bus driver. I told him Gus Arnold was still on my list, but right now I was 99.44 percent sure that Louis Brossard was my man. Then the phone rang. It was Charlie Reese, looking for me. I slipped into the phone booth and closed the folding door.

"What is it, Chief?" I said.

"The sheriff's looking for you. He said he and the DA got a search warrant for Louis Brossard's place, and he's going over there now. Olney says you can't go in with him, but he may have a statement for the press if you wait outside."

"I'm on my way," I said and hung up.

⁂

Three county cars and the DA's Chrysler New Yorker were parked outside the Northampton Court Apartments. Frank and the Thin Man were inside Brossard's place, while Pat Halvey and Stan Pulaski stood guard outside, warding off the curious.

The evening sky was clear, and the mercury had fallen below freezing again. I chatted with Stan and Pat for over an hour while the search went on inside. Brossard had called a lawyer, Joe Murray, who was inside making sure the search was kosher. Deputy Spagnola showed up a while later with some coffee for his pals, and Stan offered me his. I told him I'd just had some before arriving, but I wouldn't mind holding the cup for him. My hands were cold.

Finally, at eight o'clock, the sheriff and DA exited the apartment building with Joe Murray in tow. They made their way over to a red-and-white Chevrolet sedan and proceeded to unlock it with some keys the sheriff was holding. Using flashlights, two deputies climbed inside the car and scanned the floor and seats for evidence. They shoved their hands between the seat cushions, examined the glove box, and then popped open the trunk. They spent a good forty-five minutes going over the car, without any success. At least none that I could see from my distant vantage point.

In the end, Joe Murray was beaming, obviously happy with the results of the search. He bade the sheriff and the DA good night and went back inside to confer with his client. Frank and Don made their way over to me and the deputies.

"You boys can head back to the jail," said the sheriff. "Don and I have discussed it, and I want you to release Ted Russell. We don't have anything on him."

"Just let him go?" asked Pat Halvey.

"Yes. And give him a ride home."

"Let me guess," I said once Stan and Pat had gone. "Nothing in the car."

"Nothing," said the sheriff.

"Well, what can you expect after four weeks?" said the DA. "To tell you the truth, I didn't think we'd find anything tonight. If he's guilty, he's had plenty of time to dispose of the evidence."

"Do you think he's guilty, Don?" I asked.

The Thin Man looked up at the sky and gave it a good think. "I'd put my money on him," he said. "Proving it is going to be a lot harder, though. No witnesses and no physical evidence linking him to the girl."

"And no indication that he even left the office early that day," said the sheriff. "We interviewed the staff and his boss a couple of hours ago. No one can remember that at all."

"So you think I'm wrong?" I asked.

The sheriff looked down at me and pursed his lips. "No, Ellie. I think you're right. He's your man. I spoke to the Hudson chief of police by phone this afternoon. He said Brossard was one of their top suspects. Had the girl in his office for some kind of detention after school that day. But there was another student. A boy, a senior, in the office with them as well. Brossard told the police he dismissed the girl first, but the boy said he was sent away first. Later, the kid changed his story to match Brossard's, and the cops just couldn't break their alibis."

"My God," I whispered. "That poor girl."

"Yeah. So now we've got to figure out how to nab this guy."

"You're going to need some proof," said the DA. "Because as things stand now, he walks."

I arrived home a little past ten. I read and reread the AP article Norma had dug out of the archives. It was only twenty lines long, and there was no mention of Louis Brossard or the other student. Still, to no avail, I tried to wring some kind of clue out of that old story. Then I retraced in my head Darleen's steps on the day she died, hoping for inspiration. But still nothing. Not even a couple of stiff drinks helped. Brossard was guilty, I was convinced. But I had no hope of proving it.

I switched on the television to clear my mind. *What's My Line?* or *This*

Is Your Life. I switched it off again, and the phone rang. It was after ten thirty on a Monday. Well past normal New Holland visiting hours.

"I've got to speak to you," came a vaguely familiar voice from the other end. I couldn't place it immediately. Shaking and vulnerable, the inflection was confusing me. Then he said it was urgent and called me "Miss Stone."

"Where are you, Ted?" I asked.

"Fiorello's," he answered. "Please. I need to see you right away."

"I'm in the upstairs apartment across the street. Number forty-six."

Moments later, the bell rang, and I descended the stairs to open the newly installed door. Ted Jurczyk stood in the cold night air, breathing heavily, as if he'd just finished running line drills on the basketball court. When our eyes met, he started to cry.

"Come on in, Ted," I said, wrapping an arm around him.

I made him some hot chocolate and waited for him to compose himself. Something had knocked him for a loop. Finally, he wiped his eyes and drew a restorative breath.

"Tell me. What happened?" I asked.

He looked up at me, eyes and nose red, lips chapped. "She's gone," he said, and more tears spilled over his eyelids. "I can't believe she's really dead."

I put a hand on his and let him talk.

"I was still hoping, you know. Just hoping she'd left like she said she would."

"She told you she was leaving?"

He nodded. "The day she disappeared. I met her by the bus. I'm sorry I lied to you that night at the gym," he said. "I was so scared. I was sure you would try to pin the whole thing on me."

"I wasn't gunning for you, Ted."

"I know that now," he said, wiping his nose on a napkin.

"What did Darleen say to you that day?" I asked. "It must have been pretty important to risk missing her bus."

Ted Jurczyk reached into his coat pocket and pulled out a brown paper bag. He placed it on the kitchen table.

"What's that?"

"It's Darleen's diary."

"She gave this to you?" I asked, picking up the bag. "The day she disappeared?"

Ted nodded. "She told me she had a secret to tell me. She said she was running away for good with Joey Figlio. She wasn't sure when, but soon, she said."

"Why did she give you her diary?"

"She said she didn't want her father to find it. That would spoil everything. She told me not to read it, but to keep it until she sent for it."

"So, have you read it?" I asked.

"No. I gave her my word."

"Then why have you brought it to me?"

Ted looked down into his hands. "Because she's gone. Someone needs to read what she didn't want her father to know."

CHAPTER TWENTY

I drove Ted home. It was a school night, and he was out late. As things stood, he was sure he'd be grounded if his father caught him sneaking back in. I pulled to a stop outside the darkened duplex on Polack Hill.

"I just couldn't read it," he said. "I didn't want to know."

"I won't lie to you, Ted. It still might have to come out."

He nodded one last time and popped the door open. He climbed out and disappeared into the dark pathway alongside the house.

Back home at midnight, I tore the cover off the diary; the lock didn't stand a chance. I poured myself a long drink and settled in on the sofa. The diary took up where the one I'd found in her room had left off more than three years earlier. The months drifted by without anything of interest; Darleen was eleven and twelve at the time, and the entries were about games, friends, and farm animals. But somewhere in the fall of 1958, when she was about to turn thirteen, she started writing about boys. First there was Edward, who, she wrote, was in love with her. She liked Edward very much, but like a brother. Still, it was flattering to have a boy carry your books, send you notes, and buy you sodas in the cafeteria. Darleen got braces on her teeth in September of that year. She liked her dentist, who was a handsome married man. Then she started writing about "crazy Joey Figlio" who was in her seventh-grade homeroom. "He's in love with me," she wrote. "I sure do get a lot of attention from boys all of a sudden."

In October 1958, her entries stopped for three months. Then they resumed tentatively, with short, almost impersonal details. What she wore to school, who she sat with at lunch, what movie she saw. Finally, in the middle of February 1959, her reticence broke wide open. I gasped when I read the matter-of-fact entry: "Dad made me do it again." Again three weeks later, another brief mention: "Again. I wish he'd leave me alone. I don't like it, but he goes away if I do what he says."

The next eighteen months catalogued a string of late-night visits to her room by her stepfather. He watched her bathing, made her "do things" to him, "did things" to her, and threatened her to keep quiet. As the months passed, the frequency of his visits increased, but she was no more descriptive in her accounts. Just the same vague words like "again" and "things." I found at least sixty distinct occasions in the diary where she wrote about his visits. She described how he talked of "lying" with her as soon as she was old enough, but for now, he was satisfied with the "disgusting things he made me do."

In May 1960, Darleen wrote that she'd met an older boy who liked her a lot. Wilbur Burch was eighteen and had a car. "Wilbur's a simple boy," she wrote, "but he's going to get me out of here. He's going into the army in Arizona. I sure would like to see Arizona." Darleen went on to explain that Wilbur was crazy for the "tricks" she did with him. She wrote that he fell head over heels for her after that.

I put the diary down and downed another drink before I could continue. Drawing a deep breath, I resumed. Later that summer, Joey Figlio emerged as Darleen's steady and best hope for escape. She wrote that he was "a little weird," but he loved her and "had a plan" to take her away from the farm and her stepfather. Wilbur had turned out to be "a dud" and "kinda slow." By all accounts, Darleen had never shown her "tricks" to Joey, who seemed to love her anyway. She wrote that they planned to run away and get married.

But in September, Darleen forgot all about Joey Figlio and gushed for weeks about Mr. Russell, the dreamy music teacher. She fantasized about marrying him and moving out of her nightmare and into his dream. There was nothing in the diary to suggest that Ted Russell shared any of her interest. In fact, after about a month and a half, Darleen pronounced herself over Mr. Russell, who was kind of boring and had a way of wrinkling his mouth that "looks dumb and annoys me." I knew what she meant. Ted Russell had a funny habit of pressing his lips together on the left side of his mouth for no apparent reason. Darleen was right. It did look dumb, and it annoyed me, too.

From that point to the end, Joey Figlio was her man.

"I guess I love Joey," she wrote in early December 1960. "He loves me, and I'd rather marry him than that dolt Wilbur Burch."

She even mentioned Louis Brossard. In reference to the rumors about

Darleen and Ted Russell, the assistant principal interviewed her to find out if something was going on. She told him there was nothing between her and the music teacher.

"Mr. Brossard is kind of gross. I don't like talking to him. But he's been nice to me."

In early December, Darleen related her attempt to get money from Ted Russell and Louis Brossard. Russell caved immediately when she threatened to say he'd had his way with her and left her pregnant. Brossard got really angry, refused, and advised her to pray to Jesus for guidance.

Darleen continued to mark the visits from her stepfather with sickening regularity. By the end, she would simply write, "Again" and nothing more.

I threw the diary down on the end table and hung my head. In the gloom of my apartment, the night had closed in around me as I read the wretched account of what he'd done to her. Two hours had passed. Two hours of revolting accounts of the worst crimes I could imagine against a child. What dies inside a man to make him do such things? How far from decency must he turn to lay his hands on a girl that way? How black must his soul be? I could imagine all manner of cruelty and selfishness and even understand them to a degree when compared to molesting a child. Dick Metzger was a monster. My instinct about him had been right all along. And right behind him was the despicable Wilbur Burch. Child molesters, both of them. Base and worthless human beings. I would be happy to do my part to help send them both away forever.

I couldn't sleep for the longest time. And when I dozed off, terrible nightmares invaded my head. Horrible visions that I won't repeat. Dreams that twisted my insides until I tore at my pillow, gnashed at its cover with my teeth, and wept for Darleen Hicks and Geraldine Duffy. I promised justice for them both. And that's when I realized how confused and emotional I'd become. I was hunting two different fiends, and I didn't know what to think, whom to accuse, which to hate more. Dick Metzger was a lowlife child molester. I had proof of that. But now I needed to prove that either he or Louis Brossard was a killer as well.

I took two hours to write the article that would blacken Dick Metzger's name with the foulest tar I could conjure. Even if he never faced prison for his crimes, he would forever be known as a monster who'd molested his daughter. My heart raced as I detailed his abuse of a pubescent girl. For obvious reasons, the paper would never publish the ugly words I wanted to write. But I made sure the perversion and depravity came through in every sentence.

Once I'd finished, I photographed several of the more telling passages, including Darleen's plans to escape with Joey and Wilbur. I made sure to document many of the nauseating entries about her stepfather. I might even find one or two where the language was moderate enough to be printed along with my article as powerful visual evidence.

ॐ

TUESDAY, JANUARY 17, 1961

It was six. I showered and dressed. By seven, I was sitting outside Frank Olney's office, waiting for him to arrive. In my purse was the diary. In my head, I was turning my facts and theories over and over, looking for the answer that was so elusive. It seems trite, but I compared the impasse to the hardest crossword puzzles I'd ever solved. I recalled how they'd stumped me, then suddenly a crack appeared, giving way to a trickle, then the flood gates opened, and the game was won, as suddenly and unexpectedly as a dam bursting. But this was no crossword puzzle. The clues had not been devised to lead to an eventual solution. Quite the opposite. There was a dearth of clues, and the killer was more interested in burying evidence than engaging in an intellectual game.

Frank finally lumbered into the office at eight fifteen. He hung his coat on the stand and looked at me.

"What are you doing here at this hour?" he asked, his expression betraying a premonition that I had a very good reason for the early start.

"Can we talk inside?"

I laid out the diary on his desk, and he eyed it with dread.

"I see you took the liberty of breaking the lock," he said, reaching for it. "Okay, give me the abridged version."

"Darleen planned to run off with Joey Figlio. She collected money from various people."

"That's nice," he said, thumbing through the first few pages. "But we already knew that. What's the punch line?"

"Dick Metzger had been molesting her for two years."

The sheriff groaned as I filled him in and showed him some of the more telling passages. He turned green as he read the chilling, almost non-chalant descriptions written in Darleen's hand. "Last night he made me do it again," was the one that prompted Frank to slam his right hand down on his desk and rise to his feet. He grabbed his coat and hat from the stand, then reached into his desk for his gun.

"Where are you going?" I asked.

"I'm going to haul that son of a bitch in here."

"Why are you taking your gun?"

Frank stared at me, face impassive. "Because I'm hoping he gives me a reason to shoot him."

It was ten o'clock when I presented Charlie Reese with my story and the photos I'd rushed through the lab moments earlier. He read my copy carefully, then examined the photos one by one. When he'd finished, he pushed back in his chair and sighed.

"The world is a terrible place for people like Darleen Hicks," he said. "I've never understood how a human being can be so rotten as to do that to a child."

"Then you'll print it?" I asked.

Charlie looked up at me. "No, Ellie. We can't print this. Not in this form anyway. Ours is a family newspaper. We can't write that her father made her do . . . Oh, God, it makes me sick to think about it."

"How would you write it then?" I demanded, my hackles rising.

"Well, if the sheriff arrests him, we can say what the charges are. But we can't give this kind of detail."

"Can we at least print a photograph of the diary? Here, where she says, 'He came to my room again last night.'"

Charlie gazed at the picture for a long time. "Maybe," he said. "I'll have to run it by Artie."

At noon, I phoned Frank Olney for an update. He told me that Dick Metzger was cooling his heels in a cell downstairs on suspicion of statutory rape, sodomy, corruption of a minor, and child molestation.

"What about Wilbur Burch?" I asked.

"He's still in city jail," said Frank. "But I spoke to the DA. He says that Burch is under nineteen, and, therefore, is considered an underage offender. Don't hold your breath waiting for him to pay for this."

This was crazy. The newspaper refused to publish the salient details of Dick Metzger's crimes against nature, and the state considered a nineteen-year-old child molester underage. Plenty of folks were looking out for the rapists and the molesters, but no one seemed to care for the fifteen-year-old girl.

"Did Don say anything about Metzger?" I asked.

"You're not going to like it," said Frank. "He said that the diary alone probably isn't enough to charge him."

"What?"

"The language in the diary is too vague, he says. The girl never actually spelled out what he was doing to her or what he was making her do. And Don says the diary is hearsay anyway and inadmissible as evidence."

I swore at Frank down the line, and he urged me to calm down. "Don't shoot the messenger," he said. "I'm on your side here. And, though I shouldn't be telling this to the press, I took the opportunity to bang Metzger's head into the doorframe of my cruiser when I was putting him inside."

"That seems to be your usual way of helping criminals into cars," I said, remembering how he done the same to Frankie Ralston.

"Not officially. But I can tell you it felt damn good." He paused. "For me, not him. He swore a blue streak at me, and he's got a nice shiner under his right eye. Oh, and I gave him a ticket for an expired registration on his truck, too."

Sometimes I wished I were as big as Frank Olney. I would have loved to bounce Dick Metzger's head off the car door. And maybe slam the door two or three times more on his head while I was at it.

"So when do you have to let him out?"

"I'll release him in a couple of hours. I just don't have enough to keep him locked up."

"What can we do, Frank?"

"I wish I could tell you," he said. "But can I ask you a question?"

"Go ahead."

"Do you think Dick Metzger killed Darleen?"

I took my time before answering. Not that I was considering the question at all, but I was trying to find an answer that would derail what I assumed Frank was going to say next. Finally I had to admit that, for all the hatred I harbored for him, I did not think Dick Metzger had murdered his stepdaughter.

"Then let me tell you something that I think you should consider. Darleen is gone. Metzger can't harm her anymore. But there is a murderer on the loose, and we both want to catch him. I suggest you swallow your disgust and disappointment and concentrate on finding something that will stick to Brossard."

After a suitable pause to digest his advice, I had to admit that it was the most practical course to follow. Dick Metzger may or may not molest another young girl. Maybe he was an opportunistic rapist, who took advantage of Darleen because she was handy. Had there ever been talk of him bothering other children? I didn't know. But one thing I did know was that Louis Brossard had killed before and probably would again if he weren't stopped. But how to catch him? The trail had gone cold in the four weeks since December 21, and I didn't know where to turn for ideas.

"Okay, Frank. For now, I'll put that pervert to one side. But once we nail Brossard, I'm going to make a nuisance of myself and investigate every last detail of Dick Metzger's worthless life until I get him."

At two thirty, I was outside the junior-high-school parking lot again, this time waiting for Gus Arnold and Carol Liswenski. I wanted to retrace my steps and badger the witnesses until one of them gave me something new to go on. Perhaps the bus driver was frightened and holding back what he knew. If he could just place Louis Brossard in the snow hills after four thirty on December 21, I was confident the DA could make a case against him.

And then there was Carol Liswenski, the weak link in the circle of Darleen's friends. She knew a lot, some of which she'd shared with me, and more still she was keeping to herself. I was sure of it.

The buses had started to arrive, and number 63 pulled into its usual parking space along the wall. I switched off the ignition of my Royal Lancer and climbed out. Gus Arnold was not happy see me.

"I already told you everything," he whined.

"Come on, Mr. Arnold," I said. "You were parked behind the snow hills, not fifty yards from where Darleen Hicks was killed. And, it seems, at the exact same time. The sheriff found her gloves right there."

"But I told you, it was dark. And I was hidden behind those trees. I couldn't see the car."

"What?"

"I mean, if there was a car there, I couldn't have seen it."

"You saw a car," I accused.

"I didn't see nothing."

I glared at him. "So far, you're the only person we know who was there that day. You have no alibi, and the sheriff's getting heat to arrest someone for this crime. If I were you, and if I hadn't seen a car there, I'd jolly well invent one."

"I didn't see a car. I can't lie and say there was one." He paused. "But I thought I heard one."

That was new.

"I went to the back of the bus and opened the pint," he continued. "I laid down and took my time to drink it. Then I must have fallen asleep for a bit. I thought I heard a car arrive, but I never looked. And I didn't hear any voices or anything funny."

This was a dead end. I was getting nowhere with the most recalcitrant, least reliable witness I could imagine. Just then, Carol Liswenski climbed into the bus. Wanting to get her away from her friends, I convinced her to let me give her a lift home.

"I'm sorry about Darleen," I said as we pulled away from the school. "It must be a difficult time for you."

"Yeah," she said. "I kind of already accepted that she was gone. One way or another. But it's sad to know that she's really dead. And that someone killed her on purpose."

"Can I ask you a question?" I said.

"I figured you would."

"Are you and your friends on the outs? Susan and Linda?"

Carol looked away. I took that for a yes.

"Did Darleen ever talk to you about her stepfather?"

"How do you mean?"

"Did she ever tell you anything really personal about him? Like secrets?"

Carol watched me from her seat. I couldn't tell what she was thinking, in part because I had to keep my eyes on the road. She finally said that Darleen had told her and Susan and Linda about her bath time.

"She said he sometimes barged into the bathroom without knocking. She said she didn't like that, especially if she was undressed."

"Anything else?" I asked. "Maybe even something more secret, more personal?"

"Like what?"

I needed Carol to give me information without my putting words or ideas into her head. It had to come from her, and I had already tried to steer her to the answer. I changed gears.

"What about other men?" I asked. "Did Darleen ever tell you about men? Older men, not boys."

Carol shrugged. "Sure. We talked about men sometimes. Elvis, Bobby Darin . . . Darleen had a real thing for Anthony Perkins for a while."

"No, I meant men from around here."

"You already know the stories about Darleen and Mr. Russell."

"Yes, and I don't believe they're true. Anyone else?"

"Wilbur Burch," she said.

"Not old enough. Try again."

She shrugged once more. "I'm sorry, but I don't know of anyone else. Oh, except Paul Newman. Darleen was in love with him after we saw *Exodus*. As a matter of fact, it was just a few days before she disappeared."

I pulled over to the side of the road. We were approaching Carol's house on County Highway 58, and I still needed some answers.

"Carol," I began, "did Darleen give you a package to hold for her?"

She looked at me, startled.

"Did she give you money to hold for her?"

Carol looked down, her eyes darting from side to side as she searched for an answer.

"That's how you got the sweater and the hairdo and the charm bracelet, isn't it?"

Still nothing.

"And that's why your friends are giving you the cold shoulder. How much money was there?" I asked.

"Twenty dollars," she said suddenly. "I wouldn't have spent it, honest, but she was dead. I just knew she was dead."

"When did she give you the money?" I asked.

"It was the day she disappeared. In Canajoharie at the factory. She gave me an envelope and said to keep it for her, just for a while. She said she was leaving, and she didn't want her father to find the money."

"Why not put it in her locker?" I asked.

"Because Mr. Russell gave it to her in the parking lot that morning. Right before she got on the bus.

So much for Ted Russell telling me everything. I still didn't think he'd killed Darleen, but I wondered why he'd lied to me about not having seen her that day.

Putting that coward's lie to one side, I had little to go on, other than Mike Palumbo's sighting of Louis Brossard on the Mill Street Bridge. And I needed more than that to prove he was Darleen's killer. I tried to imagine what kind of physical evidence might have been created or left behind by Brossard, but I couldn't come up with anything that would still be present four weeks later. And the sheriff had searched his car already. It was clean. Where else could the evidence be?

I stopped in to see Fadge and have a look at the paper. My story on Darleen's diary had made the front page after all. Upper right-hand corner. I could get used to this. Charlie had made several edits, removed all references to the molestation except the most clinical descriptions I had managed. But my boss's one brilliant stroke bowled me over. He included one of the photographs—in fact the one with the most chilling passage I could remember: "Last night he made me do it again." You could read the date, a few details about her day at school, and the beginning of the heartrending line. Charlie had the lab blur the second half of the sentence, leaving only "Last night he ..." It was even more powerful without the offending words, as if the reader would make the crime worse in his own mind. In moments like this, I realized how much I still had to learn about the newspaper business.

"When are you going to wrap this up?" asked Fadge, taking a seat with me.

"I don't know if I will," I said, shaking my head.

"What are you looking for?"

"Something that's no longer there."

I spent the evening thinking about Darleen Hicks. For the thousandth time, I reviewed the details in my head. And I thought about the girl I had grown to know so well in the past weeks. None of it helped me break the logjam.

Having polished off three glasses of whiskey and several crossword puzzles, I trudged off to bed. Within minutes, I was asleep, dreaming of the first time I met Darleen Hicks in the girls' bathroom at the high school. The particulars were different. She was older, with no braces on her teeth, and we were best friends, planning to steal some liquor from Corky's. And Ted Jurczyk was there, but none of Darleen's other friends. We were laughing about something, then a phone rang in the girls' room.

Late night calls rarely bring good news. I don't recall ever having appreciated one, and this night was no different. I woke suddenly from my dream and needed a couple of seconds to find my bearings. Disoriented from the drink and the deep sleep, I wasn't sure where I was until the phone pealed again.

"Hello," I said into the receiver.

"You dirty, little slut," came the voice. "I will get you for what you did," and the line went dead.

In my daze, I couldn't quite place the voice and, as my wits returned, I realized that I couldn't be sure who it was. I suspected Dick Metzger, of course. The sheriff had released him earlier in the day, and he must have seen the article in the newspaper by now. But it could have been Louis Brossard, as well. Or Wilbur. Was he still in jail? I wasn't at all sure, especially in my current state.

I went to the kitchen, checked the bolt, and moved the kitchen table to block the door. But I felt no safer. It was a little past one, and the long night stretched out before me. The prospect terrified me, and no new lock downstairs or furniture in front of the door provided comfort.

Pulling the curtains aside, I looked up and down on Lincoln Avenue from my bedroom. The street lamps glowed in the cold night air. Nothing looked out of place. There were several cars parked along the street, their hoods covered with a dusting of frost, indicating they'd been still for hours. I switched on all the lights and sat in the parlor trying to figure out what to do.

I could call the police or Mike Palumbo or Fadge. But I feared I was becoming a nuisance. I no longer worried about Joey Figlio—or Frankie Ralston, for that matter—and I was pretty sure Wilbur Burch was still locked up. To date, no one other than those three had actually breached my door. But I had never provoked anyone the way I had Dick Metzger and Louis Brossard. And both on the same day.

Arming myself with the longest knife in my drawer, I went back to bed and tried to sleep. But the tension was too great, and I struggled to calm myself. Time passed. After what seemed like hours, I checked the clock: two thirty. Then the noises began. I thought I heard a car in the street, but nothing was visible from my window. Next, the house creaked, and I got up to investigate, knife at the ready. Nothing. At three fifteen, the wind blew a branch or something off a tree onto the roof. At least that's what I assumed and prayed it was.

At four, I made myself some tea, thinking it might soothe my nerves, and returned to bed. I laid my head on the pillow and stared at the ceiling. My eyes felt heavy, and Darleen was helping me to the sink in girls' bathroom. She patted my back and smiled at me. She was wearing braces again.

The noise that woke me was in my dream, I realized soon enough. It was a bang. A gunshot, perhaps, but I woke with a start, and the carving knife fell to the floor with a great clatter. Mrs. Giannetti would surely give me an earful in the morning.

But on the bright side, as I sat up in my bed, I had my answer.

CHAPTER
TWENTY-ONE

WEDNESDAY, JANUARY 18, 1961

The fear must have cleared my head. Or perhaps it was like a crossword puzzle after all. Eventually, even the toughest word falls. Even the hardest puzzle can be solved.

It was still dark, but morning wasn't far off. I couldn't call the sheriff at this hour, so I plotted out what needed to be done. Frank would need to arrest Brossard and get him to sign a statement in the presence of his lawyer. That would take several hours, I figured, but it couldn't be helped. It was essential to the integrity of my plan, which was still just a hunch and almost a shot in the dark. But I had nothing else. And if this didn't pan out, Brossard would be in the clear. Without witnesses and with no physical evidence, he may have achieved the perfect murder. For the second time. But only if I was wrong. The other help I needed from the sheriff was a second search of Brossard's car.

At seven, I dialed Frank Olney's home number and told him my idea. It took a few minutes to convince him that there was no harm in trying it and that the alternative was to do nothing at all. In the end, he thought he could get Brossard and his lawyer to give a statement by early afternoon.

"There's one more thing, Frank," I said hesitantly. "Last night I got a threatening phone call. I'm not sure if it was Brossard or Dick Metzger, though I'm leaning toward Metzger."

"What did he say?"

"He called me a dirty, little slut and said he was going to get me for what I did."

"Holy hell," he said. "I'll post someone to watch your place tonight. In the meantime, get a locksmith and a carpenter in this morning and replace your kitchen door with something more secure. Will your landlady let you do that?"

"Not likely," I said.

"Well, put it in and ask for forgiveness later."

I phoned Charlie Reese next and told him my plans. He, too, was uncertain, but agreed it was the only option at the moment. He also thought I should secure my kitchen door, and he recommended Milchiore's Hardware on Main.

I soon realized that a new door was out of the question on such short notice, but by noon, Dave Milchiore had installed a big brass Segal deadbolt on my kitchen door. He told me Segal had gone out of business, but this was still the best lock on the market. He lost me when he started talking about pins and cylinders. I just wanted something to keep people out.

"Of course a professional lock picker could open this," he said. "But we don't have any of those in New Holland."

"I thought you said it was the best on the market."

"Well, the best in the store, anyway," he said. "But don't worry. This will keep people out. And the bars on the window and the three surface bolts I put in make this door the safest in the city."

It did appear to be secure. Burglar bars on the kitchen window, a new deadbolt, and three surface bolts anchoring the door to the head, the jamb, and the threshold.

"Thank you, Mr. Milchiore," I said. "Just one more thing. Could you come back after dark and sleep on the landing?"

Looking both ways as I stepped off the porch, I could see no green Ford pickup truck anywhere on the street. I wasn't worried about Louis Brossard's red-and-white Chevy; Frank Olney had phoned me at ten thirty to say the assistant principal was safely in custody. He phoned again at eleven to tell me Joe Murray had showed up to spring him. Frank played his part well, saying he was going to hold Brossard no matter what Murray said, but in the end agreed to let him go after he gave and signed a statement.

In the meantime, Don Czerulniak had managed to secure a second search warrant for Brossard's car. The judge was disinclined to grant it, but finally agreed, stipulating that this was the last search he would authorize. The State could not continue harassing the man without good cause.

I showed up at the sheriff's office, just as Brossard was being released to his lawyer. He wouldn't look me in the eye, and he said nothing. That's when Don and Frank emerged from Frank's office and broke the news to Joe Murray that they were going to have one more look at Brossard's car.

"Go ahead," said Murray, once he'd given the warrant the once over. "You're spinning your wheels."

Brossard seemed confident this was a fishing expedition. Still, he was eager to get the search over with. He'd been dragged out of the junior high by the sheriff in front of his colleagues, his boss, and dozens of students, and he was itching to return as soon as possible to flaunt his innocence.

Frank announced to everyone present that the car had already been towed to the jail by a wrecker and was sitting in the impound garage out back. Murray told him to get on with it. Brossard looked impatient.

I, on the other hand, was a bundle of nerves. It was one thing to come up with a clever guess, but quite another to prove it. And what if I was dead wrong? This could end up a major embarrassment for me and the sheriff. My empty stomach growled as we stepped outside and circled around to the garage.

Frank asked for the keys, and Brossard produced them. The sheriff handed them to Deputy Brunello, who unlocked the door. Frank invited Joe Murray to observe with him as a mechanic appeared with a tool box.

"Okay," said the sheriff. "I want the front seat of the car removed." He looked at Brossard then Joe Murray. "Very carefully."

The mechanic stuck his head into the car, first from the driver's side, then from the passenger's side. Using a wrench, he unbolted the seat from the floor, and then two deputies helped him slide the bench seat out of the car.

"Lay it down on its back," said Frank to the men. Then to Joe Murray. "Let's have a look."

My heart was galloping, and I thought I might faint from the anticipation and my hunger. This was the moment when I would know if Brossard had slipped the knot and would escape, or if he would pay for his crime.

"What is this circus?" asked Joe Murray as they reached the seat.

Frank stooped to look under the seat. His face betrayed no emotion. Joe Murray scanned the underside from the driver's end to the passenger's. He squinted. The first sign that my career might survive another day. Then he reached out to touch the fabric, but the sheriff stopped him.

"Don't touch it," he said. "That's evidence."

A tingle crawled up my neck. I closed my eyes and stifled a short gasp.

"What is it?" asked Murray.

"That," said the sheriff, "is gum. Black Jack chewing gum, if I'm not mistaken."

I actually lost my balance and stumbled. Stan Pulaski was standing nearby and caught me before I hit the ground. I was starving, my blood sugar low again, and I felt overwhelmed by emotions.

"So what's that prove?" asked the lawyer. "Anyone could have put that there."

"That's true," said Frank. "But whoever put it there left a perfect fingerprint right in the middle."

Brossard collapsed to the ground. No one caught him.

⁂

There really wasn't much Louis Brossard could say. His lawyer, Joe Murray, was also at a loss for words. His client had just signed a statement, swearing that Darleen Hicks had never been in his car. Not on the day she disappeared and never before then either. Now, with a perfectly preserved fingerprint squashed into a wad of Black Jack gum stuck to the underside of his car's front seat, Brossard knew it was over. He didn't try to deny it any longer. Frank told me the whole story after the assistant principal had confessed.

"The guilt was too much for him," said the sheriff, sipping his coffee. "Once he realized that Darleen had stuck her gum under the car seat, he just wanted to get the whole thing off his chest."

"What about the St. Winifred's girl?" I asked.

"Yeah, he copped to that, too. Hudson police are sending a man up to take a confession from him."

"So how did it all happen?"

"Pretty much like you thought," said Frank. "Brossard investigated the

Ted Russell thing and said he couldn't stop thinking of the girl. He said she was so cute and mischievous. That's what gets his motor running, it seems. He likes young girls, but only the ones with the devil in their smile. That's how he put it."

"He didn't like me at all. I was convinced he didn't like girls, but it turns out I was too old for him."

Frank shook his head. "I feel sorry for guys like him."

"What?"

"Not like that," he said. "A deviant may be able to stop himself from committing these 'abominations against God,' as Brossard put it. But he can't help having the urges in the first place. They just come to him. From Satan, he says."

"So he was beguiled by a fifteen-year-old temptress," I said sarcastically. "How did it all play out?"

"Like I said, he became obsessed with her. Tried to talk to her at school, sent some notes asking to meet her, called her down to his office on the slightest pretext, phoned her at home a few times. She asked him for money, and he refused. Then, on the day she disappeared, he saw her from his office window getting off the bus in the parking lot. He watched her talking to a boy, then the bus drove off. She loitered around for a few minutes, and she left the parking lot. He had the idea he could give her a lift home. He swears he had no other intentions but to give her a ride." Frank wiped his dry mouth. "He saw her get into a taxi on Mill Street, and he followed in his car."

"Then the cab dumped her on the side of the road, and the vulture swooped in."

"That's about right," said Frank. "He drove her to the snow hills and tried to get friendly with her. She wasn't interested. But the devil had taken control of his mind, he said. He touched her, fondled her, reached under her dress and . . ." Frank stopped. "Well, you get the picture. She slapped him hard and called him names, then managed to pull away and jump out of the car. She ran through the woods alongside the hills. That must have been when she lost her gloves. He chased after her, caught her in the woods near the clearing on the other side. She screamed and he put his hand over her mouth to shut her up. When she went limp, he kissed her, and she screamed again. He grabbed her by the neck, and she was dead before he realized what he was doing."

I listened with horror. I had known that she'd been strangled, of course, but the sheriff's hoarse-voiced narrative brought it painfully to life. I took a sip of water, cleared my throat, and wiped my eyes.

"Then he buried her in the snow?" I asked.

Frank nodded. "Brossard had the superintendent's banquet that evening, and it was getting late. He couldn't dispose of the body at that moment, so he buried her in the snow, thinking he would come back later that night to move her."

"But he forgot the lunch box."

"Exactly. He was quite drunk when he returned to the hills after the banquet. 'The devil had commandeered my soul,' he kept saying. Over and over. None of it was his fault. It was the devil. He grabbed the body but forgot the lunch box."

"And then he drove to the Mill Street Bridge?"

"He had the idea of dumping her in the river because the ground was too hard to dig. He knew the snow would melt by spring, exposing the body, and he thought why not flush her down the river instead. She'd end up miles from here by the time someone found her. So he drove down to the river near Lock 11. But the river was frozen, so he doubled back to New Holland. He saw the river running under the Mill Street Bridge and, in his drunken, possessed state, thought that was his best option. It was late. The town was asleep, and it would only take a minute to toss the body over."

"And that's when Officer Palumbo came across him."

"Missed him dumping the body in the river by a couple minutes, according to Brossard."

We fell silent for a while, both lost in melancholy thoughts or hopeless disgust for all mankind. Finally, Frank spoke.

"I've been meaning to ask you," he said. "How did you figure out that Darleen left her gum under the seat?"

"It came to me in a dream. Well, sort of," I said. "I'd been racking my brain, reviewing the timeline, and thinking of everything I knew about Darleen, including my one meeting with her. Over and over, I went back to that time she'd helped me in the girls' room at the basketball game, trying to remember every last detail. Then, in the calm of my dream, she was there, smiling at me with the braces and the black gum. Everyone said she was always chewing that black gum: her teachers, her friends, even her mother. And when she was done with it, she would stick it wherever was handy—under desks, mostly. Even under the shelf in her locker. It just occurred to me in a moment of clarity that she was just as likely as not to be chewing gum when Brossard picked her up. It was a guess."

Frank whistled. "Damn good guess, Ellie."

"What's the DA's plan?" I asked, blushing a bit, but delighting in his praise nonetheless.

"He's thinking voluntary manslaughter, attempted rape, and battery. Probably a few more. He's working on it."

"And Dick Metzger?"

Frank shook his head. "Nothing for now. He denies it, and there's no witness, no victim to level an accusation."

"Can't you bash his head into the car door again?"

He smiled sadly, then turned serious. "Listen, Ellie, about Metzger. Brossard says he never called your house."

"I see. But still no proof to charge Metzger?"

"I'm afraid not. Tell you what, though. I'm going to have one of my boys watch your house for a while."

"I don't need babysitting, Frank."

"Come on, don't be a hero. Stan will sleep on the landing outside your door. He wants to."

"Absolutely not. I won't hear of it."

〽️

I wrote a long piece for a special Thursday morning edition, outlining the arrest of, and the evidence against, Louis Brossard. I wrote a second article on the Geraldine Duffy disappearance. Earlier in the week, on Monday, my Girl Friday, Norma, had requested everything the *Hudson Star-Register* had on the St. Winifred girl's disappearance, and Wednesday afternoon a box of clippings arrived at the office to my attention. I summarized the details of the case, tying it up with a neat bow and Brossard's confession. According to Frank, Brossard had indeed sent the boy away first. An hour later, Geraldine Duffy was dead, raped and strangled, buried near the railroad tracks along the Hudson River. Again, the blame went to Satan, who used Brossard as the instrument of his evil. When I reached the

Columbia County DA by telephone, he promised a first-degree murder charge. And if Satan didn't appear to stand trial, Brossard would have to take the rap himself.

I dropped my stories off at the office, along with film of Brossard's car and the gum under the seat. Charlie worked up the front page and selected the photos, then sent them off to Composition, who were working late for the special edition. I was drained. The long hours, lack of sleep, and emotional beatings I'd endured over the past three weeks had taken their toll. I could barely summon the energy to switch some new keys on George Walsh's typewriter.

CHAPTER
TWENTY-TWO

FRIDAY, JANUARY 20, 1961

We sat in the City Room Friday morning, watching the Kennedy inauguration on the television, as the torch was passed to a new generation of Americans, to echo the words of the new president. I felt inspired and full of hope as Kennedy stood there in his morning coat, hatless in the frigid cold, and told the nation that "we shall pay any price, bear any burden, meet any hardship, support any friend, oppose any foe to assure the survival and success of liberty." He moved me when he called upon our fellow citizens of the world to work together for the freedom of man, and I truly believed we were on the cusp of a new era. A better era.

Then I went home, put on a black wool dress and gloves, and drove to the Wilson Funeral Home in the Town of Glen. I wasn't expecting a warm welcome from the Metzgers, but that couldn't be helped. I intended to pay my respects to Darleen Hicks.

The funeral parlor was a large, white clapboard colonial house that sat on the shoulder of Route 161. Its paint was cracked and peeling as if it had been baked and frozen again and again for decades. Which it had. There was a small gravel parking area behind the house with a handful of cars and trucks. I noticed Dick Metzger's green Ford pickup parked near the back of the lot. I climbed out of my warm car and slipped inside the vestibule of the funeral home. A heavy velvet curtain hung half open, and I could see the simple casket and several mourners inside. It was cold, so I kept my coat on and entered.

Dick Metzger saw me, and I fancy his nostrils flared. I took a seat in one of the folding chairs and bowed my head. I recognized Winnie Terwilliger, the lady I'd met at the Metzger farm after Darleen's body had been found. The Sloans were also there, and a few other locals, too. Susan, Carol, and Linda sat together, and I noticed Ted Jurczyk right behind them, accompanied by Coach Mahoney. Clarence Endicott, principal of the junior high school, had come. Probably the last place he wanted to be, but realistically he had no other choice. Mrs. Nolan, Darleen's former English teacher, sat alone off to the side, dabbing her nose with a handkerchief.

Joey Figlio was nowhere to be seen. I figured he was probably locked up at Fulton, but I also thought he was the type to disdain formal ceremonies like this one. He was more likely to grieve on his own. Or try to kill someone who'd hurt Darleen.

No Ted Russell. Perhaps that was for the best; the tasteful, if cowardly, thing to do.

"Excuse me, miss," came a whispered voice in my ear after I'd been sitting there for several minutes. I looked up to see a man in his fifties, poorly shaven, with a black overcoat and tie.

"Yes?" I asked.

"I'm sorry, miss, but the family would like you to leave."

"I understand," I said, rising from my chair. I tried to make eye contact with Irene Metzger, but she was weeping into a handkerchief and not looking my way. I felt certain that she was avoiding me on purpose. And I knew that I would never see her again. My role in Irene Metzger's life had played out, and I'd unwittingly caused the poor woman even more sorrow than she'd expected. She'd known her daughter was gone, but never imagined that she'd lose the man she loved as well.

Her husband, on the other hand, was staring directly into my eyes with his lizard gaze, black eye and all, courtesy of the sheriff. He had demanded that I be thrown out, but I sensed he was daring me to say something, to approach them, anything, just so he could beat me senseless or choke the life out of me. Out of respect for the dead, I said nothing. But Dick Metzger wasn't satisfied with my quiet departure. He rose to his feet and hollered for me to get out, using the foulest language I'd ever heard outside a navy freighter. I resisted the temptation to answer back, determined that Darleen's wake should not become a circus. I turned slowly and walked out trying to maintain my dignity as all eyes watched me go. It's not easy to hold your head high when someone calls you a whore at a wake. But I did.

The New Holland Bucks tipped off in Johnstown at eight. Ted Jurczyk played the finest game of his short career, scoring thirty-two points with ten assists and five steals. He was masterful, and New Holland won going away, 76–58. I congratulated him after the game, and he smiled.

"One last question for my profile, Ted," I said. He nodded. "How do you do it? How do you manage to play so beautifully on such a sad day?"

He wiped his sweaty brow with a towel and sighed. "It's hard," he said. "Until the whistle blows. Just like my butterflies, everything else disappears. My nerves, Darleen, Patricia's leg braces, my mom . . . The court is a sanctuary for me. The most peaceful place on earth."

I knew I would end my feature with that line.

"You showed a lot of courage this afternoon at the funeral parlor," he said. "Gosh, I admire you, Miss Stone."

Outside the gym, I fumbled for my keys in the cold. The door nearly wouldn't open, again the residual effect of the dunking the poor car had taken in Winandauga Lake. I drove off, heading for the office to finish my story on Ted and to write the summary of the game as well. I wanted to be free of work responsibilities the next day. There was my big date with Mike Palumbo, after all.

I was cruising east along Route 67, through the desolate farm country between Johnstown and New Holland, when I first noticed the thumping of my right rear tire. A flat, damn it. I pulled over to the shoulder and cursed my bad luck. It was bitterly cold, but the tire needed to be changed.

I climbed out, nearly breathless from the frozen air, and retrieved the jack and spare from the trunk. Positioning the jack carefully, I began to crank it up. A motorist slowed and pulled over to give me a hand. That was welcome. I stared back into the burning headlights behind me, squinting to see. Why didn't the idiot switch them off? Then he did, and I dropped the tire iron and ran.

I raced for my life as I sensed the man gaining on me. My legs felt leaden, and it seemed the harder I pushed, the slower and more palsied my movements became. It was like running in water. The icy air seared my throat and lungs, but I couldn't stop, I knew that much. The steps drew closer, terrifyingly near, and I could hear his breath and the pounding of his boots behind me.

Dick Metzger corralled me after about thirty yards, grabbing me by the neck and nearly yanking me off my feet. He dragged me back to his truck as I kicked and screamed, losing both my shoes, but we were in the middle of nowhere, and no one heard. Once we reached his pickup, perhaps tiring of my resistance, he reared back and plowed his fist into my face. I saw stars. I went limp, and he opened the tailgate and threw me into the flatbed. I wanted to climb over the side immediately, but I couldn't move; my head was still swimming from his punch. He seized my ankles and pulled me into position atop a heavy tarpaulin, which, to my horror, he began rolling up on me like a cocoon. He turned me over and over until I was trapped tight, rendered immobile and unable to escape. My head hurt, but my senses returned. There was not much air, and I feared I would be smothered if I continued to struggle. Somehow, even in that desperate moment, I couldn't shake the image of an old cartoon from the *New Yorker*. Two men in pith helmets up to their shoulders in quicksand, and one says to the other, "Quicksand or not, Barclay, I've half a mind to struggle." I tried to steady my breath and think and, of course, resist the urge to struggle. Wrapped in the tarp, I heard Metzger climb into the cab and drive off.

It was a cold, bumpy ride, and I rolled from side to side whenever the truck turned sharply. From time to time, I yelled for help, but my screams were suffocated by the heavy, foul-smelling canvas. I doubted there was anyone near to hear me anyway. We drove for about thirty minutes, and I thought he intended to freeze me to death. I tried to think of a way to extricate myself from the tightly wrapped tarpaulin but realized that the only chance I had was to roll, and there wasn't enough space in the flatbed to unravel the canvas.

Eventually we slowed down. I could feel the truck bouncing over an unpaved surface; I had still no idea where he was taking me. Then he stopped and switched off the engine. The night was silent, but my heavy breathing resounded under the tarpaulin, and the close cover and terror of anticipation were exacerbated by a growing claustrophobia. I waited on my side for him to come for me. I listened, wondering where he was. What was he doing?

I intended to scream as soon as he returned and freed me, but in that moment, I just listened. Finally, after three or four agonizing minutes, I heard his footsteps approach, his boots crunching over the frozen ground.

I have never experienced such abject panic. I screamed and rolled and writhed on the flatbed of the pickup. I can't exactly say my life passed before my eyes, but there were flashes of images from my youth. I saw a pair of patent leather shoes and then a schoolbook. Elijah's guitar. My father's back and my mother's face, smiling, all as I thrashed. Then the tarpaulin was peeled away, and I loosed a cry with all my might and scratched and spat and kicked as if my life depended on it. And it did.

Or so I thought.

He threw his heavy body on top of me, trying to still my flailing. I punched and shrieked, but he didn't strike me. He just tried to restrain me. And his voice was deeper and familiar.

"Ellie, it's me!" he yelled, holding me down. "It's Frank Olney!"

I fell still, my eyes clenched shut, my lungs gasping for air. Then I opened my eyes. The night was bright with headlights and spinning cherry tops. There were three county cruisers surrounding Dick Metzger's pickup truck and five deputies standing by. Dick Metzger lay face down in the crusty snow, his hands cuffed behind his back, an ax and a shotgun lying about ten feet away.

"What happened?" I stammered. "Where are we?"

"Metzger's farm," said Frank. "He was just about to shoot you, chop you into little pieces, and bury the leftovers under some new concrete."

"How did you get here just in time?"

"We've been following that son of a bitch for three days. Night and day. I've had a man on him ever since you told me about that late-night phone call."

"Following him? Why didn't you tell me?"

"I didn't want to worry you. And I needed to catch him with something we could put him away for. Now we got kidnapping, assault and battery, and attempted murder."

I stared in horror at the man on the ground. His head was turned away from me, as if he didn't want to give me the satisfaction of seeing him defeated. His breath puffed into the cold air, rising above him like an evil steam from a foul manhole. Not far beyond him was the horse shed he'd been building. There was a hole in the ground and a hand-turned cement mixer sitting at the ready. That was my grave.

"You mean you saw him pick me up on the road?" I asked.

"Brunello was tailing him this evening. Saw him fiddling with your tire at the high school in Johnstown. Must have put a nail in it to make it leak. When Metzger drove off after you, Brunello radioed us and followed him, and we converged on him here."

"But what if he'd killed me on Route Sixty-Seven?"

Frank chewed on that one for a moment. "Hadn't thought of that. Anyways, he's busted. He'll go up for thirty to life, and he'll be dead before he gets out."

Stan Pulaski joined us and winced at the bruise on my cheek. He offered me a handful of snow for the swelling. I pressed it to my skin.

EPILOGUE

MONDAY, JANUARY 23, 1961

I spoke to the DA about Dick Metzger, wondering if child molestation couldn't be tacked on to the charges. Don said that was impossible without a witness or a confession. He also felt awkward discussing with a third party what charges should be filed.

"This is a matter of law," he said. "It's not up for public debate."

"But you're convinced he molested her, aren't you? So, what if you got him to cop to that charge instead of the one for trying to kill me?"

Don shook his head in disbelief. "You want to get him a lighter sentence? After what he did to you? Look at your face."

I brought a hand up to my bruised cheek and touched it without realizing. It was pretty sore, and the resulting headache had forced the postponement of my date with Officer Mike Palumbo. I put that thought to one side.

"No," I said, returning to the DA's question. "I want him to admit that he molested that little girl. It's quite different."

Don didn't like the idea. He droned on in his typical voice that it smelled funny, he wasn't sure how the voters would react, and he wanted to put the bastard away for the rest of his life. But in the end, he agreed to float it by Metzger's lawyer.

In lieu of forty years for kidnapping, assault and battery, and attempted murder, the DA offered a twenty-five year sentence for child molestation. After a week to think about it, Dick Metzger took the deal.

~

I finally made my trip back to New York—the one I'd put off three weeks earlier, when I'd discovered the unused bus ticket in Darleen's locker. It was a nice balm of nostalgia to be back in my family's lower Fifth Avenue apartment, the home I'd grown up in. It felt different this time. Not tragic, as it had been the last time I'd visited. A year had passed. My visit was to be a short one. Just the weekend, then back to New Holland and the life I'd started to build for myself.

The place was spic and span. No dust covers this time; I'd arranged with Nelda, my father's cleaning lady, to continue coming every week. I knew I'd return from time to time, maybe permanently one day, and I hated the sight of shrouded furniture and the smell of dust.

I spent Thursday evening at home, listening to music in Dad's study. Then Friday, I walked around the Village, had coffee, and did some shopping uptown. After so long in New Holland, I was stunned by the styles and the selection at Macy's and B. Altman. In a fit of impracticality, I chose several dresses, including an extravagant red chiffon number with a billowy skirt and a flounce of bird feathers. But a pang of guilt brought me back to earth. The dresses were far beyond what I could afford on my salary, and I couldn't bring myself to spend so much of my inheritance on an indulgence. In the end, I disappointed the salesgirl when I changed my mind and bought a winter pullover and a hair band instead.

⌀

SATURDAY, JANUARY 28, 1961

I stood before the fireplace, hands on hips, and stared at the two vases, together in the middle of the mantelpiece, the curves of their bodies touching just below the shoulders. I smiled. Then I gently took them down and placed them into a sturdy, wooden box in the foyer. Rodney, my dear old friend who manned the elevator and guarded the door, helped me take the box down to the lobby and place it in my car. An hour and a half later, I rolled to a stop on the alley beneath the bare oak trees of the cemetery in Irvington. Moises Rafael opened my car door and lent me a hand as I stepped out. A small crew of diggers waited next to Elijah's stone. Dad's sister Lena and his cousin Max were there, seated in folding chairs. I hadn't called a rabbi, and reciting the Kaddish was out of the question for many reasons, not the least of which was the lack of a quorum of ten males. It was three days short of one year since my father's death. I had reached the end of the mourning period. The yahrzeit was here.

Mr. Rafael retrieved the vases from the backseat of the car and placed each into a small, ebony box. He sealed them, nodded to me, and we proceeded to the gravesite. On either side of Elijah's restored stone were two simple granite markers. "Abraham Stone" and "Libby Stone." I'd had my mother's stone engraved with "Libby" instead of "Elisheba Merkle Stone," as no one knew her by that name. She was Libby.

I stood there solemnly as the men placed the ebony boxes into the ground. Max stood by my side, and my Aunt Lena held my hand. No one spoke. That wasn't on the agenda. But I said good-bye to my mother in my head, thinking how lucky I'd been to have her. How glad I was that she had never had to bury me as Irene Metzger had done for her daughter. I said goodbye to the joys and the memories we'd shared. I said goodbye to my dear brother Elijah, who was never far from my thoughts. To this day, whenever someone calls me "El," I think of him and smile. And I said good-bye to my father, to the tears and regrets and sorrow we'd shared and inflicted upon each other. The disappointment I'd caused him should have died with him. Instead I'd kept it alive through all the years when we hardly spoke, and now for the year since his death, flogging myself with his regrets. I drew one last breath of bitterness then blew it out. I loved my father, and he was gone; whatever torture he'd made for himself had ended for him when he died. And now, at his graveside, this was where it ended for me.

ACKNOWLEDGMENTS

I owe a debt of gratitude to many people who have played a role in bringing this book to life.

Thank you, Bill Reiss of John Hawkins & Associates, my agent, you offer the wisest advice in the business.

From Seventh Street Books, I'm indebted to Dan Mayer, editorial director, who took a chance on the Ellie Stone mysteries and makes each book better with his judicious edits and challenging questions; Jill Maxick, vice president of Marketing and director of Publicity, for her support, her enthusiasm, and her efforts to promote my books; Jackie Nasso Cooke, senior graphic designer, who has outdone herself yet again with a chillingly beautiful cover design; Melissa Raé Shofner and Jade Zora Scibilia, my editors, for their fine-tooth combs; Jake Bonar, publicist, for working so diligently to get the book into the right hands; and Pete Lukasiewicz, editorial assistant, for securing blurbs from such talented authors.

My very heartfelt thanks go to some people who gave advice and lent expertise on *Stone Cold Dead*: Dr. Kunda and Dr. Hilbert for all things medical; Lynne Raimondo, legal and plot; and Dianne Tangel-Cate, editorial.

And for reasons that go far beyond anything to do with books, my deepest appreciation is reserved for Lakshmi.

ABOUT THE AUTHOR

James W. Ziskin is the author of the Ellie Stone mysteries *Styx & Stone* and *No Stone Unturned*. A linguist by training, he studied Romance languages and literature at the University of Pennsylvania. He lives in the Hollywood Hills with his wife, Lakshmi, and their cats, Bobbie and Tinker.

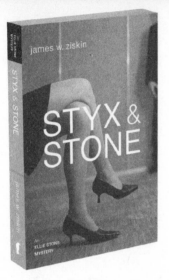
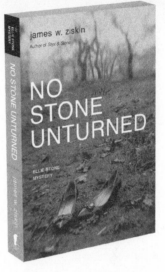